TEN-THOUSAND-DOLLAR KISS

"Don't cry, Kay," Jesse said quietly. "I won't take you back."

"You mean it?" Hope flared in her eyes, chasing away her tears, making her look young and vulnerable and beautiful, so beautiful.

"I said it, didn't I?"

"Oh, Jesse, thank you," she exclaimed softly, and kissed him.

It was a light kiss, a token of gratitude, nothing more, but it hit Jesse like a bolt of lightning. He could scarcely recall the last time a woman had kissed him of her own free will, and it seared a path to his heart and soul. Ten thousand dollars was a small price to pay for such a kiss, he thought.

Other *Leisure* and *Love Spell* books by
Madeline Baker:
UNDER A PRAIRIE MOON
WARRIOR'S LADY
LOVE FOREVERMORE
LOVE IN THE WIND
FEATHER IN THE WIND
CHASE THE WIND
THE ANGEL & THE OUTLAW
LAKOTA RENEGADE
APACHE RUNAWAY
BENEATH A MIDNIGHT MOON
CHEYENNE SURRENDER
WARRIOR'S LADY
THE SPIRIT PATH
MIDNIGHT FIRE
COMANCHE FLAME
PRAIRIE HEAT
A WHISPER IN THE WIND
FORBIDDEN FIRES
LACEY'S WAY
FIRST LOVE, WILD LOVE
RENEGADE HEART
RECKLESS DESIRE
RECKLESS LOVE
RECKLESS HEART

Writing as Amanda Ashley:
EMBRACE THE NIGHT
SHADES OF GRAY
A DARKER DREAM
SUNLIGHT, MOONLIGHT
DEEPER THAN THE NIGHT

Spirit's Song

MADELINE BAKER

LEISURE BOOKS   NEW YORK CITY

FOR SPIRITWALKER

*Thanks for the inspiration,
and for bringing
SPIRIT'S SONG
to life.*

A LEISURE BOOK®

March 1999

Published by

Dorchester Publishing Co., Inc.
276 Fifth Avenue
New York, NY 10001

ISBN 0-8439-4476-5

The name "Leisure Books" and the stylized "L" with design are trademarks of Dorchester Publishing Co., Inc.

Printed in the United States of America.

SPIRIT SONG

The Spirit's Song was lost in me,
my heart was sinking low,
I drifted on the winds of change,
I had nowhere to go.
But, then you came and with your voice,
you spoke in tones so soft,
That in my heart, I found my choice,
you set this bird aloft.

The eagle soared above my head,
my spirit guide was free,
I felt the pull but could not reach,
he was too high for me.
But, then you came, and lifted me,
with love as pure as light,
My feet left the ground, you gifted me,
again you gave me flight.

I could not say I'd ever reach
the goals I once had held,
I knew for me there was no use,
my spirit was impaled.
But, then you came, and freed my soul,
you righted what was wrong,
You are my dream, you made me whole,
you are the Spirit's Song.

—SpiritWalker

Spirit's Song

Chapter One

Summer, 1873

Jesse Yellow Thunder rested his hand on the butt of his gun. "Dead or alive, Barnett, it's up to you."

"I'm not going back to prison!"

"Like I said, it's up to you."

Phil Barnett took a deep breath, wondering if the bounty hunter would really shoot him in the back.

"Get those hands up where I can see 'em. Now."

"Who the hell *are* you?"

"The man who's gonna haul your dead carcass to the sheriff if you don't get those hands up."

"I got a right to know!"

"You've got no rights at all."

It was the sound of a gun being cocked that put

11

all thought of flight from Barnett's mind. There was an ominous quality in the harsh rasp of metal against metal, a grim finality, like the sound of dirt clods being shoveled into an open grave.

Raising his hands to shoulder level, Barnett slowly turned to face the bounty hunter. "Yellow Thunder," he muttered, only then recognizing the man he had played poker with earlier that night.

"Right the first time."

Barnett shivered. Everything he had ever heard about Jesse Yellow Thunder was true, he thought bleakly. The half-breed was as unfeeling as stone and as ugly as sin, what with that jagged white scar that started at the edge of his left temple, cut across the outer edge of his left eye, curved down his cheek, and ended just below his jaw. There was no mercy in the half-breed's cold gray eyes, no emotion in his face at all, except maybe boredom. Damn. Why hadn't he recognized him earlier?

Yellow Thunder pulled a set of handcuffs from his back pocket. "Turn around."

With a sigh of resignation, Barnett did what he was told.

Moments later, he was mounted on his horse, his hands securely cuffed behind his back.

"Would you really have shot me in the back?" Barnett asked as he watched the half-breed swing aboard his own mount.

"Damn right."

"Just like that?"

The bounty hunter nodded as he took up the reins to Barnett's horse. "Just like that. Poster says dead or alive. Dead's easier."

Phil Barnett looked into the half-breed's unblinking gray eyes and knew without a doubt that the man meant every word.

Jesse Yellow Thunder closed and locked the door to his hotel room. Tossing his hat on the room's single chair, he dropped his saddlebags beside the bed, then sat down on the edge of the mattress and pulled off his boots. His prisoner had been delivered to the local law, safe and sound. The necessary papers had been signed. He had collected the reward. Three hundred dollars.

He grinned as he sat back on the bed. Easy money, considering the fact that he had stumbled over Barnett quite by accident.

Jesse smothered a yawn as he pulled a thick sheaf of wanted posters from his saddlebags. Sometimes Lady Luck just perched on a man's shoulder. Like tonight. He'd been minding his own business, playing draw poker with a couple of the local cowhands, when who should slide into the chair across from him but Phil Barnett. They had played poker together for an hour. When Barnett left the saloon, Jesse followed him.

Jesse ran a hand across his jaw, thinking he needed a shave. In addition to the three-hundred-dollar bounty he had collected for Barnett, he had also taken Barnett for better than a hundred dollars at the poker table. A profitable evening, indeed.

Sitting back against the headboard, he began thumbing through the wanted posters. He grunted softly as he read the first one. Some fool in San Francisco was offering a ten-thousand-dollar reward for information regarding his runaway wife's whereabouts.

Jesse shook his head as he tossed the flyer on the floor. Ten grand. That was a pile of money any way you looked at it.

He glanced through the rest of the flyers, then plucked one from the bunch. Joseph Ravenhawk, wanted for bank robbery and assault. The price on his head was a thousand dollars. Ravenhawk shouldn't be too hard to find. Whenever he was on the run, he headed straight for Indian country to hole up with his Lakota relatives.

Jesse shoved the flyers back into his saddlebags. He hadn't been home in over a year, he mused as he shoved a pillow behind his head and closed his eyes. He could kill two birds with one stone. It was the time of the Cherry Ripening Moon. The Morning Star People would be gathering near *Mo'-ohta'vo'honaaeva*, the sacred Black Hills, to celebrate the Sun Dance with their allies, the Lakota. If he was lucky, Ravenhawk would be at the rendezvous by the time Jesse got there. If not . . .

Jesse grinned ruefully. He was ready for a little tipi living; ready to hear the language of his childhood, to eat cooking that wasn't his own, to smell the fresh, clean scent of pines and earth instead of air that reeked of stale smoke and booze.

He left early the following morning. Like a snake shedding its skin, he felt the constricting layers of civilization fall away as he rode deeper into the heartland of the Morning Star People. Riding toward the only place that had ever felt like home, he wondered, as he always did, why he had stayed away for so long. This would be his last bounty, he decided. He had a fair-sized bank account. He would find Ravenhawk, collect the reward, then return to the Land of the Spotted Eagle and settle down with his mother's people.

He had been away from the Cheyenne for too long, done too many things he was ashamed of. Somewhere along the way, he had lost his sense of who he was. Perhaps he could find the man he had once been before it was too late.

It was beautiful country, all green and gold at this time of the year. The air was clearer, sweeter; the sky more blue. Even his horse seemed to know they were headed home. The mare tugged on the reins, eager to run, and he let her go, reveling in the speed and power of the big blue roan as she stretched out, in the feel of the wind stinging his cheeks and whipping through his hair.

He bent low over the mare's neck. The rhythmic sound of hoofbeats flying over the earth seemed to be saying *home, home, home*.

Chapter Two

The Black Hills
Summer, 1873

Kaylynn Summers grimaced as she stooped to pick up another piece of wood. Adding it to the pile in her arms, she noticed that she'd broken her thumbnail. She would have complained, if she had thought it would do any good, but there was no one to hear her, and no one to care. Besides, another broken fingernail was the least of her worries.

Tired of walking, she dumped the wood on the ground and sat down in the shade of a gnarled cottonwood tree. Old Mo'e'ha could wait a few more minutes, and if she couldn't wait, well, she could darn well get down here and collect the wood herself.

With a sigh of exasperation, Kaylynn dug a splinter out of her finger. Just looking at her hands really did make her feel like crying. The nails were all broken and uneven; there was a large blister on her left palm, a shallow cut on her right thumb.

She stared at her hands, at the wide gold band on the third finger of her left hand. Her hands were a symbol of her life, she thought with wry amusement. The gold represented the wealth and life of ease she had left behind, the calluses stood for the poverty and hardship in which she now lived. No one seeing her now would ever believe that her hands had once been soft and smooth and lily-white, her nails neatly manicured. She looked down at her doeskin tunic and moccasins. Alan would be horrified if he could see her now.

She wondered how long he had searched for her, if he had told her parents she was missing. Strange, how life turned out. She had gone against her parents' wishes to marry the man of her dreams. Like a prince in a fairy tale, he had met her at a ball, wooed and won her and carried her away to his castle by the sea. He had dressed her in costly gowns, given her riches beyond compare.

And then he had turned into a monster, a fiend who demanded perfection, who lashed out at her if she dared voice an opinion that contradicted his; an ogre who wanted her love but only on his terms, who hit her when she failed to please him. He had been obsessed with the idea of having an heir to carry on the Summers name. He had constantly berated her because she was unable to give him a son, because she wasn't woman enough to accomplish the one thing women were good for. Well, she was glad now, glad that she was barren.

She glanced over her shoulder at the Cheyenne village sprawled near the banks of the river. Never, in her wildest dreams, had she imagined she would find herself in such a place.

The attack on the stagecoach had been a nightmare of noise and fear. One minute, she had been safe and secure, albeit terribly uncomfortable, bouncing around inside a coach headed for her parents' home in New York, and the next she had been cowering on the floor, certain she was about to be killed and scalped. She would never forget her terror as the battle raged around the stagecoach—the hiss of arrows, the popping sound of gunfire, the cloying smell of blood and the acrid stink of gunpowder, the palpable fear of the three men who had shared the coach with her. She had never been so afraid in her life.

When the fighting was over, the three men inside the coach were all dead. Riddled with arrows, they had stared at her through wide, unseeing eyes, their faces frozen in identical expressions of horror.

One of the warriors had yanked her from the coach and taken her up on his horse. The driver of the coach and the guard were dead, too, their lifeless bodies sprawled facedown in the dirt. She had never seen death up close before, but that day it had been all around her.

Numb with fear and in terror for her own life, she had watched as the Indians dragged the dead men from inside the coach. They had stripped the bodies of their clothing and weapons. One of the men had been carrying a large sum of cash. The Indians had tossed it into the air, laughing as they watched the greenbacks flutter in the breeze. She had turned away, her stomach clenching, when one of the warriors lifted the scalp of the shotgun guard.

Two of the Indians had freed the horses from the traces, then set the stagecoach on fire.

And now she was here, little better than a slave in an Indian village. It was unthinkable, unbelievable, that the daughter of Elizabeth Victoria Dearmond and William Thomas Duvall the Third should find herself in this place, forced to do menial labor for a bunch of savages. She had to admit, in all fairness, that even though some of their customs were barbaric and their way of life was, in many ways, primitive and uneducated, the people weren't really savages. They might be merciless to their enemies, but they were warm and caring toward their own, loyal to those they considered friends.

The warrior who had captured her had given her to his mother, making it perfectly clear to Kaylynn that she was to do whatever the old lady said. He had warned Kaylynn, using sign language and a few words of stilted English, that she would be punished if she tried to run away.

He didn't have to tell her twice. If she hadn't run away from Alan, she wouldn't be here now. There was no telling what fate would befall her if she tried again!

At first, she had hated it here, hated everything—the food, the people, the land itself. She hadn't known which was worse—the work she was made to do, the horrible skins she was forced to wear, the awful food they gave her to eat, or not being able to speak the language. She had told herself that she should have stayed with Alan, that being a punching bag in a big house surrounded by servants of her own was better than this.

But after a few weeks, when the strangeness had worn off, when she realized that no one was going to hurt her, she had come to an amazing discovery. She was happier here, living in a hide lodge, than she had ever been living in luxury with her husband. She might be a slave, but she was a person here, of value to Mo'e'ha. True, she worked hard, but it satisfied a need deep within her and gave her a sense of worth, of accomplishment, that she had never before experienced. Not that she wouldn't go back home to her parents in a minute, if given the chance.

Well, she had wasted enough time for one day, she thought with a grin. If she didn't hurry, old Mo'e'ha would scold her. Mo'e'ha meant magpie, and Kaylynn thought the woman was aptly named. If she was late, old Mo'e'ha would take a stick to her, but that wasn't so bad. Unlike Alan, the woman was too frail to hit her very hard. For Kaylynn, the humiliation of being punished like a child hurt far more than the beating itself.

Gathering the wood into her arms once more, she headed back toward the village. There was some sort of big celebration underway. It had been going on for over a week now. There had been lots of feasting and singing and games as the Cheyenne renewed acquaintances with their allies, the Lakota. She wondered vaguely what all the fuss was about, but it didn't really matter. She wasn't a part of it. All she knew was that it was some sort of religious celebration.

A large, circular dance arbor had been established in the center of the village. To the right of the camp, a special lodge had been erected, though she wasn't sure what its purpose was. There had been a flurry of excitement one afternoon, followed by a Buffalo Dance. The next day, a procession of warriors and women had paraded into the village bearing the trunk of a cottonwood tree that was at least forty feet long. She had watched as several prominent warriors counted coup on the tree. Then one of the medicine men had ordered the tree "killed," and it had been carried into the center of the Sun Dance lodge, where the trunk had been painted; the side to the west had been painted red, the north blue, the east green, and the south yellow. Rawhide figures had been placed in the fork of the tree, along with sixteen cherry sticks, some tobacco, an arrow for killing buffalo, and a picket pin. Rawhide ropes had been attached to the top of the pole. She could only wonder why.

There seemed to be an unusual amount of excitement when she reached the village. Several warriors were gathered into a tight group, all talking at once. The camp dogs were barking. Kaylynn blew out a sigh. She had never seen so many dogs in her whole life. Big ones, little ones, they all seemed to be half wild, always yapping, always underfoot. It had made her sick to her stomach the first time she had seen one of the Indian women catch a young dog and club it over the head, and even sicker when she realized the poor animal was going to be dinner.

Now she had not only eaten dog meat, but cooked it, and worse things as well. Creatures she would never have considered as a food source regularly showed up in the cook pot: porcupines, magpies, raccoons, prairie dogs, skunks, and beavers, along with ducks, eggs, and fish.

She kept her head lowered as she passed by the group of warriors. In all the months she had been here, she had avoided the men as much as possible. None of them seemed interested in her, for which she had been wonderfully grateful. She had heard stories, of course, of savage Indian men ravishing white women, but either the stories weren't true, or the warriors didn't find her attractive. Whatever the reason, she was glad none of them seemed to want her. She had learned the hard way what a man wanted from a woman, and she was glad to be done with it.

She glanced surreptitiously at the warriors as she passed by, wondering who the newcomer was. She didn't remember ever seeing him before. He stood a few inches taller than the men he was talking to. A jagged white scar cut across the left side of his face, giving him a fierce, angry look.

He glanced up, his gaze meeting hers, and for a fleeting moment it was as if everything else ceased to exist. The sounds of the camp, the people, all seemed to fade away until there were just the two of them standing there, staring at each other across a stretch of barren ground. Kaylynn had the eerie feeling that his soul brushed against hers, that he knew her every dream, her every fear. That he was the answer to her every prayer.

Chiding herself for imagining such nonsense, she hurried into Mo'e'ha's lodge and closed the door flap behind her. But she couldn't shake the feeling that something extraordinary had passed between her and the stranger.

Jesse Yellow Thunder stared after the girl, wondering who she was, wondering if she had felt what he had felt when their eyes met. She hadn't been in the village the last time he came home, he'd bet his last dollar on that. Her hair alone made her stand out. In a village where most everyone had straight, inky-black hair, that rich, deep, curly red stood out like a candle flame on a cloudy night.

Hardly aware of what he was doing, he touched the scar on his face. He didn't care how pretty the girl was, he was through with white women.

With a shake of his head, he turned his attention back to what his cousin, Gray Wolf, was saying.

When the first rush of excitement at his return had died down, Jesse took Gray Wolf aside. "There's a white woman in camp," he said, trying to keep the interest from his voice. "Who is she?"

Gray Wolf gave him an enigmatic look. "Two Dogs captured her in a raid. She belongs to his mother."

Jesse nodded. He had figured it was something like that, and then cursed himself for asking. It didn't matter who the redhead was. He had no need for a woman, any woman, other than the quick physical release that any whore could provide, and yet he couldn't shake the feeling that they were destined to meet.

Amused by such a fanciful thought, he put the white woman from his mind as he followed Gray

Wolf to his lodge. The Sun Dance was tomorrow, and he had preparations to make.

Kaylynn stood on the edge of the crowd, her curiosity stronger than her revulsion as she watched the shaman move among those who were going to participate in the Sun Dance ceremony. She had been intrigued by much of what she had seen during her stay with the Cheyenne, repulsed by some, but this was by far the most gruesome thing she had witnessed. A dozen young warriors stood together, their expressions solemn, as the medicine man moved among them.

She was about to turn away when she saw the shaman approach the stranger she had noticed the day before. She had asked Mo'e'ha who he was and learned that his name was Yellow Thunder and he was cousin to Gray Wolf.

Pinching the skin between the stranger's left breast and collar bone between his thumb and forefinger, the shaman lifted it as high as possible and then ran a narrow-bladed knife through the fold of skin. With the knife still in place, the shaman inserted a skewer of bone, and then withdrew the blade. A rawhide thong was fastened to the skewer, and the loose end was attached to one of the ropes dangling from the Sun Dance pole. A similar incision was made in the stranger's right breast.

The shaman moved on. He inserted skewers into the backs of three of the dancers, and then, instead of attaching the ends of the thongs to the Sun Dance pole, the rawhide was attached to a buffalo skull, which the men would drag around the dance arena.

The sound of drumming filled the air, and the participants began to move. Those who were attached to the Sun Dance pole began to dance back and forth, their faces turned up to the sky as they tugged against the thongs that bound them to the pole. The other men danced in a wide circle, dragging the heavy skulls behind them. From time to time, the dancers blew on eagle-bone whistles that hung from cords around their necks.

Fascinated and repulsed, Kaylynn's gaze rested briefly on each man before settling on the tall stranger. She didn't know anything about him except that he was Gray Wolf's cousin, but he looked as fierce and untamed as all the other dancers, maybe more so with that hideous scar on his cheek.

Face turned up to the sun, he moved with cat-like grace, his feet hardly seeming to touch the ground as he danced back and forth. She stared at the blood and perspiration trickling down his chest, at the rapt expression on his face, and knew if she lived with the Cheyenne for the rest of her life, she would never truly understand them. And yet, for the first time since her captivity, she felt herself wanting to know more. What did the dancers hope to gain by submitting themselves to such torture? What did Yellow Thunder hope to gain?

She noticed that his hands and feet had been painted red and blue; stripes were painted across his broad shoulders. He wore a long red kilt. There were bands of rabbit fur on his arms and ankles.

The drumming engulfed her like a living thing. The sound made the hair rise along her arms. She felt its power surround her, felt it go deep into the heart of the earth, felt the beat of it in the soles of her feet.

The sun rose higher. Oblivious to the perspiration trickling down her back, oblivious to everything and everyone but the scar-faced man, she watched him dance. Body sheened with sweat, muscles taut with pain, he moved forward and back with unconscious grace as he tugged against the rawhide thong that bound him like an umbilical cord to the sacred tree. It was barbaric. It was beautiful.

Once, his gaze found hers, and she felt again that surge of recognition. The drumming faded. The light of the sun bathed him in a soft golden glow, making him look otherworldly somehow. He was a lonely man, she thought. A dangerous man. With a shiver, she turned away.

She gathered wood for the evening fire, she walked down to the river for water, but no matter where she went, the drumming followed her, as did the image of the scar-faced man, until she was again drawn back to the sacred circle.

Night had fallen before all the dancers freed themselves. One of the men needed assistance from his relatives before he could tear himself free; another fainted so that a friend had to come forward and remove the skewers from his chest.

The scar-faced man required no help. Head high, chest bloodied, body sheened with sweat, he gave one final pull against the thongs and freed himself from the Sun Dance pole. He stood there for a moment, his expression victorious, and then, head hanging, he dropped to his knees.

Kaylynn stared at him, overcome by a sudden inexplicable urge to go to him, to wipe the perspiration from his brow, to gather him into her arms and ease his suffering.

As though feeling her gaze, he looked up, his dark eyes filled with pain and triumph.

She smiled uncertainly, then turned away, conscious of his gaze on her back.

Chapter Three

Alan Summers sat at his desk, fingertips drumming impatiently on the arm of his chair as he regarded the detective standing in front of him.

"What do you mean you can't find her, McCarthy? It's been eight months! She can't have vanished without a trace."

"I'm sorry, sir."

"You're keeping an eye on the house?"

"Yessir, round the clock, just as you ordered."

"You're certain she's not there?"

"Yessir, quite certain."

"And she hasn't contacted them?" Neither had he. He couldn't bring himself to write her parents, asking if his wife—*his wife, dammit*—had shown up on their doorstep crying for her mother.

"No, sir. I have someone inside the house checking the mail, both incoming and outgoing."

"And you feel you can trust this person?"

"Yessir. It's one of the maids. I offered her a rather large sum. She assures me there has been no letter from Mrs. Summers."

"Very well. Keep looking. Tell your men there will be a bonus for the one who finds her."

"Yessir." With a bow, Amos McCarthy turned and left the room.

Alan stared after him, his eyes narrowed. Eight months, and no trace of her. He had expected her to run home to New York, but if McCarthy was to be believed, and there was no reason to doubt the man, she wasn't there. So, where had she gone?

"Why don't you just forget about her?"

"Forget?" Alan whirled around, his gaze resting on the woman sitting in the plush velvet chair in the corner. "Forget?"

"You don't need her."

"She's my wife. Mine," he repeated, his voice curt. "And I keep what's mine."

"Her coming back will only complicate things."

"Afraid you might lose your place in my affections, Claire?"

She met his gaze squarely. "Yes. I don't want to share you with anyone. Not even your wife."

He laughed softly, pleased by her answer, by the jealousy in her eyes.

"Kaylynn belongs to me," he said. "Bought and paid for, just like you, my dear. She will be made to see the error of her ways when she returns."

"I could give you a son."

"You?" He laughed again, a harsh sound devoid of warmth or humor.

"Why not me? You could divorce Kaylynn. We could be married."

"Marry you? I had no idea you possessed such a wry sense of humor, my dear." He crossed the room to stand in front of his mistress. "You don't really mind sharing me, do you, my lovely Claire?"

Fear replaced the jealousy in her eyes. "No, Alan. Of course not."

"I knew you would see things my way," he replied. "Everyone does. Sooner or later."

Chapter Four

The day after the Sun Dance, the ceremonial camp disbanded. The tipis were moved from the great ceremonial circle to the usual camp circles of families within families. Kaylynn learned from Mo'e'ha that over the next week or so, the Cheyenne and the Lakota would begin to move back to their own hunting grounds in preparation for the fall hunt.

But on this day, there was to be a horse race. Kaylynn had learned that the Lakota and the Cheyenne loved contests of all kinds. Games of skill, foot races, horse races, wrestling, competing with bow and arrow and lance, they excelled at them all.

Kaylynn stood on the edge of the crowd, watching the preparations for the race. In the early days of her captivity, she had stubbornly refused to make any effort to learn the Cheyenne language. Foolish as it seemed now, she had told herself it would be a waste of time. She wasn't staying here. Surely, she would be rescued soon. She had dreamed of the Army riding in to save her, dreamed of a knight on a white horse risking life and limb to carry her to safety. She knew now that such an event was unlikely. No one knew she was here. It grieved her to think her parents would never know what had happened to her.

When she finally accepted the fact that she was probably going to spend the rest of her life with the Cheyenne, she had made an effort to learn their language. She had always been a quick study and she had learned quickly, though there were times, like now, when everyone seemed to be talking at once, that she missed more than she understood. From the enthusiastic gestures and the words she caught, she realized there was a lot of betting going on. Men and women were wagering robes, horses, and blankets on the outcome of the race.

She saw old Mo'e'ha talking excitedly with one of the men, and once she pointed in Kaylynn's direction and nodded.

Kaylynn had a sudden, sinking feeling that Mo'e'ha was offering her as part of a bet, and while Kaylynn wasn't particularly fond of the old woman, she had grown accustomed to her and her ways.

Those who were going to ride in the race began to mount up. The men, wearing nothing but clouts and moccasins, rode bareback, their dark, copper-hued skin gleaming in the sunlight. Her gaze was drawn to the stranger she had watched the day before. She felt a shiver run down her spine, a sense of trepidation, of excitement.

For a moment, with her gaze trapped by his, she forgot everything else. Like a rabbit mesmerized by a snake, she stood unmoving, her whole being quaking from the force of his steady gaze. What was there about him that filled her with such unease, that made her feel as though she were teetering on the edge of a precipice?

She breathed an audible sigh of relief when he turned away and swung onto his horse.

She didn't see or hear a signal, but suddenly the race was on. Excitement rippled through the crowd as men and women cheered for their favorites. As unobtrusively as possible, Kaylynn pushed her way to the front of the crowd.

The riders were in a close bunch, but she had no trouble picking out the stranger as the horses rounded a turn and started back toward the village. Gradually, the stranger and another warrior pulled away from the rest. Racing neck and neck, they crossed the finish line together.

A tie. Kaylynn felt a moment of relief. All bets were off.

She was turning away when she realized that the race wasn't over. The two who had crossed the finish line together were going to race again to determine the winner.

There was a great deal of noise and commotion as some of the onlookers wagered additional goods. Dogs barked. Children raced each other while waiting for the new race to begin.

Kaylynn watched Yellow Thunder as he slid off the back of his horse and began to walk the animal back and forth near the starting line.

He was tall and lean and moved with a slow, almost sensuous grace. He frightened her, though she couldn't say why. It was more than his scarred face, more than the fact that he was Cheyenne.

"Mao'hoohe. *Nenaasestse!*"

Kaylynn turned as she heard Mo'e'ha calling her.

"*Ne'aahtoveste!*" the old woman said as Kaylynn approached. "Listen to me! You belong to Bear Robe now."

Kaylynn stared at Mo'e'ha in disbelief. "What? How can that be? It was a tie."

"I did not wager on who would win the race," Mo'e'ha replied with an air of resignation, "but that Black Cloud would beat Bear Robe. Bear Robe won. You belong to him now." With a shrug, the old woman turned away.

Kaylynn stared after Mo'e'ha, stifling the urge to call after the old woman.

A deep voice drew her attention. Glancing over her shoulder, she saw the scar-faced man talking to her new owner. The stranger looked at her once, a hard, assessing glance, and then he swung aboard his horse and rode to the starting line.

Kaylynn stared after him, the hard, cold hand of fear tying her stomach in knots. *Please*, she prayed, *please don't let him win.*

A hush fell over the crowd. Kaylynn knew it was in anticipation of the start of the race, but it seemed ominous somehow, the quiet before a storm.

She bit down on her lower lip as the two horses sprang forward. She was vaguely aware of the shouts and cries of the spectators, but she felt as though she were standing there alone, her fate resting on the outcome of a race between two savages.

The horses were running neck and neck as they rounded the halfway point.

A distant part of her mind registered the primal beauty of the scene before her: the deep blue sky, the green grass that spread as far as the eye could see, the slender cottonwoods that grew along the river, the raw speed and power of the two horses as they thundered over the hard-packed earth. The stranger was bent low over his mount's neck, and she thought that she had never seen anything so visually stunning as the dark-haired stranger astride the powerful blue roan. They moved together with perfect rhythm, almost as if they were one creature. Though it was probably her imagination, she fancied the man was talking to the horse, urging it on. And slowly, slowly, the big blue roan moved ahead. Ears flat, neck stretched out, its hooves seeming to fly over the ground, the mare streaked across the finish line several yards ahead of the other horse.

A feeling of dread washed over Kaylynn as she released the breath she was holding.

The stranger had won, and she had lost.

Jesse accepted the congratulations of those around him. Filled with the exhilaration of a hard-won contest, he dismounted, smiling and nodding to the last of the well-wishers. He scratched the roan between the ears, grinning as the mare pushed her nose against his arm. It was a sad thing, he mused, when the only girl who loved you was your horse.

"I should never have bet against you."

Jesse looked at Bear Robe and grinned. "That's right."

"Here is the woman." Bear Robe pushed the white woman forward. "She answers to the name of Mao'hoohe."

Red Fox. Jesse grinned wryly as his gaze swept over the girl's long red hair. The name suited her. "You also owe me a lodge," he reminded his friend.

Bear Robe nodded, his expression glum. "It will be ready tonight."

"Good." Jesse slapped his childhood friend on the shoulder, then turned to the girl. "How long have you been a captive?"

Kaylynn stared at him through rebellious brown eyes, somewhat taken aback by the fact that he spoke fluent English. "Almost eight months." Sometimes it seemed like years.

Jesse stared at her, wondering where she had come from. She had that innate look that meant money. She was probably used to living high on the hog, he thought. No doubt she hated it here. Most white women did. He thought fleetingly of Abigail. Once, they had planned to make a home here. . . . He shoved the thought from his mind. It didn't matter how this girl felt. She was here and, like it or not, she was his. He handed her the mare's reins, turned, and headed for the river.

Kaylynn stared after him. Did he expect her to go with him?

He paused and glanced over his shoulder. "You coming?"

Sullenly, she followed him down to the river.

He walked for quite some distance, finally stopping when he came to a place that was screened by an overgrowth of brush. The mare tugged on the reins, reaching for the water.

"Don't let her drink," he said sharply.

Grimacing, Kaylynn tugged on the reins, pulling the horse away from the edge of the water.

"She needs to be cooled out," he said, then frowned when he saw she didn't understand. "You need to walk her until her coat's dry and her chest feels cool."

"She's your horse," Kaylynn retorted, then bit down on her lower lip, wondering where that bit of defiance had come from. She had learned long ago not to argue.

"And you're my slave," he replied, his cold, dark eyes daring her to deny it. "I'd advise you to do as you're told. You won't like what happens if you don't."

He turned away from her and Kaylynn gasped when, without warning, he stripped off his clout and moccasins and plunged into the water.

She stood there for a moment, wondering why she was so shocked. The Indians didn't seem to be overly concerned with modesty. Men, women, and children swam together in the summer; Mo'e'ha's son and his wife had coupled in the lodge when they thought everyone else was asleep.

With a sigh, she tugged on the horse's reins and the mare followed her downriver.

For a moment, Kaylynn contemplated climbing on the horse's back and making a run for it. There was no one there to stop her. She could be miles away by nightfall.

She looked at a fallen log lying near the river's edge. It would be easy to climb up on the log, then pull herself onto the mare's back. The roan seemed to be a docile creature.

It was tempting, so tempting, but her fear of the unknown was stronger than her fear of the stranger called Yellow Thunder. There were wild animals out there, and wilder Indians—Crow and Blackfoot. She had no food, and no guarantee she could find enough to sustain her until she reached a town, assuming she could locate one. She had no blanket, no coat. And though the days were warm, the nights were sometimes cool. She didn't relish the idea of freezing to death, or starving, or being taken prisoner by another tribe.

Chiding herself for being a coward, she turned around and started back the way she had come. Someday, she vowed, someday she would find the nerve to run away.

But not today.

Jesse swam briskly for fifteen minutes, then climbed out of the water. It was good to be home, good to hear the language of his mother's people again, to see the faces of men and women he had grown up with. Even though he had always felt himself a man apart because of his mixed blood, this was the only place on earth where he felt he belonged, the only place where he could relax, where the bad dreams didn't bother him, where he slept the whole night through. No one was gunning for him here.

Standing on the edge of the riverbank, he closed his eyes and let the sun's warmth dry him off. Taking part in the Sun Dance had restored his inner spirit, reminded him of who and what he was. Gazing at the sun, lost in a hazy world of pain, he had seen a vision which had made no sense to him and which he could not now clearly remember save that it had concerned a red-tailed vixen who had sung a song he could not now recall, a gentle creature who had seen beyond the hideous scars on his face and body and had, with a single touch, healed the scars on his soul. Perhaps it had not been a true vision at all, but merely a dream born out of a desperate hope for redemption.

Opening his eyes, he shook the vision from his mind. He had not seen Ravenhawk at the Sun Dance ceremony. He would start asking after the man's whereabouts when he got back to the village. He was certain his quarry would show up sooner or later. Once he found Ravenhawk, he would sell the woman, then haul the Lakota into Red Creek to collect the reward. And then . . . An awareness that he was no longer alone prickled over his skin. Glancing over his shoulder, he saw the woman.

His gaze traveled over her. She was tall and lithe and lovely. The sunlight emphasized the red in her hair, making him think of autumn leaves. Her eyes were dark brown, her mouth a tempting, pouty pink. Long hours in the sun had tanned her skin a smooth golden brown. He felt a warm rush of desire pool in his groin as he watched the subtle sway of her hips.

He hadn't had a woman in a long time.

And this one was his to do with as he pleased.

Ravenhawk could wait one more day.

Kaylynn came to an abrupt halt when she saw Yellow Thunder. He was standing on the river-bank, as naked as a jay bird. She tried not to look, but she couldn't seem to draw her gaze away. He was tall and lean and well muscled, with a broad back and firm buttocks. He had a birthmark on his derriere. It was about an inch long, dark brown, in the shape of a dagger. His body, the color of burnished copper, was as badly scarred as his face.

She felt a rush of heat flood her cheeks when he turned to face her, felt her mouth go suddenly dry when she saw the desire in his eyes. She gasped, one hand covering her rapidly beating heart, when she saw his body's reaction to what he was thinking.

With a low cry, she dropped the horse's reins, intending to run to Mo'e'ha's lodge, only to recall that she was no longer welcome there. She belonged to this stranger now.

She stared at him a moment longer, then turned on her heel and bolted back the way she had come.

With a grin, Jesse pulled on his clout and swung onto the roan's back. The conquest would be all the sweeter for the chase.

Chapter Five

Kaylynn ran as though pursued by a thousand devils. She had lived with the Indians for nearly eight months. In the beginning, she had been afraid of them. Back East, there had been talk about the Indian problem, about how savage they were. Godless, inhuman creatures, people said, who wore animal skins and feathers and ate raw meat. Indian men were said to lust after white women, and she had lived in constant fear that she would be raped by every man in the village. She'd been surprised when it hadn't happened.

Apparently the stories about Indian men lusting after every white woman they saw had been false. Either that, or she just didn't appeal to Cheyenne men. None of the warriors had ever approached her, not even the warrior who had captured her.

He had brought her home to be a slave in his lodge, and that was all.

She ran blindly on, heedless of the coming night, of the branches that scratched her skin and legs. Propelled by a nameless fear, she ran deeper into the woods, certain she would rather face whatever wild beasts lurked there than the man she had left behind.

It seemed she had been running for hours. Her sides hurt, her lungs hurt, she was seeing spots before her eyes. She would have to stop soon, find a place to rest, to hide.

And then, through the fog of fear, she heard the sound of hoofbeats coming up fast behind her. She risked a quick glance over her shoulder, felt a new surge of terror rise up within her when she saw the stranger riding toward her. He was leaning over his horse's neck, his long black hair streaming behind him.

"No," she gasped. "No, no."

Fear lent wings to her feet, but she couldn't outrun the big blue mare. She screamed as the horse brushed her shoulder, knocking her to the ground. She rolled over twice, the breath knocked from her body.

Quick as a cat, he was beside her, jerking her to her feet, his hands imprisoning her arms.

"Where do you think you're going?" His voice was silky-soft, low and dangerous.

Kaylynn stared into his cool gray eyes, unable to think, unable to speak. She couldn't draw her gaze from the scar on his face, could hardly draw a breath for the fear congealed in her throat. A shiver slid down her spine.

A muscle throbbed in Jesse's cheek as he endured her scrutiny. Most of the women he met were repulsed by his appearance; whores always charged him extra. He had thought himself used to it by now.

He leaned toward her, until their faces were only a breath apart. "Go ahead," he said gruffly. "Take a good look."

She blinked at him, a slow blush heating her cheeks. "I'm sorry." She spoke automatically, years of schooling in etiquette and manners coming to the fore. "It was rude of me to stare."

Rude? Jesse almost laughed out loud. No one had ever apologized for staring at him before. But he wasn't interested in her good manners now; he didn't care if she was sincere. He was only aware of the soft feminine curves brushing against his chest, of the nearness of her lips.

Muttering an oath, he pulled her body up against his and kissed her. There was nothing of softness in his kiss, no gentleness, no tenderness. He cupped her head with one hand and ground his lips against hers, his tongue plunging into her mouth.

Kaylynn struggled against him, beating at his face with her fists, scratching his cheek, his neck. And when that didn't stop him, she bit down on his tongue, recoiling when she tasted his blood in her mouth.

With a vile oath, he jerked away, his gray eyes filled with rage. "Damn you! Don't ever do that again." His hands closed over her shoulders and he shook her. "Do you understand me? You belong to me now, and that means you'll make yourself available to me whenever and however I want you."

43

She stared at him, her eyes wide, her face pale. For a moment, it was Alan staring down at her, Alan's voice ringing in her ears, his hands like claws where they gripped her shoulders. *You're mine, do you understand? Mine . . .*

"No." She formed the word, but no sound issued from her lips. "No."

"Yes," he said, his expression as implacable as his tone. "I don't want to have to beat you, but I will."

Kaylynn felt the blood drain from her face as she remembered the sound of Alan's fist repeatedly striking her flesh as he accused her of being frigid, barren; the pain that had engulfed her before she fainted; the ugly bruises his fists left behind. She clenched her hands. She wouldn't cry, not in front of this stranger, wouldn't let him see how frightened she was. And she was frightened. More frightened than she had ever been in her life. Because she had no doubt at all that, like Alan, this man meant every word. And she knew the pain of a man's hand all too well.

"Do we understand each other?" he asked.

She nodded, once, curtly. She understood. Understood that she was going to run away at the first opportunity. She would rather take her chances out on the prairie with the wolves and the snakes than stay here, at the mercy of this savage. It had taken her years to find the courage to run away from Alan, but on that day, her mouth bleeding and her eye blackened from his fist, she had vowed that no man would ever lay a hand on her in anger again.

"Go back to camp and wait for me," he said, his voice gruff.

She didn't have to be told twice. Eager to be away from him, she turned and ran back to the village.

There was a tipi waiting for Jesse when he returned to the village, compliments of Bear Robe's wives.

He found the white woman sitting in the shade, her knees drawn up to her chest. Dismounting, he beckoned her with a look, then thrust a rabbit and two quail into her hands.

"I'm hungry," he said. "Cook the rabbit tonight. We'll have the quail tomorrow."

Kaylynn felt a rush of resentment as she entered the lodge. She belonged to this man now. She would be spending the night in this lodge, alone, with the stranger.

She glanced around. There was wood laid in a fire pit near the center of the floor, two willow backrests, a few cook pots and utensils, several baskets of raw vegetables.

Refusing to think of what might happen later that night, she knelt beside the pit. Pulling a flint from her sash, she lit the fire. She found a knife in the cooking utensils. Testing the edge against her thumb, she doubted if it would cut through butter, much less the carcass of a rabbit.

She was looking for another knife when she sensed she was no longer alone. Awareness slid down her spine, a soft tingling sensation that was oddly pleasurable.

"Here." Jesse knelt beside her, withdrew his knife from his sheath, and offered it to her. He watched her turn it over in her hand, knew she was trying to find the courage to plunge the blade into his heart. "Careful with that. It's sharp."

Jesse stared at her a moment, then rose to his feet and left the lodge.

Outside, he stood with his hands clenched, unable to believe he had threatened to beat her. He had never hit a woman in his life, but something in her eyes—the fear, perhaps, or the repugnance—had triggered his rage, making him want to lash out. He had thought himself used to it by now, he mused bleakly, used to the looks, the shudders, the pity. Used to taking what he wanted whenever he wanted. So why did this woman's reaction disturb him so much?

He swore, using every foul word he had ever heard, but it didn't help. He'd been a fool to gamble for the woman, but there was something about her that called to him. He had known he would win the race, had known that she would he his. Waiting for the race to start, he'd had a fleeting, foolish thought that destiny had brought him here, not for Ravenhawk and the reward, but for the woman.

With a rueful shake of his head, he thrust such nonsense aside. Tomorrow morning, he would give the woman back to Bear Robe and then he'd go check out the Lakota encampment and see if he could find Ravenhawk. He hadn't had a woman in almost a year; he could wait another few weeks. He would haul Ravenhawk into Red Creek and turn him over to the sheriff there, and then he'd go hole up at the saloon with his favorite whore and get good and drunk.

The smell of roasting rabbit reached his nostrils. He thought about going to eat with his cousin, then discarded the idea. He had killed that rabbit and, by damn, he was going to eat it.

The woman jumped to her feet when he stepped into the lodge. The wariness in her eyes pricked his conscience—what little he had left.

"Smells good," he said gruffly. "Is it ready?"

She nodded.

Jesse sat down, watching her while she removed the rabbit from the spit and split it in half. She placed the meat in a bowl, along with some cooked vegetables, and offered it to him.

He nodded his thanks as he took the bowl from her hand. She stood beside the fire, watching him.

"Aren't you eating?" he asked.

Kaylynn shook her head. "I'm not hungry." It was a lie, but she knew she wouldn't be able to swallow a thing with him watching her every move.

He looked up at her, one brow arched, as her stomach growled loudly.

Kaylynn stared back at him, her cheeks burning, acutely aware of his presence, his nearness. Like it or not, she belonged to him now.

With a shrug, he turned back to his dinner. He ate quickly, then stood up. "Where's my knife?"

"Here." She picked it up and offered it to him.

He wiped the blade off on the side of his trousers, then left the lodge.

Kaylynn breathed a sigh of relief when he went outside. Tonight, she thought, nibbling on a piece of meat. She was leaving tonight.

Jesse spent an hour wandering through the village, renewing old acquaintances. He shared a pipe with Gray Wolf, watched a half-dozen boys trying to outdo each other with bow and arrow.

He paused outside the shaman's lodge, stood in the shade listening as the medicine man related the Hummingbird Story to a handful of children.

"It was a long time ago," the old man said, his gaze moving over each child's face. "A time when the animals and the birds still had their voices. Hummingbird fell in love with a handsome warrior. She would fly near him and make her colors bright so he would notice her beauty. One day, she flew so close that she heard him talking to his father. The warrior said he had made a bet with Crane that he could beat him in a flight around the world.

"Now," the shaman went on, "the world was not as we know it today. There were three levels. The upper level was akin to heaven. The bottom level was chaos. But the middle was the earth as we know it. Racing around the three levels could upset the balance of all three, allowing heaven and chaos and earth to mix.

"The hummingbird was very upset when she heard this. She had always assumed that the handsome young warrior was as balanced and pure as he was beautiful. Hummingbird flew off to think about what she had heard and to see if the Willow could answer her questions. On the day that the race was meant to be run, the young warrior sat crying. He knew he would lose the race. Crane was faster and needed less sleep. He was a mere man with too much pride. Hummingbird heard his tears and cried out to the Creator to help him. She asked that he might be free of his bet with Crane. As punishment for his boastful spirit, his ears would no longer be able to hear the voices of the plants and animals. The young warrior accepted his punishment and forever after the voices of the plants and animals have been silent to man.

"Now," the shaman asked, "what have you learned from this story?"

Jesse nodded to the shaman and continued on his way. He told himself he was relaxing, that he was listening for some word of Ravenhawk, when the truth was that he didn't want to go back to his lodge, didn't want to be near the woman. Didn't want to see the apprehension and loathing in her eyes when she looked at him. No doubt she would faint dead away if he touched her again. He lifted a hand to his cheek, feeling the rough edge of the scar that puckered his flesh. Who the hell could blame her?

He walked out to the horse herd and whistled for the roan. The mare came at his call, nuzzling his arm.

"You're the only girl who loves me, aren't you?" He scratched the mare between the ears and under her jaw. "You don't care what I look like, do you?"

The mare made a soft snuffling sound as she pushed her nose against his chest.

Murmuring an oath, he gave the mare a last pat on the shoulder, then walked down by the river. He would bed down here tonight. Tomorrow, he would get rid of the woman. She wasn't his type anyway. She was too tall for his taste, too skinny. He liked a woman with a little meat on her.

With a shake of his head, he pulled off his clout and moccasins and plunged into the icy water.

He didn't need her. He didn't need anyone. Not anymore.

Chapter Six

Kaylynn peered outside. It was almost midnight, and Yellow Thunder still hadn't returned to the lodge. Clutching the small buckskin bag that held a change of clothing and all the food that had been in the lodge, she stepped out into the shadows, a rough woolen blanket draped around her shoulders.

Moving as quietly as possible, she made her way toward the river and turned east. Towns and forts were usually located near water. Maybe, if she was lucky, there was some sort of settlement nearby. Maybe, if she hadn't been such a hopeless coward, she could have found her way to civilization months ago.

Clouds hovered low in the sky, hiding the moon and stars. A dog growled as she passed the last lodge, but other than that, the night was quiet.

She walked as swiftly as she dared in the dark, her heart pounding with trepidation. She wished she'd had the nerve to try to steal one of the horses. She wished she had a weapon other than the dull knife tucked in her sash. She wished she had stayed in New York where she belonged.

A sigh of resignation escaped her lips. If wishes were horses, then beggars would ride.

It was eerie, walking alone beside the river. A cool breeze stirred the leaves of the cottonwoods. Wispy white clouds drifted before the wind like horses running before a storm. A rustle in the underbrush made her shiver with fear. There were wolves and grizzly bears and coyotes in the hills. It was a wild, unforgiving land, the strong preying on the weak, and she was definitely one of the weak. She had no defense other than her wits and the knife in her belt.

Straightening her shoulders, she pushed her fears into the back of her mind. She had survived with the Indians for eight months. She was physically stronger now than she had ever been in her life, thanks to the hard work she had been forced to endure. Her hands were callused. She could carry heavy loads of wood. She knew how to skin and gut a deer, though it still made her stomach churn to do so. She knew how to start a fire with a flint. Knew that bees would lead her to water.

She laughed softly. No doubt her mother would be shocked when she saw her again, with her callused hands and sun-browned skin. Her mother had always said you could tell a lady by her hands. Well, she hadn't been a lady for quite some time.

"You can do this, Kaylynn," she said aloud.

"There's nothing to be afraid of." Nothing but the stranger with his cold gray eyes and scarred face.

She wondered if he would come after her. The thought made her walk faster. She would rather face a mama grizzly defending her cub than be at the stranger's mercy.

She walked for hours, stopping only briefly to rest and drink from the river. To pass the time, she thought of her room at home, of all the dresses and shoes and hats she had once had.

Her mouth watered as she thought of sitting down to one of Mrs. Moseley's elaborate dinners. Ah, what she wouldn't give for a slice of thick, succulent ham, or a plate of chicken and dumplings. And one of Mrs. Moseley's heavenly apple pies . . . It would be wonderful to have crepes and sausages and hot cocoa for breakfast. To sleep in her old feather bed as late as she pleased. To spend her days shopping with her friends, taking tea at La Parisienne, having Christmas again, parties again.

She wondered how Grandmother Dearmond was doing, and if she still spent long hours working in her garden. Kaylynn had loved to spend time with her grandmother, had loved listening to Grams tell stories of the old country and how her parents had sold everything they owned and left England to come to America.

With those pleasant memories of home, the time passed quickly.

At dawn, she found a secluded thicket and crawled inside. She ate a little of the jerky she had packed, then curled up on a makeshift bed of leaves and closed her eyes.

*   *   *

Jesse stood inside the empty lodge, his eyes narrowed. She was gone, there was no doubt of that. The ashes were cold; one of the blankets was missing, and all the foodstuffs were gone.

He loosed a long, shuddering sigh. So, rather than stay with him, she had run away. He grunted softly. It didn't matter. He was well rid of her.

Turning on his heel, he left the lodge. Outside, he mounted his horse and rode toward the Lakota encampment. He had wasted enough time. It was time to get on with his reason for coming here.

It was early morning and the people were just beginning to stir. Blue-gray smoke from hundreds of cook fires rose skyward.

He rode among the lodges, nodding to men he knew. And then he saw Ravenhawk walking toward the river, alone.

Jesse grinned. Sometimes, Fate was kind.

Ravenhawk floated lazily in a quiet part of the river. After days of hard riding, it felt good to relax, to do nothing but gaze up at the sky. Maybe he would stay here this time. His mother had been glad to see him. He knew she would welcome his company. Living alone was hard on a woman. With no man in her lodge, she was forced to rely on the generosity of others for meat and protection.

Grunting softly, he stood up. He might as well stay. He had nowhere else to go, and plenty of time to get there.

He turned at the sound of hoofbeats, then swore under his breath when he recognized the scarfaced man sitting astride the big blue roan mare. Jesse Yellow Thunder. Damn!

"What do you want?" Ravenhawk asked. He glanced at his knife, lying on the riverbank beside his clout and moccasins.

Yellow Thunder grunted softly as he pulled a set of handcuffs out of his back pocket. "What do you think?"

Ravenhawk shook his head. "I'm not going back to jail."

A slow smile spread over the bounty hunter's face as he drew his revolver. "I think you are."

"You're crazy if you think my people will let you take me."

"That's up to you. The reward says dead or alive. Dead's easier."

"Dammit, I didn't do it."

"Yeah, that's what they all say."

"All right, I robbed the damn bank. I was drunk and broke."

"Been there a time or two myself," Jesse admitted. "But I never robbed any banks."

"I'm not going back." Ravenhawk shook his head. "You know what it's like, being locked up. I've done enough time. I can't do any more."

"Like I said, we can do this easy or hard. If we have to do it the hard way, you're gonna end up dead, and some innocent people are likely to get hurt. But that's up to you."

"You bastard."

Jesse nodded. "What's it gonna be?"

"I'll go with you, on one condition. You let me tell my mother good-bye, and you don't put those cuffs on me until we're out of the village."

"No."

"Dammit, I won't try anything. I give you my word."

"As what? A bank robber?"

Ravenhawk drew himself up to his full height, his black eyes narrowed and angry. "My word is as good as yours, bounty hunter."

"All right. Your word that you'll come peaceably, right now. But you make one false move, and you're dead where you stand. We understand each other?"

Ravenhawk nodded.

"Let's go." Jesse shoved the handcuffs back into his pocket and holstered his gun, then rested his forearms on his saddle horn while he watched Ravenhawk step out of the water.

The Lakota were a handsome people, and Ravenhawk was no exception. He was tall and broad-shouldered, well-muscled but not bulky. He wore the faint white scars of the Sun Dance on his chest.

Under other circumstances, they might have been friends, Jesse mused. They were both half-breeds, both hunted men. But Jesse worked mostly within the law, while Ravenhawk traveled the outside.

"I'll take that knife," Jesse said.

Ravenhawk picked up the sheathed blade and tossed it to the bounty hunter, then pulled on his clout and moccasins. Anger churned deep within him. He'd been a fool to let his guard down. He should have known that Yellow Thunder would be on his trail as soon as that wanted poster came out, but the last he'd heard, the bounty hunter had been over in Colorado chasing down the Dawson gang.

He swore softly, wondering if maybe he should make a run for it now and take his chances with a bullet. Anything would be better than going back to jail. He had already decided he had taken his last bank. It was time to try another line of work.

"Let's go," Yellow Thunder said.

Blowing out a sigh of resignation, Ravenhawk headed for the village.

Yellow Thunder rode up alongside him. "Where's the money?"

"It's gone."

"What do you mean?"

"There was only a few hundred dollars." Ravenhawk shrugged. "I spent some. Lost the rest in a poker game."

"You robbed a bank, and then blew the take in a poker game?" Jesse shook his head. "You really should find a new line of work."

"Go to hell."

"All in good time. All right. This is how we'll play it. We'll mosey over to your lodge. You tell your mama good-bye, and we're out of here. Nice and quiet."

Ravenhawk nodded.

The village had awakened in his absence. There was a sense of anticipation in the air as the people contemplated the last four days of the Sun Dance festival. It was the high point of the year, a time for renewing the sacred arrows, a time for seeking power. Ravenhawk had planned to take part in the Sun Dance, to offer his blood and his pain to *Maheo* as a token of his vow to return to the ways of the *Tsis-tsistas*, but he had gotten sidetracked by a pretty little girl in Twin Bluffs and arrived two days too late.

He saw his mother sitting in front of her lodge. She had aged since his last visit a year ago. There was gray in her hair now, fine lines in her face that he had never noticed before.

She looked up and smiled as he approached. *"Hinhanni waste, cinksi."*

Ravenhawk smiled back at her. *"Hinhanni, waste, ina."* Good morning, my mother.

"Will you eat?"

Ravenhawk glanced over his shoulder, then shook his head. "I must leave."

His mother stood up, her brow furrowed, her eyes worried. "Leave? So soon?"

He jerked a thumb in Yellow Thunder's direction. "This man needs my help. I must go with him."

She turned and looked at up Yellow Thunder, who nodded at her. She studied him a moment, then looked at her son again. "How soon will you return to us?"

"I don't know. As soon as I can." Ravenhawk glanced over his shoulder at the bounty hunter. "Just let me get my gear," he said, in English.

Jesse placed his hand over the butt of his Colt, then nodded. "You do that."

Ravenhawk ducked inside his mother's lodge. He stood there for a moment, his hand caressing his rifle, his honor warring with his revulsion at going back to jail. He lifted a corner of the lodge flap and peered outside. Yellow Thunder had dismounted, and now his mother stood between the lodge and the bounty hunter.

Swearing softly, he picked up his saddlebags, slid a knife inside his left moccasin, pulled on a long-sleeved buckskin shirt, and left the lodge. "I'm ready."

Jesse regarded Ravenhawk a moment, then gestured toward the horse herd. "Let's go."

Ravenhawk embraced his mother, wondering if he would ever see her again, then grabbed his saddle and bridle and walked toward the herd. The bounty hunter walked behind him, one hand brushing his gun butt. The blue roan followed Yellow Thunder.

When they were out of sight of the lodges, Jesse said, "Hold on."

Ravenhawk stopped, every muscle taut.

"Get your hands up where I can see 'em."

Ravenhawk dropped the saddle and bridle on the ground and lifted his arms, his jaw clenching as the bounty hunter searched him. Yellow Thunder made a clucking sound when he pulled the knife from Ravenhawk's moccasin.

"All right," Jesse said. "Let's go get your horse."

When they reached the herd, Ravenhawk whistled up his mount, a long-legged, deep-chested Appaloosa gelding. He quickly bridled the horse, cinched the saddle in place, and lashed his gear behind the cantle; then, taking up the reins, he swung into the saddle.

Jesse had mounted his own horse and now he fixed Ravenhawk with a hard stare. "Remember, you gave me your word."

Ravenhawk nodded curtly. "Until we're out of the village."

The bounty hunter nodded, and a look of understanding passed between them.

Ravenhawk intended to make a break for it when they left the village behind.

And Jesse intended to stop him.

* * *

It was late morning when Kaylynn crawled out of the thicket. Brushing the dirt from her hair and clothes as best she could, she made her way to the river and rinsed her mouth, then took a long drink.

A handful of berries plucked from a nearby bush, together with a chunk of pemmican, eased her hunger.

The sun felt warm on her face, and she sat down at the river's edge. The water sang a cheerful tune as it tumbled over the rocks. She looked to the west, wondering how far she had come the night before, and then looked ahead, wondering how far she would have to walk until she reached civilization.

It had taken her hours to get to sleep the night before. She had started at every sound until, at last, exhaustion had claimed her. She had slept restlessly, her dreams troubled, yet she couldn't remember them when she woke.

She gazed into the slow-moving river, smiled when she saw the silver flash of a fish dart past. What was the old saying, something about the journey of a thousand miles beginning with a single step? Her legs felt as though she had already walked a thousand miles.

She sighed, knowing she should be on her way, but reluctant to move. It was so quiet and peaceful here. . . .

Her head jerked up and she glanced over her shoulder as she heard the muffled sound of hoofbeats coming toward her.

Scrambling to her feet, she ducked into the thicket where she had spent the night, her heart pounding wildly in her breast. Peeking through a break in the brush, she saw two men riding in her direction. She sucked in a breath as she recognized the scar-faced stranger, choked back a cry when she realized she had left her pack at the river's edge.

Please, please don't let him stop here.

Jesse reined his horse to a halt, his gaze sweeping the ground.

Ravenhawk watched the bounty hunter, whose attention, at least for the moment, was focused elsewhere. This would be the perfect time to make a break for it, except for two things—his right hand was shackled to the saddle horn, and the bounty hunter had hold of the Appaloosa's reins.

Jesse wrapped the gelding's reins around the pommel of his saddle, then dismounted and picked up a buckskin parfleche lying near the edge of the river.

Turning, he called, "You might as well come on out. I know you're in there."

Ravenhawk followed Jesse's gaze to a thicket a few yards away.

"Don't make me come in after you," the bounty hunter warned.

Ravenhawk looked at the ground, only then noticing the small footprints that led back and forth from the water to the thicket.

A moment later, a woman emerged from the brake. She was a pretty thing, tall and slender. A tangled mass of dark red hair fell over her shoulders. She stared at Ravenhawk through eyes that were as brown as tree bark, as frightened as those of a mouse facing a mountain lion.

"Things are looking up," Jesse muttered as he tied the parfleche to his saddle horn.

"No." The word rose in the girl's throat and exploded in a harsh cry. "No!"

Turning on her heel, she ran downriver, her hair streaming behind her.

Jesse watched her go, his desire quickening as he watched her. She was as fleet-footed as a young doe. He grinned as he tied the Appaloosa's reins to a tree, then pulled a second set of handcuffs from his hip pocket and cuffed Ravenhawk's hands together so he couldn't use his free hand to reach forward and untie the Appaloosa. The Lakota would have to be a fool to take off with one hand cuffed to the saddle, but desperate men sometimes did stupid things.

"What the hell are you doing?" Ravenhawk demanded.

"Making sure you'll be here when I get back," Jesse said as he vaulted onto the back of his own horse.

Feeling a sense of déjà vu, he touched his heels to the roan's sides and gave chase. The girl glanced over her shoulder when she heard him coming up behind her.

A cry of victory rose in Jesse's throat as he rode up alongside the girl and swept her off the ground, much the way a warrior rescued a wounded comrade from the field of battle.

She screamed as he dropped her, none too gently, over the horse's withers. Reining the mare to a halt, Jesse grabbed the woman under the arms and set her upright on the saddle in front of him.

She turned toward him, her eyes blazing as she lashed out at him, her small fists beating at his face and chest, her nails raking his cheek, tearing the skin. Muttering an oath, Jesse lifted a hand to his face; he felt a swift, unreasoning anger boil up inside him when he saw the blood on his palm. For an instant, he relived the humiliation and pain he had suffered at the hands of Abigail's father. Reacting without thinking, he backhanded the girl across the face. Once. Hard.

The sound of the slap rang like thunder in Jesse's ears. The girl was staring at him through eyes wide with fear. All the blood had drained out of her face, and the imprint of his hand stood out on her cheek like a bright red tattoo. Damn. He had not meant to strike her. Shame boiled up inside of him. He covered it with anger.

"Don't you ever run from me again," Jesse warned, his voice gruff with self-reproach. "Understand?"

She nodded, refusing to meet his eyes.

"Good." Reining his horse around, Jesse rode back to where he'd left his prisoner.

Dismounting, Jesse dragged the girl off the back of his horse and deposited her on the Appaloosa, behind Ravenhawk.

Jesse remounted his horse. Leaning forward, he took up the Appaloosa's reins, then fixed the girl with a hard stare.

"You were stupid to run away," he said, keeping his voice calm. "Don't try it again."

He clucked to his horse and the roan moved out at a brisk walk. The Appaloosa fell into step behind.

With a gasp, Kaylynn grabbed at the man in front of her to keep from toppling over the Appaloosa's rump.

He was a prisoner, too. His hands were cuffed to the saddle horn.

"Hold on to my waist," he said.

She didn't want to touch him any more than she wanted to touch the scar-faced man, but she had little choice. Keeping as far away from him as possible, she slid her arms around his waist, cursing the day she had left home.

They rode for hours across the broad, flat prairie. The sun beat down on her back. Her thighs ached. Her shoulders ached. She was hot and thirsty. Perspiration trickled down her back and pooled between her breasts. It made her scalp itch.

Finally, when she thought they would never stop, the scar-faced man reined his horse to a halt beside a shallow stream. He lifted her from the back of the horse, then drew his gun and unlocked the two sets of handcuffs shackling the prisoner.

When the prisoner dismounted, Yellow Thunder cuffed his hands together again. "We'll rest here for a while," he said. "Mao'hoohe, water the horses."

Tamping down her resentment, Kaylynn took the reins and led the animals down to the stream.

The prisoner went upstream a ways, dropped down on his belly, and drank from the stream, then buried his face in the water.

She slid a glance at him, wondering why he was the other man's prisoner, wondering what he had done. He was tall and broad-shouldered, as handsome as the other man was ugly.

When he looked up and caught her staring, she quickly looked away.

When the horses had drunk their fill, she led

them away from the stream and tethered them to some scrub brush, then went back to the river. Kneeling, she sipped water from her cupped hands, wondering if she would ever drink from a cut-crystal glass again.

"We'll bed down here for the night," Yellow Thunder said. He removed the saddlebags from his horse and tossed them at Kaylynn's feet. "Fix us some grub."

She wanted to argue, would have argued, but for the warning gleam in his eye. His next words made her wonder if he could read her mind. "You are my woman," he said softly. "Don't forget that."

With a curt nod, she picked up the saddlebags and began rummaging through them.

Yellow Thunder hobbled the horses, then removed their bridles, leaving them free to graze.

"Ravenhawk, get over here."

Kaylynn watched the man called Ravenhawk, saw the defiance that blazed in the depths of his eyes. He hesitated a moment, his body poised for flight, until the scar-faced man drew his weapon. With a sigh of resignation, the prisoner approached his captor.

"Turn around."

Ravenhawk did as he was bidden, his face set in hard lines as Yellow Thunder shackled his ankles.

"Unsaddle the horses."

"Do it yourself," Ravenhawk retorted.

"You don't work, you don't eat."

"All right by me."

With a shrug, Yellow Thunder went to unsaddle the horses.

Kaylynn cast surreptitious glances at both men

as she heated a couple of cans of beans. She didn't think Yellow Thunder was a lawman. He looked more like an outlaw than did his prisoner. Watching them, thinking about them, took her mind off her own troubles.

When the beans were hot, she made fry bread and coffee. There was only one plate and a knife, fork, and spoon in the pack.

"Take what you want," Yellow Thunder said. "I'll eat from the pan." He looked at her, one brow raised. "We'll have to share the cup."

"What about him?" Kaylynn asked, nodding at Ravenhawk.

"He's not eating."

She took a generous helping of bread and beans and went to sit apart from the two men, wondering at the bad luck that had put her here, in this place. If only she had taken a different stage, she might have missed the Indian attack. If only she had married the man her parents had picked for her instead of insisting on marrying Alan Summers. . . . She looked at Ravenhawk, sitting with his back against one of the saddles, and at the scar-faced man eating beans from the frying pan, and wondered if she would ever see her home or her parents again.

Ravenhawk watched Yellow Thunder from beneath half-lowered lids. The man was the most feared bounty hunter in the territory. It was said he was wanted for a murder he had committed in the Indian Nations. Still, for all that he was a hard man, and as merciless as the desert sun, he was still just a man. Sooner or later, he would make a mistake. Ravenhawk loosed a deep sigh. All he had to do was bide his time and be ready to take advantage of whatever opportunity presented itself.

He looked over at the woman, wondering about the relationship between her and the bounty hunter, wondering about the odds of convincing her to help him escape. Yellow Thunder had claimed she was his woman, but she didn't seem to be overly fond of her man.

He watched her as she carried the dishes down to the stream. She was a remarkably pretty girl, and though he'd never cared for redheads, in her case he was willing to make an exception. He wondered again how she had gotten involved with a man like Yellow Thunder.

It was near dark when Kaylynn returned from scrubbing the dishes. She had made the task last as long as possible, and only the encroaching darkness had made her leave the river.

She gasped when Yellow Thunder grabbed her by the arm and hauled her over to where Ravenhawk was sitting. Pulling another set of handcuffs out of his back pocket, he shackled one of Ravenhawk's ankles to hers.

Kaylynn looked up at him in disbelief. "You can't chain me up like I'm some kind of criminal!"

"No?" Yellow Thunder glanced pointedly at the shackle linking her to Ravenhawk, then walked away. He returned a moment later and tossed a blanket over the two of them.

Kaylynn glared up at him, but he only smiled a hateful smile and drawled, "Sweet dreams, darlin'," before returning to the campfire.

Kaylynn stared after the man, wishing she knew a word bad enough to call him. Just when she was sure things couldn't get any worse, they had!

"Might as well make the best of it."

She turned slowly to face the man sitting beside her. "The best of it? And what, exactly, is the best of it?"

He grinned, displaying even white teeth. "You can cuddle up next to me if you get cold during the night."

"I'd as soon curl up beside a snake."

He shrugged. "Suit yourself."

She bit down on her lower lip to keep from screaming. This could not be happening to her. Shackled to some criminal when all she wanted to do was go back home where she belonged.

She was on the verge of sobbing when she heard a deep rumbling sound. It took her a moment to realize it was Ravenhawk's stomach growling.

"Sorry, sweetheart," he muttered.

Determined to ignore him, she turned her back to him and lay down on the hard ground, the blanket pulled over her. She was acutely conscious of the man lying beside her. She could feel his heat, his nearness, the shifting of the blanket as he sought a more comfortable position.

And then she heard his stomach growl again. With an aggravated sigh, she reached inside the sash tied around her waist and withdrew the bread she had hidden there.

"Here," she said, thrusting it at him. "Eat this."

"Obliged." Ravenhawk offered her a crooked grin as he took the bread from her hand. He glanced over at Yellow Thunder. The bounty hunter was sitting on his bedroll, staring into the fire.

Ravenhawk ate quickly. It wasn't near enough

to fill his empty belly, but it took the edge off his hunger. "I don't suppose you've got a glass of whiskey hidden in there?" he muttered.

"Hardly." She stared over her shoulder at the man sitting beside the fire. "Who is he?" she asked.

"His name's Jesse Yellow Thunder."

"I know that. Is he a lawman?"

Ravenhawk laughed harshly. "Not exactly. He's a bounty hunter."

"A bounty hunter." She had heard it said that most were little better than the men they hunted. She scooted as far away from Ravenhawk as she could get, wondering what crime he had committed.

The move was not missed by Ravenhawk. "Thanks again for the bread," he said, his voice tinged with amusement.

With a nod, Kaylynn huddled under the blanket again. A criminal and a bounty hunter. What would her father think if he could see her now?

Chapter Seven

They were on the move early the following morning. Kaylynn had rarely felt so dirty and disheveled in her whole life. Her hair fell over her shoulders in a scraggly mass. She needed a long soak in a tub of hot water. She needed a comb and a brush, though she was beginning to think she would never get all the tangles out of her hair. She needed new clothes, though she wondered if she would ever get used to wearing a chemise, pantalets, and a mountain of petticoats again. She glanced at her hands, rough and dry, the nails broken. She needed a manicure, too. And a good night's sleep in a real bed . . .

She stared at Ravenhawk's back and told herself she would not cry. But it was hard to keep her tears at bay. Living with the Indians had not been easy, but it had been better than this. At least she'd had a bed of soft furs to sleep in, clean water to bathe with, a change of clothing. She'd had to work hard, but she had been treated well enough.

She rubbed her eyes. They felt gritty from lack of sleep. She had been all too aware of Ravenhawk lying beside her the night before. She had been afraid to fall asleep for fear of what he might do, afraid she might roll over and touch him. Apparently he had not been bothered by her nearness. He had slept soundly through the night.

He had a broad back, Ravenhawk did. And long black hair, though it was not as long as Yellow Thunder's. Wisps of his hair brushed her cheek from time to time. She sat as far away from him as possible, but there wasn't a lot of room to spare on the back of a horse. She held lightly to his waist to keep from tumbling over the Appaloosa's rump.

The bounty hunter rode ahead. He had roused them from bed just after dawn that morning. He had looked after the horses while she prepared breakfast, if beans and hardtack could be considered breakfast. And now they were riding across a seemingly endless prairie of gently waving grass beneath a brassy blue sky. The sun was warm on her back. The horse had an easy, rolling gait. If she hadn't been in such dire circumstances, she might have enjoyed the ride.

"You on the run, too?"

Kaylynn sat up, startled to realize she had been dozing, her forehead resting against Ravenhawk's back. "What?"

"You sleeping back there?" There was a faint note of amusement in his voice.

It was, she thought, a very nice voice, for a criminal. Deep and rich.

He glanced over his shoulder. "You are still back there, aren't you?"

"Yes, of course," she snapped. "Where would I go?"

"No need to bite my head off, sweetheart."

She glared at him. "I really don't feel like making small talk, Mr. Hawk. And don't call me sweetheart."

"Ravenhawk. It's all one word. No mister."

She stared at him, not knowing what to say.

"So, do you wanna tell me your name? Sweetheart."

"No."

Ravenhawk laughed softly, then faced forward again. He had more important things to worry about than the woman riding behind him. He tugged on the cuff that shackled his right hand to the saddle horn. He'd be in a hell of a fix if the horse went down. He glared at Yellow Thunder's back. Damn the man. The bounty hunter was as persistent as a wolf on the scent of blood.

Damn! He never should have robbed that bank. There had only been a couple hundred dollars in the vault, hardly worth the risk involved. But he'd needed a stake. He was tired of drifting, tired of wandering aimlessly from one place to another, looking for . . . He grunted softly. He didn't know what the hell he was looking for. He'd been a restless wind ever since he could remember, always wanting to see what was beyond the next rise, always looking, searching, never finding whatever it was he was looking for.

He wasn't content living with the whites; he

wasn't content living with the Lakota. He had ties to both worlds and didn't feel at home in either. Hell, he'd never felt at home anywhere.

The girl shifted behind him. He stared down at her hands, locked around his waist. Women had never been a problem for him. He'd had more than his share. He didn't know why they liked him, but they did. All but this one. She looked at him as if he was less than the dirt beneath her feet. He wondered what crime she had committed. At first, he had thought she was Yellow Thunder's woman, but after last night it was obvious that she wasn't staying with the bounty hunter of her own free will, and he wondered how long she had been Yellow Thunder's prisoner, and if he ever used her to keep warm on long, cold nights. The thought of the bounty hunter pawing at the woman bothered him more than it should have.

They rode all that day, stopping only once to rest the horses.

Kaylynn groaned softly as she slid from the back of the Appaloosa. Her legs felt like rubber as she walked over and sat down in the shade of a thornberry bush. Sitting on the back of the horse, with nothing between her and sweating horseflesh, left her feeling sticky and dirty and itchy. She gnawed at the jerky the bounty hunter had given her, and for a moment she closed her eyes, remembering Mrs. Moseley's succulent roast beef and whipped potatoes swimming in rich brown gravy. If she ever made it back to her parents' home again, she was never, ever going to leave.

She watched the two men. Ravenhawk squatted near the water hole, filling a canteen. Yellow

Thunder stood near his horse, idly scratching the roan's ears as he stared into the distance. She wondered what he was thinking. She had never met a man as hard and cold as the bounty hunter. Merciless was the word that came to mind. She wondered how he had gotten that way, how he had gotten the dreadful scars on his face and body . . . if there was any chance of escaping him.

Her gaze moved back to Ravenhawk. He had stripped off his shirt and was splashing water over his arms and chest. He was tall and broad, though not so tall or broad-shouldered as the bounty hunter. His skin was the color of fine old copper, smooth and unblemished as far as she could see, save for one puckered white scar on his forearm and two faint scars on his chest. He looked up, catching her gaze, and smiled—a long, lazy smile that made her acutely aware that she was a woman. Lord, but he was a handsome man. For a criminal.

With a huff, she looked away. It was a sin, for a man of his ilk to have a smile like that.

"Let's go."

She watched Ravenhawk stand up at the bounty hunter's words, but she didn't want to move. It was pleasant, sitting in the shade. The grass was cool beneath her; a faint breeze kept the heat at bay. A small lizard sat on a rock, regarding her through beady black eyes, and then, in a flash, it was gone.

She sprang to her feet when she saw Yellow Thunder striding toward her.

He looked at her, his right brow raised in an expression she was beginning to recognize as mild amusement. She had the feeling he was laughing at her, that he knew exactly how afraid of him she was.

He jerked his chin toward the horses. "Let's go."

Afraid to defy him, she walked toward the Appaloosa.

Yellow Thunder rested one hand on the butt of his gun as he ordered Ravenhawk to mount up. The Lakota's expression was mutinous as he pulled his buckskin shirt over his head, then climbed into the saddle and secured the handcuff to his wrist.

Yellow Thunder lifted Mao'hoohe onto the horse behind Ravenhawk, then swung aboard his own mount.

Kaylynn frowned, wondering how long it would take to reach a town, wondering what the bounty hunter intended to do with her when that time came.

She stared across the prairie. It seemed her life had never been her own. As far back as she could remember, she'd had to answer to someone. First her mother and father. Then her husband. Then old Mo'e'ha. And now this crude, unwashed, heathen bounty hunter. Just once, she wished she could be her own boss, that she could come and go as she pleased, with no one to order her around and no one to answer to but herself. But it wasn't likely to happen. If she ever made it to her parents' home again, she would be right back where she started, under her father's thumb. One thing was certain—divorce or no divorce, she was never going back to Alan.

Lost in thought, she was hardly aware of the passage of time. It wouldn't be easy, going back home, admitting she had been wrong about Alan.

No doubt her father would say I told you so. Her mother would be appalled at the idea of a divorce in the family. Decent people did not sue for a bill of divorcement. It simply wasn't done. It wouldn't be easy. As badly as she wanted her freedom, she wasn't sure she could endure the shame, the stigma, of being a divorced woman.

It wasn't until Ravenhawk reined the Appaloosa to a halt that Kaylynn realized dusk had fallen.

They made camp as though they had been doing it for years. Ravenhawk had apparently decided food was more important than his pride, and after Yellow Thunder unlocked the cuff shackling him to the pommel, Ravenhawk unsaddled the horses and rubbed them down. When that was done, Yellow Thunder shackled Ravenhawk's feet, then led the horses down to the stream to drink.

Kaylynn fixed dinner, grimacing as she sliced bacon and fried a mess of beans. She was heartily sick of this rough fare.

The three of them ate in silence so thick she could have cut it with a knife. She had eaten first, acutely aware of the tension that simmered in the air between the two men. When she was finished, she filled the plate and offered it to Ravenhawk. The bounty hunter ate out of the frying pan. He sat a little apart, a rifle across his knees.

When the meal was over, Yellow Thunder shackled her ankle to Ravenhawk's. If she had been speaking to the bounty hunter, she would have told him there was no need. She wasn't going to try running away again. She had learned her lesson the last time. Every time she tried running away, she ended up in a worse fix than the one she had left behind.

She shuddered when she heard a wolf howl. It was a sad, lonely sound. For some reason, it made her want to cry.

Later, lying on the hard ground with Ravenhawk at her back, she did cry, even though it was a waste of time and tears, when there was no one there to comfort her, no one there to care, no one to make it better.

Yellow Thunder roused them at dawn. A quick breakfast, and they were riding again. To Kaylynn, it seemed they had been riding across the prairie for weeks instead of days. The insides of her thighs felt raw, her back ached, her shoulders ached, even her neck ached.

Ravenhawk glanced at her over his shoulder. "You'd be more comfortable if you'd just relax."

"I'm fine."

"Uh-huh. You're stiff as a post. Scoot forward a little bit and lean against me."

"No, thank you."

"Stubborn woman. What's the matter, sweetheart?" he asked caustically. "You afraid of getting too close? Afraid you might catch something from the dirty half-breed?"

She stared at his back, surprised by the bitterness in his voice. She hadn't known he was only half-Indian and wondered what difference it made.

Ravenhawk swore softly. Why the hell had he said that? He didn't care what she thought of him. All he wanted was his freedom, and he aimed to get it, one way or another, before he found himself behind bars again. He wouldn't go back to jail. Couldn't go back to jail, couldn't spend his days and nights surrounded by iron bars. Not again.

He looked at Yellow Thunder, riding just ahead. The bounty hunter seemed to have let down his guard a little since yesterday. Ravenhawk had done his best to appear resigned to his fate. He hadn't tried to escape, had done what he was told, even though it galled him to do so. Yellow Thunder hadn't slept much the first two nights; earlier, Ravenhawk had caught him dozing in the saddle. The bounty hunter couldn't go without sleep indefinitely.

Tonight, he thought. Maybe tonight.

They made camp before sunset. Kaylynn looked around. It was a pretty place. There were a few trees, some berry bushes laden with fruit, and a deep, slow-running stream. She looked at the water with longing, wishing she could take a bath and wash her hair.

"Here."

She whirled around, her hand at her throat, to find Yellow Thunder standing at her elbow. He held up a chunk of thick yellow soap.

"Go on," he said. "Wash up."

Kaylynn's eyes widened. Take a bath? Here? Now?

The bounty hunter's right brow rose slightly. "This is the only chance you're gonna get."

Kaylynn stared at him a moment, the thought of being clean a temptation she was hard-pressed to resist. But to bathe in broad daylight, with two men nearby?

Yellow Thunder pointed downstream. "There's a secluded place around the bend. Don't go any farther than that," he warned. "And don't do anything dumb."

Kaylynn stared at the soap. The prospect of being clean again was impossible to resist. The bounty hunter grinned, as if he was fully aware of her inner struggle. He laughed softly as she snatched the soap from his hand and headed downstream.

When she rounded the bend in the river, she found a shallow pool screened by an overgrowth of brush. Glancing over her shoulder to make sure she was alone, she untied the sash at her waist, slipped off her tunic and moccasins, and stepped into the water. She had expected it to be cold, but it was surprisingly warm.

She sank below the surface for several moments, enjoying the sensation of the water swirling over her bare skin. She felt wicked somehow, bathing out in the open with the setting sun glinting on the water. A sparrow landed on a nearby branch, its head bobbing up and down as it watched her. She laughed out loud, and the bird took flight.

She soaped her hair twice and her body three times, and then stared at the bank. She had two choices. She could get out of the water and put on her dress while she was wet, or she could stand on the bank and let the waning heat of the sun bake her dry. As warm as it still was, it shouldn't take long. Still, the idea of standing naked on the shore, with two disreputable strange men only a few yards away, wasn't particularly appealing.

She was still debating what to do when she heard a loud popping noise. It took her a moment to realize it was gunfire.

She stood there for a moment, the soap clutched in her fist. She didn't know what had happened back at the camp, but she knew it couldn't be good. Several possibilities ran through her mind—they were being attacked by the Crow; Ravenhawk had tried to escape and Yellow Thunder had shot him; Ravenhawk had shot Yellow Thunder.

Another gunshot rang out, and she flew out of the water and snatched up her tunic. Whatever was happening, she didn't intend to be caught naked and helpless. She pulled the tunic over her head, tugged it down over her hips, and stepped into her moccasins. What to do? she thought, grabbing her sash. What to do?

Her first instinct was to run, yet that seemed foolhardy in the extreme. She had no food, no water, no weapons. As much as she hated to admit it, she needed help to get back home.

Breathless, she hid behind a clump of brush, her heart pounding like a runaway train. She would wait, and watch. If Ravenhawk and Yellow Thunder had been killed by the Crow, she would have to strike out on her own. They had been heading east. Yellow Thunder was a bounty hunter. In order to collect a reward, he had to take Ravenhawk to a town, so it stood to reason that he had a destination in mind. Surely, if she kept going east, she would find civilization sooner or later.

She huddled in the brush for what seemed like hours, ears straining for some sound that would tell her what was going on back at their camp.

Fear shot through her when she heard the sound of hoofbeats. Just one horse, coming slow.

She peered through the brush, wondering who was riding toward her.

Ravenhawk or Yellow Thunder?

Chapter Eight

Ravenhawk reined the Appaloosa to a halt, one hand pressed against his wounded side as his gaze swept the ground, noting the chunk of soap lying on the edge of the riverbank, the hurried footprints that led into a tangled clump of brush and overgrown weeds.

"Hey, Red Fox, you in there?"

His voice shivered through her. Slowly, Kaylynn stepped out of her hiding place.

"I'm leaving," Ravenhawk said. "You wanna come along, or stay here with him?"

Kaylynn looked up at Ravenhawk, thinking the choice he offered was like asking the bacon if it preferred the frying pan or the fire.

"Make up your mind, sweetheart."

Kaylynn plucked a twig from her hair. "Will you

take me to the nearest town so I can catch the first stage headed east?"

"Can we discuss this later? We're a little pressed for time."

Ravenhawk glanced over his shoulder, regretting the fact that he hadn't killed the bounty hunter when he'd had the chance. He knew it was a decision that was sure to come back to haunt him, sooner or later.

Kaylynn looked up at him. His eyes were deep and black, with a hint of warmth, not cold and gray like Yellow Thunder's.

Ravenhawk held out his hand, and after a moment, she placed her hand in his. He groaned softly as he lifted her up behind him, but before she could ask what was wrong, he urged the horse into a gallop and they were flying along the bank of the stream.

Kaylynn slid her arms around his waist, grimacing as she felt a warm wetness against her palm. She drew her hand back, alarmed to see that her hand was covered with blood. Good Lord, he was bleeding. She knew a moment of panic, but then told herself he couldn't be badly hurt. If he was, he wouldn't be riding like the devil was at his heels.

She didn't know whether to be frightened or relieved as the miles went by. On one hand, she was glad to be away from Jesse Yellow Thunder. He scared her in ways she didn't understand. It was more than the coldness in his eyes, more than the awful scar on his face. And yet, in spite of the fact that he frightened her, there was something compelling about him, something that called to a need deep inside her. . . .

She gasped, her arms tightening around Ravenhawk's waist, as he slumped forward in the saddle. Just when she feared he was going to fall, he jerked upright.

"Are you all right?" she asked, but he didn't answer.

They rode until the horse was covered with lather. Only then did Ravenhawk allow the Appaloosa to slow, then to stop.

Kaylynn glanced at their surroundings. The stream ran shallow here, edged by a few scrawny willows and shrubs and a mound of boulders.

She felt Ravenhawk take a deep breath before he dismounted. He stood beside the horse, leaning against the animal's shoulder. He stared up at her, his face unusually pale.

"Can you make it down on your own?" he asked.

She nodded, her gaze drawn to the dark red stain that covered the right side of his shirt. As she slid off the Appaloosa's rump, she asked, "What happened?"

"What do you think?"

"He shot you."

Ravenhawk nodded. He swayed on his feet, blinking rapidly as the world seemed to spin out of focus.

Kaylynn stared at Ravenhawk as he took a step toward her, then slowly crumpled to the ground. So much blood. Was he dying? Dead?

She looked at the horse. She would never have a better chance to escape than she did now. There was a waterskin looped around the saddle horn, a bedroll behind the cantle, food in one of the saddlebags. A rifle in the boot.

She stared down at Ravenhawk. She didn't

know anything about the man except that he was an outlaw. She didn't owe him anything. For all she knew, she might be in more danger with Ravenhawk than she had been with Yellow Thunder. She glanced over her shoulder. If the bounty hunter was still alive, he was sure to come after them.

The thought eased her conscience as she reached for the Appaloosa's reins.

With a snort, the gelding tossed its head and backed away from her.

"Hold still, horse." She took a step forward.

The Appaloosa lifted its head to the side to keep from stepping on the dangling reins. And took another step back.

"Stupid horse," she muttered. She took another step forward and when the horse backed up again, she lunged forward and made a wild grab for the reins.

The Appaloosa reared, forelegs pawing the air, one hoof coming dangerously close to her head.

Kaylynn shrieked as she ducked out of the way. Hands fisted on her hips, she glared at the horse.

She was trying to figure out how to catch the beast when she heard the man groan.

She glanced over her shoulder to where Ravenhawk was lying in the dirt and knew that, even if she had been able to catch the horse, she wouldn't have been able to ride off and leave him there, helpless. Outlaw or not, she couldn't just abandon another human being.

She didn't know what she could do to help him, either. Her medical knowledge was less than impressive, although she had learned a few things while living with the Cheyenne.

She knelt beside him, trying not to be sick as she lifted the edge of his shirt to look at the wound beneath. There were two holes just above his waist on his right side, the exit wound a little larger than the other. Two holes, raw and red and oozing with blood. She supposed that meant she didn't have to worry about the bullet being lodged inside somewhere. And it was a good thing, too, because there was no way on earth she would have been able to get it out.

Rising to her feet, she looked at the waterskin looped over the saddle horn, wondering how she could get close enough to the horse to get it.

The Appaloosa eyed her warily as she took several slow steps toward it. It was a big horse, all black save for a patch of white sprinkled with irregular ebony spots across its rump. It had a short, thick mane and a scraggly tail.

"Please," she murmured. "Please, horse, just stand still."

Surprisingly, the Appaloosa did just that. Eyes wide, ears twitching, the gelding stood poised for flight as she lifted the waterskin from the saddle horn.

Returning to Ravenhawk's side, she knelt beside him. As gently as she could, she eased his shirt over his head and tossed it aside. Removing the sash from her waist, she soaked one end in water and began washing the blood from his side. The sash, made of thick red wool, had been a gift from Mo'e'ha.

A low moan rose in Ravenhawk's throat as she dragged the cloth over the wounds. Looking at them made her stomach queasy. They were red and ugly, the edges looking raw and painful.

She cleaned the wounds as best she could; then, remembering something she had seen one of the Indians do, she packed the wounds with damp tree moss to stem the flow of blood. Removing Ravenhawk's headband, she made a thick square pad and placed it over the wounds. She used her sash to hold the makeshift bandage in place. It took all her strength to lift him enough so that she could wrap the sash around his middle. She was perspiring by the time she finished.

Now what? She glanced around. At least he had picked a sheltered place to stop. Rising, she gathered an armful of sticks and twigs and one good-sized branch. She dug a shallow pit and laid a fire, then looked over at the horse.

Smiling, she walked toward the Appaloosa. "Hey, there," she said quietly. "I bet you'd like to get rid of that heavy old saddle, wouldn't you?"

The gelding snorted softly as she approached, but didn't back away. Taking up the reins, she tethered the Appaloosa to a tree, then removed the saddle and blanket. The blanket was soaked with sweat and she spread it out on the ground to dry; then, remembering Yellow Thunder's stern admonition to cool his horse, she untied the Appaloosa and gave a gentle tug on the reins. To her surprise, the gelding followed along behind her, as docile as an old dog.

A short distance from the streambed, she found some berry bushes heavy with fruit. She would come back later and pick some, she thought.

When the horse was cooled out, she led it to the stream and let it drink, then led it back to their campsite. Replacing the bridle with a horsehair halter, she tethered the Appaloosa to a tree where it could graze on the sparse yellow grass that grew beside the shallow stream. She patted the horse on the shoulder; then, knowing she had stalled long enough, she picked up the bedroll and walked back to where she had left Ravenhawk.

As far as she could tell, he hadn't moved while she'd been gone. His breathing was coming in short, shallow gasps. His face and chest were sheened with sweat. She laid her hand on his chest. His skin felt warm. What if his wound got infected? What would she do if he died? Even though she had learned a lot about survival from the Indians, she didn't think she would last very long out here on her own.

She spread one of the blankets beside him, then rolled him over until he was lying on it. Using a sharp knife she found in one of the packs, she cut a small square from the edge of the second blanket, soaked it in water, and began to sponge him off.

It seemed an odd time to notice such a thing, but she couldn't help observing that his skin was a beautiful shade of copper, that his shoulders were incredibly wide, that his stomach was hard and flat and ridged with muscle. His arms and legs were also well-muscled. To her chagrin, she found herself comparing Ravenhawk's body to Yellow Thunder's, remembering the way Yellow Thunder had looked dancing around the Sun Dance pole, the spider-web of faint silvery scars that criss-crossed his back and shoulders. She had never thought a man's body could be beautiful, but his was. He had moved with sinuous grace, reminding her of a panther she had seen in a circus when she was a little girl. The big cat had been sleek and beautiful, too. And deadly. Like Yellow Thunder.

She thrust the thought from her mind. Soaking the cloth again, she ran it over Ravenhawk's chest. She had not thought Alan's body was beautiful. She had not thought of his body at all, except when he was poised over her, grunting with animal lust, his mouth crushing hers. She had hated his touch, used every excuse she could think of to avoid allowing him in her bed. She had pleaded headaches. She had lied about the length of her monthly flow, so that three days became five, six, a week. Once, she pretended to sprain her ankle while walking down the stairs. Another time she claimed she had strained her back while rearranging the bedroom furniture.

She wet the cloth again and drew it down Ravenhawk's arms and legs. He stirred beneath her hand, a low groan rising in his throat. Looking up, she saw that he was awake and staring at her.

"How do you feel?" she asked.

He grimaced. "I've been some better."

"Are you thirsty?"

He nodded and licked his lips.

Picking up the waterskin, she lifted his head and gave him a drink. He had beautiful eyes. Surely a man with eyes like that wouldn't beat a woman just because she forgot to invite one of his friends to a party.

She put the waterskin aside, then covered him with the second blanket.

"Thanks." His voice was low and thick and edged with pain. He closed his eyes, took a deep breath, and started to sit up.

"What do you think you're doing?" Kaylynn exclaimed.

"We've got to . . . to go."

She shook her head. "You need to rest, and you should have something to eat. You've lost a lot of blood. Besides, it's dark."

"I'm not hurt all that bad. Anyway, we can't stay here." Ravenhawk closed his eyes and took another deep breath. He was hungry and tired, his side throbbed with pain, but they couldn't stay here. He had to find a place to hide, a place to heal. "Yellow Thunder . . ."

She hesitated, afraid to ask the next question, yet needing to know the answer. "He's not dead, then?"

"No. He'll come . . ." He opened his eyes and glanced around. She'd made a comfortable camp; his horse was tethered a short distance away. He frowned when he saw she'd unsaddled the Appaloosa. "Think you can saddle my horse for me?"

Kaylynn nodded. She had removed the saddle, hadn't she? How much harder could it be to put it back on?

"Hurry."

The urgency in his voice propelled her to her feet. The saddle blanket was almost dry. Picking it up, she walked toward the Appaloosa.

The horse regarded her warily, sidestepped when she tried to spread the blanket over its back.

"Ridge Walker, stand." At the sound of Ravenhawk's voice, the gelding stood stock still, ears twitching.

Kaylynn placed the blanket on the horse's back, smoothed it out, then reached for the saddle, surprised that it was so heavy. It hadn't seemed to weigh that much when she took it from the horse.

It had to weigh forty pounds, she thought as she wrestled it up onto the horse's back.

Taking a deep breath, she looked at the cinch dangling on the far side of the horse. Visions of being kicked crossed her mind as she gathered her courage, bent down, reached under the Appaloosa's belly, and grabbed the end. It took her several minutes to get it tight enough so that the saddle wouldn't fall off.

When she thought she had it right, she slipped the bridle in place, then led the gelding over to Ravenhawk. Taking hold of the stirrup, he pulled himself to his feet, then stood there for a minute, his forehead resting on the horse's shoulder, while Kaylynn looped the waterskin around the horn, tied the saddlebags in place, then folded the blankets and lashed them behind the cantle.

"Are you sure you can do this?" she asked.

"No," Ravenhawk replied, "but I damn well intend to try."

She watched Ravenhawk gather his strength as he put one foot in the stirrup, then swung his other leg over the horse's back. Fine lines of pain etched his mouth and eyes.

"Come on," he said, and taking his foot from the stirrup, he offered her his left hand.

Kaylynn put her foot in the stirrup and he lifted her up behind him.

"Ready?" he asked.

"If you are."

With a nod, he clucked to the gelding. Ready or not, it was time to move on.

Chapter Nine

His jaw clenched with anger, Jesse bound up the wound in his right shoulder the best he could. Stupid, he thought, he'd been so damn stupid. Must be getting old, going soft in the head. He knew better than to turn his back on a prisoner, especially one as desperate as Ravenhawk.

He ran his hand over the shallow furrow along his left temple. He was lucky to be alive, lucky Ravenhawk's second shot had only creased his hairline.

He glanced up at the sky, judging the time. A good three hours had passed, making it close to nine o'clock. He supposed he should be grateful Ravenhawk hadn't slit his throat while he was unconscious, that he hadn't tied him up so tightly that he couldn't get loose, that he hadn't taken his revolver and the roan and left him unarmed and afoot. But he didn't feel grateful. He was mad clear through.

Grimacing with pain, he tied off the end of the makeshift bandage on his shoulder, then took a long drink from his canteen, wishing it was whiskey instead of water.

He gathered some wood and built a fire, then hunkered down on his heels and stared into the flames. Ravenhawk had taken his rifle and the saddlebags that held the food and cooking gear. It didn't matter. He had lived off the land before; he could do it again.

He would go after them tomorrow at first light.

He stared into the flames. Abigail had been taken from him on a night like this, a night when the wind moved restlessly through the trees and a full moon hung low in the sky like a ball of thick yellow butter.

Abigail. When he'd recovered from the brutal beating her father had given him, he had gone looking for her, but it was as if she had disappeared from the face of the earth. Try as he might, he hadn't been able to find her, hadn't been able to find anyone who knew what had happened to her. He sometimes wondered if, in a fit of rage, her father had killed her.

He had searched for Abigail for over two years. Somewhere along the way, he had taken up bounty hunting. It had seemed an easy way to earn money while he was on the move. In the last seven years, he had hunted and found over two dozen men who had not wanted to be found, but he had never been able to find a trace of Abigail.

He lifted a hand to his scarred face, remembering the last night he had seen her. They had met at the end of town, determined to run away. He never knew how her father discovered their plans. But suddenly the old man was there, waiting, along with several other men. When Abigail realized what her father meant to do, she had gone down on her knees, begging her father to let Jesse go. Her pleas had cut into Jesse with more force than the long black snake whip her father had used on him. He would never forget the humiliation of having the woman he loved beg for his life, never forget the way Abigail's father had looked at her, his cold blue eyes filled with disgust. He had ordered her taken away. He could still hear Abigail crying his name, her voice choked with fear, vowing that she loved him, would always love him.

He had endured the brutal whipping in silence. *I am a Cheyenne warrior,* he had told himself. *I will not be afraid. I will not show weakness in front of my enemy.*

Nor would be ever forget the cold satisfaction that blazed in her father's eyes as he pulled a knife from his pocket and waved it in front of him.

No white woman will ever be taken in by that handsome face of yours again, you dirty half-breed, her father exclaimed. *You'll be lucky if they don't faint.*

Sick with fear, Jesse glared up at the man, his stomach churning with nausea as the razor-sharp blade sliced into his flesh. One of the men nearby began to retch. Jesse choked back the bile that had risen in his own throat.

Be strong. A warrior does not surrender to pain or fear. His grandfather's voice, strong and vibrant, as he instructed his young grandson in the ways of a warrior. *A warrior is strong and brave. He does not flinch from danger. When faced with a challenge, he does not back down, he does not back up. You must cling to the wisdom of your ancestors, Little Spirit, feel them standing behind you, giving you their strength.*

Only when they left him, alone and bleeding in the dirt, did he give in to the pain that hummed through him. Like a wounded animal, he crawled away to lick his wounds. . . .

Jesse shuddered as the images faded. Raven-hawk and the girl were out there. He felt a rare twinge of jealousy as he thought of the two of them together.

He would find them. Both of them. The woman was his. Since the night of the beating, he had allowed no one to take anything he considered his. He would not start now.

Chapter Ten

It was scary, riding across the vast grassy plains with nothing but the moon and the stars to light the way. Kaylynn clung to Ravenhawk, reassured somehow by the solid feel of him. He was wounded, he was an outlaw, but at the moment, he was all that stood between her and whatever dangers lurked in the ever-changing shadows of the night.

The gelding stumbled once, jarring them. Certain they were going to fall, she tightened her hold on Ravenhawk's waist, heard him swear as her hand pressed against the wound in his side.

"I'm sorry," she said, and quickly loosened her hold.

He blew out a breath between his teeth. "It's all right."

Hour after hour, mile after mile, they rode through the night. Her eyelids grew heavy; her eyes began to play tricks on her. A clump of bushes became a bear rising up from the earth; a branch became a snake.

Finally, unable to stay awake any longer, she rested her head against Ravenhawk's back and closed her eyes.

Ravenhawk felt Kaylynn's cheek against his back and knew, by the way she slumped against him, that she was asleep.

She had probably saved his life. The thought did not sit easy on his spirit. He did not want to be beholden to a woman, especially a white woman with hair as red as autumn leaves and eyes as brown as the earth where he'd been born.

He wondered why she hadn't run away when she had the chance. She had been afraid of Yellow Thunder; he knew she was afraid of him, as well. Was she afraid of all men, or just Indians?

Her hands began to slide away from his waist, and he caught them both in one of his, anchoring her against him. The night was cool and quiet, lit by a full yellow moon and a million twinkling stars. Her breasts were soft and warm against his back, warmer than the fever that burned through him.

He was bone weary, hungry, thirsty. The pain in his side seemed to throb to the rhythm of the pounding hoofbeats of the Appaloosa. He longed to stop, to wrap up in a blanket and surrender to the weariness that weighed him down, but the thought of Yellow Thunder spurred him onward. The bounty hunter had all the tenacity of a wolverine. He would be on their trail again as soon as he was able. Ravenhawk cursed softly. They had to find a place to hole up for a day or two while he regained his strength. . . .

The stars were fading from the sky when he reined Ridge Walker to a halt and looked around. To his right ran the stream they had been following. It was wider and deeper now, a slow-running river that snaked through the grasslands. Heavily wooded hills rose to the left. He frowned as a memory tried to surface. He had been here before. If he remembered correctly, there was a small cave near the crest of the hill, a ceremonial cave revered by the Lakota.

The river curled around the base of the hills. He clucked to Ridge Walker, urging the horse into the stream in an effort to hide his trail. Yellow Thunder was a tracker without equal; Ravenhawk hoped this would throw the bounty hunter off their trail, or at least slow him down.

Ravenhawk swore as the Appaloosa slipped in the mud, sat down hard, then scrambled to its feet and plunged into the river. He rode in the water for half a mile until he came to a beaver dam. It stretched halfway across the river. Ravenhawk leaned forward in the saddle, his hand gripping the girl's as he urged the horse out of the water.

The big Appaloosa plunged gamely up the sloping side. When they gained the bank, the horse shook itself.

"Damn, Ridge Walker," Ravenhawk muttered, pressing one hand to his injured side. "Quit that!"

Kaylynn came awake with a start. "What is it?" She glanced around, afraid Yellow Thunder had overtaken them, but there was nothing to see save the river and a wooded hillside. The blackened shell of a burned-out oak stood like a sentinel at the base of the hill. "What's happening?"

"Nothing. Everything's fine."

"Is it?"

"Yeah." He took a deep breath. "I need your help."

"My help? What can I do?"

"I want you to gather up some wood chips from the dam and use them to cover our tracks. At best, it'll keep Yellow Thunder from knowing we left the river here. If not, maybe it will at least slow him down and buy us some time."

Kaylynn glanced over her shoulder. In the faint light of early dawn, she could make out a domed mound of sticks and twigs in the midst of the water. One side was attached to the river bank.

She slid over the horse's rump. Ravenhawk urged the Appaloosa forward, heading toward the base of a high hill. Kaylynn collected an armful of small chips of wood and twigs and then, walking backwards, she covered the horse's tracks and her own with pieces of bark and tufts of grass. She didn't know if it would fool Yellow Thunder, but to her untrained eye, it looked as if they had never been there.

When she reached the base of the hill, Ravenhawk pulled her up behind him once again.

It was a long, slow climb up the side of hill. There were places where the pines grew so close together that they had to detour around them, places where tree branches and deadfalls made the way treacherous.

Kaylynn held tightly to Ravenhawk's waist, afraid that if she let go, she would slide over the horse's rump and go tumbling head over heels down the hillside.

Faint sounds rose on the wings of the morning breeze. Leaves rustled in the trees, whispering secrets to the wind. Something stirred in the underbrush. There was a high shriek, and then a dark shape burst out of the trees, wings flapping.

Startled, Kaylynn cried out. The Appaloosa snorted and shook its head, and only Ravenhawk's sure hand on the reins kept the horse from turning and bolting down the hillside.

"Easy, Ridge Walker," Ravenhawk murmured, his voice low and soothing. "Easy, boy, it's just an owl."

Kaylynn sighed. Eyes closed, she rested her forehead against Ravenhawk's back and waited for her heartbeat to return to normal.

"We'll camp here," Ravenhawk said.

"Here?" She glanced around, seeing nothing but trees and rocks and detritus. In the distance, the sky was growing lighter.

"Here."

She heard the utter weariness in his voice and then realized that her right arm was wet. She didn't have to look to know that it was blood. His side was bleeding again.

Ravenhawk offered her his hand, and she slid from the back of the horse. He took a deep breath and, jaw clenched, he dismounted. For a moment, he stood braced against the horse, his eyes closed. Then she saw him take a deep breath, as if he were gathering strength from deep within himself.

"There's a cave," he said. "Over there. I need to rest a few hours."

She looked where he pointed but saw nothing.

"There." He pointed again. "Take the saddlebags inside. I'll bring the rest."

"I'll do it." She released the ties that held the bedroll in place and thrust the blankets into his arms. "You go lie down before you fall down. I'll look after the horse."

Ravenhawk looked at her a moment. Sliding the rifle from the saddle boot, he turned and walked toward the cave.

Kaylynn watched him, surprised when he suddenly seemed to just disappear.

She looked up at the horse. "Don't give me any trouble, all right?"

The Appaloosa's ears twitched back and forth, but it stood quietly as she removed the waterskin and canteen from the pommel, then struggled with the cinch. Darn saddle seemed heavier every time she picked it up. Huffing and puffing, she carried it toward the place where she had seen Ravenhawk disappear. Only when she was right on top of it did she see the opening—a small hole cut into the side of the hill and screened by trees and brush. She dropped the saddle inside the entrance, then went back to the horse. Removing the blanket, she tethered the Appaloosa to a sturdy tree around a bend in the trail, screened by heavy brush, then took the blanket and the waterskin and returned to the cave.

She found Ravenhawk inside, sprawled facedown on the floor. He was quite a man, she thought, to have ridden so far without complaint. She only hoped his stubborn male pride wouldn't be the death of him.

She made one more trip outside to gather some kindling and wood for a fire and then, kneeling beside Ravenhawk, she shook his shoulder. "Wake up."

With a groan, he rolled onto his back. "Damn, woman, leave me alone."

"You're bleeding again."

He looked down at his side and shrugged. Better to bleed to death within the walls of the ceremonial cave than go back to the white man's prison; better to die here, now, than spend a single day behind bars.

As though she had read his mind, the girl shook her head. "Don't you even think about dying and leaving me out here all alone," she warned.

Rising, she laid a fire, spread the blankets on a smooth stretch of ground, then turned and looked at him.

Biting back a groan, Ravenhawk crawled over to the blanket, removed his shirt, and lay down, eyes closed, as she removed the bloody bandage.

Kaylynn rinsed out the old bandage, then used it to wipe away the blood oozing from the edges of the wound. It seemed to be healing, and not bleeding as badly as she had feared. She tossed the bloody square of cloth away when she was through, cut a new piece from the blanket, folded it and placed it over the wounds, then used the sash to hold it in place again.

When she was done, she offered him a drink of water and covered him with the second blanket.

"Wake me about noon," he mumbled. Moments later, he was asleep.

She looked up, her gaze settling on the cave wall. It was covered with drawings and carvings of horses and people. One scene seemed to depict a battle.

Stifling a yawn, she glanced at Ravenhawk. She had two choices—share the blankets with him or sleep in the dirt. It didn't take long to decide. Crawling under the blanket, she turned her back to Ravenhawk and closed her eyes.

Strangely, it was Jesse Yellow Thunder she dreamed of.

Chapter Eleven

Jesse woke with the dawn, loath to open his eyes, reluctant to banish the last vestiges of the dream images that lingered in his mind.

He had dreamed of the red-haired woman. Mao'hoohe. He wondered what name she had been born with, where she had come from, if her people thought her long dead.

He recalled how she had watched him during the Sun Dance. Even when his back was toward her, he had been aware of her presence. Her nearness had strengthened him. And when it was over, when he had knelt on the ground, exhausted and hurting, he had felt her gaze on him. His sacrifice had been sweeter still because she had witnessed it.

Mao'hoohe. He would have her yet.

With an oath, he threw back the covers. He wondered about her far too much for his peace of mind. He stood up slowly, fighting a wave of dizziness.

It was awkward, saddling his horse with one hand. The mare snorted softly, her nostrils flaring at the scent of blood that clung to him.

"Easy, girl." He swore under his breath as he struggled with the cinch.

He was breathing hard by the time the mare was saddled.

Breakfast was a drink of water from his canteen, a handful of berries picked from a bush. He cursed Ravenhawk as he stepped into the saddle, cursed his own greed. But for the lure of an easy thousand dollars, he could be back in the Cheyenne camp, taking life easy. He considered letting Ravenhawk and the woman go, but only for a moment. It was more than the reward now. It was personal. Ravenhawk had taken his food, the woman—his woman—and his pride. Jesse might have forgiven the Lakota for the first two, but he would have to pay dearly for the last.

Blocking the pain of his wounded shoulder from his mind, he took up the reins and began following the Appaloosa's tracks.

Chapter Twelve

"You said he was hurt." Kaylynn toyed with a lock of her hair, her thoughts troubled. "How do you know he'll come after us?"

"He'll come," Ravenhawk replied.

"What makes you so sure he'll find us?"

Ravenhawk grunted. "He'll find us. Our only chance is to stay ahead of him."

"I don't think you're strong enough to ride." Kaylynn studied Ravenhawk's face, noting the dark shadows beneath his eyes. At least the fever was gone. That was a good sign. "Maybe we should wait another day," she suggested. "You need to rest."

"We don't have time to rest," Ravenhawk snapped impatiently.

"You're afraid of him, aren't you?"

A muscle twitched in Ravenhawk's jaw, but he didn't deny it. Jesse Yellow Thunder was a hard, unforgiving man. He would be angry that he had been caught off-guard, and Ravenhawk would bear the brunt of it. He glanced at the woman, wondering if the bounty hunter would lash out at her, too. Yellow Thunder was not a man to let what he perceived as a wrong go unpunished.

Ravenhawk swore under his breath. Maybe he shouldn't have taken all the food. Maybe he should have left the woman behind.

He stood abruptly. It was too late to worry about that now. What was done was done, and it was time to move on.

Kaylynn gathered their supplies and followed Ravenhawk out of the cave, blinking against the sunlight. The Appaloosa eyed her warily, but didn't shy as Kaylynn smoothed the blanket over its back, settled the saddle in place, tied the bedroll behind the cantle, and lashed the packs in place.

She was getting better at it, Kaylynn mused with a sense of satisfaction as she slid the rifle into the boot.

She watched Ravenhawk as he took up the Appaloosa's reins and climbed into the saddle. A grimace of pain flashed across his face. He took a deep breath, then offered her his hand.

Putting her foot in the stirrup, she swung up behind him. "Where are we going?"

"Twin Bluffs. Red Creek is the closest town, but Yellow Thunder will be expecting us to go there."

"How far is it to Twin Bluffs?"

"Two days' ride."

Two days. "Is there a train there?"

"No, but they've got a stage that comes through there pretty regular." Kaylynn shuddered at the memory of the last time she had ridden on a stagecoach. She had hoped to be able to take a train home. A fast-moving train sounded nice and safe. She had never heard of a train being attacked by Indians.

She wrapped her arms around Ravenhawk's waist as the horse descended the backside of the hill, grateful that he seemed to be getting better. The thought of being stranded out here, in the wilderness, alone with a sick man was unnerving. The Indians might be able to live off the land, but she was sadly ill-prepared to do so for more than a few days. If anything happened to Ravenhawk, she had little hope of surviving out here alone.

The prairie stretched ahead of them, miles and miles of unbroken grassland. She had heard stories of women who had followed their husbands to places like Kansas and then gone quietly insane, driven over the brink by the loneliness of the endless grassland, the everlasting sighing of a relentless wind.

They rode for hours. She dozed, her forehead resting against Ravenhawk's back, wondering if she would ever see her parents again.

Several times, she glanced over her shoulder, convinced there was someone following them, but she never saw anyone, just miles and miles of gently rolling prairie. No doubt it was just a bad case of nerves, she thought. Ravenhawk was so certain Yellow Thunder would come, he had her hearing hoofbeats that weren't there.

They rode until dusk.

Ravenhawk crawled into his bedroll as soon as

they made camp that night, and she knew that riding had taken all his strength. She knew rest was the best thing for him; still, it worried her that he seemed so weak.

Gnawing on a piece of jerky, she sat close beside him, afraid that if she left him for even a moment, he might die on her and she would be left alone, prey to wild animals and weather and a relentless bounty hunter.

She stared into the night, a prayer in her heart, quietly pleading for courage, for help, for protection.

The sound of a wolf howling sent a shiver down her spine.

Just get us through the night. Please, just get us through the night.

Nights back home had never been this dark, this quiet.

Legs bent, arms folded on her knees, she gazed up at the inky sky and tried to remember the good times, before Alan. Picnics and dances, rides in the park, overnight parties at her best friend Regina's house, teasing and gossiping with her friends. And then she had met Alan Summers. How could she have been so wrong about him? How could something that had started out so promising have ended so very, very badly? Why hadn't she listened to her mother?

He'll never make you happy, Kaylynn. She remembered standing in her wedding dress in the church, her mother at her side. *It isn't too late to change your mind,* her mother had said as she arranged the long white veil that was as sheer and delicate as a spider's web. *If you're not sure about this, you can still call it off. It's not too late.*

But she hadn't wanted to call it off. Standing there clad in a gown of antique satin and ivory lace, she had felt like the princess in a fairy tale, and Alan had been her prince. He was tall and fair, with blue eyes and a wonderful smile, and she had thought herself deeply in love. How quickly that had changed. She had seen those mild blue eyes turn dark with rage, watched that smile turn to a sneer, felt her love turn to fear, and then hatred. Now she wondered if she had ever really loved Alan at all, or if she had just been drawn to a pretty package that was all wrapping and no substance.

It would be difficult to go home to her parents and admit she had made the worst mistake of her life, but no more difficult than living with the Cheyenne. No more difficult than riding across the endless prairie.

That which does not kill us can only make us stronger.

Oh, Mother, she thought with a rueful grin. If you only knew.

Jesse rode doggedly onward, refusing to surrender to the fever that was burning through him. His shoulder ached. His head ached. He'd had nothing to eat all day. He drank copious amounts of water to replace the moisture he was sweating away. Twice, he found himself dozing in the saddle.

Several times he had contemplated giving up, but some inner demon refused to let him quit, and so he rode onward, no longer sure he was even headed in the right direction.

Maybe the roan knew the way. She followed the river eastward. It was near dusk when he spied the tracks leading into the water. Reining the mare to a halt, he studied the ground for several moments before urging the roan into the water. She picked her way across carefully before scrambling up the bank on the far side. Jesse checked the shore, looking for tracks. He saw the prints left by a couple of deer, others left by a coyote, but no hoofprints.

Resting his uninjured arm on the saddle horn, Jesse looked upriver. Had Ravenhawk backtracked? Or continued eastward?

With a sigh, he closed his eyes and put himself in his quarry's place. Then he turned eastward, his gaze searching the ground for sign. Part of being a good bounty hunter was listening to your hunches.

He'd gone about a quarter of a mile when he saw the blackened oak tree. The sight sparked a distant memory, and he glanced upward. If he remembered rightly, there was a ceremonial cave up there somewhere, the walls covered with paintings and carvings depicting ancient battles and horse raids against the Crow and the Pawnee. He had hiked up there once, when he was a boy, curious to see the drawings left by the old ones. It would be a good place to spend the night.

Dismounting, his right arm dangling limply at his side, he bent to examine the ground around the dam. Moving cautiously near the edge of the riverbank, he picked up a few pieces of bark. It didn't take long to find what he was looking for— one fresh hoofprint cut deep into the earth.

Tossing the wood chips into the river, he glanced up the hillside, and smiled.

* * *

Standing in the mouth of the cave, Jesse took a deep breath. They had been here. The acrid smell of a recent campfire lingered in the air, but it was the warm, musky scent of the woman that he inhaled. He closed his eyes, remembering the fear in her eyes, the way the sunlight had turned her hair to flame. Need quickened within him, a desire deeper than passion, stronger than mere physical desire. The need to be held, comforted.

He shook it off, refusing to think of how long it had been since he had been held in a woman's arms, heard a woman's voice whisper his name.

Mao'hoohe. She would be his, willing or not.

Desire burned within him, hotter than the fever raging through his flesh.

Leaving the cave, he went outside and swung into the saddle.

Uncapping his canteen, he took a long drink. He would rest later. If he rode through the night, he might be able to catch them by this time tomorrow.

Chapter Thirteen

"We'll rest here." Ravenhawk drew the Appaloosa to a halt in a sheltered hollow between two low hills. A couple of scrawny cottonwoods grew alongside a shallow seep.

Kaylynn nodded. She practically fell into Ravenhawk's arms when he lifted her from the back of the horse. He was the one who had been wounded, yet he seemed to have far more strength and stamina than she did. She couldn't remember ever being so tired, so sore, so homesick.

She unsaddled the horse, wrapped one of the blankets around her shoulders, and sat down, her back against a tree.

"I'll fix us something to eat in a few minutes," she said, and closing her eyes, she fell asleep.

Ravenhawk stared at her. He had expected her

111

to be more trouble than she had been. In his experience, white women were spoiled and weak, but this one hadn't complained once. She had cared for him when he needed help.

His gaze moved over her face. She was a pretty woman, and women had always come easily for him. A smile, a few sweet words, and they were his for the taking.

He grinned. If only banks came as easily.

He watched her sleep a moment more, then went in search of fuel for a fire. It was not yet dark, but he would let her rest. She would need it later.

Jesse had ridden all through the night and into the day. He had stopped only once. Stretching out on the ground, the mare's reins looped around his left wrist, he'd slept while the horse grazed. He woke an hour later, feeling worse instead of better. The pain in his shoulder throbbed monotonously, his head ached, and he was sick to his stomach.

I will not surrender. I will not back down.

Climbing into the saddle, he urged the roan eastward. Ravenhawk's tracks were easy to follow now. Apparently thinking himself safe, the Lakota wasn't making any effort to cover his trail.

Jesse felt a grin twitch his lips as he examined the Appaloosa's droppings. Ravenhawk and the woman were less than an hour ahead. Riding double was slowing them down.

Jesse grunted softly. He would have them before nightfall.

Kaylynn woke with a start to find Ravenhawk leaning over her.

"What is it?" she asked. "What's wrong?"

He smiled down at her. "Nothing's wrong, sweetheart. Dinner's ready."

"Oh." She stared at him, her heart pounding, as his hand tunneled up into her hair.

"Pretty," he said, his fingers gently massaging her scalp. "Real pretty. Soft, too."

"Thank you."

"Where's home for you?"

"New . . . New York City."

"Never been there." He ran a finger down her cheek. "I could go with you. Make sure you get there safely."

She swallowed hard, his nearness making her uncomfortable. "Why would you want to do that?"

"Why not?" His lips brushed her cheek. "A woman as pretty as you are shouldn't be traveling alone."

"Oh." He had beautiful eyes, large and dark and filled now with a look she had seen in Alan's eyes all too often. Fear spiraled through her as Ravenhawk bent lower, closer, his breath fanning her cheek.

He was going to kiss her. The thought spurred her to action. Rolling to the left, she scrambled to her feet, and backed away, truly afraid of him for the first time.

He smiled up at her, a lazy, roguish smile. She knew it was meant to be enticing, but all she could think of at that moment was Alan. He had wooed her with sweet smiles, charmed her with his good looks and flowery words, made her think he was wonderful, but it had all been a lie, and she had the scars to prove it.

"I'm hungry," she said, and with a show of bravado, she turned her back on him and went to see what he had fixed to eat. She should have known. Jerky and beans and hardtack.

She helped herself to a plateful, poured a cup of coffee, and sat down.

Ravenhawk rose to his feet with a wry grin. She'd won that round.

He was reaching for a hunk of jerky when the short hairs prickled on the back of his neck. A moment later, a voice cut across the stillness.

"Don't even think about it."

Ravenhawk swore. He knew that voice all too well.

"Get those hands up."

Ravenhawk thought of making a dive for his gun, thought of plunging into the sheltering darkness beyond the firelight, but the sound of a .44 being cocked put any thought of resistance out of his mind. Yellow Thunder wasn't likely to miss at this range, and there was no way to outrun a bullet. He should have killed the bounty hunter when he had the chance, he thought bleakly. When his second shot went high and wide, he could have finished him off with a bullet to the heart, but he'd never been a cold-blooded killer. More's the pity, he thought now as, with a sigh of resignation, he raised his arms over his head.

Jesse stepped out of the shadows, his hooded gaze moving from Ravenhawk to the woman. She stared at him as if she was seeing a ghost, her mouth agape, her brown eyes wide and scared.

He swayed on his feet, exhaustion and fever burning through him. He hadn't slept in almost two days; he was weak from the blood he'd lost. He wished he could forget Ravenhawk, that he could put his revolver down, that he could stretch out beside the woman, lay his head in her lap, and go to sleep. He was so tired, so damn tired.

He stared at the woman and everything else seemed to fade into the distance. Mao'hoohe. Red Fox . . .

He took a step toward her, then felt himself falling, endlessly falling, into a deep black void.

"Well, I'll be damned," Ravenhawk said.

Kaylynn looked over at Ravenhawk. He was standing with his hands on his hips, a smirk on his face.

Ravenhawk gestured at the fallen bounty hunter. "If that don't beat all!" He grinned at her as he picked up Yellow Thunder's .44 and shoved it in the waistband of his trousers.

Kaylynn put the plate aside and stood up. "He's hurt."

"Yeah, he is that," Ravenhawk said, looking pleased. "Gonna be dead soon."

"What do you mean?"

"Wound's festering. I can smell it from here. Come on, let's go."

"Go? You can't just leave him here to bleed to death."

"Hell I can't. We'd be doing him a favor if we put him out of his misery right now."

Kaylynn stared up at him, unable to believe her ears. "You can't mean that! He's hurt. He needs help."

"Well, you can stay and help him, if you've a mind to. But I'm leaving. And if you've got any sense at all in that pretty head of yours, you'll come with me."

Kaylynn looked down at the bounty hunter, a shiver rippling down her spine as she recalled the

first time she saw him, the sense that his soul had
brushed against hers. She remembered watching
him at the Sun Dance. Lifting a hand to her cheek,
she remembered how he had slapped her, the look
in his eyes when he warned her not to run away
again. He was a violent man, but so was Ravenhawk.

"You coming?"

Kaylynn met Ravenhawk's gaze and nodded. He
was right. There was nothing she could do for the
bounty hunter.

She packed their gear while Ravenhawk went
in search of Yellow Thunder's horse, and all the
while, she was aware of the man lying unconscious in the dirt. Fresh blood oozed from the
wound in his shoulder. His face was deathly pale
beneath his sun-bronzed skin. His breathing was
shallow, rapid, and uneven. A low groan rumbled
in his throat. His eyelids fluttered open, and he
gazed up at her for a moment before his eyes
closed again. He didn't look so forbidding or so
frightening now.

He had slapped her. She lifted a hand to her
cheek, remembering. He hadn't meant to hit her.
She knew it without knowing how she knew. Perhaps it had been the look of horror in his eyes
when he realized what he had done.

She looked up as Ravenhawk materialized out
of the shadows, leading the bounty hunter's horse.

"I'm staying here," she said, surprising them
both.

"What?"

She shook her head, hardly able to believe what
she was saying. She couldn't ride off and leave
Yellow Thunder any more than she had been able

to resist looking after Ravenhawk when he needed help. Maybe she had missed her calling in life, she thought wryly. Maybe she should have taken up nursing the sick and infirm. Heaven knew she had loved to pretend she was a doctor when she was a little girl, always bandaging her dolls, pretending she was setting broken arms and legs. Once, she had found a baby bird and taken care of it until it was old enough to fly away. She had been sorry to see it go, but had felt a deep sense of satisfaction that she had saved its life.

"I can't just leave him," she said.

"Don't be a fool."

"He needs help."

Ravenhawk glanced at Yellow Thunder, then at her, and shook his head. "There's nothing you can do for him. You'd best come with me. I'll see that you get home."

"I'm staying here."

"I don't think so." He made a grab for her.

With a cry, Kaylynn twisted out of his grasp and grabbed the rifle he had left propped against a tree. She swung it to her shoulder and leveled it in his direction. "I'm staying."

He laughed softly, mockingly. "You don't even know how to use that."

"Yes, I do." Mo'e'ha had taught her how to load and fire a rifle, saying it was good for a woman to know how to shoot in case she had to protect herself or her children from the Blue Coats.

Kaylynn jacked a round into the breech and leveled the gun at Ravenhawk's chest. "I may not be a very good shot, but this close, I don't think I can miss. You make a pretty big target."

He stared at her, his amusement turning to disbelief, then anger. "Suit yourself, sweetheart. I'll leave the food."

"Thank you."

"Don't thank me. You'll both be dead inside a week." He looked at her, his eyes hot. "It's a damn shame. We'd have been good together."

Ravenhawk tethered the bounty hunter's roan to a tree. Moving to his own horse, he quickly saddled the Appaloosa. "Sure you won't change your mind and come along?"

"I'm sure."

He looked at her for a moment, his expression one of regret. Then he swung into the saddle and rode into the darkness.

Kaylynn watched him ride away, a sudden cold fear knifing through her. Hands shaking uncontrollably, she let the rifle fall to the ground, relieved that he had not called her bluff. She could never have pulled the trigger. She looked down at the bounty hunter. What madness had made her stay with a man who was most likely dying? She could scarcely take care of herself, let alone a wounded man.

Yet even as the thought crossed her mind, she knew that wasn't true. She had learned a lot in the last eight months. She wasn't helpless, not anymore. She knew how to tell which plants were poisonous and which were safe, how to locate water, how to erect a lodge, how to start a fire with a flint. Of course, the things she had learned from the Cheyenne wouldn't be of much use to her in New York, but out here they just might keep her alive.

Yellow Thunder groaned softly, and she forgot everything else but the fact that he needed her help. Placing the rifle within easy reach, she added a handful of wood to the fire, filled the coffee pot with water, and placed it in the coals to heat.

Kneeling beside Yellow Thunder, she removed his shirt and the bandage beneath, then felt her stomach churn as she looked at the ugly wound on his shoulder. It was red and swollen, oozing blood and pus.

She pulled a knife from one of the packs, heated the blade in the fire until it glowed white hot. *You can do this*, she told herself, and slid the point of the knife into the edge of the wound. Yellow Thunder groaned deep in his throat as dark red blood and thick greenish pus spurted from his shoulder. The sight, the smell, made her gag, and she turned her head away. She took several deep, calming breaths; then, turning back to the task at hand, she let the wound drain until the blood ran a bright crimson.

When she was satisfied that all the pus was gone, she washed his shoulder with hot water. She dried it with his shirt, then cut a strip of cloth from the edge to use as a bandage.

When she was finished, she sat back on her heels and closed her eyes. She had done all she could do. The rest was up to him.

Rising to her feet, she covered Yellow Thunder with a blanket, added more wood to the fire, and unsaddled his horse. And then, hardly able to keep her eyes open, she crawled under the blanket beside him and went to sleep.

Jesse came awake slowly, aware of a dull throbbing in his shoulder, of a warm body pressed against his back. He frowned, trying to remember where the devil he was.

He glanced over his shoulder, blinked, and blinked again. What the hell was Mao'hoohe doing lying beside him?

He swore under his breath as his memory returned with a jolt. He had caught up with Ravenhawk and then passed out.

Propping himself up on his good arm, he surveyed the camp. His roan stood hip-shot a few yards away, tethered to a tree. There was no sign of the Appaloosa, or of the Lakota. Or his .44. Damn and double damn.

He glanced at the woman again, surprised that Ravenhawk hadn't taken her along. The Lakota had quite a reputation as a ladies' man. It wasn't like him to leave one behind.

His gaze moved slowly over her face. Her brows were finely sculpted, delicately arched. Her lashes were thick and long. She had fine, clear skin, a nice nose, a beautiful mouth.

His gaze slid lower, following the line of her throat, watching the shallow rise and fall of her breasts beneath the rough blanket.

He was hungry and tired. His shoulder burned with all the fires of an unforgiving hell. He cursed softly as he felt a warm rush of desire. He was in no condition to take what he wanted by force, and he knew without doubt that she wouldn't be offering it to him any time soon, if ever.

Damn Ravenhawk. With a sigh, Jesse sank back down on the blanket and closed his eyes. Why hadn't Ravenhawk taken the woman with him? She was a distraction he could ill afford, Jesse mused, and perhaps that was the best explanation of why Ravenhawk had left her behind.

* * *

It was daylight when Jesse woke again. The smell of beans and coffee hovered in the air, reminding him that he was alive and hungry enough to eat a bear, hide and all.

With a low groan, he lifted himself up on one elbow. The woman knelt beside the fire, her hair falling in a riotous mass of auburn waves over her shoulders and down her back. He clenched his hands, resisting the urge to crawl toward her, to run his hands through the heavy fall of her hair.

Damn. Why hadn't Ravenhawk taken the woman with him?

She looked over her shoulder and their gazes met. Awareness arced between them, sizzling like bacon frying in a pan. The woman felt it, too. He saw it in the sudden widening of her eyes, heard it in her startled gasp.

He held her gaze for a timeless moment and then, swearing softly, he fell back on the blanket.

Kaylynn stared at Yellow Thunder, her stomach churning. She didn't know what it was that had passed between them, but it frightened her more than the lust she had seen smoldering in Ravenhawk's eyes, more than the thought of going back to Alan. Frightened her because it was unknown, because, whatever it was, it left her feeling anxious and excited at the same time.

She stared at the beans warming in the pan. When she got home, she was never eating beans of any kind again. She glanced at Jesse Yellow Thunder and wondered if maybe she should have gone with Ravenhawk, after all.

She filled a plate with beans, added a hunk of jerky, poured a cup of coffee, and carried it to Yellow Thunder.

"Does your shoulder hurt very much?" she asked, kneeling beside him.

He lifted one brow. "What do *you* think?"

"I did the best I could."

He glanced at the bandage on his shoulder. "You did fine. Thanks."

"Are you hungry?"

He nodded.

"Can you sit up?"

"Of course I can sit up," he said crossly. "I'm not dead yet."

She watched as, very slowly, he pulled himself up, being careful not to jar his injured shoulder. He was sweating by the time he made it.

"I don't suppose you're left-handed?" Kaylynn mused.

"No."

She scooped up a spoonful of beans and offered it to him. He scowled at her, and she knew he was thinking of refusing her help.

"Oh, for goodness sakes, just eat it," she snapped.

A glimmer of amusement flickered in the depths of his eyes as he obediently opened his mouth.

"Why are men so foolish?" she muttered. "Women bring you into the world. We feed you and bathe you and kiss your hurts, and yet you always get your feathers ruffled when you need our help."

"Yeah," he drawled. "That's true enough, but you're not my mother." His gaze met hers, bold and direct. "But you can kiss my hurt, if you've a mind to."

A rush of heat suffused Kaylynn's cheeks. "That's not what I meant."

"No? Too bad."

"Just be quiet and eat, all right?" She thrust another spoonful of beans into his mouth.

Jesse coughed. "Damn, woman, what are you trying to do?" He glared at her. "Choke me to death?"

"I'm sorry."

She fed him the rest of the meal in tight-lipped silence. When he looked at her like that, his expression harsh, it was all she could do not to run away. Alan had often looked at her like that, his face distorted, his eyes narrowed and dark with anger.

Jesse frowned. She was quite a puzzle. He yelled at her, and all the color drained from her face. He knew she had been ready to cut and run, yet she sat there, wary as a doe poised for flight, while he finished eating.

He wiped his mouth with the back of his hand. "Obliged."

"You're welcome." She put the plate aside. She regarded him a moment, a question in her eyes.

"Go ahead, ask it."

"Ask what?"

"Whatever it is you're wanting to know."

She worried her lower lip a moment, then said, in a rush, "How did you get to be a bounty hunter?"

"How?" He grunted softly. "I don't know. Just sort of fell into it. Seemed like an easy way to earn a living."

"Easy?"

"Yeah." He smiled faintly. "Beats herding cattle, or working for wages in a store."

She glanced at the bandage on his shoulder.

"Maybe, but at least you wouldn't have to worry about the cattle shooting you."

He laughed, and it felt good. "I guess that's true."

"Have you known Ravenhawk very long?"

"Long enough to know how he thinks."

"But you're not friends?"

Jesse frowned. "Not exactly," he said, though he had often thought that they could have been, had their circumstances been different.

"What happened back there?"

A muscle twitched in his jaw. "I got careless."

"Oh?"

His gaze drifted over her face. The truth was, lack of sleep and thoughts of Mao'hoohe had distracted him. He had been thinking of her bathing in the river covered by nothing but soap and sunshine when he should have been watching his prisoner. He had known Ravenhawk was just biding his time, waiting for a chance to make a break for it. He hadn't been fooled by his prisoner's submissive attitude, not for a minute.

Jesse muttered an oath. It was his own fault Ravenhawk had got away. He had been daydreaming like some empty-headed schoolboy when some sixth sense had warned him of danger. He had turned as Ravenhawk jacked a round into the rifle. He had drawn his gun as Ravenhawk fired. Ravenhawk's first shot had taken him in the shoulder. His first round and Ravenhawk's second had sounded as one. Ravenhawk's second shot had just creased his temple, knocking him off his feet. He had lost consciousness, and when he woke up, Ravenhawk was gone. He should be grateful the man hadn't killed him when he had the chance, or left him out there, handcuffed and helpless. But he didn't feel grateful. His shoulder hurt, his head ached, and he was madder than hell.

He met her gaze, knew she was waiting for an answer. "I got careless," he said again. "I turned my back on him when I shouldn't have. He grabbed my rifle . . ." He shrugged his left shoulder. "It won't happen again. I don't suppose he told you where he's headed."

"No."

One brow arched upward in wry amusement. "But you'd tell me if he had?"

"No."

"Why didn't you go with him?"

"How do you know he asked me?"

"I know Ravenhawk." His gaze ran over her, slow and hot, like warm molasses. "I know what he likes."

Heat suffused her from the soles of her feet to the roots of her hair as she recalled Ravenhawk bending over her, telling her she was pretty.

"Why didn't you go with him?" Jesse asked again, his voice sharp.

"It's none of your business."

"The hell it isn't."

"It isn't," she said, her voice equally sharp. "He could have killed you when he had the chance, but he didn't."

"True enough."

"You would have killed him, wouldn't you?"

"Is that what you think?"

"Wouldn't you?"

"Damn right. And if he'd been smart, he'd have done the same thing."

"Then I guess I should have gone with him and left you out here to rot."

"Why didn't you?"

She met his enigmatic gaze. Why was he looking at her like that? What did he want her to say? His face was pale, making the scar across his left cheek more pronounced.

"Why didn't you?"

She looked away, unable to meet his eyes any longer. Why had she stayed? She didn't know, didn't want to know.

Before he could ask her any more questions she didn't want to answer, she scrambled to her feet.

"I'd better look after your horse," she mumbled. She hurried toward the roan, took up the reins, and led it out of the hollow.

Chapter Fourteen

Jesse stared after her, plagued by his unanswered question. Why hadn't she gone with Ravenhawk? He had never yet met a woman who could resist the man's enigmatic charm.

Lying back on the blanket, he closed his eyes. It was peaceful, lying there with the sun warm on his face. If he were smart, he would forget about Ravenhawk. He would take the woman and spend what was left of the summer and the winter with the Morning Star People.

For a moment, he let himself imagine what it would be like to live with the People again, to hunt the curly-haired buffalo, to sit around the campfire on warm summer nights and listen to the ancient ones sing the old songs and tell the old stories, to hear the pride in the voices of the young warriors as they told of raiding parties and counting coup against the Crow, to feast on roast buffalo hump and tongue, to feel the heartbeat of the People in the singing of the drum and the sighing of the wind over the plains.

His thoughts turned back to the woman, with her smooth, suntanned skin and wavy red hair and warm, gentle hands. He imagined those hands moving over him, gentling him, healing old hurts, old wounds . . .

Muttering an oath, he pushed the thought away. She would no more caress him of her own free will than she would pick up a rattlesnake, and he was a damn fool to think otherwise.

He would rest here a few days, and then he would take the woman to Red Creek and drop her off. And then he would go after Ravenhawk.

Kaylynn stood beside the blue roan, staring out over the prairie while the horse grazed. She had spent the last eight months yearning to go home, yet she knew she would miss this place. There was a beauty here, a sense of peace, of awe, that she had never felt back East. The sky seemed bigger out here, a vast blue vault that stretched away into eternity. She had loved to sit beside the river and listen to the summer wind whisper secrets to the cottonwoods, to lie back and watch the clouds drift like puffs of cotton candy across the sky. Living with the Cheyenne had taught her to appreciate the simple things of life—a warm fire on a cold night, a full belly, the satisfaction that came at the end of a hard day's work.

She looked at her hands. Every callous was a badge for a lesson learned. Now that there was a chance she might get back home, she could admit that she would miss the Cheyenne people. She had expected them to be cold, cruel savages, but they were a warm, caring people. Indian women loved their children as dearly as her own mother loved her. Indian men took pride in the accomplishments of their sons. Grandparents told stories to their grandchildren. The children themselves were adorable, happy wide-eyed boys and girls who laughed and played, who had sometimes followed her around the camp, begging to touch her hair, pretending that the reddish-brown strands burned their fingers.

With a sigh, she wondered how long it would take her to get used to living inside four walls again, to sleeping on a fluffy feather mattress, to bathe in hot water, to wear clothes that smelled of soap and starch instead of wood smoke, to wear stockings and shoes instead of soft moccasins.

She laughed softly. Not long. Even though her stay with the Cheyenne had not been unpleasant, she was eager to go home, to see her parents and her grandmother, to be with her own people again.

Her stomach growled, reminding her that she hadn't eaten since the night before. She would be glad when she finally made it back home, glad to eat something besides beans and jerky and hardtack. But for now, even that rough fare sounded good.

Tugging on the reins, she led the horse back to their camp.

She was glad to see that Yellow Thunder was asleep. She warmed up what was left of the beans, then sat beside the fire pit, studying Yellow Thunder while she ate, wondering again how he had gotten the scars that marred his face and body, wondering how and why he had become a bounty hunter. He had said he "fell into it." She wondered exactly what that meant, and if he had killed many men. She wondered why she had really stayed here with him, when Ravenhawk had promised to take her home.

It was a long day. Yellow Thunder slept most of the time, and she was content to do nothing more than watch him, her gaze drawn to the scar on his face, to the width of his shoulders. He was a big man, an inch or so taller than Ravenhawk. Older, too, she thought. But for that awful scar, he would have been a nice-looking man, though Ravenhawk was by far the handsomer of the two. Still, of the two, she had to admit that she found the strong, rugged features of the bounty hunter vastly more appealing than Ravenhawk's boyish good looks.

To her chagrin, she found she rather enjoyed watching the shallow rise and fall of Yellow Thunder's chest as he slept. His skin was a deep, warm bronze; the sun drew blue highlights from his hair.

He woke at dusk, struggling to sit up, cursing his weakness.

"What are you doing?" Kaylynn asked.

"I'm getting up."

Kneeling beside him, she placed her hand on his brow. His skin felt hot and damp. "I don't think that's a good idea."

"Yeah, well, you won't think it's a good idea when I piss in the blankets either."

"Oh." Feeling as though her cheeks were on fire,

she scrambled to her feet and turned her back to him, appalled by what he had said.

She was wishing she could magically conjure up a roast beef dinner when she heard him swear. Glancing over her shoulder, she saw that he had gained his feet and now stood swaying unsteadily, his face pale and covered with sweat.

Hurrying toward him, she slid her arm around his waist. "You look like you're going to faint."

He scowled at her. "Hardly."

"Maybe you'd better lean on me."

He didn't need her help, but, deciding he rather liked the feel of her arm around him, he didn't object.

Kaylynn moved a few steps away and turned her back, her cheeks burning while he relieved himself. She had been married to Alan for six years, but this was the first time she had ever seen a man answer nature's call. It was embarrassing. She thought it ironic that Yellow Thunder was also the first man she had ever seen fully naked. Alan had always come to her bed in the dark of night, making her feel as though their coupling had been shameful somehow.

Staring into the distance, she felt her cheeks grow hotter as she recalled the day she had seen Yellow Thunder standing on the riverbank, drops of water glistening on his long, lean body.

She shook the image from her mind, confused by the shivery feelings that engulfed her when she thought of him. "Are you . . . ah, ready to go back?"

"Yeah."

He forced back the urge to grin as, face carefully averted, she came to help him back to the bedroll.

Her cheeks were rosy with embarrassment as she eased him down onto the blankets.

"Obliged."

"You're welcome." Still refusing to meet his eyes, she went back to the fire and began preparing the evening meal.

Jesse grinned faintly as he watched her. It was obvious that she had led a sheltered life. There was an innocence about her that he found endearing.

It amused him that she wouldn't meet his gaze when she brought his dinner.

"Why?" he asked when he had finished eating.

"Why what?"

"Why didn't you go with Ravenhawk?"

She glared at him. He had asked her that before, and she'd had no answer. She still didn't.

"What difference does it make?" she replied irritably. "I'm here."

He didn't know what he wanted her to say, but like a dog worrying a bone, he couldn't let it go. "Did he leave you behind?"

She shrugged.

"Did he?"

"No! He tried to make me go with him."

Jesse lifted one brow. "Tried?"

"Yes."

"And you refused? Why?"

"My reasons are none of your business, but I'll tell you one thing. Ravenhawk said we should just leave you here to rot, and you know what? I'm beginning to think he was right!"

With a huff, she stood up and flounced back to the fire.

Jesse stared after her. She had stayed of her own

free will. Why? He was still wondering when sleep claimed him.

Kaylynn awoke abruptly, the last remnants of a nightmare trailing cold fingers down her spine. It had seemed so real. She could still hear Alan's voice echoing in the corridors of her mind, see his face, distorted with rage, as he struck her again and again. *Why?* he screamed. *Why do you make me hurt you like this?*

Wrapping her arms around her body, she rocked back and forth.

"It was only a dream."

She spoke the words aloud, hoping they would dispel the terror within her. She was free now. Yellow Thunder would take her to a town, and she would go home, and she would never leave again. Never.

She glanced across the fire, the last vestiges of her nightmare fading away when she saw that Yellow Thunder wasn't there. Fear shot through her. Where had he gone so early in the morning?

She scrambled to her feet, her fear dissipating when she saw that his horse was still there. He hadn't ridden off and left her.

She filled the coffee pot with water from the canteen, added a handful of coffee, and set the pot on the coals to heat.

She ran a hand over her tunic, thinking fleetingly of the closets full of clothes and shoes and hats she had left at home. Alan had insisted she leave it all behind, saying he wanted to buy her a whole new wardrobe. And he had. He had picked it out himself, choosing colors and styles, not asking her advice, not caring what she thought.

Lifting a hand to her hair, she wished for the silver-backed brush that had been lost when the stagecoach was attacked.

The roan made a soft snuffling sound, and she glanced over her shoulder to see Yellow Thunder walking toward her.

She smiled uncertainly as he knelt beside the fire and thrust a rabbit into her hands.

"I got tired of jerky," he said with a shrug.

Kaylynn's mouth began to water as he reached inside his shirt and pulled out a head of squaw cabbage and a handful of wild onions. She would make stew.

"I'm gonna go lie down," he remarked.

Kaylynn nodded. He looked a little better, she thought, not quite so pale. But haggard. As if he wasn't sleeping well. She wondered if he was plagued by nightmares, too.

She watched as he eased himself down on his blanket and closed his eyes, wondering why she found so much pleasure in watching him.

Turning to the task at hand, she quickly skinned and gutted the rabbit, her mouth watering again as she imagined having savory stew for lunch instead of the inevitable beans and jerky.

Later, she led the horse out on to the prairie to graze. She had been afraid of Ravenhawk's Appaloosa, but Yellow Thunder's blue roan was a much more tractable beast. She had big brown eyes and a sweet disposition.

She stood beside the horse, one hand idly stroking the mare's back while the animal grazed on the thick yellow grass. How strange life was. She had been so anxious to get married, to get away from her parents, to have children of her own.

She'd had such big expectations when she married Alan. Her parents were well-to-do, but Alan Summers was rich. Their wedding had been beautiful. Like a storybook princess, she had gone off with her prince, looking forward to a life of ease and luxury and love.

Instead, she had lived in constant fear of her husband's temper. She wondered if life ever turned out the way people expected. Certainly she had never, in her wildest dreams, imagined she would wind up as a slave in a Cheyenne village, or that she would find herself out in the middle of nowhere, caring for a man who was not only a bounty hunter, but was under the illusion that she belonged to him because he had won her in a horse race.

Some time later, she led the roan to the seep and let it drink, noticing as she did so that Yellow Thunder was awake and sitting up.

Tethering the mare to a branch, she went to check on the stew, smiling at the savory aroma.

"Are you hungry?" she asked, glancing over her shoulder at Yellow Thunder.

He nodded. "Yeah. Smells good."

She filled the coffee cup with broth and carried it to him.

"I was hoping for something a little more substantial," he muttered.

"Broth is better for you."

"Is it?"

She nodded as she handed him the cup. She stood there, waiting while he took a sip, then drained the cup in several long swallows.

"It's good," he said. "Got any more?"

"Sure." She refilled the cup for him, pleased that

he had complimented her, though she couldn't imagine why she should care. Maybe it was because compliments had been practically nonexistent since she married Alan. Maybe she was just hungry for a little attention, recognition, appreciation. She shook her head, disgusted with herself. She'd never been one who needed praise before. She certainly didn't need it from this man. Whether the stew was good or not was immaterial.

When he'd had his fill, Kaylynn sat down beside the fire to eat. Jesse watched her, noting how gracefully she moved. She might have been seated at a fancy table eating off fine china instead of sitting on a log drinking out of a dented tin cup.

Desire stirred within him, making him shift uncomfortably on the hard ground. It had been a long time since he'd had a woman. He watched her as she sipped the last of the broth from the cup, noticing the slender curve of her throat, the softly rounded feminine shape of her, and wondered how he had ever thought her too skinny.

He wondered again where she had come from and how she had come to be with the Cheyenne. He could easily imagine her living in a big house, with an army of servants to answer her every need. She didn't belong out here, in the wilderness.

A soft sigh escaped his lips as he realized that she would never really be his. He could take her by force, now, if he was of a mind to, but he would not have what he really wanted.

When they reached Red Creek, he would let her go. He could always buy a woman to ease his desire. In the past, Lula had satisfied his needs. . . .

With stunning force, he realized that he wanted more than mere physical satisfaction from this woman. He wanted her to look at him with adoring eyes instead of eyes filled with fear and revulsion. He wanted her to caress him with hands of love instead of hands of mercy and pity. He wanted her to kiss him willingly, with passion, instead of recoiling from him in fear. He wanted all this and more, but he would never have it. She was as out of his reach as the stars that filled the night sky, as unattainable as the moon.

And like a child crying for the moon, he knew she would never be his.

Sinking back on the blanket, he closed his eyes. She would never be his, he thought ruefully. But he could dream.

Chapter Fifteen

They stayed where they were until the food ran out and the seep went dry. The rest had done Jesse good, and though his arm was still tender, he felt stronger than he had in days.

Now he stood near the roan's head, idly scratching the mare's ears, while Mao'hoohe gathered their meager supplies and saddled the mare. He had asked her again what her white name was, but she had refused to tell him, making him wonder if she had something to hide, or if she was just plain stubborn. The Cheyenne believed a man's name held power, and he wondered if she felt that way, felt that, by giving him her name, he would have some kind of power over her. Maybe she was more Cheyenne than she knew.

When all was ready, he climbed into the saddle.

His shoulder was still sore, but it was on the mend. Reaching down, he pulled the woman up behind him, then clucked to the mare.

If they rode hard, they could be in Red Creek sometime tomorrow afternoon. It wasn't much of a town, but they would be able to pick up some supplies and a change of clothes. He was pretty sure Mao'hoohe would enjoy a long soak in a hot bath. He knew he would. He enjoyed a fleeting image of the woman reclining in a tub of hot water, her hair falling over her shoulders, her skin rosy, before he pushed it from his mind.

But he couldn't ignore the reality of the woman riding behind him, or the touch of her hands at his waist, or the heat of her breasts pressing against his back.

Desire stirred within him, and he swore under his breath. As soon as they reached Red Creek, he was going to have a hot bath, a hot meal, and a hot woman, in that order.

Kaylynn frowned as she heard Yellow Thunder curse softly. "What's wrong?" She glanced around anxiously, wondering if he had seen some cause for alarm. But there was only blue sky and waving prairie grass as far as she could see.

"Nothing."

"Are you sure? You sound kind of . . . I don't know. Upset."

"I'm fine."

Put off by his curt tone, she lapsed into silence again. Men. There was no understanding any of them.

Lulled by the rocking motion of the horse and the warmth of the sun, she dozed fitfully.

* * *

Jesse laid his hand over Kaylynn's as he felt her slump against his back. He had been so determined never to let himself care for another woman, and then she had come along, with her big brown eyes and her pouty pink lips. He had known from the first moment he'd seen her that she was going to be nothing but trouble. Big trouble. And yet he had been unable to resist her.

He had gambled everything he'd had with him to win her in that damn race, and then hadn't had the guts to take what he wanted.

He looked down at their hands: his big and brown and shaped by violence; hers, small and delicate in spite of her callused palms. He wondered what had put the fear in her eyes. He had seen it several times, a fear that went deeper than just being afraid of him. Mulling it over, he wasn't sure it was him she was really afraid of, but she was afraid of something. He had seen fear enough to know it when he saw it.

They arrived in Red Creek early the following afternoon. The town rose up from the prairie like a row of children's blocks. Rough buildings of varying sizes lined a wide, dusty street.

Jesse was familiar with the town and most of the inhabitants. It was a regular stopping-off point for him when he was in the territory. There was no law here, and he had found more than one bounty hiding out in the saloons that made up the bulk of the town's establishments.

He glanced over his shoulder at Mao'hoohe. She was staring at the town, a look of disbelief in her eyes.

Jesse chuckled softly. "Not much of a place, is it?"

Kaylynn shook her head. When Jesse had mentioned a town, she had imagined a city like San Francisco, or maybe Boston. But this . . . She had never seen such a collection of shoddy-looking buildings in her life. There were only about a dozen or so ramshackle structures, and more than half of them appeared to be saloons. She read the names as they rode by. The Dirty Shame. Lady Ace. The Four Queens. The Lucky Deuce.

"Do we have to stop here?" she asked.

" 'Fraid so."

She glanced up at the balcony of the Lady Luck. A young woman with dyed red hair and ruby-red lips was leaning over the rail. She wore a gaudy red-and-black silk wrapper that gaped open to reveal the tops of her ample breasts. Her eyes were outlined with kohl.

The woman leaned farther over the railing. "Hey, Thunder!" she called, waving. "Hey!"

Reining the mare to a halt, Jesse turned his head and looked up at the woman on the balcony.

Kaylynn saw him smile.

"I've been missing you, Big Indian," the woman called with a salacious grin. " 'Bout time you got back here."

Jesse winked at her. "How's it going, Lula?"

"Better, now that you're here." The woman glanced at Kaylynn and frowned. "Don't tell me you brought your own girl this time?"

"No."

"Good. I've got enough competition." The woman smiled again, revealing a dimple in her left cheek. "Will I see you later?"

Jesse nodded, acutely aware of the fact that Kaylynn was listening intently to every word.

Kaylynn glanced over her shoulder as Jesse clucked to the mare. "Is she a . . . you know?"

"Yeah."

"Is that a sporting house?"

Jesse cleared his throat, not liking where the conversation seemed to be headed. "Yeah."

There was a moment of silence. He could almost hear the wheels turning in Mao'hoohe's head.

"What's it like? Inside."

"Most of 'em are a lot fancier than that one. Carved furniture, red velvet drapes, rugs on the floors, mirrors. Good whiskey, honest gambling."

"How does it work?"

"How does what work?"

"When a man wants a woman. Does he just . . . just take his pick?"

Jesse cleared his throat. "Are you sure you want to be talking about this?"

Kaylynn nodded. "Yes." Like most chaste women, she had always been curious about how her fallen sisters plied their trade, always wondered what really went on in those places men whispered about.

"Well," Jesse said, "the first floor in a fancy house is usually a saloon. A man can get a drink there, or spend a few hours gambling or dancing with a pretty girl." He paused, hoping she'd be satisfied with that.

"Go on. How do you decide which—ah, girl you want?"

"When a man's ready to go upstairs, whatever girls are available line up." Jesse swore under his breath. "When a man makes up his mind, he pays the madam and then he takes the—the lady of his choice upstairs."

"I see." Kaylynn thought a moment. "What does it cost?"

"You planning on going into business?"

"Of course not!" Kaylynn exclaimed, glad she was sitting behind him so he couldn't see her flaming cheeks.

Jesse chuckled. "The standard fee in a fancy house is ten dollars; overnight is thirty." In most places, the madam took half of the girl's fee, and then charged an additional five or ten dollars a week for room and board.

And then there were the cribs, but Jesse didn't think Kaylynn needed to hear about those. They were little more than a room made of rough lumber with a tin roof and the girl's name on the door. Cribs were rented to the girls for two or three dollars a day, payable in advance. There was no bonded bourbon there, no soft bed. Usually, a man just removed his hat. The fee for a Chinese girl was two bits, a Mexican was four bits, a French tart was six bits.

He remembered seeing one sign that read: "Big Minnie Faye. Two hundred pounds of passion. Fifty cents each. Three for a dollar."

Jesse had never visited one of the cribs, but he had, on occasion, visited Lula. He breathed a sigh of relief when no more questions were forthcoming.

"That . . . that girl on the balcony. She knew you."

He didn't miss the curiosity, or the accusation, in Mao'hoohe's voice.

Jesse cleared his throat. "Yeah. We're old friends."

"Friends?"

Jesse reined the mare to a halt in front of the hotel. Swinging his right leg over the mare's neck, he dropped to the ground, then reached up and helped Kaylynn dismount.

He could feel her watching him while he tethered the roan to the hitch rack, obviously waiting for him to explain his relationship with Lula.

Jesse removed the saddlebags from behind the cantle, slid the rifle from the boot, then climbed the stairs to the hotel and stepped inside. Kaylynn followed close behind him.

The lobby was dimly lit. Going to the reception desk, Jesse dropped his saddlebags on the floor, then rang the bell. A few moments later, a man with a pencil-thin mustache emerged from the office behind the counter.

"Can I help you?"

"I need two rooms. One with a bath."

The clerk grunted as he opened a register and slid it toward Jesse. "Rooms are a dollar a day. Two bits for the bath."

Jesse nodded. "Send up some hot water right away."

"Sure." The clerk glanced at the register. "Mr. Thunder."

"Where's Abe?" Jesse asked.

"Got hisself killed last week."

"You the new owner?"

"That's right."

"I'd like someone to look after my horse."

"I'll take care of it. How long will you be staying?"

Jesse glanced at Mao'hoohe. "I'm not sure. A day or two. See that my horse gets a good rubdown, will you, and a quart of oats."

With a nod, the man plucked two keys from the board behind the desk. "Rooms 201 and 203, adjoining."

Jesse draped his saddlebags over his shoulder, then reached for the keys. "Obliged. Which one has the tub?"

"Room 201."

"Obliged."

Kaylynn followed Jesse up the narrow stairway. She couldn't believe he was paying a dollar a day to stay in a place like this. Old Mo'e'ha's lodge had been cleaner, and smelled better.

Jesse stopped in front of Room 201 and opened the door. "Home, sweet home."

Kaylynn stepped inside. It was a small, white-washed room, with a narrow iron bedstead covered by a multi-colored quilt. There was a small window, a three-drawer chest, and a straight-backed chair.

"About that girl . . ." She hadn't meant to ask him again, but the words slipped out.

"Let me know when you get done with your bath," Jesse said, quickly changing the subject. "I'll be wanting to use the water."

Kaylynn nodded. It was obvious he wasn't going to tell her what she wanted to know. And maybe she didn't really want to know, anyway.

"After we get cleaned up, we'll go down and get something to eat. Tomorrow, we'll see about getting you some new clothes."

She nodded again, uncomfortable at the thought of spending the night alone. From outside came the sound of a gunshot, the tinny, off-key notes of a piano, the raucous laughter of a saloon girl.

"I'll be right next door," Yellow Thunder said. "Holler if you need me."

She nodded again, somewhat reassured by the knowledge that he would be nearby.

Closing the door, she glanced around the room. A flimsy Chinese screen painted with dragons and water lilies hid a cheap zinc bathtub.

For a moment, she closed her eyes. It was only temporary. She would be home soon, in her own room. She would wear nice clothes and bathe in scented water in an enamel tub, and she would never, ever have to ride a horse or eat buffalo meat or see Jesse Yellow Thunder again.

For some reason, the thought made her feel like crying.

Jesse dropped his saddlebags on the floor near the highboy, laid the rifle across the arms of the chair beside the bed, then went to stand at the window. Maybe, instead of taking seconds on Mao'hoohe's bath water, he'd go over to the saloon and have a good long soak in the pretty enameled tub Lula had ordered from St. Louis. She would scrub him from head to foot, wash and trim his hair, massage the soreness from his back, and ease his other longing, too.

He turned away from the window and took three strides toward the door, then paused. He couldn't let Mao'hoohe wander around alone. He doubted the town of Red Creek had ever seen a decent woman.

With a sigh, he removed his gunbelt and holster

and hung it over the bedpost. One of the first things he needed to do was see about buying a pistol and ammunition to replace what had been stolen by Ravenhawk.

Stripping off his blood-stained shirt, boots, and thick wool socks, he tossed them in a corner, then stretched out on the bed. There would be time enough to see Lula later, once Mao'hoohe was bedded down for the night.

He closed his eyes, his thoughts drifting toward Ravenhawk. He was certain the man wouldn't come here. Would he head for Twin Bluffs? And if so, how long would he stay?

He heard the door to the next room open, heard the muffled sound of voices as a couple of hired boys began to fill the tub.

Thoughts of Ravenhawk slipped from his mind, and he found himself thinking of the woman again, imagined her shrugging out of her travel-stained tunic and moccasins, stepping into the tub, sighing as the hot water closed over her.

Mao'hoohe . . . with her smooth skin and hair as soft and shiny as that of the little red fox for which she'd been named. Mao'hoohe . . .

Kaylynn reclined in the tub, wishing she had some lilac bath salts to add to the water. But she wasn't complaining. It was the first hot bath she'd had in over eight months, and it felt like heaven.

Closing her eyes, she let her thoughts drift.

Soon, she would be home again. Safe again.

For the first time, it occurred to her that Alan might have gone to New York looking for her. If he had, her parents would be worried sick. She was their only child, and they had always been protective of her. She would have to ask Yellow Thunder if she could send her parents a message to let them know where she was and that she was safe, and to ask them not to say anything to Alan about her whereabouts.

Alan. She was afraid her parents would never believe her when she told them how awful her marriage had been, the times he had locked her in her room, the numerous times he had beaten her. He had always been sorry afterward, begging her forgiveness, promising it would never happen again. She had believed him in the beginning. But no more. If her parents wouldn't take her in, if Alan refused to grant her a bill of divorcement, then she would just have to find somewhere else to go.

She smiled grimly. If all else failed, she could always go back to the Cheyenne.

Thoughts of the Indians brought Ravenhawk and Yellow Thunder to mind.

If she were totally honest with herself, she found them both attractive, though in vastly different ways, but it didn't matter. She was through with men.

Finally, with a great deal of reluctance, she stepped from the tub. No doubt Yellow Thunder was also anxious for a bath. The least she could do was get out of the tub he was paying for while the water was still warm.

She toweled off, grimacing as she pulled on her tunic and moccasins. She hoped Yellow Thunder had been serious when he'd offered to buy her some new clothes. Though she hated to be beholden to him, she wasn't about to board a stage dressed in a dirty tunic and moccasins.

Wrapping her hair in a towel, she crossed the floor and rapped on the door that connected her room to his.

Nothing. She rapped on the door again; then, wondering if he had gone out, she opened the door and peered into his room.

He was sprawled face down on the bed, asleep. She tiptoed toward the bed, her gaze moving over him in a long, sweeping glance, noting the blood-stained bandage on his shoulder, the inky black of his hair, his long, long legs. Even relaxed, he looked dangerous.

Should she wake him? He hadn't gotten much sleep in the last few days.

She was turning toward the door when his voice stopped her.

"Did you want something?"

"I . . ."

"What?"

"I was just wondering . . . that is . . ." She gestured toward her room. "I'm through with the . . . uh, tub."

She felt her cheeks flush as a slow smile spread over Yellow Thunder's face.

He slid his legs over the edge of the bed and sat up. "Is the water still hot?"

She chewed the inside of her lip, feeling suddenly guilty for lingering in the tub so long.

"Not really," she said. "I stayed in longer than I should have. I'm afraid it's . . ."

The words died in her throat as he raised his arms over his head, stretching. She watched the play of muscles beneath his dark coppery skin, the way his muscles flexed. She didn't understand her attraction to this man. He scared her in ways she didn't comprehend, made her yearn for something for which she had no name.

Heat flooded her cheeks when she realized he was watching her watch him.

"Like what you see?" he asked, his voice edged with amusement.

Kaylynn swallowed hard as he stood up, his body unfolding with unconscious grace. He towered over her, close enough to touch. The musky male scent of him stung her nostrils. She tried not to stare at him, tried not to notice the width of his shoulders, his flat belly, the fact that he was half-naked. She curled her hands into fists to keep from reaching for him, to keep from running her fingertips over the muscles in his arms.

He grinned at her. "I don't suppose you want to wash my back?"

She shook her head, dislodging the towel to reveal a mass of damp red curls.

He caught the towel and slung it over his shoulder. "I didn't think so. Why don't you wait in here? I won't be long."

She nodded, then moved quickly out of his way as he took a step toward the door.

"I won't bite you, you know," he muttered as he moved past her. Although, he thought as he closed the door behind him, the idea definitely had merit.

Chapter Sixteen

Kaylynn put her fork on the table and sat back in her chair. She never should have had that second piece of apple pie, but apple pie had always been her favorite, and it had been so long since she'd had a dessert of any kind. And the pie had been so good and oh, so sweet. The crust had been almost as light and flaky as one of Mrs. Moseley's.

Surprisingly, the whole meal had been wonderful, something she had not expected to find in a town like Red Creek. She had ordered chicken and dumplings. Yellow Thunder had ordered a steak, rare, with all the trimmings. It was the biggest, thickest steak she had ever seen. He had watched her, his brow arched in amusement, as she asked for a second piece of pie. She had wondered what he was thinking, but lacked the nerve to ask.

Earlier in the day, they had gone shopping at the General Store. He had told her to buy whatever she needed, and when she had summoned the nerve to ask how much she should spend, he had frowned and told her not to worry about the cost; he could afford to buy her whatever she wanted.

It had seemed strange, wandering through the store on her own. Alan always hovered over her when she shopped, criticizing her choices, replacing them with his own. She had often wondered why she bothered to shop at all, since she rarely went home with anything she had picked out.

She looked down at her dress. It was just a simple cotton frock, blue with tiny white flowers, with a square neck and a bit of lace at the throat and the sleeves, but it was the first dress she had chosen for herself since her marriage. She had bought a few other items, too: a plain white petticoat, undergarments, shoes and cotton stockings, a comb and brush, a package of pins for her hair. She had bought a dark green traveling suit, too, along with a matching hat with a jaunty black feather, a pair of gloves, and a pair of black half-boots.

She looked at Yellow Thunder. He was leaning back in his chair, one hand curled around a cup of coffee. He had been shopping, too. The dark gray of his new shirt emphasized the gray of his eyes and complimented the color of his hair. He wore a pair of black whipcord britches, also new, and a pair of boots, scuffed but freshly polished.

He lifted his gaze to hers, and a slow smile spread over his face as he gestured at her empty pie plate. "Gonna go for thirds?"

A warm rush of color suffused Kaylynn's

cheeks. "No. I'm afraid I've already made a pig of myself."

Yellow Thunder shook his head. "I like a woman with a healthy appetite."

"Do you?" Alan had often complained that, if he let her, she would eat everything in sight. He had told her time and again that he wouldn't abide having an obese woman for a wife. Living with Alan, she had been hungry for sweets all the time.

Yellow Thunder nodded.

"Do you think I'm . . . I'm fat?"

"Fat! You?" He shook his head. "A little too thin, for my taste. Maybe you *should* have another piece of that pie."

His words, accompanied by an easy-going grin, sent a warm feeling spiraling through her. It wasn't just sweets Alan had denied her, she thought. She was starved for affection, for attention, for kind words and friendly smiles.

Yellow Thunder's gaze moved over her. "Pretty dress. You look real nice."

"Thank you." His compliment, completely unexpected, surprised and pleased her even though it made her a little uncomfortable. Even though they had spent several days together, he was still a stranger. She cast about for some topic of conversation, but couldn't think of anything interesting to say, and so she asked, "How does your arm feel?"

He lifted his arm and flexed his fingers. "Fine. A little sore. You ready to go, or should I call for another piece of pie?"

"No, I'm ready."

Jesse signaled for the waiter and paid the check and they left the dining room. He'd never made it

to Lula's last night, though he'd planned to. He
had taken Kaylynn to get something to eat after
they got cleaned up, fully intending to take her
back to the hotel, then pay Lula a visit. Instead,
he'd made sure Kaylynn was settled in her room,
then had gone to bed himself. Must be getting old,
he thought, when a good night's sleep held more
appeal than a romp in Lula's feather bed.

Jesse paused in the lobby. "It's a nice night," he
remarked. "You wanna go for a walk before you
turn in?"

Kaylynn nodded, and Yellow Thunder offered
her his arm and escorted her outside. She was
keenly aware of him beside her as they left the
hotel. The heat of his hand penetrated her sleeve
and warmed the skin beneath.

The sun had set. There was nothing to be seen
but darkness beyond the edge of the town. Yellow
Thunder released her arm and they walked side
by side down the street, close but not touching.
Lamplight and raucous laughter spilled out of the
saloons.

"How long have you been a bounty hunter?"
Kaylynn asked after a while.

Jesse shrugged. "Going on seven years, I
reckon."

"Have you . . . ?"

"Have I what?"

"Never mind."

Jesse glanced over at her. "Go on, spit it out.
What do you want to know?"

"Have you killed very many men?"

He grunted softly. "Not as many as I could
have."

Kaylynn frowned. "What does that mean?"

"Most bounties say dead or alive. Dead men don't give you any trouble."

Kaylynn shuddered. She had a quick mental image of him shooting Ravenhawk in the back, then hauling his body in to the nearest lawman for the reward. But he hadn't done that.

"Hey," Jesse said, "I was just joshing." They were at the end of town now. He stared out into the darkness. "I've killed a few men in my time, but only in self-defense, or in battle."

"In battle? Were you in the Army?"

"No, but I've fought the bluecoats a time or two."

She looked up at him, her eyes wide. "Really?"

"Really." He had been a young warrior then, filled with the juice of life, eager to prove himself in battle, to count coup against the enemy.

"Why don't you live with the Cheyenne?"

He shrugged. "My mother died of smallpox when I was sixteen. My father was a white man, and when she died, he decided to go back home and see if any of his folks were still alive. His mother was still living but she was crippled up and needed help running the farm, so we stayed there with her until she died. My dad married a widow woman from a neighboring farm. I was almost nineteen then, and restless, and I took off."

He shoved his hands into his pants' pockets. He'd seen a good deal of the country. He had been living in Texas when he met Abigail. He had been smitten with her at first glance, mesmerized by her yellow-gold hair and sky-blue eyes. He had followed her around like a puppy dog, eager for her attention, hungry for any scrap of affection she was willing to throw his way. She had teased him and flirted with him and kissed him in the moonlight. He had told her of life with the Cheyenne, and she had called him her Mighty Warrior. He had basked in her love, never dreaming she would love him in return, but she had, and they had spent long hours planning for the day when they could be together. And then, on the eve of Abigail's eighteenth birthday, her father had caught them together. . . .

"Are you still going after Ravenhawk?"

Her question drew him back to the present. "Yeah."

"Can't you just let him go?"

Jesse looked at her. Her face was a pale oval in the moonlight. "You sweet on him?"

"Of course not!"

"You never told me why you didn't go with him."

"It doesn't matter."

He shrugged. "If you say so. Are you ever gonna give me your name?"

She hesitated a moment. "It's Kaylynn."

"Kaylynn." He frowned, wondering why the name sounded familiar.

"Mama named me after my two grandmothers."

"It's a right pretty name." He took a step toward her, grateful for the darkness that shadowed his scarred face from her view. "For a pretty woman."

She stared up at him, her eyes wide and scared, like a mouse hypnotized by an eagle, as he slowly bent his head and kissed her.

She tasted like warm sweet apples and cinnamon. The moment his lips touched hers, heat flooded through him, hot and quick, like chain lightning sizzling over the prairie.

Wanting, needing, he drew her into his arms and deepened the kiss. For a moment, she stood passive in his embrace and then, with a low cry, she wrenched out of his arms and fled down the street.

Jesse watched her go, and then, fearful for her safety, he followed her back to the hotel.

When he was sure she was safely inside, he headed for the nearest saloon. He paused in the doorway, his gaze sweeping the interior. It was Saturday night, and the place was crowded.

Pushing through the doors, he went to the bar and ordered a whiskey.

"Hey, Yellow Thunder."

Jesse glanced over his shoulder. "Sandler."

"Long time no see."

Jesse grinned good-naturedly. He and Sandler shared a rough camaraderie. "Not long enough. You on the hunt?"

"Me?" Sandler shook his head. "What about you?"

Jesse shrugged. "Huntin' for Lula. You seen her tonight?"

Sandler jerked his thumb over his shoulder. "She's back there, watching Old Zeke fleece some young tinhorn."

"Obliged. No offense, but I think I'd rather spend the night with her."

Sandler laughed. "Don't blame you a bit."

With a nod, Jesse finished his drink and put the glass on the bar. Lula was exactly what he needed right now.

Kaylynn closed the door to her room and turned the key in the lock. Sitting down on the bed, she

157

stared at the door that connected her room to Jesse Yellow Thunder's.

Why had he kissed her?

Why had she let him?

Heart pounding, pulse racing, she lifted her fingertips to her lips. She could still feel his mouth on hers, warm and firm and gentle. Not like Alan's kisses . . .

She put the thought from her mind. She wouldn't think of Alan, not now, not ever again if she could help it. But Yellow Thunder . . .

"Jesse." She smiled as she said his name aloud, liking the way it sounded, the taste of it on her tongue. "Jesse."

She glanced at the door to his room, wondering if he was in there, wondering how she would face him in the morning.

A knock on the door set her heart to pounding. She couldn't face him, not now. She needed time.

He knocked again, louder this time. She thought of pretending to be asleep; then, taking a deep breath, she stood up. She would have to face him sooner or later. Waiting wouldn't make it easier. Her mother had always said unpleasant deeds were best done quickly.

She ran her hand over her hair, smoothed her skirt, crossed the room, and opened the door.

"Jesse. Jesse?"

"What?" He glanced over his shoulder, puzzled by Lula's angry tone.

Lula sighed. "Why did you come here tonight?"

"To be with you."

"Really? You've been staring out that window for the last half hour."

"Sorry." Moving away from the window, he sat down in the room's only chair, wondering if Kaylynn was asleep. "Guess I've got a lot on my mind."

"Like that woman you rode into town with?"

"Don't be ridiculous. She's nothing to me."

"Really?" Lula picked up one of the half-dozen fancy pillows strewn over her bed and clutched it to her chest. "When did you start lying to yourself?"

"I don't know what you mean."

She shook her head. "I don't know why you didn't just stay with her. She's the only thing you've talked about all night. When you bothered to talk at all, that is."

Hardly aware of what he was doing, he ran one finger over his scarred cheek. "That's not true."

"Isn't it?" Lula rolled her eyes. "Let's see, you wondered about her family and where she came from and what she's hiding. And you think she's just about the prettiest little cabbage in the patch, and—"

"Wait a minute," Jesse said gruffly. "I never said that."

"Maybe not," she said, pouting, "but you're thinking it."

"Like hell."

"So, you don't think she's pretty?"

"Dammit, Lula—"

She threw the pillow at him, just missing his head.

"Don't you cuss at me, Jesse Yellow Thunder. I never thought I'd see the day you'd be cow-eyed over a woman."

He scowled at her. "I am not cow-eyed."

"Hah."

"All right, I admit it. I think she's pretty."

"Go on," Lula said, her eyes narrowing ominously, "get out of here."

"What?"

"You heard me. Git! I don't want you here."

"Dammit, Lula . . ."

Scooting off the bed, she opened the door. "Go on! Git!"

Muttering an oath, Jesse grabbed his hat and stalked out of the room.

Lula closed it with an obliging slam.

Settling his hat on his head, Jesse went downstairs. Going to the bar, he ordered a whiskey, straight, and drained it in a single swallow. Women! There was no understanding any of them. What the hell reason did Lula have to be jealous? He didn't belong to her. He knew she was sweet on him, but hell, the woman earned her living on her back. He swore softly. He had always been fond of Lula, always thought she was a good-looking woman. Until he met Kaylynn. Lula's dyed hair, rouged cheeks, and painted lips seemed garish in the extreme when compared to Kaylynn's quiet beauty.

Ordering another drink, he made his way to the back of the saloon, where a poker game was in progress. He'd had enough of women for one night.

Taking a vacant seat, he bought into the game. He grinned to himself when he won the first hand with four queens.

Women, he mused. God love 'em.

Chapter Seventeen

It was after midnight when Jesse decided to call it a night. He bought a round of drinks for the table, then bade his companions a good night. It had been a profitable four hours. He'd won better than two hundred dollars, and he was feeling good when he left the saloon.

He stood on the boardwalk a minute, enjoying the night air, and then he crossed the street and headed for the hotel.

He paused outside Kaylynn's door and then passed on by and went into his own room. He tossed his hat on the bedpost, ran a hand through his hair, then glanced at the connecting door. She had probably been asleep for the last hour or so, but he knew he wouldn't rest until he was sure she was safely tucked in for the night. It surprised him, the protective instincts she aroused in him. There was a vulnerability about her that made him want to wrap his arms around her, to shield her from the ugliness of the world.

Chiding himself for being a damn fool, he knocked softly on the door between their two rooms, not wanting to wake her if she was asleep. When there was no answer, he knocked again, then opened the door.

The lamp beside the bed was lit. The room was empty.

Frowning, he crossed the threshold. The bed hadn't been slept in. Her tunic and moccasins were in a neat pile on the chair beside the window. The hairbrush and other odds and ends she had bought were on the dresser.

Where the hell was she?

Leaving her room, he went downstairs.

The hotel clerk was dozing behind the desk. He sprang to his feet when Jesse thumped on the bell.

"Yes, sir?"

"The woman I came in with. Did you see her leave the hotel?"

The clerk ran a finger inside his shirt collar. "Why, yes, she left with a gentleman."

"When?"

"I'm not sure. Perhaps three hours ago." The clerk pulled his timepiece from his pocket and frowned. "Four hours at the most."

"Did she say where she was going?"

"No, sir."

"Did you recognize the man?"

"No, sir. Is anything wrong?"

"I don't know. Do you remember what the man looked like?"

The clerk frowned thoughtfully. "He was about my height. Brown hair. Wore a black duster and a fancy two-gun rig."

Jesse swore a short, pithy oath. "Obliged for your help."

Vance Sandler. Jesse swore again as he turned away from the desk and headed for the stairs. What was Kaylynn thinking, to go off with some man she'd never met? And why had Sandler sought her out?

Damn the man. For all that they were friends, they'd always been competitors, vying for the prettiest saloon girls, chasing the highest bounties. . . .

Shit! Taking the stairs two at a time, Jesse ran down the corridor and burst into his room. He should have known better than to believe anything Sandler said. The man lied with all the finesse of a seasoned whore.

Rummaging through his saddlebags, Jesse pulled out the sheaf of wanted posters, tossing them left and right until he found the one he was looking for.

Staring at the wrinkled piece of paper, he called himself every dirty name he could think of.

Ten Thousand Dollar Reward
For information regarding the
whereabouts of Kaylynn Summers.
Description: Age 23
Height—5' 7" Weight—135 pounds
Long auburn hair, Brown eyes
If found, contact Alan Summers
First Bank of San Francisco

Jesse wadded the poster into a ball and hurled it against the far wall. Damn. Damn, damn, damn.

How could he have been so stupid? He'd had the answer to who she was in his possession the whole time, only he'd been too blind to see it!

Cussing mightily, he gathered his gear and jammed it into his saddlebags, picked up his rifle, then went into Kaylynn's room and gathered her few belongings as well. And all the time he cursed himself for being a fool. Ten thousand dollars right under his nose, and he'd been too blind to see it!

He tried to tell himself that was the cause of his anger, that it had nothing to do with the fact that she was married to another man. Nothing at all to do with the tiny spark of hope that had flickered to life when she had stayed behind to look after him. He had clung to a faint, foolish hope that maybe she wasn't totally repulsed by his ruined face, that in time she might even learn to care for him, that they might be able to build a life together.

With his saddlebags draped over one shoulder and his rifle under his arm, he stalked out of the hotel. His first stop was the livery.

Sean Murphy didn't like being roused out of a warm bed in the middle of the night, but one look at Jesse's face kept him from saying so. The bounty hunter looked as though he had just caught a glimpse of a hot and unforgiving hell.

"Did a man and woman ride out of here tonight?" Jesse asked.

"Maybe."

"Don't play games with me, Murph. I'm not in the mood."

"Sorry, laddie. They rode out about four hours ago."

"You see which way they headed?"

Murph shrugged. "I didn't pay much attention, but it might be they headed west."

"Were they ridin' double?"

"No. Sandler bought a little dun-colored mare for the lady."

"Saddle my horse. I'll be back in ten minutes."

The man who owned the General Store wasn't any happier about being roused out of bed in the middle of the night than Murphy had been, but old Lon didn't see fit to argue either.

Jesse rounded up enough supplies to last for a couple of days, dumped it all in a gunny sack, and headed for the door.

"Hey, wait," the shopkeeper called. "You didn't pay for—"

"I'm good for it," Jesse hollered over his shoulder.

Murphy was standing outside the stable, scratching the roan's ears, when Jesse arrived.

"She's important to ye, the lass," Murphy remarked, and it wasn't a question.

"Anyone ever tell you to mind your own business?" Jesse asked as he took the mare's reins and swung into the saddle.

"All the time, boyo. All the time. I hope ye find her."

"I'll find her," Jesse said, sliding the rifle into the boot. "I'll find her."

Kaylynn stared at the man sitting across the fire from her. He was tall and thin, with brown hair and green eyes. He had told her his name was Sandler, and that he was taking her home.

Home to Alan.

165

Feeling numb, she wrapped her arms around her body. Ten thousand dollars. Alan had put up a reward of ten thousand dollars for her return. A bubble of hysterical laughter rose in her throat. Jesse would probably be as mad as a wet cat when he found out he had let ten thousand dollars slip through his fingers.

Jesse. She closed her eyes, the thought of him warming her more than the flames. They had shared little, said little, yet she felt as though she had known him all her life, been waiting for him all her life. His image rose up before her, tall and lean, as rugged and enduring as the hills, his face as scarred as her heart.

A tear slid down her cheek. She would never see him again. She told herself it was just as well. They were worlds apart—culturally, ethnically, financially. She was bound by the laws and restrictions of the society in which she lived; he was bound by nothing at all. She was afraid of life, of living. He wasn't afraid of anything.

She was a married woman, shackled by the vows she had spoken with such hope and conviction. Jesse was as free as the wind, but she belonged to Alan. As his wife, she was his property, just like his fancy house and his shiny carriage.

Alan. She feared and hated him as much as she had once thought she loved him. She watched the dancing flames, wondering if she had ever really loved Alan Summers. With startling clarity, she realized that she had never really known him. She had been overwhelmed by his attention, flattered that such an important man, such an extraordinarily handsome man, would be interested in her. She had been blinded by his smile, charmed by his courtly manners, thrilled at the thought of moving to San Francisco, living in a mansion, having a dozen servants to wait on her. She had been so enamored of the package, of the pretty colored paper and bright shiny ribbons, that she had never lifted the lid, never taken the time to look inside the box and see that it was filled, not with beauty, but with ugliness and cruelty.

"It's time to turn in."

With a start, Kaylynn looked up to see her captor standing beside her, a short length of rope in his hand. He meant to tie her up, she thought, suddenly frantic.

"Please," she said, "please don't take me back there."

"You pay me ten grand, and I'll take you anywhere you want to go."

"I don't have that kind of money."

"Too bad."

"Please. You don't understand. . . ."

"Lady, all I understand is money. And ten thousand dollars is a heap of money."

She nodded, her expression resigned. "Could I have a cup of coffee before I go to bed?"

He looked at her for a moment, then nodded. She poured herself a cup of coffee, then cradled the mug between her palms.

With a sigh of impatience, Sandler sat down. Pulling a knife from a sheath inside his boot, he began to clean his fingernails.

Kaylynn stared into the dwindling flames. She couldn't go back to Alan. The very thought of what he would do to her made her sick with fear.

She sipped the coffee, then put the cup on the

ground. She couldn't go back to Alan. She had to get away from here.

Now.

Tonight.

Sandler picked up the rope. "You ready now?"

"I have to . . . to . . ." She felt her cheeks burn. "You know?"

Sandler grunted. "Be quick about it."

With a nod, she walked into the darkness until she was sure she was out of sight, and then she began searching for a stick, a rock, anything she could use as a weapon.

"Hurry up, lady!"

Heart pounding, she picked up a rock the size of her fist and tiptoed back toward the fire. Sandler was still sitting there, his back toward her.

It was now or never.

He turned as she brought the rock down on his head, his expression one of utter astonishment. With a sharp cry of surprise and pain, he toppled to the ground. Blood oozed from the side of his head.

Oh, Lord, had she killed him? She bent down and placed her hand over his heart, reassured by the strong, steady beat. Thank God, he was still alive.

Rising, she hurried to where the horses were tethered. She had to get away, now, before he woke up. Saddling her horse would take too much time. Climbing on a large boulder, she pulled herself onto the back of the horse she had ridden earlier. It was a pretty little dun mare, with three black stockings. Taking up the reins to Sandler's horse, she rode out of camp, the thought of going back to Alan far more frightening than anything she might encounter in the dark.

It felt strange, riding bareback. Taking a deep breath, she urged the horse in the direction she hoped was east. She tried to remember the few landmarks they had passed earlier. With any luck, she would find her way back to Red Creek.

Jesse swore under his breath. It hadn't been easy, tracking in the dark. Fortunately, Sandler wasn't making any effort to hide his trail; still, even with the help of a full moon, it had been slow going. But the sign was there—two horses headed west. The nearest town was Bourdrie. No doubt Sandler figured to catch a stage headed west from there.

He swore again, wondering if the bounty hunter would ride straight through to Bourdrie. If that was the case, Jesse knew he would never catch them, not with the lead Sandler had. He had to hope that Kaylynn would slow the other man down or that Sandler had made camp for the night.

The sky was turning gray when the roan snorted, her ears pricking forward. Straightening in the saddle, Jesse peered into the distance. Had he heard something? The roan made a soft snuffling noise, and then Jesse heard it, the sound of hoofbeats off to the left.

He slid the rifle out of the saddle boot, his ears tracking the sound. A horse whinnied in the distance. There was the sound of brush being trampled, and then two horses crested a small rise.

Jesse slid the rifle back into the boot as he recognized the woman on the back of the dun mare.

"Hey," he drawled.

Kaylynn's eyes grew wide as Jesse dismounted and walked toward her. He looked up at her for a long moment, and then, slowly, he reached for her. With a sigh, she slid into his arms.

"Are you all right?" he asked.

Kaylynn nodded, too close to tears to speak.

"Did he hurt you?"

She shook her head, wondering why this man, of all men, should make her feel so safe.

"Where's Sandler?"

"Back there somewhere."

"How'd you get away?"

She burrowed deeper into his arms, remembering how afraid she had been when she had opened the hotel door expecting Jesse and found a stranger with a gun instead. "I hit him over the head with a rock. I thought I'd killed him."

"He's got a hard head. I doubt if you did him much damage. I'd like to be there when he wakes up, though," Jesse remarked, grinning. Sandler had always been a cocky sonofagun. No doubt his pride would take a beating when he came to and found his bounty had ridden off in the middle of the night.

Kaylynn shifted in his embrace, and all thought of Vance Sandler fled Jesse's mind. She was warm and soft, shivering a little. More from nerves than the cold, he thought, and held her closer. She felt good in his arms. Holding her like this, he realized she wasn't too skinny, not by half. A wisp of her hair tickled his chin.

Kaylynn closed her eyes, content to be held. His touch was so gentle. It had been years since anyone had held her just to comfort her.

She shivered again as a light breeze wafted over

the land. Jesse took a deep breath. He knew a good way to warm her, to make her forget about Sandler and everything else, and before he could change his mind, he put his forefinger under her chin, tilted her head up, and kissed her lightly.

For a moment, she stood stiffly in his embrace, and then she leaned into him, her arms slipping around his waist.

His hands skimmed over her back as he deepened the kiss, and she pressed herself against him, her breasts warm against his chest, her lips sweet, so sweet.

She gasped when his tongue teased her lower lip, then slipped inside to duel with her own. He felt her hesitation, and then her surrender.

With a low groan, he crushed her to him, one hand cupping her buttocks, drawing her up hard against him.

With a little cry, she pulled away, her eyes suddenly wild. "Don't!"

"Kaylynn . . ." He reached for her again, hungry for her touch.

"No!" She stared at him, her hands clenched into tight fists. "I . . . I can't."

He nodded, one hand stroking his scarred cheek. "Sure," he said. "I understand."

He didn't, but she couldn't explain, couldn't tell him that it wasn't him. It was the sudden sense of being imprisoned in a man's arms, of being helpless, that sent panic spiraling through her. Alan had held her like that, crushing her, hurting her, delighting in causing her pain if she didn't please him, if she didn't do everything he asked of her.

Jesse swore under his breath. He hadn't meant

to frighten her, but it was easy to see that he had, and badly.

"Why don't you ride my horse?" he said. "I think you'll be more comfortable in a saddle."

Kaylynn nodded. Jesse brought his horse up and lifted her into the saddle. Swinging onto the back of Sandler's big chestnut gelding, he took up the reins of the dun mare.

"Ready?"

She nodded, a shiver sliding down her spine.

"Here." Jesse shrugged out of his sheepskin jacket and handed it to her.

Kaylynn slipped it on, grateful for its warmth. "Where are we going?"

"Back to town."

"Do you think Sandler will try again?"

"Not if he's smart. I'll leave word with Murph that you're with me." He'd worry about Sandler if and when the time came, but he didn't think the bounty hunter would give him any trouble. Once Sandler knew Jesse had staked his claim, he'd most likely ride on.

Kaylynn nodded. "And when we get back to town, what then?"

"I don't know." Jesse held her gaze a moment, then reined his horse east, toward Red Creek.

It was early afternoon by the time Jesse got Kaylynn settled into bed at the hotel. He warned her not to open her door for anyone but him, then took the horses down to the livery.

Murph frowned as Jesse handed him the chestnut's reins. "Where's Sandler?"

"He'll be along."

"Don't guess ye want to tell me what the hell's goin' on?"

"Nope."

"Didn't think so."

"Give my horse an extra ration of oats. She's earned it."

Murph grunted. "Ye look like ye've been rode hard and put away wet your own self."

"Yeah. One more thing. Tell Sandler the bounty on the girl is mine."

Murphy grinned, well aware of the friendly rivalry between the two bounty hunters.

Jesse patted the roan on the shoulder, then left the barn. Ten thousand dollars. Kaylynn was worth ten thousand dollars to a man in San Francisco. And not just any man. Her husband.

Damn and double damn.

Ten thousand dollars. Why had she run away from home?

Why the hell did he care? He was a bounty hunter, and she was wearing a right pretty price tag.

He was in a foul mood when he reached the hotel. He'd get a few hours' sleep, then go check the schedule for the next stage headed west. He would take Kaylynn back to her husband, and then hightail it out to spend the winter with the Cheyenne.

Entering his room, he locked the door, tossed his hat on the chair, then sat on the edge of the bed, wishing he had a drink.

Why had she run away from home?

He ran a hand through his hair. It was none of his business. Too restless to sit still, he began to pace the floor. He thought fleetingly of going to the saloon, but he doubted Lula would have anything to do with him right now, and none of the other girls appealed to him.

If he was going to be totally honest, he had to admit that even Lula didn't appeal to him now. He wanted Kaylynn.

"Jesse?"

Startled, he whirled around, his hand automatically reaching for his gun. He swore when he saw Kaylynn standing in the doorway between their two rooms.

"Damn, girl, don't creep up on me like that."

"I'm sorry."

"What do you want?"

"I want to go home."

"They why did you run away?"

"I don't mean back to my husband. I mean home, to my parents."

"He's put up a ten-thousand-dollar reward for your return. Did you know that?"

Kaylynn nodded. "Yes. Sandler told me." She had known Alan would be upset when she left. She had expected him to look for her, maybe even offer a reward. But ten thousand dollars . . .

"It's a lot of money," Jesse remarked. "Is your husband good for it?"

"Yes."

"Guess he wants you back pretty bad."

"Please don't take me back there."

"What did he do to you?"

Kaylynn folded her arms over her breasts. "Nothing. I just don't want to go back."

"Nothing?"

She shook her head. She couldn't tell Yellow Thunder of the beatings she had endured, of the times Alan had locked her in her room, deprived her of food and water. It was too humiliating, too degrading. She was ashamed to admit her husband had treated her like that, ashamed she hadn't had the courage to leave sooner.

"Get some sleep. We'll talk later."

She nodded, but didn't move, just continued to stand there, staring up at him through eyes filled with sadness.

"Kaylynn, I . . . Dammit, girl, talk to me."

"I can't go back. Please don't make me."

Hardly aware of what he was doing, he crossed the floor and folded her into his arms. She huddled against him, and his arms tightened around her.

"Kaylynn, you can tell me. Whatever it is, you can tell me."

"I can't. I'm too ashamed."

He stroked her hair, her back, while silent sobs wracked her body. Swinging her into his arms, he carried her to the chair in the corner and sat down, cradling her against him as if she were a child in need of comfort.

Kaylynn snuggled closer, needing his warmth, his strength. Somehow, she had to convince him to take her to her parents. Somehow. But how? What could she offer a man like him?

His lips brushed her cheek, and she knew then what he wanted, what she could offer him, if she only had the courage. As soon as the thought crossed her mind, she knew she couldn't do it. Knew he would laugh at her if she even offered. Alan had told her on more than one occasion that she was a failure in bed, a failure as a woman. *I could get more heat from a block of ice,* he'd often said. *More affection from a stone.*

What made her think Jesse Yellow Thunder would consider a night in her bed a fair exchange for ten thousand dollars?

She should have gone with Ravenhawk. He would have taken her back to her parents. The thought brought a fresh wave of tears.

"Kaylynn . . . Dammit, girl, tell me what's troubling you."

"I can't. Please, don't ask me."

He drew back a little so he could see her face, felt his heart constrict at the utter misery in her expression. Her gaze met his, frightened, discouraged, resigned.

Jesse drew a deep breath and blew it out in a ragged sigh. "Don't cry, Kay," he said quietly. "I won't take you back."

"You mean it?" Hope flared in her eyes, chasing away her tears, making her look young and vulnerable and beautiful, so beautiful.

"I said it, didn't I?"

"Oh, Jesse, thank you," she exclaimed softly, and kissed him.

It was a light kiss, a token of gratitude, nothing more, but it hit Jesse like a bolt of lightning. He could scarcely recall the last time a woman had kissed him of her own free will, and it seared a path to his heart and soul. Ten thousand dollars was a small price to pay for such a kiss, he thought.

Instinctively, he drew her closer, seeking to deepen the kiss. He expected her to pull away, maybe slap him for his boldness. Instead, she pressed herself against him, her hands clutching at his back, a little purr of enjoyment rising in her throat.

Sweet, he thought, indescribably sweet.

For a long moment, Kaylynn clung to Jesse, enraptured by the sensations flooding through her as his mouth moved over hers. Hungry for love, she surrendered to his touch, her body seeming to come alive as his hands moved over her back, cupped her breast. Gentle, she thought. His hands were so big, yet so gentle. Alan had never kissed her like this, never made her feel like this, her pulse racing and butterflies of excitement dancing in her stomach. Alan made her feel ugly and unworthy of his attention; Jesse made her feel beautiful, desirable.

Alan. With a little cry, she twisted out of Jesse's arms and stood up. No matter how wonderful it felt to be in Jesse's arms, she was still a married woman. No matter that Alan had abused her, no matter that he had been unfaithful to her, she was still his wife, bound to him by the words she had spoken when they wed. No matter that he had not seen fit to live by them.

Jesse stared up at her, his hands clenched. "I'm sorry." He ran a hand through his hair. "Go to bed."

With a nod, she turned and went back into her own room and quietly closed the door behind her.

Chapter Eighteen

Ravenhawk stood near the end of the long mahogany bar, one foot braced on the rail, his gaze fixed on the shot of whiskey in his hand. He had to make a decision, he mused, had to decide what to do next, where to go next. He'd been holed up in this dirty little no-name town long enough. He should have stayed in Twin Bluffs, but the chances of Yellow Thunder showing up there had been too great.

He glanced over at the six men gathered around a table across the room. Four of them were involved in a high-stakes poker game. They were planning to hit the stage out of Twin Bluffs, and they had asked him to ride with them. He knew one of them. Paul Nash. Nash was a good man to have behind you in a tight spot. He was fast on the draw, a quick thinker.

Ravenhawk had never met the other five men, though he knew one of them, Victor Mazza, by reputation. Mazza was a cold-blooded killer. It was his idea to hit the stage. He'd come into town with a couple of his men to buy supplies and had heard a rumor that the coach might be carrying a large sum of cash. Rather than take the time to go back to his hideout for more men, he had asked Nash and the two men with him to ride along, and Nash had asked Ravenhawk.

Ravenhawk swallowed half the whiskey in his glass, savoring the taste. After his last encounter with Yellow Thunder, he had decided to go straight, but his interest in becoming an upstanding citizen had waned when faced with the hard reality of finding a job. Truth was, he didn't know what he wanted to do. Clerking in a store held no appeal. Working cattle was hard, dirty work with little to recommend it. Dealing cards in a saloon was a possibility. The pay wasn't bad and the hours suited him, but it meant working for someone else, and he'd never been good at that.

Draining the glass, he set it on the bar behind him.

He was out of money and already wanted for bank robbery. One more job wouldn't hurt. He'd get a good stake and light out for parts unknown. He wouldn't drink his share away this time, or spend it on his favorite whore, or wager it on the turn of a card. He'd find a woman, a job, and settle down before it was too late.

His mind made up, he crossed the room. "So,"

he said, sliding into the vacant chair across from Nash. "That offer still open?"

Nash laughed softly. "I knew you'd come around."

"Did you?"

Nash made a vague gesture with his hand. "Men like us, we weren't meant to live by the clock. We're like the wind."

Ravenhawk nodded, but the words left him feeling unsettled. He didn't want to be like the wind. Nor did he want to be like the trees, rooted to one spot.

"You in?" Mazza asked, shuffling the cards.

Ravenhawk shook his head. "I'm busted."

"He's in." Nash pushed a stack of silver dollars in front of Ravenhawk, and then winked. "You can pay me back after we take the stage."

With a nod, Ravenhawk watched Mazza deal the cards. What did he want? he mused as he picked up the cards he was dealt. Three aces, a deuce, and a ten. He tossed the deuce and the ten into the center of the table. What did he want? he asked again. And thought that, at the moment, a fourth ace to go with the three in his hand would suit him right down to the ground.

Face impassive, he tossed a dollar into the pot. The future would take care of itself.

Chapter Nineteen

Kaylynn was still subdued the next morning. She'd taken a long nap the day before and eaten supper in her room. Jesse had spent the evening in the saloon, buying drinks for Sandler, who'd had a long walk back to town. He was as mad as hell, but not mad enough, or foolhardy enough, to try to take Kaylynn a second time.

Eyes narrowed, Jesse sat back in his chair, regarding her across the dining room table while she picked at her breakfast.

"Kaylynn, why don't you tell me about it?"

"I can't."

He finished his coffee and put the cup aside. "I'm giving up ten grand to take you back to your parents. I think that buys me the reason."

She looked up at him then. "He . . . My husband

181

. . . he . . ." She took a deep breath and finished in a rush. "He beat me."

Jesse frowned. "Beat you?"

Kaylynn stared at the fork clutched in her hand. "All the time."

Jesse swore under his breath as he recalled the day he had slapped her. Damn.

"I'll see you get back to your parents," he said quietly.

Relief washed through her, pure and sweet and clean.

"Thank you."

"You about done there?"

"Yes." She put her fork on her plate, folded her napkin, and placed it on the table.

Rising, Jesse dropped a dollar on the table, then reached for his hat. Taking Kaylynn by the arm, he led her from the dining room.

Jesse paused in the lobby. "I need to go over to the stage depot. You want to go with me, or stay here?"

"I'd like to go with you."

There wasn't much activity in the street at this time of the day. The stage depot was located at the west end of town. A long counter divided the small one-room building. According to the schedule, the next stage headed east was due to leave at half past one that afternoon.

Several posters had been tacked to the side of the building. Kaylynn read them while waiting for Jesse to purchase their tickets.

One was an advertisement for forty acres of "prime grazing land" in Texas.

Several were wanted posters. One Victor Mazza was wanted for robbing a number of trains and stages. The reward for his capture "dead or alive" was five-hundred dollars. Another poster was for the James-Younger Gang. She had heard of them. They were notorious in Kansas and Missouri. The poster said they were wanted for robbing the Chicago, Rock Island and Pacific Railroad in Adair, Iowa, of six thousand dollars, as well as for several other bank robberies in Kansas and Missouri. She recalled reading somewhere that the James Gang had been responsible for the first train robbery ever committed.

Another flyer was titled "Hints For Plains Travelers." She read this one with interest.

1. The best seat inside a stage coach is the one next to the driver.
2. Never ride in cold weather with tight boots or shoes or close-fitting gloves.
3. When the driver asks you to get off and walk, do it without grumbling. He will not request it unless absolutely necessary. If a team runs away, sit still and take your chances; if you jump, nine times out of ten you will be hurt.
4. In very cold weather, abstain entirely from liquor while on the road; a man will freeze twice as quick while under its influence.
5. Don't growl at food stations; stage companies generally provide the best they can get.
6. Don't smoke a strong pipe inside, especially early in the morning. Spit on the leeward side of the coach.

7. Don't snore, nor lop over on your neighbor when sleeping.

Kaylynn laughed softly, wondering how a sleeping person was supposed to know when he was "snoring or lopping over on his neighbor's shoulder." Shaking her head, she read the next one.

8. Never attempt to fire a gun or pistol while on the road; it may frighten the team. Don't discuss politics or religion, nor point out places on the road where horrible murders have been committed.
9. Don't linger too long at the pewter wash basin. Don't grease your hair before starting or dust will stick there in sufficient quantities to make a respectable 'tater' patch. Tie a silk handkerchief around your neck to keep out dust and prevent sunburns. A little glycerin is good in case of chapped hands.
10. Don't imagine for a moment you are going on a pic-nic; expect annoyance, discomfort and some hardships. If you are disappointed, thank heaven.

Apparently wanting to make sure that no point was missed, someone had posted a second list entitled "Stagecoach Riders Nine Commandments."

Kaylyn read the list quickly. Most of them were just repeats of the previous list, with the additonal warnings that gentlemen must refrain from the use of rough lanuage if women or children were present.

Number seven warned passengers to remain

calm in the event of runaway horses and went on to say that leaping from the coach in a panic will "leave you injured, at the mercy of the elements, hostile Indians, and hungry coyotes."

Number eight warned against discussing stage-coach robberies and Indian uprisings.

She read number seven again, shuddering at the part about being at the mercy of hostile Indians. She had survived one attack. Surely Fate would not subject her to another.

Jesse turned away from the counter and slipped their tickets into his back pocket. "So, would you like to take a walk?" he asked.

"A walk?" Kaylynn looked around. "Where to?"

"We've got some time to kill before the stage leaves. There's a pretty little lake not far from here."

"All right."

He took her hand, surprised that she didn't object. It made him feel suddenly young and care-free, to be walking hand in hand with a pretty girl.

"What will you do with your horse while we're gone?" Kaylynn asked as they left the depot.

"Take her with me."

"Oh?"

Jesse nodded. "I'll tie her to the back of the coach. It's done all the time."

Away from the town, there was only green grass and blue sky. Kaylynn was acutely aware of the man walking beside her, of his large callused hand holding hers. His nearness filled her with an odd excitement. Her every nerve seemed to be humming, her skin felt extraordinarily sensitive.

Walking on, they neared a stand of slender willows. Beyond the trees was a small blue pool surrounded by a carpet of grass. Sunlight danced on the quiet surface of the water, sparkling like diamonds tossed by a careless hand. She smiled as a fish jumped, its tiny silver body glistening wetly.

Jesse sat down on a log, and after a moment, she sat beside him, her insides trembling, her heart pounding.

Silence stretched between them. It made her nervous. She glanced at him, then looked away. What was he thinking?

"It is pretty here," she remarked, unable to endure the silence any longer. Her voice sounded loud in her ears.

"Yeah. Peaceful."

Kaylynn nodded. Being a bounty hunter, she thought it unlikely that he had known much peace in his life. She studied him from the corner of her eye. His profile was sharp and clean.

He really was a handsome man. She hardly even noticed the scar on his cheek any more.

An odd sensation uncurled within her stomach, like a rosebud opening its petals to the light of the sun. She had a sudden urge to touch his cheek, to feel the warmth of his skin beneath her hand, to make him smile.

Abruptly, he turned to face her. "What?"

She blinked at him, startled by his curt tone.

Jesse dragged a hand over his jaw. "I'm sorry."

Kaylynn smiled tentatively. "I wasn't staring, really."

"It's okay. I'm used to it."

"Are you?"

"I thought I was."

"Do you like poetry?"

He lifted one brow. "Poetry?" He laughed softly.

"Do I look like a man who reads poetry?"

He grinned as her cheeks turned a rosy shade of red.

"I guess not."

"Why'd you ask?"

"Never mind."

"Tell me."

"This place." She made a gesture that encompassed the lake and the grass. "It reminded me of a poem, that's all."

"How does it go, that poem?"

"I don't remember."

"Sure you do."

"Well . . ." She chewed the inside of her lip a moment, wishing she had never mentioned it. It was a love poem from a book titled *Love Poems and Sonnets to Win a Lady's Heart*.

"I'd like to hear it."

She looked away, her gaze settling on the lake.

"Walk with me, Spirit's Song, and sing gently
     to me in the night of your love.
 Tell me of grasses sweet and lying in the sun
     together.
 Tell me of moonlight and starlight somehow
     joined as one, forming an endless blanket
     of light for our roof.
 And then, my lady fair, tell me that it will
     never end."

"That was pretty," Jesse said. "Real pretty."

Kaylynn nodded, unable to meet his eyes.

"Do you know any more?"

"Part of one."

"Recite it for me."

"When the morning awakes you, listen as my
  voice softly calls, beckoning you to arise
  to new wonders.

Listen for my footsteps as I arrive with the
  dawn.

I will not delay my coming to you.

Warm yourself in my memory. With each
  breath of the day, I whisper your name
  on the wind.

I will be there. As the sun shines, and the
  birds sing, my love will prevail."

Hesitant, she turned and met his gaze. She felt
a rush of heat engulf her as his gaze met hers.

"Kaylynn . . ."

"I . . . It's just . . ." She stared at him, mesmerized, her body yearning toward him, her heart
thundering in her ears as she waited. Waited, hoping and afraid.

"Kaylynn."

"We should go back." She spoke quickly, afraid
of the feelings rioting within her, afraid of being
hurt, of being rejected, ridiculed, found wanting.
She was afraid he would reach for her, kiss her.
Afraid he wouldn't.

Slowly, so as not to frighten her, Jesse took her
hand in his. "Kaylynn, don't run away from me. I
won't hurt you."

She looked up at him, her eyes wide. "Jesse,
I . . ."

"What is it? You can tell me."

She shook her head, knowing she could never
put her feelings, her fears, into words.

"Touch me," Jesse said, his voice whisper-soft.
"I need to feel your touch. Just once."

She looked into his eyes and knew she couldn't refuse his request, or deny the urgings of her own heart. Gently, she caressed his right cheek, her fingertips trailing down his neck, over his shoulder, down his arm.

A sigh escaped Jesse's lips and then, unable to resist, he bent his head and kissed her.

For a moment, their gazes met and then, with a sigh, Kaylynn closed her eyes, the wonder of his touch swallowing her fear.

It was a moment steeped in magic and sunlight. The rest of the world fell away, and she felt herself being reborn in Jesse Yellow Thunder's arms. She felt his spirit touching hers, felt his need, his loneliness, and she knew, in the deepest part of her being, that this man would never hurt her, never belittle her, never make her feel worthless. He would live for her and die for her.

"Kay." He drew back a little, his voice ragged, his eyes filled with the same wonder she knew must be reflected in her own.

She smiled tentatively, her heart filled to overflowing. "You felt it, too?"

He nodded, his mind echoing the words she had spoken earlier. *Walk with me, Spirit's Song, and sing to me gently in the night of your love. . . .* He could hear her heart singing in his soul, the soft, sweet notes lighting corners long dark, healing old hurts, old wounds.

Unable to put his feelings into words as eloquent as the poetry she had recited, he drew her into his embrace and kissed her again, hoping she would hear the words he could not say, be warmed by the love he was incapable of speaking aloud.

189

Kaylynn sighed as she put her arms around him, her spirit soaring like the red-tailed hawks that glided over the Black Hills as Jesse held her close. It filled her with a sense of wonder she had never known before to think that this man, this strong beautiful man, needed her. Wanted her.

They sat there for a long quiet time. Jesse held her close, knowing that, in the last few moments, the entire course of his life had been changed.

Kaylynn rested her cheek on Jesse's shoulder. If only she could stay there, locked forever in his arms. Wrapped within the safe haven of Jesse's embrace, she knew she need never fear anything, or anyone, again. Nothing could hurt her now. Not Alan. Not anyone.

She closed her eyes as Jesse stroked her hair, his touch gentle, tender. How wonderful it was to feel so safe, to know the touch of a man's hand, not in anger or violence, but in a soft expression of caring. For he must care. Surely he would not kiss her so tenderly, hold her so sweetly, if he didn't feel some degree of affection for her.

And what, she wondered, did she feel for him? Was it only gratitude because he had agreed to take her home, or was it the first gentle stirring of something deeper, richer, more lasting? She had thought herself in love with Alan. What if she was wrong again?

She felt Jesse's lips move in her hair, felt his hands roam lightly up and down her back. His touch, light yet sensual, made her shiver with delight.

"Kay?"

"Hmm?" She smiled at him. No one else had ever called her Kay. She rather liked it.

"Do you want to go back to the hotel?"

"No." She snuggled a little closer. "I like it here."

Jesse glanced up at the sun. They still had a couple of hours until it was time for the stage to pull out.

"Can I ask you something?" she asked, not meeting his gaze.

"I reckon you can ask me anything."

"You won't get mad?"

"No."

"How did you get that scar on your face?"

He drew in a breath, his arm tightening around her waist.

"I'm sorry," she said quickly. "I shouldn't have asked."

"No, it's all right."

In a voice devoid of emotion, he told her about Abigail, about the night they had planned to run away, and how her father had caught them. He told the story as though it had happened to someone else, but she heard the underlying pain in his voice, the sense of helplessness and loss.

"And you never found her?"

Jesse shook his head. "No." He shrugged. "I guess I never will."

"I'm sorry," Kaylynn said, and knew it for the lie it was. If Jesse had found his Abigail, he wouldn't be here, with her, now.

"It was a long time ago. I'm no longer the man she fell in love with."

"I'm sure it wouldn't matter," Kaylynn replied. "Not if she loved you."

Jesse laughed softly, bitterly. "I'm sure it would." The boy Abigail had loved had died that night, and there was no going back. Even had he wanted to, there was no way to turn the clock back, no way to erase the bitter memories, or wash the blood of the last seven years from his hands.

"Jesse." His name was a whisper on her lips as she reached out to caress his scarred cheek.

"Don't." He caught her hand before she could touch him, imprisoning it tightly in his.

"Let me."

He gazed deep into her eyes and then, very slowly, released her hand, his body stiffening as her fingertips traced the long white scar that was a constant reminder of a night he would never forget. Her touch left him feeling weak, vulnerable, needy for more.

"Kay . . ."

Taking her hand in his, he kissed her palm. And then, very lightly, he ran his tongue over her skin. Heat sizzled through her, awareness flooded through every nerve ending, making her pulse race and her heart beat fast. Excitement fluttered like butterfly wings in her stomach.

"Jesse." She gasped his name. "Oh, Jesse."

"It's all right." He wrapped her in his arms again, holding her close, closer. He had promised to take her home, he thought, and wondered how he would ever let her go.

Thrill to the most sensual, adventure-filled Historical Romances on the market today...

FROM LEISURE BOOKS

As a home subscriber to the Leisure Historical Romance Book Club, you'll enjoy the best in today's BRAND-NEW Historical Romance fiction. For over twenty-five years, Leisure Books has brought you the award-winning, high-quality authors you know and love to read. Each Leisure Historical Romance will sweep you away to a world of high adventure...and intimate romance. Discover for yourself all the passion and excitement millions of readers thrill to each and every month.

SAVE AT LEAST $5.00 EACH TIME YOU BUY!

Each month, the Leisure Historical Romance Book Club brings you four brand-new titles from Leisure Books, America's foremost publisher of Historical Romances. EACH PACKAGE WILL SAVE YOU AT LEAST $5.00 FROM THE BOOKSTORE PRICE! And you'll never miss a new title with our convenient home delivery service.

Here's how we do it. Each package will carry a 10-DAY EXAMINATION privilege. At the end of that time, if you decide to keep your books, simply pay the low invoice price of $16.96 ($19.98 CANADA), no shipping or handling charges added.* HOME DELIVERY IS ALWAYS FREE.* With today's top Historical Romance novels selling for $5.99 and higher, our price SAVES YOU AT LEAST $5.00 with each shipment.

AND YOUR FIRST FOUR-BOOK SHIPMENT IS TOTALLY FREE!

IT'S A BARGAIN YOU CAN'T BEAT! A Super $21.96 Value!

LEISURE BOOKS A Division of Dorchester Publishing Co., Inc.

GET YOUR 4 FREE* BOOKS NOW—
A $21.96 VALUE!

Mail the Free* Books
Certificate
Today!

Get Four Books Totally
F R E E* —
A $21.96 Value!

(Tear Here and Mail Your FREE* Book Card Today!)

PLEASE RUSH
MY FOUR FREE*
BOOKS TO ME
RIGHT AWAY!

Leisure Historical Romance Book Club
P.O. Box 6613
Edison, NJ 08818-6613

AFFIX
STAMP
HERE

Chapter Twenty

Alan Summers sat back in his chair, his voice deceptively low and calm, his eyes narrowed. "You're telling me you lost her?"

Amos McCarthy shuffled his feet nervously. "Yessir."

Alan swore a pithy oath. His temper had grown considerably shorter as the weeks had gone by.

"What kind of men are you hiring these days, that they can't hold on to one woman?" Alan asked disdainfully.

McCarthy felt his cheeks grow hot. "One of my men spotted Mrs. Summers in a little town called Red Creek. He was about to close in, but . . ." McCarthy cleared his throat. "A bounty hunter by the name of Vance Sandler beat him to it."

"I don't want excuses," Alan snapped. "Why

didn't your man just take her from Sandler and be done with it?"

"Well . . ." McCarthy ran a pudgy finger around the inside of his shirt collar. "The truth is, she got away from Sandler. I heard she left him afoot out on the plains." McCarthy started to smile, but one look at his employer's face changed his mind.

Alan drummed his fingers on his desk top, his anger growing. "Where . . . is . . . she?"

"Well, according to my last report, Mrs. Summers is now in the hands of another bounty hunter." McCarthy pulled a small black leather-bound book from his inside coat pocket. "Name of Jesse Yellow Thunder."

"Dammit!" Alan surged to his feet. "Where the hell is she now?"

McCarthy took an involuntary step backward. "Still with Yellow Thunder, last I heard. Two of my best men, Andrews and Porter, are in Red Creek keeping an eye on them. Yellow Thunder is sticking to Mrs. Summers like a tick on a dog. My men can't get close to her."

"Imbeciles!" Alan exclaimed, his voice rising. "Incompetents!"

"I'm sorry, sir, but from all we've learned, Jesse Yellow Thunder is a man to be reckoned with."

"So am I."

"Yessir." McCarthy cleared his throat. "Do you want Porter to take your wife if the opportunity presents itself?"

Eyes narrowed thoughtfully, Alan ran a hand through his hair. "Get out of here, McCarthy."

"Sir?"

"Get out."

"Shall I take my men off the case?"

Alan considered that a moment, then shook his head. "No. Stay in touch with them. Now get out."

With a curt nod, Amos McCarthy left the room.

Alan slammed his palms down on the desk top. He didn't know where his foolish little wife had been hiding since she'd run away, but it was obvious to him that she was on her way back to New York, running back home to daddy like a scared little girl.

Rounding the desk, he began to pace the floor. Now that he knew she was alive, he needn't bother with McCarthy and his incompetent fools any longer. He knew where Kaylynn was headed. He would tie up the loose ends at the bank, and then take a little vacation.

Going to the window, he stared out into the night, hands clenching and unclenching as he anticipated his reunion with Kaylynn.

She would never leave him again. He would see to that.

Chapter Twenty-one

Kaylynn climbed into the coach and settled her skirts around her. The stage, which was to have left at half-past one, hadn't arrived until almost three. It was a good thing the stage hadn't left on time, she mused, or they would have missed it. Thinking of the reason why they had been late getting to the depot made her blush.

She glanced around, glad the Concord wasn't crowded. Though designed to seat nine people, there were only three other passengers besides herself and Jesse: two dark-haired businessmen in city suits who introduced themselves as John Porter and Bill Andrews, and a rather stout traveling salesman who stammered that his name was Saul Jackson. It made her uncomfortable, being the only woman in the coach, and she sat close to

Jesse, reassured by his presence. The window shades, meant to keep out sun, rain, dust, and tobacco juice spat by passengers on the roof, were up. From past experience, she knew they were totally inadequate.

She wasn't looking forward to the trip. The last one she had taken had been long and uncomfortable, rumbling along over rutted roads—when there had been roads—stopping every twenty miles or so to change horses, stopping twice a day to eat. The food, which had usually consisted of boiled beans, salted meat, hardtack, and coffee, had cost a dollar a plate, and the passengers had been given seven minutes to eat it. Sometimes supper consisted of tough beefsteak, boiled potatoes, stewed beans, and dried apple pie. She didn't know which menu was worse.

She put the memory aside, reminding herself that the trip, however tiresome it might be, would be worth it when she was home again.

She slid a glance at Jesse. Dressed all in black, he looked like the angel of death. She noticed that the other men in the coach were careful not to meet his gaze. It was hard to remember that she had once been afraid of him, that she had been repulsed by the scar on his face. Looking at him now, she saw only the man she loved. . . .

The revelation struck her like a bolt from the blue. She loved him. Acknowledging it filled her with a sense of rightness, of peace. She loved him. Oh, but it was impossible. Like it or not, she was married to another man. Not only that, but they were worlds apart. Jesse was a man of the West, a man of violence. As much as she had enjoyed the Indian people, she was anxious to return to the East, to the myriad comforts and luxuries of civilization. Even if Jesse loved her in return, even if they could bridge the differences between his world and hers, Jesse had no home, no roots, nor had she ever heard him express a desire to settle down in one place. She didn't think she could be happy living like a vagabond, with no place to call her own.

She pushed her doubts aside. Alan had given her a home, clothes, jewelry fit for a queen. None of it had made her happy.

She looked up at Jesse, wishing they were alone so she could tell him how she felt. Would he be pleased? What if he didn't feel the same? What if he kissed every woman he met the way he had kissed her? She dismissed the thought as soon as it occurred to her.

If only they were alone, she could nestle against him and feel the strength of his arm around her, but she couldn't snuggle up to him, not now, not with three other men in the coach.

With a sigh, she looked out the window. She was going home at last. For some reason, the thought didn't make her as happy as it should have.

Jesse stared out the window, trying to ignore the curious stares of the other passengers. None of the men dared to meet his gaze, yet he was aware of their furtive glances, their speculation about his scarred face. More maddening than their covert looks was the open admiration in their eyes when they looked at Kaylynn. Not that he could blame them. Dressed in the dark green traveling suit she had bought, she looked good enough to eat. It was, he thought, the best money he had ever spent. She had promised to repay him when they reached her home in New York. As if he'd take it. Money was the last thing he wanted from her.

He swore a silent oath, knowing that the one thing he did want was the last thing he was likely to get.

He would never fit into her world, and she couldn't live in his. Yet people changed. He certainly had. He would be willing to change again, for her, if she would have him.

They pulled into Twin Bluffs the following afternoon. There was a short layover at the depot, during which time a fresh team of horses was hitched to the coach. They also took on two new passengers. Bill Andrews went to sit topside, while the salesman who had been sitting across from Kaylynn moved to sit beside her so the new arrivals, obviously newlyweds, could sit together. They introduced themselves as Ben and Doris Whiteside.

Kaylynn offered them a tentative smile. Doris Whiteside was tall and thin. She had pale blue eyes and fine, honey-gold hair that she wore in a tight bun at her nape. She looked about sixteen. Ben Whiteside looked as if he could have been her brother. He had the same pale blue eyes, the same honey-gold hair.

Jesse looked out the window, wondering if Ravenhawk was in town. It didn't sit well with him that his bounty had gotten away. In the last seven years, he had brought in every man he'd gone after. He glanced back at the livery as the driver stowed the newlyweds' baggage in the boot, wondering if old Ron Hays was still running the stable in Twin Bluffs. It had been a while since he'd seen the old man. Hays was one of the few men Jesse considered a friend.

Kaylynn shifted on the seat beside him as the coach lurched forward, drawing his mind back to matters at hand. The most important thing to him now was taking Kaylynn back home, where she belonged, making sure she was happy.

His gaze moved over her. When had he fallen in love with her? How had she come to mean so much in such a short time?

She looked up, a shy smile curving her lips as her gaze met his.

He hadn't been afraid of much in his life, but he was suddenly afraid of her, afraid of the power she had over him, a power she didn't even realize she held. A word, a gesture, and she could destroy him.

She rocked against him as the coach went over a deep rut in the road. Instinctively, he put his arm around her and drew her up close. And knew again that he never wanted to let her go.

For a moment, nothing else in the world existed but the two of them. He forgot about the newly-wed couple who were staring adoringly into each other's eyes, forgot about the other two men inside the coach.

Hungry for the touch of her, the taste of her, he lowered his head and kissed her lightly, hardly more than the brush of his lips over hers, yet he felt a spark ignite deep within him, knew by her sudden intake of breath that she had felt it, too.

When he drew back, he felt as if his heart would break. She was a wild rose among thistles, a delicate flower like those that grew wild on the prairie. He had no right to pluck that flower and make it his own, no right at all. Looking into her eyes, he saw his dreams, his vision of a future that could never be, and though pain gripped his heart, he knew he loved her too much to ask her to stay.

"Are you newlyweds, too?"

"What?" Jesse looked at the woman across from him.

"I asked if you were newlyweds, too."

Jesse glanced at Kaylynn. She was staring down at her gloved hands. Her cheeks were bright red.

He shook his head. "No."

"Engaged?"

He swore softly, wishing the woman would mind her own business. "Not yet." It was a lie, but it was the only thing he could think of to salvage Kaylynn's reputation.

"You look good together," Doris remarked, then turned her attention back to her husband.

Jesse started to lift his arm from Kaylynn's shoulder, but she placed her hand over his, holding it in place.

She looked up at him, cheeks still pink. "The road's so rough, I'm afraid if you let go, I'll slip off the seat."

It was a lie and they both knew it. But it gave him all the excuse he needed to keep holding her.

Jesse blew out a sigh. It was late afternoon. They had been traveling almost nonstop for the last three hours, and everyone else inside the coach had fallen asleep.

He glanced down at Kaylynn, a surge of tenderness rising within him. What had he done to make her trust him so? He thought of the poetry she had recited to him and wondered what had ever possessed her to do such a thing.

Walk with me, Spirit's Song, and sing to me gently in the night of your love . . .

If anyone else had said something like that to him, he would have laughed. His gaze moved over Kaylynn's hair, as thick and red as a vixen's winter coat, and he knew, in that moment, that Kaylynn was the answer to his vision. Mao'hoohe. Red Fox.

Before he could ponder it further, he heard a shout from the stagecoach driver, followed by several gunshots.

The passengers inside the coach came awake with a start.

Kaylynn jerked upright, her eyes wide. "What was that?"

"I think we're about to be robbed."

"Robbed!" Doris Whiteside shrieked. Sobbing hysterically, she clung to her husband, who didn't look capable of defending himself, let alone anyone else.

John Porter drew a snub-nosed pistol from beneath his coat. The drummer sitting beside Kaylynn cowered in the seat, his pudgy face drained of color.

Jesse slid his Colt from the holster as the stage shuddered to a stop. "Kaylynn, get down on the floor. You, too, Mrs. Whiteside."

Wordlessly, Kaylynn did as she was told. The other woman clung to her husband, dragging him down on the floor beside her, where they huddled together like frightened puppies.

There was the staccato bark of gunfire from outside the coach. A man cried out, his voice edged with pain.

Jesse leaned forward and looked out the window. He could see five masked men armed with rifles. One of them had his weapon aimed upward, apparently at the driver.

Jesse glanced at the man sitting across from him. Wary of putting the women in danger, neither of them had risked shooting at the bandits.

"How many?" Jesse asked, his voice low.

"Two on this side," Porter replied.

Jesse glanced outside again.

The man covering the driver shouted, "Throw down your weapons and no one will get hurt. You people in the coach, keep your heads inside."

The driver tossed his pistol to the ground; Jesse assumed the guard had surrendered his shotgun.

"Throw down the strongbox."

The box landed with a dull thud. Painted a dark green, made of Ponderosa pine, oak, and iron, the box weighed about a hundred pounds. Jesse shook his head. Nothing was quite as irresistible to outlaws as a Wells Fargo treasure box. They were invariably filled with gold dust, gold bars, or payrolls.

Two of the bandits dismounted. One of them shot the lock, and then they began passing bags of money to their companions.

The box was nearly empty when there was a gunshot from the top side of the coach and a sharp cry of pain, quickly followed by a second gunshot. Kaylynn gasped as Bill Andrews's body toppled over the side of the coach.

"Kill 'em all!" The cry came from one of the bandits.

"Like hell!" Jesse muttered as he lifted his gun and fired at the nearest outlaw. He swore as a man mounted on a flashy Appaloosa rode into view. Ravenhawk!

Jesse swore again as he fired at the Lakota and missed.

For a moment, their eyes met, and then Ravenhawk rode out of sight.

Jesse fired again, then grunted with satisfaction as one of the outlaws tumbled from the saddle.

John Porter thrust his pistol into the drummer's hand. "Defend yourself!" he said, and reaching under his seat, he withdrew a rifle and began firing out the window.

The sound of gunfire and the stench of gunsmoke filled the air.

One of the outlaws hollered, "Let's get the hell out of here!"

Jesse threw himself across Kaylynn as a hail of gunfire exploded into the coach. Pieces of cloth and splinters of wood rained down on them, covering Jesse with a layer of debris. Jesse felt the drummer's foot jerk spasmodically, but his only concern was for Kaylynn, and he knew he would die before he let anything happen to her.

There were more gunshots and then an abrupt silence.

Jesse waited a moment; then, rising to his knees, he risked a look outside. The outlaws had fled. He caught a glimpse of the last rider, slumped over his horse's neck, heading north, toward the river.

Inside the coach, the drummer was sprawled across the seat. Blood trickled from a neat hole in his left temple. John Porter was cradling his shoulder.

Jesse's gaze moved over Kaylynn. "Are you all right?"

She looked up at him, her face pale, her suit badly rumpled, her hat askew, the delicate black feather bent at an odd angle.

"Never again," she said, her voice low and shaky. "I'm never riding on a stagecoach again."

She had been through hell and she was making jokes. He could have kissed her.

"What about you?" Jesse said, looking over at Porter. "How bad are you hit?"

"I'm all right. Just nicked me."

Jesse holstered his Colt, then opened the door of the coach and stepped outside. Turning, he offered Kaylynn his hand and helped her out. A faint dust cloud hung in the air.

The newlywed couple scrambled out of the coach behind Kaylynn. John Porter descended more slowly.

Jesse knelt beside the driver and the shotgun guard. Both were dead, as was the man who had been riding on top of the coach. One of the holdup men was dead; a second one lay in the dirt. Blood poured from a wound in his chest. Jesse doubted if he'd live much longer.

Jesse glanced in the direction the robbers had gone. If he hurried, he might be able to catch them.

With that thought in mind, he moved toward the back of the coach.

Kaylynn followed him. She frowned as he checked the saddle cinch on the roan, then replaced the halter with a bridle. "What are you doing?" she asked.

"I'm going after them."

"No."

"Ravenhawk was with 'em."

"Ravenhawk!" she exclaimed. "Are you sure?"

"I'm sure. You might want to bandage him up," Jesse said, nodding at John Porter, who stood near the coach, clutching his shoulder.

"Please don't go."

"I've got to." Jesse glanced at the other passengers. "There's plenty of water on board. Just sit tight till I get back."

"What if you don't come back?" John Porter asked.

Jesse shrugged. "You can try taking the coach back to Twin Bluffs, or you can just sit tight." He untied the roan from the back of the Concord. "When the stage doesn't show up at the next stop, they'll send someone looking."

"Jesse. Don't go."

"I have to." He kissed her, hard and quick, then swung aboard the roan and rode after the bandits.

Chapter Twenty-two

The outlaws' trail was easy to follow. Five horses headed north, moving fast. He recognized the tracks of Ravenhawk's big Appaloosa gelding among them.

He hadn't gone more than a mile or so when he found one of the bandits lying facedown across the road. The man's horse stood a few feet away, grazing on a patch of short grass.

Reining his horse to a stop, Jesse dismounted, one hand resting on his gun butt as his gaze swept the surrounding area. There was no cover here, and little chance of an ambush, but years of bounty hunting had taught him to be cautious.

He approached the outlaw warily, prodded him in the side with the toe of his boot.

The man groaned softly.

Reaching down, Jesse plucked the man's Colt from his holster and shoved it into the waistband of his pants; then he rolled the man over.

Jesse grunted softly. The outlaw was just a kid, probably not more than sixteen years old.

"Got any water?" the kid asked.

"Sure, in a minute. How bad are you hurt?"

"I don't know. Feels like I'm . . . I'm dyin'."

Jesse lifted the boy's shirt, then shook his head. The boy lifted his head, trying to see.

"Don't look," Jesse said. He dropped the boy's shirt back in place.

"Is it bad?"

"Real bad. I doubt you'll last more than an hour. You got any kin that needs to be notified?"

"Sister in Kansas City."

"What's her name?"

"Rosemary Clemens."

"And your name?"

"Jimmy Claudill."

Jesse grunted softly. Unless he was mistaken, there was a three hundred dollar bounty on Claudill's head.

"Give me some water."

"Not a good idea. Water now will just speed things up. Where are the rest headed?"

The kid shook his head. "Go to hell."

Young and stupid and scared, Jesse thought. "Tell me where they're going, and I'll see you get a decent burial."

"No." The kid licked his lips. "Dammit, gimme some water."

With a nod, Jesse went to get the canteen from his saddle. Returning to the wounded man, he hunkered down on his heels beside him and shook the canteen. "Tell me what I want to know."

"Bastard."

Jesse shrugged. "Your friends left you here to die. I don't know why you feel you owe them any loyalty."

Claudill laughed, a dry hollow sound. "You're right. They're headed for Mazza's place."

Jesse grunted softly. Victor Mazza was a cold-blooded killer. "Where's that?"

"Outside Twin Bluffs. Mazza and his brother have a spread in a box canyon about twenty miles out of town."

"How long will they be there?"

"I don't know."

"Who's ramrodding the gang?"

"Victor Mazza."

Jesse uncorked the canteen, lifted the man's head, and let him drink. "That's enough. Come on, let's go."

"Go? Go where?"

"I'm taking you back to town." If what Claudill said was true, then the bandits would be holed up for a few days. He could see Kaylynn safely back to Twin Bluffs, claim the reward for Claudill, then alert the sheriff as to the whereabouts of the Mazza gang after explaining that Ravenhawk belonged to him.

"I thought you said I was dying?"

"I lied. That bullet just nicked a rib. You'll be all right in a day or two." Rising, Jesse grabbed Claudill by the arm and pulled him to his feet.

"You really are a bastard."

Jesse chuckled softly as he pulled a set of handcuffs from his saddlebags and cuffed the kid's hands together. "So I've been told. Let's go."

* * *

Kaylynn sat in the scant shade offered by a wind-blown pine. Earlier, she had bandaged John Porter's arm. As he had said, it wasn't a bad wound, just a shallow furrow along his shoulder.

Doris Whiteside sat beside her, her hands clasped in her lap. Earlier, with much sweating and straining and more than a little swearing, Ben Whiteside and John Porter had secured the bodies of the driver, the shotgun guard, and the two dead outlaws on top of the coach. Now Whiteside and Porter stood a few feet away, trying to decide whether they should attempt to drive the coach back to Twin Bluffs or wait for help from the station at Logansville.

Kaylynn hoped they decided to wait for help. Neither Porter nor Whiteside had any experience driving a six-horse team. Of the two, Kaylynn thought that, even with his injured arm, Porter was the better man for the job. Ben Whiteside had all the self-confidence of a turnip.

Porter glanced up at the sun. "Well, we need to make a decision. It'll be dark in a couple of hours."

"I think we should go on," Ben Whiteside said. "I don't like the idea of spending the night out here."

"Me, either," Doris agreed.

"All right then," Porter said. "Let's get moving."

Kaylynn glanced in the direction Jesse had gone. Was he all right? Had he found the outlaws? Would she ever see him again?

The thought had no sooner crossed her mind than he was riding toward her, a second horse and rider in tow.

Kaylynn stood up, relief at seeing Jesse alive and well sweeping through her.

"Did you find them?" Porter asked.

"No, but I know where they're headed." His gaze swept the area. "What did you do with the bodies?"

"Up there," Porter said, jerking a thumb toward the roof of the coach.

Jesse nodded. Dismounting, he fixed his prisoner with a hard stare. "Step down."

With a grimace, Jimmy Claudill slid from the saddle.

Kaylynn laid her hand on Jesse's arm. "Are you all right?"

"Fine. You?"

"Fine, now." Now that you're here, she thought.

"We're going back to Twin Bluffs," Jesse said. Pulling the halter and lead rope from his saddlebags, he removed the bridle from the roan, slipped the halter in place, and tethered the mare to the rear of the coach. He dropped a rope over Claudill's horse and tied her to the coach beside the roan.

"All right," Jesse said. "Everybody inside. Porter, keep an eye on the kid, will ya?"

"Sure."

"Jesse, do you know how to drive a stagecoach?" Kaylynn asked.

"Sure."

"Really?" she asked dubiously.

"Would I lie to you?"

"I don't know," she replied tartly. "Would you?"

"I'd never lie to you, Kay," Jesse said quietly. "Believe that if you believe nothing else."

"I do. Would you mind if I rode up front, with you?"

"No, I don't mind." He smiled at her. "Be glad for the company."

He held her gaze a moment more, then walked toward the coach window and looked inside. "Everybody settled?"

Porter nodded. "Let's go."

Jesse helped Kaylynn climb up to the driver's box. She slid across the seat and smoothed the skirt of her rumpled suit as Jesse took a seat beside her. "Ready?"

"I guess so." She grinned at him. "No stage I've been on yet has reached its destination."

"Well," he said, grinning back at her, "that's about to change."

Taking up the reins, he turned the team back toward Twin Bluffs.

The ride back to town was uneventful. Occasionally, Jesse could hear Claudill complaining about the ride, his bad luck, the fact that Jesse had lied to him.

Jesse glanced at Kaylynn. She sat close beside him, one hand holding down her skirts. Every time they hit a rut in the road, her knee bounced against his.

"You sure you don't want to ride inside?" he asked. "Less breezy in there."

"No, thank you. I'd rather be out here."

He didn't argue. He liked having her close. He wished he could slip his arm around Kaylynn and draw her closer, but handling a six-horse hitch was no easy task for someone who wasn't used to it. Still, he was ever aware of the girl beside him, of her constant glances in his direction. She had a lot of spunk for a gently reared city girl.

It was going on nine o'clock when they pulled into Twin Bluffs.

The unexpected arrival of the coach caused quite a stir at the depot. As quickly as possible, Jesse told the agent what had happened. The agent sent for the sheriff, the doctor, and the dentist, who was also the town undertaker, then hovered over the Whitesides, assuring them that they wouldn't have to pay for another ticket, offering to pay for their hotel room for the night.

Claudill sat on the bench against the wall, muttering under his breath. Porter sat beside him, rubbing his injured arm.

The sheriff arrived first and Jesse told his story again, saying he'd stop by the lawman's office to fill out the form for the reward on Claudill after he got Kaylynn settled in the hotel.

"Fine, fine," the sheriff replied. He glanced at the other passengers. "I'll need to see all you down at my office at your convenience."

Jesse took the sheriff aside. "I reckon you'll be going after them."

The sheriff nodded. "I'll get a posse together. We'll ride out at first light."

"Mind if I ride along?"

"Glad to have you."

"Obliged." It wouldn't be easy, but somehow he was going to have to find a way to get Ravenhawk away on his own. He had come too far now to lose the reward to someone else.

The doctor arrived as Jesse and Kaylynn were heading out the door. Outside, Jesse stopped at the coach and untied the mare, then pulled Kaylynn's valise from the boot.

"Do you want me to carry that?" she asked.

"I've got it."

"That boy seems awfully young to be an outlaw," Kaylynn remarked as they made their way down the street.

"Lots of young kids on the wrong side of the law," Jesse remarked. He'd brought in a few of them in his time, boys who ran away from home looking for adventure and wound up robbing banks and stagecoaches.

They left the roan at Hays Livery. Kaylynn smiled as Jesse introduced her to the owner of the stable, and then gave the man instructions, admonishing Mr. Hays to be sure to give the horse a double helping of oats. He sure loved that horse, she thought. It was obvious, from the way the two men bantered back and forth, that they were old friends.

Jesse gave Hays a friendly slap on the arm, settled his saddlebags over one shoulder, and picked up her valise, again refusing her offer to carry her own baggage.

The clerk at the hotel seemed to know who they were. Jesse was always surprised at how fast bad news spread.

"We need a couple of rooms." Jesse said.

"Yes, sir," the clerk said. He glanced at Kaylynn and smiled. "Sorry to hear of your ordeal."

"Thank you," Kaylynn replied.

"Terrible thing, when decent folk can't travel in safety," the clerk remarked. He plucked two keys from the board behind the desk. "Just terrible."

"Terrible," Jesse agreed. "We'll be wanting some hot water."

"Yes, sir."

The clerk handed the keys to Jesse.

"Don't forget about that water."

"No, sir. Right away, sir."

Jesse took Kaylynn's hand and they went up the stairs.

"Home sweet home," Kaylynn muttered as she opened the door and stepped into her room.

Jesse grinned at her as he dropped her valise and his saddlebags inside the door. "Seems like we've been through this before. I'm going over to the sheriff's office. I won't be gone long. Lock your door when I go, and don't open it unless you're sure who's on the other side. Here." He handed her the Colt he had taken from Claudill. "Keep this handy."

"Jesse . . ."

"I won't be gone long. Save me some hot water."

"I will."

"Damn," he said, and sweeping her into his arms, he kissed her, his lips scorching hers like the hot winds that blew across the prairie.

She was breathless when he released her. "Jesse."

He winked at her, and then he was gone.

Chapter Twenty-three

The sheriff, whose name was Joe Keegan, ran a hand over his jaw. "Victor Mazza. He's a mean one."

"Yeah," Jesse agreed. He glanced around the office. It looked pretty much like every other jail he'd been in: a scarred desk, battered filing cabinet, gun rack on the wall, pot-bellied stove in the corner. "I've heard of Mazza a time or two, but he's of no interest to me now. I just want Ravenhawk."

"Well." Keegan leaned forward in his chair. "I don't reckon that will be a problem. I've got a dozen men ready to ride out at first light."

"I'll be here. How soon can I get that bounty on Claudill?"

"It should be ready by the time we get back from Mazza's place." The lawman shook his head. "Taking Mazza won't be easy now that they've joined up with Nash."

"Nothing's ever easy," Jesse said, rising. "I'll see you in the morning."

"Right."

Jesse left the sheriff's office and headed for the hotel. If all went as planned, Ravenhawk and the others would be in custody by this time tomorrow. He'd collect the bounty on the Lakota, see Kaylynn safely back to her parents, and then . . . what? He'd planned to go back to the Cheyenne, but even that had lost its appeal now. All he could think of was Kaylynn, and how important she had become to him.

Entering the hotel, he crossed the lobby. Pausing at the desk, he asked the clerk to send up some more hot water, and then he ran up the stairs, anxious to see her again, to make certain she was all right.

He knocked lightly on her door. "Kay?"

Anxiety twisted in his gut when she didn't answer right away and he knocked again, louder this time. "Kaylynn, it's me."

"I'm coming."

A moment later, she opened the door and he felt a rush of sweet relief. She was wearing the blue dress he had bought for her in Red Creek. Her hair, freshly washed, fell in damp waves down her back.

She smiled as she took a step back. "Come in."

Jesse stepped inside and closed the door behind him. "Everything all right?"

"Yes, fine. Why wouldn't it be?"

Jesse shrugged. "Last time I left you alone, you weren't here when I got back."

"I'm fine. What did the sheriff say?"

"Not much. He wants you to stop by before we leave town and make a statement."

"I'll go in the morning."

"You'll have to wait until he gets back. We're riding out after Mazza and his gang at first light."

She didn't want him to go. Would he stay if she asked him to?

Her gaze ran over him. Had she ever in her life been this happy to see anyone? Certainly Alan hadn't affected her like this. Even when she had loved him, or thought she had, his nearness hadn't made her pulses race, hadn't caused her heart to swell. She had never wanted Alan's kisses. At the time, she hadn't thought it strange that he sparked no desire in her. She had been ignorant of what went on between a man and a woman. She had assumed that her desire for Alan would bloom when they were married, but it never had. Was it desire that she felt for Jesse? Was it desire that made her think of him day and night, that made her burn for his kisses, that made her hungry for the touch of his hands on her flesh?

And what if it was? She could never surrender to the passion he aroused in her. She was a married woman, bound by vows of fidelity and loyalty to another man. And even though that man had betrayed her, had abused and abased her, she was still his wife.

The thought made her want to cry.

"Kay?" Jesse took a step toward her. "What's wrong?"

"Wrong?" She looked at him, torn by what she wanted and what she knew was right. "Nothing."

"You can tell me."

She shook her head. She couldn't say it, couldn't tell him that she loved him. With an effort, she swallowed the words she longed to say.

"Kaylynn." Closing the distance between them, he took her in his arms. "Tell me what's bothering you."

She rested her forehead against his chest so she wouldn't have to meet his gaze. "Nothing."

"Dammit, Kay, don't shut me out."

"Why do you have to go with the posse?"

"You know why."

"Because of Ravenhawk."

"Yeah. That kid, Claudill, told me where the gang's holed up. I'm going after him."

"Where are they?"

"Some ranch not far from where they held up the stage."

"I wish you wouldn't go."

Was it his imagination, or was there a faint note of worry in her voice?

"Why?" Jesse asked, his voice sharp. "You afraid he'll get hurt?"

"I don't want anything to happen to either of you."

"That's up to him."

"How long will you be gone?"

Jesse shrugged. "Two, three days at most." It would take them a day to reach the canyon. They'd spend the night outside, then go in at dawn. Another day to get back.

"Jesse . . ." She looked up at him, confused by the underlying note of anger in his voice.

"Are you sweet on him?" Jesse asked gruffly. "Is that why you're so worried?"

"Of course not. But he helped me—"

"Helped you run away from me." There was no mistaking the anger in his voice this time.

"I'm not running now, Jesse."

She spoke the words so softly, he wasn't sure he heard them right.

With a sigh, he drew her closer. "Dammit, Kay, do you know what you're doing to me?"

She shook her head, her brown eyes wide as she gazed up at him. "Tell me," she whispered, and he felt her breath move across his skin, warm and sweet.

"I've never wanted a woman the way I want you."

His voice, low and husky and filled with yearning, sent a shiver down her spine. Her heart began to pound as he bent his head and kissed her. And she was kissing him back, clinging to him, pressing herself against him, wanting him more than she wanted her next breath. A wild tide of desire flooded through her, making her forget everything but the touch of his lips, the erotic thrust of his tongue meeting hers in a dance as old as time.

"I've never needed a woman the way I need you." His hand moved restlessly up and down her back. "You remember that poem you told me?" he asked.

"Yes."

"That's how I feel about you, Kay. You're my spirit's song. You make me feel alive again." He pulled her closer, molding the length of her body to his, letting her feel the evidence of his desire.

And in that moment she experienced a thrill of excitement she had never known before. She wrapped her arms around him, wanting to be closer, closer, wanting to feel his body against hers.

"Ah, Kay," he murmured, "what have you done to me?" He had never felt like this before. Never. Her touch moved through him, warm, welcome, making him feel weak and vulnerable. He ached for the taste of her.

She felt the sting of tears in her eyes as his lips claimed hers. It was a gentle kiss filled with tenderness and a soul-deep yearning, a hunger that went deeper than the desire of the flesh. There weren't words enough to describe the way she felt, her heart filled to overflowing with emotions she had never known before. No one had ever needed her. Alan had wanted her, but he had not needed her. She had the feeling now that he had married her simply because she had refused to give in to him until they were man and wife. Alan had wanted someone to bear him a son, and she had been young and pretty and smitten with his charm. It hadn't hurt that she came from a good family. Sad, that neither of them had found what they were looking for.

She pressed herself more fully against Jesse, wanting to be closer still, reveling in his strength, in the strength and assurance of his arms tight around her.

She slipped her hands under his shirt, delighting in the warmth of his skin beneath her fingertips. She didn't argue when he carried her to the bed. Lying beside her, he drew her into his arms, drawing her body up against the length of his while he rained kisses on her brow, her cheeks, her lips.

A wild longing suffused her, frightening and

thrilling at the same time. This was passion, she thought. This was what love should be like, this soaring sense of freedom and desire, the burning urge to taste and touch, to caress and explore. She wanted to touch him, to feel his skin against hers, to feel his weight pressing her into the mattress. Jesse wouldn't hurt her. He wouldn't vent his lust on her and then turn away in disgust, the way Alan had done. Jesse would be gentle and kind and patient.

"Kay?" His voice was low and urgent, his breath warm against her ear.

It was wrong, she thought, wrong to want him this way, but she didn't care. He was going after Ravenhawk in the morning. What if he was killed? What if she never saw him again, never had this chance again?

"Love me," she murmured. "Please, Jesse."

"I do. God help us both, I do."

"Show me."

"Kay!" Words had never come easily to him, and he kissed her long and hard, hoping she would know how deeply he had come to love her, how desperately he needed her.

He held her close, his hands lightly caressing her. He didn't want to rush her, didn't want to frighten her. He groaned with pleasure as her hands explored his body, her fingers trailing fire as they ran over his chest, slid up over his shoulders and down his back. She caressed the muscles in his arms, a smile hovering over her lips when he flexed.

"Nice," she murmured, and he grinned at her.

"You're beautiful," he said, his lips feathering across her cheeks.

"So are you."

Her words erased the smile from his face and he looked away. "Yeah," he muttered. "Beautiful."

Gently, she cupped his face in her hands. "You are beautiful to me, Jesse Yellow Thunder. The most beautiful man I've ever known."

He shook his head.

"When I look at you, I don't see your scars anymore. I just see you."

"Kay . . ."

"I'm not beautiful, either."

"You are."

"Only because you love me." Drawing his head down, she dropped feather-soft kisses over his scarred cheek.

He looked down at her, at the love shining as bright as the sun in her eyes, and wondered if he could ever find the words to tell her just how much he loved her.

And he knew, just as surely, that he could not take what she was offering. She might want him now, but later, when she'd had time to think, she would hate herself, and him.

He was trying to think of a way to ease away from her without hurting her feelings when there was a knock at the door.

Kaylynn's eyes widened. "Who can that be?" she asked.

"I asked the clerk to send up some hot water."

"Oh!"

He smiled as her cheeks turned crimson. "I'll get it."

Rising, he crossed the room and opened the door. Two boys stood in the hallway, each bearing two buckets of hot water.

"Just leave it," Jesse said.

"Sure, mister, whatever you say." The two boys smirked at each other as they lowered the buckets to the floor. Jesse scowled at them, and they hurried away, giggling.

Jesse carried the buckets inside and dumped the water into the tub, thinking as he did so that a cold soak would suit him better right now.

When he turned around, Kaylynn was standing at the window, looking out.

"Why don't you go wait in my room?" Jesse suggested.

She nodded, but didn't move, and he knew she was embarrassed by what had almost happened between them.

"Kaylynn, it's all right."

"No, it isn't."

He went to her then, and drew her into his arms. "Kay, look at me. I'd never do anything to hurt you."

"I know. It was my fault."

"It's nobody's fault."

"I can't love you!" she exclaimed. "It's wrong."

"Why?"

"Because I'm married to someone else."

"He doesn't deserve you."

"What difference does that make? I belong to him."

"Is that what you want?"

"No." She looked up at him, her eyes filled with anguish. "I want to belong to you." She could never go back to Alan, not now, not when she had finally found what she had been missing, looking for, dreaming of, her whole life.

"I know." He wanted it, too, more than he had

ever wanted anything, but he had nothing to offer her. Not a damn thing.

With a sigh, he folded her into his arms and held her tightly and knew that, because he loved her, he would have to let her go.

Chapter Twenty-four

Ravenhawk sat on a bench outside the Mazza ranch house. Victor Mazza and his younger brother, Rafael, had a nice place. The back of the house was tucked against the rear wall of the canyon. There was a fair-sized barn, a sturdy corral. There was no cover between the front of the house and the entrance to the canyon, providing a clear view of anyone who might try to approach the house uninvited.

Ravenhawk propped his foot on the porch rail. If he had a spread like this, he'd be raising horses, not risking his life robbing stagecoaches.

The sound of angry voices drifted through the open window. Inside, Victor Mazza and Nash were arguing over how to split the loot. Mazza figured he was due a bigger cut than the others since he had planned the robbery. Nash disagreed. He felt they were all due equal shares. Rafael agreed with his brother, saying they should get an extra cut for providing Nash with a place to hole up.

Ravenhawk ran a hand through his hair. The strongbox had yielded a little over sixty thousand dollars. Depending on how Nash and Victor decided to split the take, he figured his cut would be somewhere around four or five grand. It was a good-sized chunk of change; more money than he'd ever had in his life, and it weighed heavily on his conscience. He had robbed a number of banks and stages in the past, but he'd never killed anyone. Victor Mazza had killed the stagecoach driver in cold blood; Nash had killed the shotgun guard when the man made a furtive move. Two of Nash's men had been killed. A third, a young kid named Claudill, had been wounded and left behind.

Ravenhawk swore softly. Robbery was one thing. Cold-blooded murder was something else entirely. Damn.

He stared into the distance, torn between the thought of staying with Nash and riding on. There was safety in numbers. He hadn't realized until they got here that Mazza and his brother had a gang of their own. He had learned from one of Nash's men that Victor and Rafael never worked together. One of the brothers always stayed at the ranch with part of the gang, ready to ride to the rescue if there was trouble.

Ravenhawk had planned to stay on at the Mazza place until things quieted down. Before the robbery, staying here had seemed like a good idea.

But that was before Mazza had gunned the driver.

Before he had seen Jesse Yellow Thunder inside the coach.

He swore softly. Talk about bad luck and bad timing. He wondered if Kaylynn had been on the stage, too. Somehow, the thought of her being there, knowing that he had been part of the robbery, left him feeling ashamed, the way he'd felt when he'd been a boy and his mother had caught him in some act of mischief.

There would be no safety for him here if Yellow Thunder decided to come after him. And the bounty hunter would come. Ravenhawk knew it as surely as he knew good whiskey from bad.

He would ask Nash for his cut and leave tonight, or first thing in the morning. He'd had enough of riding the outlaw trail. He was going back to the Lakota and he was never leaving there again. It was time to find a willing woman, settle down, raise a couple of kids, and count himself damn lucky he'd gotten away with a whole skin.

A woman. He closed his eyes, and an image of Kaylynn floated across his mind. Ah, Kaylynn, with her wide, innocent eyes and tempting pink lips.

If Jesse Yellow Thunder was here, could the woman be far behind?

Chapter Twenty-five

Kaylynn stood at the window of her room, looking down into the street below. She could see the sheriff and his posse mounting up, but she had eyes only for Jesse. Dressed all in black, he stood out from the others, a tall, dark man mounted on a sleek roan mare.

As though feeling her gaze, he glanced up at her window. Last night she had begged him not to go, but to no avail. It was more than the reward, she thought. It was a personal vendetta.

She watched as the sheriff and his men rode out of town. Jesse gazed up at her a moment longer and then, with a wave of his hand, he turned and followed the posse.

She stared after him until the dust settled, a nagging feeling that she should go after him worrying the edges of her mind. What if he killed Ravenhawk? What if Ravenhawk killed him?

It was a thought that haunted her as she watched the eastern sky brighten. Dressing, she went downstairs for breakfast, and all the while her mind was conjuring images of Jesse and Ravenhawk. Sometimes Jesse killed Ravenhawk. Sometimes Ravenhawk killed Jesse. Sometimes they killed each other. Last night, her dreams had been filled with violence and bloodshed and death. Jesse . . . She should have gone with him.

Returning to her room, she began to pace the floor. Even if Jesse had let her ride along, what made her think she could do anything to stop the inevitable confrontation between the two men? She had asked Jesse not to go, and he had gone anyway, driven by a sense of duty, a need to salvage his pride. And yet she couldn't shake the feeling that something awful would happen if she wasn't there to stop it.

She paced the floor for ten minutes, her agitation growing. She couldn't just stay here and wait and wonder. She had to know what was happening, had to know that Jesse was all right.

She rolled two blankets into a tight bundle, grabbed the gun Jesse had given her earlier, and left the hotel. She stopped at the mercantile and bought some foodstuffs with the money Jesse had left her, then ran down to the livery.

Ron Hays looked surprised to see her, and even more surprised when she asked if he would rent her a horse.

"Leaving town, are you?" he asked, his disapproval at the thought of her riding out alone clearly etched on his face.

"Not exactly. Do you have a horse I can borrow?"

"I'm sure I can find you one, though I don't think you should be traveling by yourself."

"I know, but it's urgent. Can you help me?"

Hays looked her over from head to foot. "Do you know how to ride?"

"Of course."

He nodded. "I have a horse I think will fit you well enough."

Fit me, Kaylynn thought with a grin. What a peculiar way of putting it.

Minutes later, Hays emerged from the stable leading a long-legged brown horse with three white stockings and a white splotch on its forehead.

"This here's my horse," Hays said. "His name's Rufus."

"Your horse!" Kaylynn explained. "I couldn't—"

"Well, he's the only broomtail I've got that I'd trust you with." Taking her blanket roll, he secured it behind the cantle, then put the pistol in one of the saddlebags. "Climb up there so I can adjust the stirrups."

He held the reins while Kaylynn mounted and then adjusted the stirrups to the proper length.

"Does that sour-faced Indian know you're leaving?"

"Of course."

"I don't mean any disrespect, but you're a poor liar," Hays said gruffly. "If you lose your way, just give Rufus his head, and he'll bring you safely home."

"Thank you, Mr. Hays."

"Hays, just call me Hays."

"Thank you, Hays."

He grunted softly. "Be careful."

"I will." She looked down at him. "Why are you being so nice to me?"

"Yellow Thunder did me a favor once. He's never let me repay it." Hays shrugged. "Don't let that gruff exterior of his fool you for a minute. He's a good man underneath."

"I know. Thanks again."

Hays nodded. "Have a care now."

Kaylynn smiled at the livery man. Then, taking up the reins, she rode out of town after Jesse.

The trail of the posse was easy to follow. It occurred to her that she had learned more than she realized while living with the Cheyenne. Some things she had learned by doing, some by watching, and some she seemed to have absorbed without conscious thought. If she couldn't catch up with Jesse, she'd have to spend the night in the wilderness alone. She didn't relish the idea, but it didn't scare her.

One of Mo'e'ha's grandsons had taught her what she knew about tracking. He had been a precocious boy of about ten, eager to show off what he knew. He had showed her how to distinguish between dog and wolf tracks, deer and elk tracks, and how to tell, from the way grass had been flattened in passing, which way a horse was going. When a man walked, he pushed the grass down ahead of him, so it lay in the direction he was going, but when a horse walked, it pushed the grass backward. Mo'e'ha's grandson had also taught her how to tell time by the position of the sun and the stars, and how to locate water.

It was peaceful, riding alone across the land in the quiet of a new day. The last streaks of sunrise trailed across the sky, the rich golds and pinks gradually fading until they disappeared altogether. She had never paid much attention to sunrises or sunsets until she was captured by Two Dogs. Living with the Cheyenne had taught her to appreciate the beauty of the world around her, to find pleasure in simple things.

Pleasure . . . She had found pleasure of another kind in Jesse Yellow Thunder's arms, in the gentle touch of his hands, the intoxicating taste of his mouth on hers.

She couldn't believe how she had melted in his embrace, hated to admit, even to herself, that she had been ready, eager, to give herself to Jesse, body and soul. She knew in her heart that she would have given him anything he asked for if those two boys hadn't interrupted them when they did. It had felt so right to hold him, to let him kiss her, and to kiss him in return. Even now, the mere thought of him filled her with a warm, rosy glow, as though she had swallowed a ray of early morning sunshine.

She urged the horse into a gallop, wondering how far it was to the ranch where the outlaws were hiding out, wondering if she would get there in time. She had a feeling Jesse would not be happy to see her, but she didn't care. She could tolerate his anger, but she knew she would never forgive herself, or him, if he killed Ravenhawk simply to assuage his pride.

There were a dozen men in the posse. Jesse recognized a couple of the men as shopkeepers, though he didn't know their names. They had spent the night a few miles from the canyon, then ridden the rest of the way that morning. Now the canyon was just ahead, awash in the early light of a new day.

The entrance was narrow, only wide enough to allow one horse through at a time. Two well-armed men, posted on either side of the entrance, could probably keep an army at bay for quite a while, but try as he might, he couldn't find any sign of a lookout.

Keegan's deputy, Hank Frey, went to check it out. He returned a short time later. Using a stick, he drew a diagram of the layout inside the canyon.

"Any lookouts?" Keegan asked.

Frey shook his head. "I didn't see any."

Sloppy, Jesse thought. Or maybe they thought they were invincible.

Keegan grunted. "We'll play it like this. Yellow Thunder, you take two men and come down near the barn. Hank, you take two men and circle in from the right. The rest of you will ride with me." Keegan pulled a silver-backed watch from his vest pocket. "Yellow Thunder, how long do you think it will take you to get in place?"

Jesse shrugged. "Maybe twenty minutes at the outside."

"All right. Just to be safe, we'll wait thirty minutes before we make our move."

"How many men do you think are in there?" Hank asked.

The sheriff shrugged. "No way of knowing. I'd guess ten or twelve." He looked at Jesse. "You ready?"

"Yeah."

"Hank?"

"Let's do it," the deputy said.

Jesse urged the roan up the rocky slope that formed the back side of the canyon wall. Two of the men followed him.

He thought about Kaylynn as he rode toward his destination. She occupied his every thought, his every waking moment, his every dream. He tried to tell himself it was impossible, that he couldn't have fallen so deeply, so hard, in such a short time, and yet he couldn't deny the feelings of his heart. Just his luck, he thought bitterly, to fall in love with a woman who belonged to another man. No matter that she had left her husband; she was still another man's wife, and he had no right to love her, to want her, to think they might have a life together. And even if she loved him in return, he had nothing to offer her. He was thirty years old, and what did he have to show for his life? Nothing. He had one horse, one saddle, a Winchester rifle, a .44 Colt, and some cash in the bank. He had no home, no family to speak of other than his cousin. He was a loner, a drifter, and likely too old to change his ways, even if she'd have him.

He put all thought of Kaylynn from his mind as he crested the ridge. A narrow shelf hung out over the canyon.

Dismounting, he dropped to his hands and knees, crawled toward the edge, and peered over the side. The barn was directly below him. The ranch house was situated to the left. It was L-shaped, with a tile roof. A lazy column of blue-gray smoke rose from the chimney. He counted nine horses in the corral; six of them were saddled, leading him to believe that at least part of the gang was getting ready to ride out. He didn't see Ravenhawk's Appaloosa among them. A half-dozen or so skinny chickens were scratching in the dirt near the barn. A big gray cat was curled up on a rock on the side of the house.

Glancing toward the east, he saw the sheriff and his men riding through the entrance, one by one. He shook his head, unable to believe that Mazza didn't have one of his men keeping watch at the entrance to the canyon. The man was either unbelievably arrogant or just plain stupid.

A movement from below caught his eyes, and he smiled faintly when he saw Ravenhawk leave the house and enter the barn. Once again, luck was with him.

A shot rang out. One of the sheriff's men clutched his chest and toppled over the back of his horse.

Someone inside the house shouted, "We've got company!"

He heard the sheriff holler, "Take cover!" and then the air was filled with the sound of gunfire.

Jesse glanced over his shoulder at the two men who had accompanied him. "You two, get on down there and cover the back of the house."

"Where are you going?"

"Don't worry about me," he replied, and launched himself from the overhang to the roof of the barn, hands and feet scrabbling for purchase on the sloped roof.

Keeping his head down, he inched toward the front of the roof and peered over the edge. The pulley system used to lift hay from the ground up into the barn's loft jutted out just above a small door, which was open.

Swearing under his breath, Jesse lowered himself over the edge of roof and dropped onto the arm of the pulley. Swaying back and forth, he gathered momentum, then propelled himself toward the loft, feet first, trying not to think of the consequences if he missed.

He landed on his butt just inside the loft door. Off balance, he managed to grab hold of the door frame to keep from tumbling over backward and crashing to the ground. Damn, but that had been close!

The interior of the barn was dim and smelled of hay and horseflesh and manure. Taking a deep breath, he rolled onto his stomach and crawled toward the edge of the loft. Ravenhawk was standing near the barn door, looking out. His Appaloosa, saddled and ready, was waiting in a nearby stall.

Quick and quiet, Jesse descended the ladder and crept up behind his quarry. One sharp blow from his gun butt rendered Ravenhawk unconscious. Moving quickly, he plucked Ravenhawk's Colt from his holster and tucked it into the waistband of his own pants; then he tied Ravenhawk's hands together with a length of rope. That done, he took Ravenhawk's place at the door.

Several bodies lay sprawled in the dirt between the entrance to the canyon and the house. Three of the posse members were holed up on the far side of the house behind a pile of wood, firing at a handful of outlaws who were riding for the entrance. He recognized Nash and Mazza among the fleeing outlaws. Apparently, the last man out of the corral had neglected to close the gate and the other horses had scattered.

The sound of gunfire came from the back of the house. A moment later, the front door burst open and four men ran outside, only to be cut down by the remaining members of the posse.

A few minutes later, the two men who had climbed the canyon wall with Jesse stepped out from behind the barn. The three men alongside the house stood up. Two more posse members, both wounded, emerged from the back of the house.

The fight was over.

Jesse glanced over his shoulder. Ravenhawk was sitting up, a sour expression on his face.

"Damn," Ravenhawk muttered. "I knew I should have left last night."

Jesse grunted softly. Grabbing Ravenhawk by the arm, he pulled him to his feet and shoved him toward the door, then took up the Appaloosa's reins and followed Ravenhawk outside.

The posse had gathered on the porch. Hank was bandaging one of the men. All eyes turned toward Jesse and his prisoner as they emerged from the barn.

"Where's Keegan?" Jesse asked.

"Dead."

"Too bad. Keep an eye on this one for me, will ya? I'll ride up on the rim and get our horses."

Jesse swung onto the Appaloosa's back and rode out of the canyon.

His mare and the other two horses were where they had left them. Taking up the reins, he rode around the rim to where the other members of the posse had left their horses.

Leading the horses, he rode back toward the canyon, his thoughts again centered on Kaylynn.

He wondered how she had spent the day, wondered if her husband was still looking for her. He tried to tell himself she was none of his business. She belonged to another man and he would be worse than a fool to get involved, but it was too late. He was already involved.

When Jesse got back to the canyon, Ravenhawk was sitting on the porch, his expression glum. The bodies of the dead men had been carried into the barn. Hank Frey informed Jesse that the money taken from the stage had been found hidden beneath the floor in the barn.

"It was all there," the deputy remarked, pleased.

Jesse dismounted. Handing the reins to the posse's horses to one of the men, he checked the cinch on the roan. "I'll be leaving now," he told Frey.

"Leaving?"

Jesse nodded. "Some of your men are wounded. They're gonna slow you down. I don't have time to wait for you."

"What's your hurry?"

"I've got someone waiting for me in town."

Frey grunted softly. "You might wanna let Doc Gordon know what happened out here. Tell him to let Harvey know we've got some business for him."

"Right," Jesse said. Harvey was the undertaker

"I don't look forward to telling Keegan's wife about this."

"Yeah, there's never any easy way to say it." Jesse looked up and met Ravenhawk's gaze. "Let's go."

"Hold on," Frey said. "Where are you taking him?"

"I had a deal with Keegan," Jesse said. "Ravenhawk, here, was to be mine. He's wanted in Durango."

Frey shook his head. "I don't know anything about that . . ."

"I've been chasing him for months," Jesse said, his voice hard. "I don't aim to let him out of my sight."

Frey cleared his throat. "Well, if Keegan said it was all right . . ."

"Obliged," Jesse said. He looked at Ravenhawk again. "Let's go."

Ravenhawk stood up, his face impassive as he walked toward Yellow Thunder. Despair sat heavily on his shoulders as he mounted his horse. For a moment, he thought about making a break for it. He had no doubt Yellow Thunder would gun him down if he did. But at least a bullet in the back would be quick. Better than rotting in jail.

"Don't even think about it," Yellow Thunder said.

"I don't know what you're talking about."

"Uh-huh." Jesse swung aboard his own horse, then took up the Appaloosa's reins. "I've seen that look too many times not to know what it means."

Jesse looked over at Hank Frey. "Good luck to you."

"We'll be all right."

With a nod, Jesse touched his heels to the roan's flanks. There was nothing more to be done here. He had what he'd come for and now all he wanted was to get back to Twin Bluffs, and Kaylynn.

Chapter Twenty-six

A light rain began to fall as they cleared the canyon. Jesse urged the roan into a gallop, eager to get rid of his prisoner and get back to Kaylynn. In spite of what he'd said to her earlier, he hadn't worried overmuch about leaving her behind. She was a smart girl, smart enough to stay put until he got back.

But now, suddenly, he felt a sense of unease, an urgency to see her again, to assure himself that she was all right.

He glanced over his shoulder to check on Ravenhawk. It was then that he saw it, a long strip of blue cloth fluttering from a bush.

He gave a sharp jerk on the reins, bringing the roan to an abrupt halt. Behind him, the Appaloosa reared, almost unseating its rider.

"What the hell are you doing?" Ravenhawk exclaimed. "Trying to kill me?"

Jesse didn't answer. He was leaning out of the saddle, reaching for the cloth, turning it over in his hands.

Ravenhawk urged his mount up alongside the roan. "What've you got there?"

Jesse shook his head. It couldn't be. But it was. He was sure of it. "Kaylynn's been here."

"Here? What the hell would she be doing out here?"

"I don't know." Jesse looked at Ravenhawk. "Worrying about you, I reckon."

"Me? Don't be a fool."

"She was afraid I'd kill you."

"Yeah?" Ravenhawk mused. "I thought the same thing myself a time or two."

But Jesse wasn't listening. Dismounting, one hand wrapped around both sets of reins, he began to walk in an ever-widening circle, searching the ground for sign.

Ravenhawk leaned forward over the Appaloosa's neck, his gaze sweeping the ground. "I'd say six horses."

"Yeah." Jesse swung into the saddle and followed the tracks. They were easy to read. Five sets of hoofprints riding hard from the direction of the canyon, gradually slowing. One set of tracks coming from the opposite direction. A change in pace as five horses went in pursuit of the lone rider. Some chewed-up ground where the riders had overtaken the single horse.

"You don't really think it's her, do you?" Ravenhawk asked.

Jesse clutched the scrap of cloth in his hand. "I know it is."

"Victor will most likely kill her, you know."

"Shut up."

"They'll all have a turn at her first, and then Victor will slit her throat."

"Shut up, dammit!"

"You know it's true."

Jesse shook his head. "If they lay a hand on her, I'll cut 'em long and deep."

"Turn me loose."

"No chance."

"You're gonna need my help."

Jesse reined his horse to a halt, then turned in the saddle to face the other man. "You must take me for a fool if you think I'm gonna turn you loose and put a gun in your hand."

"I'll side you. All I want is your promise that you'll let me go when it's over."

"No."

"You may be the best bounty hunter in the territory, but even you can't hope to go against Mazza and his gang alone. Not when they've got Kaylynn for a hostage."

Jesse considered that a moment and knew Ravenhawk was right. "Who's out there?"

Ravenhawk frowned, trying to remember who'd been hurt in the fight and who'd been killed. "Near as I can tell, Victor and his brother. Nash. Two others whose names I don't recall. But they're all cold-blooded killers."

"Good company you picked to ride with."

Ravenhawk shrugged. "It seemed like a chance to make a little easy money."

"Yeah," Jesse retorted. "That's what I thought when I started after you."

"So, how about it?" Ravenhawk asked. "I'll help you get Kaylynn back and you turn me loose when it's over."

Jesse muttered a crude oath as he shoved the piece of cloth into his back pocket. He hesitated a minute, then drew his knife and cut Ravenhawk's hands free. He didn't like the idea of making deals, especially with a man like Ravenhawk, but right now he didn't have much choice. He would have made a deal with the Devil himself if it meant getting Kaylynn away from Mazza's cutthroats.

Ravenhawk rubbed his wrists, then held out his hand. "I'll be needing my iron."

"I've got your word as a warrior, right?"

Ravenhawk nodded. "You've got it. I'll side you until we get the girl, and then I'm gone. And you won't be coming after me again. I've got *your* word on that, right?"

"You've got it," Jesse said gruffly, "but if you cross me, I'll shoot you on sight the next time I see you. No call, no questions. Understood?"

Ravenhawk nodded curtly, knowing that Yellow Thunder meant every word.

Jesse handed Ravenhawk his Colt and the Winchester rifle he had taken from the saddle boot earlier. "Let's ride."

The rain let up before it washed out the tracks. Oblivious to the cold and damp, Jesse followed the tracks of the outlaws. He refused to think about Kaylynn, about how scared she must be. Refused to think of Victor Mazza's men leering at her, wanting her, touching her. He tamped down his rage, his fear, and concentrated on the task at hand. Mazza and his men had taken his woman and for that they would die, and their deaths would be slow indeed if they had dared defile her.

He smiled faintly. There were numerous ways of inflicting excruciating pain while prolonging the victim's life. He had never practiced them, but he knew how they were done.

Kaylynn stared straight ahead, trying to still the awful panic that threatened to engulf her. She had to keep her wits about her, had to think. Had to find a way to escape from these men before it was too late.

She had been frightened before, many times, but never like this. She had been afraid when she ran away from Alan, afraid he would find her. She had been terrified when the Cheyenne attacked the stagecoach and took her captive, though none of the horrors she had imagined back then had come true. Indeed, those fears all seemed foolish now. But these men were outlaws, killers, totally without remorse. One look into their eyes and she knew they were capable of every atrocity known to man.

Shifting in the saddle, she wrapped one arm around her body in an effort to warm herself, to ease the violent tremors of fear that racked her from head to foot. There was no one to come to her rescue this time. By the time Jesse returned to Twin Bluffs and discovered she was gone, it would be too late. Too late . . .

Oh, Jesse, Jesse, I'm so afraid. . . .

Why hadn't she stayed at the hotel and waited for him? What had she hoped to accomplish by riding after him? What had made her think that she could reach Mazza's hideout in time to prevent bloodshed or, even if she had managed to catch up with Jesse, that she would have been able to make him change his mind? How could she have been so stupid? But none of that mattered now, and she was faced with the knowledge that she would never see him again, never be able to tell him how she felt.

Jesse, I hope you know how much I love you. . . .

She could hardly believe her bad luck. She had managed to follow Jesse's trail without any trouble and then had ridden right into the outlaws' hands. Too late, she had made a grab for the gun Jesse had given her, but one of the outlaws had snatched it out of her hands.

Her horse stumbled and she found herself hoping that the animal would fall and crush her. Surely death would be preferable to suffering the unspeakable lust she had read in the eyes of the men who surrounded her.

They had been riding hard for over two hours. She prayed fervently that they would never stop, that they would just ride forever. As long as they were moving, she was safe.

But stop they did. The leader, Victor Mazza she thought his name was, slowed his mount to a trot, then a walk. It was early afternoon. It had drizzled earlier, then stopped. Overhead, the clouds hung low and gray and heavy. Thunder rumbled in the distance.

Victor Mazza reined his horse to a halt. The man riding beside Kaylynn reached over and grabbed hold of her horse's bridle. Releasing her hold on the reins, Kaylynn lowered her head so she wouldn't have to look at any of them. Wrapping her arms around her body, she tried to make herself small, wished she could just disappear.

"How much farther?" one of the outlaws asked.

"Three, four miles," Mazza answered.

"How do you think they found us?" another of the men asked.

"Had to be Claudill," Victor replied, his voice laced with anger. "Leo, why the hell didn't you finish him when he fell behind?"

"I thought he was dead."

"Next time make sure."

"Yeah," Leo said gruffly. "Next time. What are we gonna do about that posse?"

"What about them?" Victor asked with a sneer.

"Do you think they're following us?"

"No. They've got wounded to look after, and there's a storm brewin'. We'll hole up at Ma's place until it's over, then split up and meet later."

"Whole damn deal was a bust," one of the outlaws muttered.

"Buck up, Nash. It happens."

The man called Nash swore a vulgar oath.

"Besides, it ain't a total loss," Victor remarked. "At least we've got a way to pass the time."

A cold chill snaked its way down Kaylynn's spine as she realized she was suddenly the center of attention.

Rough hands pulled the pins from her hair so that it tumbled down her back.

She jerked away before the man could touch her again.

Victor laughed. "She's got some spunk. I like that."

"You will not touch her. Not yet."

Kaylynn glanced at the man who had spoken. His name was Rafael, and he looked enough like Victor to be his twin.

"You are not thinking, any of you," Rafael went on.

"Go on," Victor said.

"We may need the woman later." Rafael held up a hand to silence his brother. "We can't be sure the posse has quit. And we can't go to Ma's. Claudill may have given them that location, as well."

Victor nodded, his expression sullen, and Kaylynn realized that for all his bold talk, he was not the leader of the gang.

"We'll ride for Broken Rock," Rafael said.

"Broken Rock!" Nash exclaimed. "Now, wait just a minute. That's Injun country."

"Exactly. No posse will follow us there." Rafael smiled at his brother. "Once we're out of danger, you can do whatever you want with the woman, as long as you don't kill her."

"Go on," Victor said.

"Use her lightly, and we can sell her to the Comancheros. They pay a high price for white women."

Victor considered his brother's words a moment, and then nodded. "Let's go, *hombres*. We can reach Broken Rock by tomorrow night."

Jesse studied the pile of horse droppings at his feet, then swung aboard the roan.

"How long ago?" Ravenhawk asked.

"Less than an hour, I'd say."

Ravenhawk looked up at the sky. "If this storm breaks, it's gonna be a real gully-washer."

"Yeah. Any idea where they're headed?"

248

"No. But they've been riding due west for the last five miles."

Jesse nodded again. If the storm hit, the tracks would disappear. Until the outlaws' trail had abruptly changed direction, he had figured Mazza was headed for a two-bit hangout called Ma's. Now he thought they might be riding for Broken Rock, which was a notorious hideout for gun runners and Comancheros and the like. Earlier, Ravenhawk had mentioned that the Mazza gang often did business with the Comancheros, who traded whiskey, women, and rifles to the Indians. Holing up at Broken Rock seemed like the Mazza gang's best move. He didn't like to think what the consequences would be if he was wrong.

Jesse glanced up at the sky. The clouds were moving, slowly drifting toward the south. A cool wind blew across the face of the land, whispering softly to the tall prairie grass.

Relieved that the storm seemed to be passing them by, Jesse urged the mare onward. It would be full dark soon. He wondered if Mazza and his bunch would find a place to hole up for the night, or ride on until they reached their destination. He wondered how Kaylynn was doing. She had endured much in the past few weeks, but she was a strong woman. She would be all right. Dammit, she had to be all right.

The roan snorted and tossed her head as a rabbit bounded across its path. He heard Ravenhawk curse as the Appaloosa shied.

There was a flash of lightning, a rumble of thunder, followed by a few raindrops.

Needing to do something to release the tension building within him, Jesse slammed his heels into the mare's flanks, leaning low over the roan's neck as she lined out in a dead run, his only thought to reach Kaylynn before it was too late.

He let the mare run until she slowed of her own accord, and then he reined her to a halt in the lee of a cliff to wait for Ravenhawk to catch up.

A stiff wind chased the clouds across the sky then died away, and a heavy stillness lay across the land. It was then that he saw it, a brief flicker of light off to his left, as though someone had struck a match. He caught the scent of tobacco drifting on the wind.

Peering through the moonlit night, he made out the shape of a rocky overhang jutting from a hillside several yards away.

Moments later, Ravenhawk rode up.

Jesse motioned for him to be quiet. "I think they're over there," he whispered.

Ravenhawk glanced over his shoulder, then nodded.

Side by side, they rode until they came to a small stand of timber, where they left the horses; then, on cat-quiet feet, they made their way back to the rocky overhang.

A cold excitement rose up inside Jesse as they neared the outlaws' camp. It reminded him of his days as a young warrior, of creeping up on a sleeping Crow camp to steal war ponies and count coup. The prize he was after now was of far more worth than a few horses.

The moon had gone behind the clouds again by the time they reached the overhang.

"So," Ravenhawk whispered. "Do we go in shooting?"

Jesse shook his head. "No. Nice and quiet. I

don't want to take a chance on Kaylynn getting caught in a crossfire."

Ravenhawk nodded. "Nice and quiet," he said with a wink. "No prisoners."

"No prisoners," Jesse said.

Keeping low, Jesse moved to the left. He'd gone only a short distance when he saw one of the outlaws standing near where the horses were tethered. He was standing with his back toward Jesse, smoking a cigarette. A thin column of gray smoke rose above his head.

Picking up a small rock, Jesse tossed it over the man's head. It landed in the grass with a dull thud.

The man grabbed his rifle and stared toward the sound.

Silent as the shadows moving over the land, Jesse ghosted up behind the outlaw. Bending over, he grabbed the man by the ankles and gave a sharp jerk. The man fell forward. His head struck the ground, hard, the force snapping his neck.

One down. Four to go.

Cold, hungry, and tired, Kaylynn stared up at the drifting clouds, feeling as though she were caught in a nightmare from which she would never awake. Her hands, tightly bound, were almost numb. Victor Mazza slept beside her, snoring loudly. The other outlaws were bedded down not far away. The fifth man was standing guard.

A faint sound drew her attention. Wriggling onto her side, she stared into the darkness and watched, stunned, as the man keeping watch suddenly pitched forward.

Struggling to a sitting position, she glanced around, felt her heart begin to race when she saw

Ravenhawk slip up behind Rafael Mazza, who had fallen asleep sitting against a rock. Her eyes widened as Ravenhawk reached over the rock and slipped a garrote around the outlaw's neck.

The outlaw twitched once and lay still. Moving swiftly and silently, Ravenhawk edged around the rock and padded toward the man called Nash.

Kaylynn held her breath, waiting, felt her heartbeat increase as the outlaw suddenly stirred and sat up.

Nash muttered, "What the hell!" when he saw Ravenhawk moving toward him.

Grabbing his rifle, Nash jacked a round into the breech and then, with a grunt, he fell forward, lifeless as a rag doll, a knife protruding from the middle of his back.

At almost the same time, the man lying a few feet away from Nash came awake and began fumbling for his gun. Ravenhawk dove forward, jerked the knife from Nash's back, turned, and plunged it into the outlaw's chest.

Kaylynn gasped and looked away. It was then she saw Jesse step out of the shadows.

She blinked at the two men, unable to believe her eyes. She didn't stop to wonder why Jesse and Ravenhawk were working together, or how they had found her. They were here, and that was all that mattered. She had never been so glad to see anyone in her whole life.

Jesse was pulling his knife from the dead outlaw's chest when a harsh voice cut across the stillness of the night.

"Hold it right there," Victor Mazza said. "Drop your weapons, or the girl dies."

Ravenhawk glanced over his shoulder to see

Victor Mazza sitting beside Kaylynn, his gun aimed at her head. There was no doubt in his mind that Victor meant what he said.

The color drained from Kaylynn's face as she looked into the barrel of Mazza's pistol.

Slowly, Ravenhawk tossed his Colt away.

"You, too," Victor said, jerking his chin in Jesse's direction.

A muscle twitched in Jesse's jaw as he dropped his gun, and then his knife.

Victor Mazza stood up and took a step forward. He stared at Ravenhawk through narrowed eyes. "Traitor," he hissed. "I will enjoy killing you." He took another step forward.

Ravenhawk spat into the dirt at Mazza's feet. "You gonna gun me down in cold blood? Just like that?"

"It is the fate of traitors. Yesterday you were one of us. Today you ride against us."

"I came because of the woman," Ravenhawk said.

Mazza flicked a glance at Kaylynn. "The woman? What is she to you?"

"She was mine," Ravenhawk said, stalling for time. "At least she was until this man took her away from me."

Victor shook his head, obviously unconvinced.

Ravenhawk jerked his head in Jesse's direction. "He's a bounty hunter. I was his prisoner not long ago, but the woman and I escaped. He thinks I'm on his side, but I'm not." He laughed softly. "You don't really think I'd be sidin' a lawman, do you?"

Mazza took a few steps forward as he studied Ravenhawk, doubt showing in his eyes.

Jesse's hands clenched into tight fists as he lis-

tened to the exchange between Ravenhawk and
Mazza. Damn! He had known the Lakota couldn't
be trusted.

He was weighing his chances of rushing Mazza
when he saw Kaylynn pick up a good-sized rock,
then struggle to her feet. She was far enough behind Mazza that he couldn't see her.

"Dammit, Mazza," Ravenhawk said loudly.
"There's a price on my head." He threw his hands
up in the air, his voice rising. "Why would I be
ridin' with a man who's anxious to collect it?"

Mazza glanced briefly at Jesse and then back at
Ravenhawk.

Jesse held his breath as Kaylynn stood up. Taking a step forward, she brought the rock down
hard on the back of Victor Mazza's head.

Mazza dropped like a poleaxed steer.

"Hot damn!" Ravenhawk exclaimed. He looked
at Kaylynn and smiled. "Nice work, sweetheart."

"Hot damn indeed," Jesse repeated. Grabbing
his gun, he eared back the hammer of the Colt and
leveled it at Ravenhawk. "Get those hands up."

"What the hell . . ."

"Don't make me tell you again."

"Dammit, we had a deal."

"Yeah, I thought so, too. Now I'm not so sure."

"You didn't fall for all that stuff I was tellin'
Mazza? I was trying to save our hides."

"Uh-huh."

"It's true. I was just stallin', giving Kaylynn time
to make her move." He smiled at Kaylynn. "Nice
going."

"Thank you," Kaylynn replied, looking pleased.

Jesse glanced over at Kaylynn. He didn't have
any faith in Ravenhawk, but he trusted Kaylynn.

With a sigh, he holstered his gun. "Kaylynn, come here."

Kaylynn made a wide berth around Victor Mazza. "Is he . . . he isn't dead?"

"I doubt it," Jesse replied regretfully.

"Too bad if he ain't," Ravenhawk said.

Jesse took a step forward and nudged the outlaw in the ribs, then shrugged. "He's still breathin'."

"Why don't you untie Kaylynn?" Ravenhawk suggested. "I'll look after Mazza."

Jesse regarded Ravenhawk for a long moment, wondering if he was making a mistake; then, retrieving his knife, he cut Kaylynn's hands free, all the while keeping one eye on Ravenhawk, who quickly lashed Mazza's hands behind his back.

Driven by a need to touch her, Jesse ran his knuckles over Kaylynn's cheek. "You all right?"

Kaylynn managed a weak smile. "Fine."

Ravenhawk glanced from Kaylynn to Yellow Thunder, then grunted softly. There was no mistaking the look that passed between the bounty hunter and the girl. A blind man stuck in a coal mine could have seen it.

With a shake of his head, he began gathering the outlaws' weapons.

Jesse cleared his throat. "They didn't . . ."

"No," Kaylynn said.

He blew out a sigh of relief; then, taking her hands in his, he gently massaged her wrists, first one, then the other.

"Kay . . ." He clasped one of her hands in both of his and then, unable to resist, he drew her up against him and wrapped her in his arms.

"You're sure?" he asked. "Sure you're all right?"

She snuggled against him. "I am now."

"Maybe you two would like to be alone."

Jesse glanced over his shoulder into Ravenhawk's smirking face.

Ravenhawk shrugged. "I'll keep an eye on things here." Bending, he picked up the blanket Kaylynn had been sleeping on and tossed it over Jesse's shoulder. "You might need that," he said with a lecherous grin.

With a nod, Jesse swung Kaylynn into his arms and carried her away from the outlaws' camp.

She didn't argue, didn't say a word, merely slipped her arms around Jesse's neck.

"I'm not letting you out of my sight again," Jesse said.

"I'm sorry to be so much trouble."

"You are that," he muttered.

She made a face at him, though she doubted he could see it in the darkness.

"Why the hell didn't you stay in town?"

"I was afraid you'd kill him."

Jesse came to an abrupt halt. His arms, a haven only moments before, now felt like steel around her.

"You put your life in danger for him?" he asked.

Kaylynn shivered. His voice was colder than the night air. "No."

"Tell me."

"I was afraid he would kill you. Or you would kill him. I just didn't want that to happen. Can't you understand?"

"I understand you must have feelings for him."

"I care for him," she admitted, "but not the way I care for you."

"Go on."

"I love you."

"Kay!"

"It's wrong, I know it, but I can't help how I feel."

"Shh." He held her tighter, wishing he had the right to hold her forever.

She cupped his face in her hands and kissed him, heard him groan deep in his throat. "Make love to me, Jesse."

"Kay . . ."

"Don't you want to?"

"Want to? Good Lord, woman, I've hardly thought of anything else."

"Then do it."

"You'll hate me if I do."

"I'll hate you if you don't."

He started to argue, to tell her it would be wrong, that she would feel different later, when she was back home where she belonged, but she covered his mouth with hers, stifling his foolish words. Her hands caressed his nape, slid down the inside of his shirt to stroke his back.

He stood her on her feet, his body coming alive as she pressed herself against his chest, her lips eager as she kissed his scarred cheek.

He held on to her tightly, afraid she would disappear if he let her go. She kissed him, and he drank from her lips as though she were life itself.

And then he was kissing her back, his clever hands stroking her hips, sliding along her rib cage, drifting over her breasts, which suddenly seemed fuller, heavier, achy.

She sighed with pleasure as a wellspring of desire rose up within her and she pressed herself against him, needing to be closer, to feel all of him.

He broke away long enough to spread the blanket on the ground, and then he was kissing her again, drawing her down onto the blanket.

"Sweet," he murmured. "So sweet."

"You are."

"Kay . . ."

"I know," she whispered. "I feel it, too."

He unfastened her dress and she shivered as the cold wind brushed her skin, and then his lips were there, kissing her neck, her shoulders, her breasts, and she was on fire.

She watched him remove his shirt and trousers, her eyes greedy for the sight of him, her hands hungry to touch him, her lips eager for the taste of him.

She lifted her arms to embrace him, sighed with pleasure as she felt his weight.

"Jesse. Jesse." His name was like a sigh, a prayer. "Tell me."

"I love you, Kaylynn," he said, his voice low and rough with desire. "God help me, I love you."

She looked up at him, her eyes slumberous with desire, her lips swollen from his kisses. "Show me."

He kissed her again, his mouth hot and hungry, and she surrendered to him without fear, without regret. He whispered that she was more beautiful than the wildflowers that grew along the Greasy Grass, that she was desirable, that he loved her, adored her, and for the first time in her life, she felt that she *was* beautiful and desirable, that she was lovable, that she had worth.

He filled her heart and her soul and she clung to him, unafraid, trusting, letting him carry her higher, higher, until she thought she would surely die and then, like lightning ripping through the dark of night, she found fulfillment in a man's arms for the first time.

I have felt love, she thought, *felt it surround me. I have tasted its sweetness, felt it moving within me, its breath upon my face . . . Jesse . . .*

A moment later, she was filled with a rush of warmth and Jesse buried his face against her neck, his body trembling, and she hugged him to her, filled with a sense of tenderness, a sense of completeness, that she had never known before. It filled her heart with a strange kind of pain, spilled from her eyes in a wash of tears.

Jesse drew back as he felt the warmth of her tears on his neck. "Kay? Did I hurt you?"

"No. Oh, no." She hurt, she thought, but not in the way he meant. Her heart was so full, so full. The memory of his touch, his taste, the sound of his voice moving through the air, dancing in her heart, his breath moving lightly over her skin, his love covering her, warm and soft.

He caught one of her tears on his fingertip and felt a sinking feeling in his heart. She was regretting it already.

"I'm sorry," he said gruffly, but when he started to pull away, she held him to her.

"Don't go."

"I knew this would be a mistake."

"No!" She covered his mouth with her hand. "These are happy tears."

"Happy tears?"

"Oh, Jesse, I never knew it could be like this." She looked up at him, her eyes wide with wonder. "I've never . . . I mean . . ."

He stared at her in disbelief. "Never?"

259

She shook her head, her cheeks flaming. "Alan said making love to me was like making love to a block of ice. He said there was no passion in me, that I was a . . . a failure as a woman."

Jesse laughed then, laughed with the sheer joy of being alive and having her in his arms.

"Believe me, honey, you've got enough passion for a hundred women," he murmured as he kissed the tip of her nose, and he couldn't help feeling a sense of pride that he had been the one to awaken it.

She snuggled against him, her head pillowed on his shoulder, one arm draped across his chest. He held her close, felt her sigh and then relax as sleep claimed her.

Jesse stared into the darkness, one hand idly stroking Kaylynn's hair. It had been a hell of a day, he mused. A hell of a night.

He brushed a kiss across the top of her head, wondering what madness had possessed him. Making love to her had been a mistake. He had known it would be, yet he had been powerless to resist the sweet temptation of her touch. She had kissed him, and he had been lost. Damn. How was he going to let her go?

He took a deep breath, and her scent filled his nostrils, warm and womanly, musky with the scent of their lovemaking. Her husband had accused her of lacking passion. The man must have been deaf, dumb, and blind if he couldn't find it. Not that he was complaining, Jesse thought with a wry grin. He was inordinately pleased that he had been the one to introduce her to the pleasure between a man and a woman. There was so much more he wanted to teach her. He wanted to spend hours making love to her, now slow and soft, now quick and urgent. He wanted to tease and caress and pleasure her, watch her eyes grow hot with desire, hear her voice cry his name. . . .

Damn, but he wanted her again.

Knowing he had to put some distance between them before desire overcame reason, he started to ease away from her, only to feel her arm tighten around him.

"Where are you going?" she asked sleepily.

"We should be getting back."

"Do we have to?"

She was just tired, he thought. She didn't mean what he was thinking.

But then he felt her lips against his neck, the heat of her tongue against his skin.

"Kay?"

"Hmm?"

"Kay, do you know what you're doing?"

"I think so," she murmured, and her voice was no longer sleepy, but low and husky. "Am I doing it wrong?"

"No."

"Do you want me to stop?"

He swallowed hard as her fingertips drifted down over his bare chest. "No, don't stop."

"Do you like it when I touch you?"

He nodded, afraid to frighten her away. She had never been the aggressor. It pleased him that she felt comfortable with him, that she wanted to explore, to test her newfound sexuality.

Kaylynn took a deep breath. It was wrong for her to be here, with him, wrong to make love to him, to let him make love to her. But she had been unhappy for so long and she might never have this chance again.

For tonight, she would forget right or wrong. Tonight, she would reach for happiness with both hands. She would worry about guilt tomorrow.

"Touch me, Kay."

Emboldened by his words, she ran her hands over his arms and chest, down his belly. She played with the dark curly hair on his chest, the wiry hair on his legs. She kissed the scar on his cheek. She pushed him until he rolled over, and then she ran her hands down the long length of his back. He had a beautiful back, well-muscled and smooth. He had small, firm buttocks, long legs.

She kissed his neck and he rolled onto his back, drawing her down on top of him, and she thought what a wondrous feeling it was, the touch of his skin brushing against hers. She reveled in the strength of his arms around her, the gentleness of his lips when he kissed her, the aching need in his voice when he said he wanted her, needed her.

She surrendered completely, her heart and soul soaring, flying, reaching. And he was there beside her to catch her when she fell, tumbling through rainbow clouds into ecstasy.

Chapter Twenty-seven

She was embarrassed when she woke in his arms in the morning. Embarrassed but not ashamed. He had given her a gift beyond price, and she would never regret accepting it.

Jesse seemed to know what she was feeling and turned his back while she dressed. Then she stood staring across the prairie while he pulled on his pants and shirt.

When he was dressed, he moved up behind her and slipped his arms around her waist. "Kay?"

"What?"

"Are you all right?"

She nodded.

Slowly, he turned her to face him. "Are you sure?"

"I'm sure."

He hugged her tightly, and then kissed her gently, tenderly. "We'd better go see how Ravenhawk's doing."

"Ravenhawk!" She had forgotten all about him. She pressed her hands to cheeks suddenly hot. How could she face him? He would know what she had done. Mazza would know.

"Hey." Jesse put a forefinger under her chin and tilted her face up. "It doesn't show," he said with a wry grin.

"But he'll know. They'll both know."

"And they'll think I'm the luckiest man on earth."

"But what will they think of me?"

"Do you care?"

She looked into his eyes and knew she didn't care what anyone else thought. She had followed her heart and she would never be sorry. She had shared a beautiful night with a beautiful man, and she wouldn't let anyone spoil it, or turn it into something shameful or sordid.

"Kay?"

"No." She smiled at him. "I don't care."

"Good." He kissed her again. "Let's go get something to eat."

Ravenhawk looked up at the sound of footsteps. It took but one look at Kaylynn's face to know how she had spent the night. There was a glow about her, a look in her eyes that said she had been well and truly pleasured. He glanced at Yellow Thunder and knew a swift rush of jealousy.

Jesse slipped his arm around Kaylynn's waist as he met Ravenhawk's gaze. It was a gesture that was not only possessive but a blatant warning, as well.

"Everything all right here?" Jesse asked.

Ravenhawk shrugged. "Why wouldn't it be?"

"No reason." Jesse nodded at Victor Mazza, who was sitting a few feet away, his arms bound behind his back. "He give you any trouble?"

"No."

"Is there anything to eat?"

Ravenhawk shook his head. "Not much. Couple cans of beans and some hardtack."

"Any coffee?"

"There's a little in the pot."

Jesse walked over to the fire and poured a cup of coffee. It was as black and bitter as an old whore's heart, but it was hot. He drank half, then offered the cup to Kaylynn, who shook her head.

She glanced around, then looked at Ravenhawk, wondering what he had done with the bodies of the outlaws.

"Victor wrapped 'em up good and tight so we could haul 'em back to town," Ravenhawk remarked, answering her unspoken question. "Gave him something to do while we were waiting for you two."

Kaylynn nodded, her cheeks heating beneath Ravenhawk's knowing gaze. "Oh."

Mazza muttered something foul under his breath, his expression feral.

Jesse emptied the dregs from the coffee pot into the fire pit. "Let's pack up and get the hell out of here." He looked at Ravenhawk. "I guess you'll be riding on."

"I was thinking there's probably a good-sized reward out for old Victor and the rest, and that half of it rightly belongs to me."

"Is that what you were thinking?"

Ravenhawk nodded. "You got a problem with that?"

"No, I guess you earned your share."

"Damn right. You wanna help me saddle the horses?"

"Sure."

"I'll clean up here," Kaylynn said.

Jesse looked at her and smiled. "Stay away from Mazza," he warned, then followed Ravenhawk toward the picket line.

Kaylynn rolled the bedding and put out the fire while Jesse and Ravenhawk tied the bodies of the outlaws to the backs of the horses. Victor Mazza's malevolent gaze followed her every move.

An hour later, they were headed toward town.

They made quite a sight, Kaylynn mused. Jesse rode on one side of her, leading four corpse-laden horses. Ravenhawk rode on her other side, leading Mazza's horse.

It was a grisly parade.

Kaylynn sat in a chair beside the window, looking down at the street below. Jesse had left her and Ravenhawk at the hotel while he went to the jail to drop off Victor Mazza and fill out whatever forms were necessary to claim the rewards on Victor Mazza and the four dead outlaws.

Jesse had warned Ravenhawk to stay in his room. He was, after all, supposed to be Jesse's prisoner.

The trip back to town had been strained. Kaylynn had been acutely aware of the tension between Jesse and Ravenhawk, and just as aware that she was the cause of it. Victor Mazza had cursed long and loudly, vowing to kill them all for what they had done to his brother, until Raven-hawk threatened to geld him if he didn't shut up. Apparently the outlaw took the threat to heart, because he hadn't said another word, though if looks could kill, they would all have been dead long since.

A knock at the door drew her attention from the window. Rising, she crossed the room and opened the door.

Ravenhawk shrugged at her look of disappointment. "I guess you were expecting Yellow Thunder."

"Yes, I was. Did you want something?"

He shook his head, thinking he wanted quite a lot from her, but he couldn't tell her that. "No. I was going crazy in my room, so I thought I'd come by and make sure you were all right."

"I'm fine."

"Mind if I come in?"

She bit down on the inside of her lower lip. She knew it was improper for a woman to entertain a man in her room, but after all she had been through in the last few weeks, such a strict moral code seemed foolish somehow.

She stepped back. "Come in."

Ravenhawk crossed the threshold, and she closed the door behind him.

"I wonder what's keeping Jesse," Kaylynn mused.

Ravenhawk shrugged. "Probably still doing paperwork and answering questions."

"Do you think there was a problem?"

"I doubt it. Maybe he stopped to have a drink at the saloon." He smiled reassuringly. "Don't worry about him. I'm sure he'll be along soon."

"I guess so." She stood in the middle of the floor, ill at ease without knowing why.

"Kaylynn, where are you going from here?"

"Home, to my parents. You know that."

"I just wondered if maybe you'd changed your mind."

"Why would I do that?"

"I thought maybe you'd decided to stay here, with Yellow Thunder."

"No." He hadn't asked, she thought, and she didn't know what her answer would be if he had. She wanted to go home. Had to go home.

"Is there any chance I could talk you into staying with me?"

"With you?" she exclaimed.

He shrugged. "I'd do my best to make you a good husband."

"I'm already married."

"What! To who?"

"A man in San Francisco." Suddenly agitated, she began to pace the floor. "I thought you knew."

"No." He frowned at her. "So, your husband lives in Frisco," he mused aloud, "and you're on your way, alone, to New York. You wouldn't be running away from him, would you?"

"I don't see as how that's any of your business."

"No, I reckon not. Does Yellow Thunder know?"

"Yes."

"Hmm."

She felt a rush of heat suffuse her, knew he was remembering the night she had spent with Jesse, knew he was thinking she was no better than a harlot.

Stiffening her spine, she met his gaze. "What does that mean?"

"Nothing." Reaching out, he grabbed her arm.

"What are you doing?"

"Nothing. Calm down, Kaylynn."

"I am calm."

He grinned at her. It was a devilishly handsome grin.

"Let me go."

"Shh." Slowly, deliberately, he drew her up against him.

She stared up at him, her heart pounding, as he lowered his head and claimed her lips with his. In all her life, she had only been kissed by two men, Alan and Jesse. Well, three men if she counted her second cousin who had kissed her in the gazebo at her thirteenth birthday party.

She struggled against Ravenhawk for a minute and then, overcome with curiosity, she closed her eyes and surrendered to his kiss. It was warm and pleasant, yet she felt none of the excitement that had coursed through her when Jesse kissed her.

"What the hell is going on?"

Guilt heated Kaylynn's cheeks as she tried to twist out of Ravenhawk's arms. "Jesse!"

He looked at her, his expression unreadable. "I knocked. Guess you didn't hear me."

She shook her head. "No."

Jesse's gaze rested on Ravenhawk. "What are you doing here?"

Ravenhawk shrugged. "I just came by to make sure she was all right."

"Yeah, I can see that."

"You jealous, bounty hunter?"

Jesse took a step forward, his hands curled into tight fists. "Get your filthy hands off her."

"Calm down," Ravenhawk said. Releasing Kaylynn, he put her away from him. "It was just a kiss. No need to—"

"Like hell!" Face flushed with anger, Jesse lunged forward.

Kaylynn screamed, "No!" as Jesse plowed into Ravenhawk.

Ravenhawk reeled backward, crashing into the window behind him, shattering the glass. In an effort to catch himself, Ravenhawk clutched Jesse's shirt, but to no avail. Driven by the bounty hunter's momentum, he fell backward over the sill, dragging Jesse with him. Locked together, they tumbled down the sloping roof, and plummeted to the street below.

Kaylynn hurried to the window and leaned out over the sill in time to see Ravenhawk gain his feet. Thank God the fall wasn't as far as she'd feared.

She shook her head in disbelief as Ravenhawk staggered over to where Jesse lay facedown in the street. He looked down at the bounty hunter a moment and then drew back his foot and kicked Jesse in the ribs.

It was a vicious blow. With a grunt of pain, Jesse rolled onto his back.

Kaylynn gasped as Ravenhawk drew back his foot to kick Jesse again, but Jesse was ready for him. With a grimace, Jesse grabbed Ravenhawk by the ankle, then rolled to the side, bringing Ravenhawk crashing to the ground once more.

Both men were breathing hard when they gained their feet.

Jesse clutched his side, his eyes narrowed as Ravenhawk lunged at him. In spite of the pain of his bruised ribs, Jesse lashed out at Ravenhawk, his fist catching Ravenhawk with a hard right cross. With a grunt, Ravenhawk stumbled backward and Jesse rushed him.

Before the Lakota could regain his balance, Jesse drove into him, driving him backward, until Ravenhawk came up short against the horse trough. As Ravenhawk lurched to a halt, Jesse drew back his arm and slammed his fist into the Lakota's face.

Blood spurted from Ravenhawk's nose as he tumbled backward, landing with a loud splash in the trough.

Ravenhawk came up cussing mightily. As soon as he broke the surface, Jesse grabbed him by the shirt collar and dunked him again and yet again before he hauled him to the surface.

Gasping for breath, Ravenhawk glared at him.

"I'm not gonna say this again," Jesse growled. "Keep your hands off what's mine."

"I reckon her husband would tell you the same thing, bounty hunter," Ravenhawk said with a sneer. "Maybe you should take your own advice."

"Damn you," Jesse hissed. "I ought to drown your sorry hide here and now."

Suddenly aware that a crowd had gathered, Jesse shoved Ravenhawk underwater one last time before pulling him out of the trough.

Jesse took a step back and drew his gun. "Just stand easy," he warned. He glanced over his shoulder at the sound of footsteps and saw Hank Frey striding toward him.

Jesse swore softly when he saw Kaylynn standing on the porch of the hotel. She started toward him, and he shook his head. She threw him a puzzled look, but stayed where she was.

"Say now, what the hell's going on here?" Frey demanded. "I don't allow no gunplay in my town. Say, isn't this one of the men from the robbery? The one you were taking to Colorado?"

"Yeah," Jesse said. "He got away from me. We'll be leaving as soon as I collect the money due me."

Frey nodded. "Maybe I should keep him over to the jail until you're ready to leave?"

"Good idea," Jesse said, suppressing a grin as Frey pulled a set of handcuffs out of his back pocket. "Thanks."

A look of dismay settled over Ravenhawk's face as Frey snapped the cuffs in place.

"No problem," Frey said. "I finished up the paperwork on those bounties you turned in. Should be ready by noon tomorrow."

Jesse grunted softly as he shoved Ravenhawk's gun into the waistband of his trousers. "Obliged."

Ravenhawk glared at Jesse, his dark eyes filled with anger and condemnation.

Frey drew his gun, then gave Ravenhawk a little shove. "Let's go."

Jesse wrapped one arm around his bruised ribs, a faint smile playing over his face as he watched Frey hustle the Lakota off to jail. Ravenhawk wouldn't be kissing Kaylynn again any time soon.

He turned as Kaylynn came up behind him.

"What are you doing?" she demanded. "Why did you let the sheriff take Ravenhawk?"

Jesse shrugged, grimacing as a twinge of pain lanced through his side. "He's wanted for robbery."

"You hate him, don't you?"

Jesse shook his head. "No, I don't hate him. But

when I saw his hands on you, I wanted to kill him."

"Jesse . . ."

"Ironic, don't you think?"

"What do you mean?"

He took her by the arm and started walking back to the hotel. "He told me to practice what I preach."

"I don't understand."

"I hit him because he kissed you." Jesse laughed softly, bitterly. He had no more right to touch Kaylynn, to kiss her, to want her, than did Ravenhawk. She belonged to another man, and it was time he remembered that.

"I still don't understand."

"Forget it."

He opened the door to the hotel and ushered her inside. "Go to your room and stay there."

"Where are you going?"

"I need a drink."

"Jesse, what is it? What's wrong?" Her gaze ran over his face. "Are you all right?"

"Right as rain, darlin'. Go along now."

She frowned at him. It was in her mind to protest, to tell him he had no right to send her off to her room as if she were a naughty child, but something in his eyes warned her not to argue, not now.

Turning on her heels, she headed for the stairs. Men! She was fed up with all of them.

Jesse watched her out of sight; then, with a sigh, he left the hotel.

Ravenhawk paced the confines of his cell, four strides up, four strides back, the air turning blue as he cursed Yellow Thunder with every foul epithet he knew. Damn the man!

He paused in front of the cell's single window, his hands fisted around the iron bars as he stared out into the alley behind the jail. He had to get out of here.

Tension coiled in his gut and he began to pace again. He'd kill Yellow Thunder for this if it was the last thing he ever did. They'd had a deal, dammit, and he'd kept his part. He should have known he couldn't depend on Yellow Thunder to keep his word, should have known the bounty hunter would double-cross him.

Damn!

Jesse spent the rest of the day holed up in a saloon, quietly working his way to the bottom of a bottle of whiskey.

He was about halfway through the bottle when it began to rain. Tilted back in his chair, a full glass of whiskey in his hand, he stared out the window. It was a light summer shower, just enough to tamp down the dust in the street. A low rumble of thunder echoed in the distance. The gray day suited his mood perfectly. He'd been a fool to fall in love with Kaylynn, to think they could have a life together. He never should have touched her, kissed her. Damn! Even now, she was all he could think about.

Emptying his glass, he left the saloon. He spent twenty minutes walking in the drizzle, hoping a cold shower would cool the aching need he felt for another man's wife, even though he knew it was a futile hope at best.

He wanted her more than he'd ever wanted anything in his life.

He needed her more than his next breath.

He loved her . . .

He paused in front of the hotel. Soft yellow lamplight spilled from the window of her room. Warm. Beckoning . . .

And he, poor fool that he was, went toward it.

Chapter Twenty-eight

Kaylynn turned onto her side and punched the hard pillow. It had been a long day, and a longer night. She had been tempted to go visit Ravenhawk in jail, but after all that had happened, she was reluctant to leave her room. It seemed that every time she took off on her own, she got into trouble.

She wondered where Jesse was; she couldn't believe he had let Ravenhawk go to jail.

She rolled onto her back again and stared at the reflection of the lamplight on the ceiling. Where was Jesse? She had expected him to look in on her, maybe take her to dinner, but she hadn't seen him for hours. Finally, she had gone to the hotel dining room to get something to eat, then hurried back to her room to wait for Jesse.

Doubts plagued her. She hated them, hated herself for entertaining them, but she couldn't help wondering if it had been a mistake to let him make love to her. She knew it had been a sin, a betrayal of her wedding vows, but in her heart, it had *felt* so right. She was hopelessly, helplessly, in love with him. Had she been wrong to think he felt the same? Had his kisses, his sweet words, all been lies?

A long sigh shuddered through her. Blinking back tears, she was about to extinguish the lamp when there was a knock at the door.

Hope flared in her heart as she jumped out of bed, wrapped a blanket around her shoulders, and went to the door. "Who is it?"

"Me. Jesse."

At last. Clutching the blanket with one hand, she unlocked the door. "Jesse!" Her gaze ran over him. His shirt and pants were damp. "What have you been doing?"

"Walking."

"In the rain?"

He nodded.

With a shake of her head, she stepped away from the door. "Come in."

He stepped inside and she closed the door.

"You'll catch a chill," she said, though it really wasn't very cold. Without thinking, she wrapped the blanket she had been using around his shoulders. Too late, she remembered she was wearing nothing but her chemise.

Jesse grinned as a becoming blush pinked her cheeks.

Kaylynn stared at him, wondering why she was so embarrassed. They had made love not long ago.

"Want the blanket back?" Jesse asked.

Kaylynn shook her head. "No. Keep it." She sat down on the bed and drew the covers over herself. "Where did you go?"

"Nowhere."

Pulling Ravenhawk's gun from his waistband, he placed it on the top of the dresser, then crossed the floor.

Kaylynn wrinkled her nose when he sat down on the edge of the mattress. "You've been drinking."

"Yeah. A little."

"A little?"

"All right. A lot."

"You smell like a saloon."

"How would you know?"

"I guess I don't. Is everything all right?"

He shook his head, his gaze moving over her. What could be right when she belonged to someone else?

"You should get out of those damp clothes," Kaylynn said. "You'll catch your death."

"It doesn't matter," he said with a shrug.

"It matters to me."

"Does it?"

"You know it does."

"Kay . . ." He clenched his fists to keep from reaching for her. She was beautiful, so beautiful. Her hair fell over her shoulders; her skin glowed luminously in the light of the lamp. Damn. He stood abruptly. "I'd better go."

"No." She reached out and grabbed his hand. "Don't leave."

"It's for the best."

"Please, Jesse, stay with me." She didn't want to

be alone anymore. Sometimes she felt as if she'd been alone her whole life, until she met Jesse.

"Kay, I can't stay here and not touch you . . . want you." He swore softly. "I'd better go."

"Stay," she whispered. "Stay with me."

He nodded, and she looked up at him, her smile more radiant than the sun, and he knew he couldn't leave her, knew he would do anything she asked, anything at all, just to see her smile.

Unbuckling his gunbelt, he tossed it on the chair, then sat down on the bed and removed his boots. He took off his shirt, too. His pants were cold and damp, but he left them on.

Leaning back against the wall, he slid his arm around Kaylynn's shoulders and drew her up against him. She snuggled close to him, her head resting against his chest, one of her legs pressed to his. He could feel the warmth of her breast, the length of her leg through the blankets, smell the faint, lingering fragrance of the soap she had bathed with.

"Kay . . ."

She looked up at him, her eyes filled with love and longing, and he felt something stir deep inside him, felt a crack in the wall he had hidden behind since he lost Abigail all those years ago.

"I love you, Jesse."

"Don't. I'm no good for you."

"You're perfect for me."

When she looked at him like that, eyes shining with hope and love, he could almost believe it.

"You're not going to leave Ravenhawk in jail, are you?"

"Still worrying about him?" Jesse asked, unable to keep the edge of jealousy out of his tone.

"He saved our lives."

"Did he?"

"You know he did. He kept Mazza busy so I could hit him over the head."

"He wants you."

"I can't help that."

"No, I guess not," Jesse allowed. He kissed the top of her head. "I guess every man who sees you wants you."

She tilted her head back so she could see him better. "But I only want you."

Jesse blew out a deep breath. "What about your husband?"

"I'm never going back to him! Never. I'm going to sue for a bill of divorcement when I get home."

"And what if he won't give it to you?"

"I don't know."

"Come away with me, Kay. We'll go away some-where, make a life for ourselves."

"That sounds wonderful," she said, sighing, "but I have to go home. I want to see my parents again. I want to divorce Alan so you and I can be mar-ried . . ."

Her voice trailed off and a rush of heat pinked her cheeks. "I'm sorry. You never . . . I mean . . ."

"Kaylynn."

"It's all right." She looked away, embarrassed. He had never mentioned marriage. Just because he had made love to her didn't mean he wanted to marry her, spend his life with her.

"Kay." He cupped her chin in one hand and lifted her face toward his. "I'd marry you now if I could. You know that, don't you?"

She looked up at him, the memory of the night they had spent making love burning bright in her memory. Her mother had always said that intimacy wasn't the same for a woman as it was for a man, that when a woman gave her body to a man, she gave him her heart and soul as well, but that wasn't always true for men, that they were often ruled by lust.

"Kay, I never meant to shame you," Jesse said. "Or hurt you."

"You didn't."

"I think maybe I did."

"No, Jesse. It was wonderful."

He held her tighter. "All right, Kay, I'll take you home."

"Jesse?" She slid her fingertips over his chest, ran her hand over the muscle in his arm. "If Alan won't give me a divorce, I'll go away with you. Anywhere you want."

"Kay!" Wrapping her in his arms, he kissed her with all the love and hope in his heart and knew that, even though he would never be worthy of her, he would never willingly let her go.

Kay snuggled deeper under the covers. She had been having the most wonderful dream and she didn't want to wake up, didn't want to face reality. She had been dreaming about Jesse, and in her dream she had composed a poem.

Eyes tightly shut, she tried to remember the words.

"In the quiet of the night," she began, "when in dreams my spirit wanders . . . his soul finds mine . . . and together we go walking.

"Hand in hand we share the night, where in dreams I'm free to say . . . the words I dare not speak . . . when we meet in the light of day.

"We walk through flowered meadows . . . and pause by starlit streams . . . and our bodies come together . . . but only in my dreams."

That wasn't true anymore, she mused, remembering the day by the lake when Jesse had kissed her. She had read him a poem that day; now she was composing one. The thought made her giggle.

"And so I hurry through each day . . . and long for sleep's embrace . . . when again our souls can touch . . . and I can see his face;

"And taste again his lips on mine . . . as our hearts and souls entwine . . . and know that here, within my dreams . . . he always will be mine."

He always will be mine. The thought made her smile.

"Kay?"

"Jesse!" Her eyes flew open and she stared up at him. "How long have you been standing there?"

"Long enough, sleepyhead." He grinned at her as he sat down on the edge of the bed. "Do you always recite poetry first thing in the morning?"

"Not always." In spite of her embarrassment, she felt a thrill of excitement stir in the depths of her being as she gazed up at him. He was dressed, his gunbelt in place. The beginnings of a beard shaded his jaw, giving him a faintly roguish look.

"Hi," she said again, and slipping her hands around his neck, she drew his head down and kissed him.

They hadn't made love last night, though they had slept in each other's arms. She knew somehow that he would not make love to her again until they were married, or until they knew for a certainty that Alan would not give her a divorce.

Joy swelled within her as his mouth closed over

hers. She loved him, loved him with every breath in her body, every beat of her heart.

"I liked the poem." Leaning down, he feathered kisses along her throat. "Is it from that book you told me about?"

"No."

"No?"

She shook her head. "I just . . ." She shrugged. "I just made it up."

"Oh?" He looked at her, one brow arched. "And what inspired you to recite poetry first thing in the morning?"

She stared up at him, mute, her cheeks redder than Georgia clay. It didn't take a genius to figure out what she was thinking.

"I think you'd better get dressed," Jesse said, his voice husky, all his good intentions of the night before weakening.

"I think you're right."

"I'll wait for you in the hall."

She nodded, saddened because they weren't going to make love, touched by his willingness to wait, by his understanding of her feelings.

He kissed her once more, quickly, and then left the room.

Hank Frey was hunched over his desk, sorting through a pile of papers, when Jesse entered his office.

Frey glanced up. "Be right with you."

There was a bulletin board on one wall. Crossing the floor, Jesse glanced over the wanted posters. He grunted softly when he saw that Phil Barnett had escaped from jail. The man was as slippery as an eel and just as hard to hang on to.

Well, some other hunter could go after him this time, Jesse mused. He was through chasing outlaws.

"You'll need to sign these forms," Frey said. He pushed a stack of papers across the desk. "The Mazza brothers were worth five hundred each. Three hundred for Claudill. Four hundred for Nash. Polk and Talbot were each worth two hundred. That brings the total to two thousand, one hundred dollars."

Jesse whistled softly. He hadn't expected it to come to that much.

Going to the desk, he dipped a pen in the ink well and signed his name where the sheriff indicated.

Frey nodded as Jesse signed the last paper. "That should do it." Opening his desk drawer, he withdrew a small money bag and handed it to Jesse. "I'll need you to count it and sign for it."

Jesse quickly did as he was bidden. Twenty-one hundred dollars. He signed the receipt, and then signed another paper for Ravenhawk's release.

"I guess that's everything," Frey said. "I'll get your prisoner."

"Obliged."

Jesse pulled a set of handcuffs out of his back pocket as Ravenhawk emerged from the cellblock, followed by the lawman.

Keeping his face impassive, he handcuffed Ravenhawk.

"Well, good luck to you," Frey said.

"Thanks. Obliged for all your help."

"No problem."

Frey and Jesse shook hands, then Jesse ushered Ravenhawk out of the jail and across the street to where Kaylynn was waiting for them. The rain had stopped during the night, and the sky was a bright, clear blue.

"I'm surprised you didn't tell him I was involved in that bank robbery in Silverton while you were at it," Ravenhawk muttered angrily.

"I thought about it," Jesse retorted, "but we made a deal."

"Yeah, we had a deal, all right. I kept my end. You broke yours when you let the sheriff lock me up."

"And just what did you expect me to do? Frey recognized you from Mazza's hideout. I could have let him take you in for the Twin Bluffs robbery, you know. The way I look at it, I saved you from doing some hard time behind bars. As far as I'm concerned, I kept my end of the deal."

Ravenhawk regarded Yellow Thunder for a moment, wondering if he could believe the bounty hunter. After all, Yellow Thunder had believed him not long ago. "So, what now?"

"We're leaving town," Jesse replied. "The stage pulls out in about ten minutes."

"Where's my horse? I'm not leaving him behind."

"I asked Hays to hitch 'em to the coach."

Kaylynn smiled at the two men as they approached. "Everything all right?"

"Fine." Jesse picked up his saddlebags and Kaylynn's carpetbag. "Let's go."

"This is damned embarrassing," Ravenhawk muttered as they crossed the muddy street toward the stage depot. "How about taking these damned cuffs off me?"

"Later," Jesse said.

When they reached the station, Jesse went to check on his roan and Ravenhawk's Appaloosa, which were tethered behind the coach. Tossing his saddlebags and Kaylynn's satchel into the rear boot, he nodded at the driver as he rounded the coach.

It was with a great deal of reluctance that Kaylynn climbed inside the Concord after Ravenhawk.

"I said I wouldn't do this again," she muttered as she sat down and settled her skirts around her.

"Third time's a charm," Jesse said as he took his place beside her.

The coach was about to leave when John Porter climbed inside.

"Morning, folks," he said. He smiled at Kaylynn. "Hope this trip won't be as exciting as the last one."

The driver poked his head inside the open doorway. "Everybody all set in there? Good."

A moment later the coach lurched forward.

"How are you, Mr. Porter?" Kaylynn asked.

"Fine, fine." He rubbed his shoulder. "Doc says I'll be good as new in a week or so."

"I'm glad to hear it."

Porter nodded. "Where are you folks traveling to?"

"New York City," Kaylynn replied.

"Business?"

"No, I'm going to see my parents."

"So, Porter, where are you headed?" Jesse asked.

"New York," Porter said. "Business for me, I'm afraid."

Jesse regarded Porter thoughtfully, a niggling

suspicion forming in the back of his mind. Porter met his gaze squarely, then settled into a corner of the seat and closed his eyes. A few minutes later, he was snoring softly.

Ravenhawk glared at Jesse. "Turn me loose, dammit," he hissed.

"Shut up," Jesse replied quietly. "You're lucky I didn't leave you in jail where you belong."

"Quit it, both of you," Kaylynn said. "Honestly, you two squabble worse than a couple of kids."

"Yeah, well, we had a deal," Ravenhawk said crossly. "I kept my part of the bargain. I'm still waiting for him to keep his."

"A deal?" Kaylynn asked. "What kind of deal?"

Ravenhawk glanced at Porter, who was still snoring. "I told Jesse I'd help him get you away from Mazza if he'd let me go afterwards. And he agreed."

Kaylynn looked at Jesse. "Is that right?"

"Yeah."

"Then why is he handcuffed?"

Jesse grinned. "I figured it was the best way to make sure he kept his hands off you."

Kaylynn blushed. "Jesse, really."

"Yeah," he said. "Really."

"What's the matter, bounty hunter? Afraid I'll steal her from you?"

"I'd keep my mouth shut, if I were you," Jesse said mildly, "unless I wanted to find myself in jail in the next town."

Ravenhawk started to speak; then, apparently deciding he had pushed Yellow Thunder as far as he dared, he settled back in his seat, took a deep breath, and closed his eyes.

* * *

The trip to the next town passed uneventfully, for which Kaylynn was heartily grateful. Ravenhawk was morosely silent. Jesse stared out the window, his face impassive. She wondered what he was thinking, but something warned her not to ask.

Upon waking from his nap, John Porter had tried to engage Jesse in conversation and when that failed, he pulled a penny dreadful from his coat pocket, and spent the rest of the time reading about the adventures of Kid Curry.

It was near dark when they reached Acworth Corners. The driver told them there would be a thirty-minute layover while they changed horses and picked up passengers.

Porter asked the driver if he knew if the telegraph office was still open, and was told he might make it, if he hurried.

Porter offered the man his thanks, tipped his hat at Kaylynn, and hurried across the street.

Jesse waited by the coach until a man came by to unhook the team. "Look after my horse, will ya?" Jesse asked. "See that she gets some grain and a rubdown."

"Sure," the man said agreeably. "What about the other one?"

"I'll be leaving the Appaloosa here."

"Yes, sir."

With the roan's comfort taken care of, Jesse turned his attention to Ravenhawk. "Let's go."

"Go where?"

"Just come with me. Kaylynn, go on over to the hotel and order us something to eat."

"What are you going to do?" she asked.

"Just do as I said. I'll be along in a few minutes."

With a sigh of exasperation, she flounced across the street.

"Now what?" Ravenhawk asked.

"Let's go." Jesse took up the Appaloosa's lead rope and started walking toward the end of town. "I'm turning you loose. I'm warning you for the last time to stay out of my way."

Ravenhawk grunted softly, but said nothing. When they reached the end of town, Jesse stepped behind the last building, dug the handcuff key out of his pocket, and unlocked the cuffs.

Ravenhawk rubbed his wrists, a wary expression on his face.

"Here." Jesse handed Ravenhawk a buckskin bag. "That's half the reward money." He thrust the Appaloosa's reins into Ravenhawk's hand. "Now get the hell out of here."

"What about my gun?"

Casually, Jesse tossed Ravenhawk his gun.

Feeling the lightness of the weapon in his hand, Ravenhawk spun the cylinder with his thumb and noted that each chamber was empty. He looked at Yellow Thunder, a faint smile curving his lips.

"I may be crazy," Jesse drawled, "but I'm not stupid enough to put a loaded gun in your hand."

With a nod, Ravenhawk swung onto the Appaloosa's back. "We've had our differences, bounty hunter," he said as he turned the Appaloosa toward the north, "but you'll do to ride the river with."

Jesse stood there until Ravenhawk was out of sight. "So will you," he muttered as he turned back toward town. "So will you."

* * *

289

Kaylynn watched Jesse enter the dining room, her expression worried as he crossed the floor and sat down beside her.

"Is everything all right?" she asked.

"Fine. What did you order?"

"Steak. What happened?"

"Nothing happened."

"Nothing? Where's Ravenhawk? You didn't take him to jail?"

"No."

"Well?" she asked impatiently.

"I let him go. Now, can we drop the subject?"

"Jesse, honestly, you make me so mad sometimes."

"Do I?"

"Why are you so jealous of him?"

It was a good question. He only wished he had a good answer. When he put his reasons into words, they sounded ridiculous. Ravenhawk was young. He was charming. He was handsome, with his dark eyes and unscarred face. But the real reason for his jealousy was the fact that Kaylynn worried about Ravenhawk far too much, and that drove Jesse wild. He didn't want her thinking of any man but him, wanting any man but him.

"Jesse, there's no reason for you to be jealous. You know that, don't you?"

He nodded. He did know, but he couldn't help it.

Their meal arrived a few moments later and they ate quickly, knowing the stage wouldn't wait for them.

John Porter was already in the coach when they climbed inside.

Jesse pulled a blanket from beneath the seat and

spread it over Kaylynn, then slipped his arm around her shoulders.

"Where's your prisoner?" Porter asked, frowning.

"I dropped him off here," Jesse replied smoothly.

"I see."

From outside, the driver yelled, "All aboard!"

Moments later, they were on their way.

Chapter Twenty-nine

William Duvall shuffled the papers on his desk; then, with a sweep of his hand, he wiped the desktop clean. How could he be expected to concentrate on business when his daughter, his only child, had been missing for almost a year? Perhaps longer, for all he knew.

He swore, long and loud, unable to believe that Alan Summers had never bothered to get in touch with them, never thought it important enough to let them know she was missing.

William had been concerned for some time, wondering why Kaylynn's letters were so infrequent. He had made excuses for her. She was busy getting settled into a new house, busy exploring an exciting new city, making new friends. Alan was a prominent man in San Francisco. There would be parties and dinners.

Three years ago they had invited Alan and Kaylynn to spend Christmas with them. Alan had sent a letter, making excuses.

Two years ago, Alan had refused another invitation to spend the holidays with them. Thinking Alan might be having financial problems, William had sent two tickets with the invitation he had sent last year. Alan had returned the tickets, along with a curt note of regret, stating that business was such that he could not afford to leave town.

William had gotten suspicious when Alan had declined to attend a party celebrating Grandmother Dearmond's seventieth birthday, but he hadn't gotten truly worried until six months ago, when he wrote Kaylynn to tell her that her grandmother was ill and had gotten no reply at all. It was then that he knew something was wrong. Even if Alan had somehow poisoned his wife's mind against her parents, Kaylynn would have come home to see her grandmother, or at least written to express her concern. Kaylynn and Grandmother Dearmond had always been close.

Rising, he began to pace the floor, the sound of his footsteps seeming unusually loud in the room. It was Sunday, and the building was empty. He had come to the office to catch up on some work, but it had been a waste of time.

Going to the window, he stared out at the street. He had never trusted Alan Summers, never liked the man. Without telling Elizabeth, he had hired a detective to go to San Francisco and check on Kaylynn's welfare. The man had been gone four months. On returning, the detective had reported that, in all that time, he had seen no sign of Kaylynn. He had gone to the house himself on one occasion, passing himself off as a census taker. A maid had answered the door and ushered him inside, where he had spoken to a woman, but it had not been Kaylynn. He had sent others to the house on various errands. None of them had ever seen Kaylynn.

William glanced at the photograph on his desk. It was a picture of Kaylynn taken on her wedding day. His little girl. She looked like a fairy-tale princess in a froth of white satin and lace.

He smiled, remembering how she had loved to play dress-up and make-believe. Once, the house had echoed with the sound of her happy laughter. She had liked to pretend she was a doctor, to lay her dolls in a row on the bed and pretend they were sick, or hurt. He recalled the baby bird she had found, the long hours she had spent caring for it, how surprised he had been that it hadn't died. She had cried the day it flew away. His heart ached when he remembered how she had followed him around the house. She had loved to wear his slippers, to play with his pipes, to sit on his lap while he read to her.

Where was she now?

Chapter Thirty

By the time the stage arrived in Cedar Junction, Kaylynn was heartily sick of the constant jarring and bouncing, the curses of the driver, the hurried meals, which always included beans, the impossibility of getting a good night's sleep aboard a moving stagecoach, and the grit that seeped inside her shoes and her clothes. The coach grew more crowded. At one time, there were nine people crammed inside, including three young children who wiggled and whined the whole time.

At one stop, while waiting for fresh horses, Kaylynn read a brief account of riding on a stagecoach that had been written by Mark Twain, which described a stagecoach as "a cradle on wheels." He went on to say, "We rode atop of the flying coach, dangled our legs over the side and leveled an outlook over the world-wide carpet about us for things new and strange to gaze at. It thrills me to think of the life and the wild sense of freedom of those fine overland mornings."

But Kaylynn found the ride neither thrilling nor exciting. Fifteen inches of seat, with a fat man on one side, and a lady with a colicky baby across the aisle, was not her idea of fun.

She stood on the stage station platform while Jesse retrieved their luggage, such as it was, and his horse.

As always, their first stop was a livery barn. From there, they went to the railway depot, where he purchased two tickets at a cost of three hundred and fifty dollars and secured a place for the roan in the stock car.

"Wouldn't it be easier for you to just buy another horse?" Kaylynn asked as they left the depot and began walking down the street.

"Maybe," Jesse said, settling his saddlebags over his shoulder, "but I spent a lot of time training that mare. We've ridden a lot of miles together."

"Oh. How long will it take to reach New York?"

"Three days. They gave me two berths, an upper and a lower. You can have your pick."

"Either one is fine."

"So, what do you want first?" Jesse asked. "A hot bath, or a decent meal?"

"A bath," she said without hesitation.

"A bath it is," Jesse said, and taking her by the arm, he led her across the street to the hotel.

It was far more luxurious than the hotel in Twin Bluffs. Thick oriental carpets covered the highly polished hardwood floors in the lobby. Heavy maroon draperies hung at the windows. Several high-backed sofas covered in rich damask provided places for guests to sit and read the newspaper or chat with other guests. An ornate chandelier hung from the ceiling.

A clerk dressed in a dark brown tweed suit and mustard-colored cravat greeted them from behind a shiny mahogany desk.

"May I help you, sir?" His voice was carefully polite as he tried not to stare at the scar on Jesse's face.

"I'd like two rooms, adjoining."

"Yes, sir." The clerk placed a thick leatherbound book on the desk and flipped it open. "If you'll just sign here."

Taking the pen the man offered, Jesse signed their names. "The lady would like a bath."

"Of course," The clerk smiled at Kaylynn. "The bathing room is at the end of the corridor on the second floor. Here is the key."

"Thank you."

"I'll have the tub filled right away. You'll find clean towels on the shelf."

Kaylynn nodded.

Turning, the clerk plucked two keys from the board behind him. "Rooms 107 and 109, adjoining. I trust you will find them satisfactory."

Jesse nodded, acutely aware of the clerk's curious gaze.

"How long will you be staying with us?"

"Just overnight."

"Very good, sir."

Taking Kaylynn's carpetbag, Jesse walked briskly toward the long curved stairway.

"Jesse, wait!"

He paused at the foot of the stairs, giving her

time to catch up with him. He was used to people staring, used to seeing the questions in their eyes, questions they didn't have the nerve to ask. He didn't know why the clerk's curious glances bothered him so much now, but they did.

Kaylynn laid her hand on his arm. "What's wrong?"

Jesse shook his head and started up the stairs, and she trailed behind him, one hand sliding up the polished banister. "Jesse?"

"Forget it." He reached the landing and glanced up and down, then turned to the left and walked down the hallway.

Room 107 was located halfway down the corridor on the left side. Jesse opened the door, then handed Kaylynn her satchel. "Leave the water in the tub."

"I'm sure they'll refill the tub for you."

Jesse shrugged. "No need. Just rap on my door when you're done."

"All right." She studied his face a moment, then went into her room and closed the door, wondering what was wrong.

Taking the blue muslin dress from her bag, she went down the hallway to the bathing room. Inside, she found a stool, a large enameled tub filled with steamy water, several fluffy white towels, and a bar of lavender-scented soap.

She sat down on the stool and removed her hat, boots, garters, and stockings. Rising, she removed her traveling suit and undergarments and laid them over the stool.

She put one foot in the tub, then sighed with pleasure as she stepped in and sank down, letting the deliciously hot water close over her. Was there anything that felt as wonderful, she mused, and then smiled. Yes, she thought. Jesse's arms around her, the gentle touch of his hand in her hair, the heat of his kisses, his breath fanning her cheek, his weight pressing her down as he whispered that he adored her. . . .

A warmth that had nothing to do with the temperature of the water suffused her. Jesse . . . He was the most wonderful man she had ever known. She thought of him constantly, dreamed of him, yearned to touch him, to be in his arms, to hear his voice. She loved the sound of his voice, his laugh. She shook her head. Admit it, she thought. You love him. You love everything about him.

She would have lingered in the tub until the water cooled but, wanting the water to still be hot for Jesse, she washed quickly and stepped from the tub.

She towel-dried her hair, then dressed in the blue muslin. Gathering up her traveling suit, she left the room and went down the hall to knock on Jesse's door.

He seemed surprised to see her. "Finished so soon?" he asked.

She shrugged. "The water's still hot, if you hurry."

"Thanks."

"Jesse, what's wrong?"

"What do you mean?"

"Why are you so distant? Have I done something wrong?"

"No, Kaylynn. You haven't done anything. Let me get washed up, and then we'll go get something to eat."

"All right."

*   *   *

He came for her a short time later, and they went down to the hotel dining room. The dining room was as plush as the rest of the hotel. Starched linen cloths covered the tables. The chairs were covered in forest-green velvet. Curtains hung at the windows. There were fresh flowers on each table, crystal and silver and china instead of the speckled blue enamel and tin she'd become accustomed to on the trail.

She ordered fried chicken. Jesse ordered a steak, rare. She asked for a glass of milk. He asked for coffee, black.

"Oh, look," she said, "there's John Porter."

Jesse grunted softly as he saw the man take a seat at a nearby table. Porter nodded at him, and smiled at Kaylynn.

"Maybe I should ask him to join us," Kaylynn suggested, "so he won't have to eat alone."

Jesse shook his head. There was something about Porter that bothered him, though he couldn't put his finger on it. Still, his instincts had never proven wrong, and there was something about the man that didn't ring true.

After dinner, they took a stroll through the town, then returned to the hotel.

At her door, Jesse drew her into his arms and kissed her. "Sweet dreams, darlin'."

She smiled up at him. "All of you."

"Good night, Kay."

"Night, Jesse."

He was about to kiss her again when he heard footsteps. Turning, he saw John Porter walking toward them.

"Evening," Porter said. He stopped at the door

across from Kaylynn's and pulled a key from his pocket. "See you two in the morning," he said, and unlocking the door, he went inside and shut the door behind him.

Jesse swore under his breath.

"What's wrong?" Kaylynn asked.

"I don't know." Jesse shook his head. He kissed her again. "Lock your door. I'll see you in the morning."

There were only two hotels in town. It could just be coincidence that Porter was staying in this hotel, that he had the room directly across from Kay's. But Jesse had never believed in coincidences.

They boarded the train after an early breakfast. Kaylynn felt a sense of excitement as she took her seat and looked out the window. For the first time, she really believed she was going to make it home again. She hadn't seen her parents in over six years. She wondered if they had changed much, if the house was the same, if Mrs. Moseley was still there.

She had written home every month, but letters from her parents had been rare. She had consoled herself as best she could, telling herself that her father was busy with his job at the bank and his nights at his club, that her mother was involved in seeing to the affairs of the house and hosting parties and organizing her charity work at the orphanage.

A cry of "All aboard!", a grinding of gears and wheels, and the train began to move.

"Here we go," Jesse said.

She grinned. He didn't sound very excited, but

she was. Home. She was going home.

She turned away from the window at the sound of a familiar voice and smiled as John Porter sat down in the seat across from them.

He returned her smile. "We seem destined to travel together," he remarked.

"Yes, indeed," Kaylynn replied.

"At least we have a nice day for it."

Kaylynn nodded. "Is this your first trip to New York?"

"Yes, it is. I'm looking forward to it. I believe you said you were visiting your parents?"

"That's right. I haven't seen them for several years."

"Will you be staying long?"

"As long as they'll let me."

"I see." Porter looked at Jesse. "I'll wager this is your first visit to New York, too."

Jesse nodded, every instinct he possessed warning him that Porter was not what he appeared.

Porter turned his attention back to Kaylynn. "Perhaps I could persuade you to show me the town."

Jesse slid his arm around Kaylynn's shoulders. "I'm afraid the lady will be too busy," he said.

Porter held up his hands in a gesture of surrender. "I didn't mean any offense. I just thought the three of us might spend a little time sightseeing."

Kaylynn looked at Jesse, puzzled by his rude behavior. He met her gaze with an imperceptible shake of his head.

"I'm sorry, Mr. Porter, but I'm afraid Jesse is right. I won't have much free time. You understand."

"Of course, of course. Well, if you'll excuse me,

I think I'll go have a cigar." Rising, he tipped his hat at Kaylynn, then made his way down the aisle toward the smoking car.

Kaylynn looked at Jesse. "What was that all about?"

Jesse looked back to make sure Porter was out of earshot. "There's something about Porter that doesn't sit right," he remarked, turning back to Kaylynn.

"What do you mean? He seems all right to me. He's certainly friendly enough."

"Yeah, a little too friendly, if you ask me."

"Are you always so suspicious of people?"

"Not always."

Kaylynn grinned at him. "Just most of the time?"

Jesse shrugged. "I guess it comes with the territory."

"What do you mean?"

"You hunt outlaws long enough, you begin to think all men are cut from the same shoddy cloth."

"Maybe it's time to quit."

He looked at her for stretched seconds, and then he nodded. "I've been thinking the same thing."

"Oh, Jesse!" Unmindful of the fact that they weren't alone, she threw her arms around his neck and kissed him.

She might have kissed him forever if the little boy sitting behind them hadn't said, in a very loud voice, "Mama, look! Those people are kissing!"

Embarrassed, Kaylynn scooted away from Jesse. "I'm sorry," she stammered. "I . . ."

"Don't be sorry on my account," Jesse replied, squeezing her hand. "You can kiss me anywhere, any time."

Face flushed, Kaylynn turned and stared out the soot-smudged window. The tall prairie grasses seemed to cover the earth like a winter blanket. The land was mostly flat and barren now. She saw a lone Indian riding in the distance. As she watched, he spurred his pony into a gallop, disappearing from sight as he descended a low hill. She wondered if there was a hunting party close by, if he was a "wolf" sent out to keep the herd moving in the right direction. Mo'e'ha had told her they called the scouts wolves because the Cheyenne had noticed the way the wolves hunted, and adopted their tactics. A lone wolf had no chance of bringing down a healthy adult buffalo, but a pack working together could circle the herd and pick off the weaker animals.

She closed her eyes, thinking of the months she had spent with the Cheyenne. Never again would she live such a simple life. New York City was like a different world. Could she really go back and take up where she had left off?

Her bittersweet memories of the past were interrupted by the shrill scream of the train's whistle, and she was suddenly aware of voices rising all around her.

She looked at Jesse. He had stood up, and now he was at her shoulder, staring out the window.

"What's happening?" she asked. She looked out the window again, but all she saw was a cloud of dust off in the distance.

"Buffalo!" he exclaimed.

"Buffalo?" Kaylynn wiped off the inside of the window, then leaned forward for a better look. The churning dust cloud now looked as though it was peppered with hundreds of black dots. She jumped as the whistle blew again, and then again.

"They're heading for the tracks," Kaylynn said. She looked up at Jesse. She had seen a buffalo stampede, seen the damage they could do.

Jesse swore a short, pithy oath. Shrugging off his long black duster, he grabbed his rifle from the overhead compartment.

"Where are you going?" Kaylynn asked.

"I'm gonna try and turn the herd." He had to shout to be heard over the incessant shriek of the whistle.

Kaylynn glanced out the window again. Unless the buffalo turned aside, the herd was on a collision course with the train. She had a quick mental image of the engine slamming into the herd, of the train derailing, killing passengers and buffalo alike.

There was a low hum of conversation as the other passengers became aware of what was going on. The little boy sitting behind her began to cry.

Jesse sprinted down the aisle and opened the door, only to come face to face with John Porter.

Porter glanced at the rifle in Jesse's hand. "What's going on?"

"Get out of my way," Jesse said, pushing past the man. "I don't have time to explain."

Jesse opened the connecting door and stepped onto the narrow platform that formed the walkway into the next passenger car. The wind whipped his hair into his face as he climbed the ladder to the top of the car. Steadying himself on the roof, he surveyed the situation.

It was a big herd, though not as big as the ones he had seen in his youth. In recent years, buffalo hunters had taken their toll on the herds, killing them by the thousands for the hides and the tongues, leaving thousands of pounds of fresh meat to rot on the prairie. Once, when he'd been young and foolish, he had crept into the middle of a herd and sat motionless while they moved around him, so close he could feel their breath on his face, so close he had felt the hair along his nape prickle at the thought of being trampled beneath the large bulls. Another time he had stood on a rock and watched them pass by, close enough that he could have reached out and touched them. Once, he had come face-to-face with a large old bull. He had stood motionless for what seemed like hours while the buffalo decided what to make of him. Finally, the animal had turned and walked away.

Jesse shook off the memories. The engineer was still blowing the whistle in a desperate attempt to turn the herd, but to no avail. They were coming hard and fast.

They were too far away for his rifle to be effective, and Jesse knew he would have to make his way to the front of the train. Bending low, he ran across the roof of the passenger car. His lungs filled with the acrid scent of smoke, and he cussed the man who had invented the iron horse. What kind of fool felt the need to travel so fast? White men were always in a hurry. They never took the time to appreciate the beauty of the land. Riding a horse was a much more satisfying way to travel, and much safer.

He jumped onto the next car and ran along the roof, cursing as his foot slipped. One more jump put him on the first passenger car, just behind the wood box. He could see the engineer leaning out the window, waving one hand in a useless attempt to shoo the herd away.

"Won't do any good!" Jesse yelled as he dropped to one knee near the front edge of the car.

Startled, the portly engineer looked over his shoulder. "What the hell are you doing?"

"Gonna shoot me a buffalo," Jesse replied. "Stop blowing that damn whistle. I can't hear myself think."

"You're crazy!"

The word stuck in Jesse's craw like an unripe persimmon, and he slowly brought the rifle to bear on the engineer. "Stop blowing that damn whistle," he repeated.

The engineer ducked back inside the car, and the whistle went silent.

With a smile, Jesse lifted the rifle to his shoulder. He had to pick the right animal. The herd, most likely stampeded by an Indian hunting party, would follow the leader in whatever direction it went. The Lakota often purposely stampeded a herd toward a cliff, knowing the main body of the herd would follow the lead animal. He recalled the lone Indian he had seen earlier. No doubt it had been a "wolf" sent out to scout the herd's whereabouts.

Jesse whirled around at a sound behind him. Looking down the barrel of the rifle, he was surprised to see John Porter crawling toward him. "What are you doing here?"

"I came to help," Porter replied.

"I don't need your help," Jesse said as he turned his attention back to the oncoming herd.

"Well, your lady was worried about you. I told

her I'd see what I could do to help. I brought my rifle."

Jesse glanced at Porter. He didn't like the man. Porter was intrusive and nosy and that didn't sit well with Jesse, but another gun would be welcome just now. "Can you use that rifle?"

"Been known to," Porter replied.

"Good. When I start shooting, drop as many of the lead animals as you can, as quickly as you can."

Porter inched up beside Jesse and leveled his rifle at the herd. "Do you think it will really do any good?"

"I don't know. All we can do is drop the animals in front and hope the others will turn aside. It's the only chance we have of turning 'em away from the tracks."

"When you're ready then," Porter said.

Jesse grunted. There was no time to stop the train now. The engineer had never even applied the brakes, apparently hoping to beat the buffalo to the point of contact. But there was no chance of that now. If the train collided with the herd, it would surely be derailed; if the herd slammed into the side of the train, there was a pretty good chance the train would remain on the tracks.

They were within range now, and Jesse was sure he had spotted the lead buffalo. It was a large bull. Its furry shanks showed the weathering of many winters. Jesse couldn't help admiring the beauty of the animal as it ran, nostrils flaring as it led its unwary followers toward certain destruction.

Jesse leaned forward, steadying his forward arm on his knee as he sighted down the barrel. If he were still living with the Cheyenne, it would be an honorable kill, one to brag about around the campfires after the hunt. He would tell of the strength of the great beast, and his own skill as he steadied himself for the shot. The women would flock to the side of the downed animal, cut out the liver from the still-warm flesh and offer it to him as a reward of the hunt. He smiled at the thought of the sweet taste.

Porter was growing more and more nervous as the seconds passed. How close were they going to allow the herd to get before they began shooting? Sweat trickled down his forehead and soaked his shirt.

Jesse measured the distance between the train and the herd. He had to be sure they were within rifle range before he began firing. They couldn't afford to waste ammunition firing at ghosts in the dust. His finger slowly squeezed the trigger.

The sound of Jesse's Winchester startled Porter for a second, and then, sighting down the barrel of his own rifle, he fired his first shot.

Jesse's rifle bucked in his hands, and with every shot, a buffalo went down. The scene was chaotic as the animals began to tumble over the carcasses at the head of the stampede. The herd seemed determined to cross the tracks, and Jesse kept firing.

Abruptly, the herd turned. Jesse ceased firing, and so did Porter. Jesse watched the buffalo run, experiencing the same sense of awe he had felt when he was a young boy seeing his first stampede, amazed anew that the buffalo, which looked so large and cumbersome, were capable of such speed, of turning so quickly. It was a sight to behold as the tail of the herd began to twist like a giant hairy snake, writhing across the prairie.

"We did it!" Porter exclaimed. He was about to congratulate Jesse on a job well done when a handful of buffalo, unable to change direction as quickly as the others, crashed into the side of the car they were on.

The impact knocked Jesse off balance. His rifle went skittering off the far side of the train as he scrambled for a handhold.

He heard Porter scream, "Help me!" and turned to see the man dangling over the side of the car.

Jesse grabbed an air vent, wincing as the sudden movement put a strain on his bruised ribs. Swinging his feet in Porter's direction, he yelled, "Grab hold of my foot!"

Hanging precariously off the edge of the train, Porter could just see the tip of Jesse's right boot. He risked a glance at the ground moving quickly beneath him and knew he was facing certain death if he lost his grip on the train. Without another thought, he lunged upward for Jesse's foot.

Jesse grunted as he felt Porter's weight tugging on his right leg as the man pulled himself up onto the car, then wrapped a hand around the air vent. Porter lay there, panting, glad to be alive. They had done it. The herd had turned and the last stragglers were moving away from the train.

Jesse looked at Porter and grinned. "Obliged for your help."

"Yeah," Porter said, with a wry grin. "Any time."

A cheer went up from the passengers when Jesse and Porter returned to the car, and then everyone was talking at once as fear turned to relief.

As Jesse made his way down the aisle toward Kaylynn, women reached out to pat his arm, calling him a hero, thanking him for saving their lives. Men slapped him on the back and offered to buy him drinks at the next stop. One man thrust a cigar into his hand.

Kaylynn smiled up at him. "You saved us."

"I had help." He glanced over his shoulder at John Porter, who was surrounded by grateful passengers. Enjoying the limelight, Porter was boasting about how they had turned the herd.

Kaylynn shook her head. "You might have fallen to your death."

Jesse shrugged, though he was pleased by her concern. "Had to be done."

Sitting down beside her, he put his arm around her, liking the way she leaned into him, the way her body felt against his. He looked deep into her eyes, warmed by the love he read there. Cupping her face in his hands, he kissed her, long and hard.

This time, no one noticed.

Chapter Thirty-one

To Kaylynn's relief, the remainder of the trip passed uneventfully. Riding on the train was much faster and more comfortable than bouncing around inside a stagecoach, though it was a little noisier. The Pullman berths were warm and snug; the food served in the depots along the way was a vast improvement over the rough fare served at stagecoach way stations.

John Porter repeated the tale of his harrowing ride atop the train to any and all who would listen. He nodded and smiled at Kaylynn when he saw her, but, apparently mindful of Jesse's unspoken warning to keep his distance, he didn't try to engage her in conversation again.

Jesse went to the stockcar once each day to check on his horse. Kaylynn found it endearing that he was so concerned for the mare. Such a gentle man, she thought, to be so brave. She would never forget how he had reacted during the crisis. He had saved John Porter, as well as the train and all its passengers. He was a true hero, and she was proud to be his lady.

They arrived in New York City shortly after ten o'clock on a warm midsummer morning.

Kaylynn collected their meager baggage while Jesse went to get his horse.

"How far is it to your parents' house?" Jesse asked.

"Not far." Kaylynn looked across from the depot, where a number of carriages for hire were parked. "Shall we rent a hack?"

Jesse's gaze slid over Kaylynn. It would have been quicker and easier to ride, but he doubted she would be comfortable on the back of his horse in her traveling suit. "Sure."

Jesse flagged down a hack. Kaylynn gave directions to the driver while Jesse tied the mare to the back of the carriage. She smiled at Jesse as he handed her into the vehicle, then climbed in beside her.

Kaylynn couldn't seem to stop smiling as the hack moved down the street. She'd made it! She looked out the window, thinking how good it was to be back where she belonged, to see women wearing fashionable clothes, to see familiar places and landmarks again.

She glanced over at Jesse. He was looking out the other window, and she wondered what he thought of the city, what he would think of her parents. What they would think of him.

Some of the joy at being back home faded when she thought of introducing Jesse to her mother and father. Her parents were nice people. She knew they would make Jesse welcome, would be grateful to him for bringing her home. But would they recognize his good qualities? Would they look past his rough exterior, his scarred face, and see him for the good man that he was?

Excitement bubbled up inside her as the hack started up the long, tree-lined road to the house. The first thing she noticed was that the shutters on the upstairs windows, which had been white when she left, were now forest green. She wondered what other changes had been made in her absence.

She fidgeted while Jesse paid the driver and untied his horse.

"Leave the mare here for now," she said, indicating he should tether the roan to a nearby tree. "Johnny will look after her."

Jesse would have argued, but he could see she was eager to go into the house. With a nod, he tied the lead rope to a sturdy branch. After picking up her satchel, he settled his saddlebags over his shoulder.

Kaylynn tugged on his hand, then turned and ran up the stairs. Opening the front door, she hurried inside, then reappeared a moment later. "Jesse, hurry!" she called impatiently.

Jesse shook his head in wry amusement as he followed her up the steps. He caught a quick glimpse of a tiled foyer papered in a dark blue print before Kaylynn grabbed him by the hand and led him into a large parlor.

"Mother? Mother, are you home?"

An elderly woman wearing a long gray dress and a crisp white apron entered the room.

"Miss Kaylynn!" she exclaimed, pressing one hand over her heart. "Lord have mercy." She glanced at Jesse, her eyes widening. "Where have you been, child? Your parents have been worried sick."

"It's a long story," Kaylynn replied. "Is mother home?"

"No, dear. She's at the orphanage. It's Wednesday, you know." Martha Moseley spoke to Kaylynn, but she was still staring at Jesse.

Kaylynn started to reprimand the woman, then bit back the words. Might as well let her look her fill and get it over with, she thought, and wondered how Jesse had stood it all these years, having people stare at him like that. She had grown accustomed to his appearance; indeed, she hardly noticed the scar anymore. When she looked at him now, all she saw was the man she loved.

"Mrs. Moseley, could you fix us something to eat, please?"

"Yes, of course, dear."

"And would you ask Johnny to look after the horse out front?" She looked at Jesse. "And make sure the horse gets a good rubdown and a quart of oats."

"Thanks," Jesse murmured.

"I'll see to it," Mrs. Moseley said. She looked at Jesse again. "Will the—uh, gentleman be staying here?"

"What? Oh, yes. Ask Cora to prepare a room, will you? The blue one, I think."

"Very well. May I take your coat, sir?" Mrs. Moseley asked.

"Sure." Jesse shrugged out of his duster and handed it to the woman.

Her eyes widened when she saw the gun holstered on his hip. Jesse looked at Kaylynn.

"You probably won't need that here," Kaylynn said, smiling. "Why don't you give it to Mrs. Moseley? She'll see that it's put in your room."

Jesse grunted softly. Placing Kaylynn's satchel on the floor, he unbuckled his gunbelt. Wrapping the thick leather belt around the holster, he held it out to the woman.

"I'll have your coat cleaned and pressed for you," Mrs. Moseley said. She draped his coat over one arm, then took the gunbelt from his hand, a look of distaste playing over her features.

"Obliged," Jesse drawled.

"I'm going to show Jesse around the house," Kaylynn said. "Ask Cora to put my bag in my room, will you?"

Mrs. Moseley nodded. She sent one last glance in Jesse's direction, then turned and left the room, holding his gunbelt away from her body as if it might bite her if it got too close.

"I don't think she likes me," Jesse remarked.

"That's all right," Kaylynn said, stroking his arm. "I like you."

"Nice place," Jesse said, glancing around. The furniture was made of gleaming mahogany covered in a dark green print that picked up the green in the flocked wallpaper. A large Oriental carpet covered most of the floor. A marble fireplace took up a good part of one wall. Knickknacks made of crystal and pewter were artfully arranged on the mantel.

"Come on," Kaylynn said, "I'll show you around."

It was a big house. Front parlor, back parlor, a dining room decorated in a deep maroon. The ballroom took up the rear half of the house. A huge crystal chandelier hung from the ceiling. One wall was mirrored, making the room seem even larger than it was. There was a large music room, a sewing room that was small only when compared to the other rooms in the house, a library stocked with hundreds of books, a den that was obviously her father's domain.

Kaylynn told him there were six bedrooms upstairs—one for her parents, hers, and four guest bedrooms.

It was the biggest, finest house Jesse had ever seen. It was also the perfect setting for Kaylynn, he thought as he watched her move from room to room, her hands touching a pillow here, a chair there, as if to prove to herself that she was really home.

Her bedroom was decorated in shades of mauve. There was a large canopy bed, a highboy made of dark cherrywood, and several shelves crowded with books and porcelain dolls and pewter figurines. A painting of a waterfall. A Tiffany lamp. There was a white porcelain tub decorated with pink roses in an adjoining room, fluffy white towels and bottles of bath salts on a shelf.

"This will be your room." Kaylynn smiled at him as she opened the door to the room across from hers.

Jesse stepped inside. Like all the others, it was

a large room. There was a comfortable-looking double bed, a four-drawer chest made of dark oak, a rocking chair, and a small table. Dark blue curtains covered the windows; a matching spread covered the bed. A small oval mirror hung over a shaving stand. There were several paintings on the walls depicting ships at sea.

"There's a sitting room through there," Kaylynn said, pointing at a door. "And a bathtub."

"It's nice," Jesse said.

"Come on, Mrs. Moseley should have fixed us something to eat by now. Wait until you taste her cooking! I hope she baked today. She makes the best pies. And cakes."

Jesse followed Kaylynn down the stairs and into a large, sunlit kitchen.

Mrs. Moseley made a tsking sound when she turned around and saw Kaylynn. "Still wanting to eat in my kitchen, I see."

Kaylynn nodded. "I'm starving."

Mrs. Moseley ran a knowing gaze over Kaylynn. "You look like you've lost some weight, but don't worry, I'll put it all back." She beamed at Kaylynn. "I must have known you were coming because . . ."

Kaylynn took a deep breath. "You baked an apple pie!"

Mrs. Moseley laughed. "Yes, I did. Now, go along with you. I can't be serving a guest in the kitchen. What would your mother say?"

Kaylynn made an aggrieved face. "She doesn't have to know."

Mrs. Moseley made a shooing motion with her hands. "Go on now."

"Come on," Kaylynn said, and taking Jesse by

the hand, she led him into the dining room. "It seems silly for the two of us to sit at this big table," she muttered.

She sat down, and Jesse sat across from her. The table was big enough to seat a dozen people comfortably.

Jesse glanced around the room. Rarely had he felt so out of his element as he did here, in this house.

A few moments later, Mrs. Moseley served them the best meal Jesse had ever eaten—sliced ham and cold chicken, potato salad, bread fresh from the oven, and warm apple pie for dessert.

"What did I tell you?" Kaylynn said, pushing her plate away.

Jesse nodded. "You were right."

The girl, Cora, came in to the clear the table a few minutes later. "Mrs. Moseley thought you might want to wash up. Kevin filled the tubs in both of your rooms."

"Tell Mrs. Moseley thank you for me," Kaylynn said. "A hot bath sounds wonderful."

"Yes, miss."

Kaylynn stood up. "Come on," she said, offering Jesse her hand.

Jesse took her hand and stood up. "I'm not sure my staying here is a good idea."

"Why not?"

He shrugged as he followed her up the stairs.

"But I want you to stay. Please, Jesse."

He nodded. If she wanted him to stay, he would.

She paused at the top of the stairs. "I'll meet you in the library in . . . hmm, an hour?"

"An hour," Jesse said.

Smiling, Kaylynn kissed him on the cheek, then

went into her bedroom and closed the door.

Jesse stared after her a moment, then went into the room that was to be his during his stay.

He stood in the middle of the floor and did a slow turn. He had stayed in some nice hotels in his time but never, in all his life, had he stayed in a room as elegant as this one.

He locked the door from force of habit. He looked at the bed, reluctant to sit on it, and then he shrugged. What the hell. Sitting on the edge of the mattress, he took off his boots, thinking they could use a good polishing. Rising, he shucked his clothes and tossed them on the bed, then padded naked into the bathroom.

Steam wafted from a porcelain tub. There were several clean towels folded on a shelf, topped by a bar of finely milled soap.

He stepped into the tub and sat down, a low sound of pleasure rising in his throat as the hot water enveloped him. Head back, arms resting on either side of the tub, he closed his eyes, imagining Kaylynn in her own room, reclining in her own bathtub. The thought flowed through him, hotter than the water that covered him.

Muttering an oath, he opened his eyes, scattering the images. He had known she came from a well-to-do family, but seeing her home, the way she lived, made him realize anew just how wrong he was for her. He would never fit in her world. She deserved a man who came from a similar background, one who had similar interests.

He glanced around the room. A man could get used to this kind of life right quick if he wasn't careful, he mused. So he'd have to careful.

* * *

Kaylynn drew her finger across the surface of the water, spelling Jesse's name, wondering if he was also taking a bath. The thought made her warm all over. Jesse. He loved her. Had made love to her. She smiled, and then giggled. She'd never been in love like this before. He was in every thought, every hope for the future . . .

They would buy a house. He would get a job, maybe working for her father in the bank. They would make love every night, take walks in the park, have Sunday dinner with her parents. It would all be so wonderful . . . unless Jesse wanted children. A familiar ache filled her heart, and her arms felt suddenly empty. She had wanted children, dozens of them, but it wasn't to be. Maybe, if Jesse was agreeable, they could adopt a child. There were so many children who needed love. She had gone to the orphanage with her mother on several occasions. It had broken her heart to see the babies that had been abandoned by the very people who should have loved them most. It wasn't fair, she thought, that she should want a child so badly and be unable to conceive when there were hundreds of women who had children and threw them away.

She shivered, aware that the water had grown cold. Stepping from the tub, she wrapped herself in a towel. It was soft against her skin and smelled faintly of soap and sunshine.

Going into her room, she opened the drawers in the bureau. Everything was as she had left it. On one hand, she had been upset when Alan insisted she leave everything behind. On the other hand, she had been glad to know that her furniture and belongings would be there, waiting for her, when she came back to visit. When she married, she had been certain they would return to visit her parents at least once a year. She had been certain of so many things when she got married, she thought sadly, and wondered how she could have been so wrong.

She pulled on her undergarments, then moved to the armoire. She had left numerous dresses behind, too. She ran her hands over them now, enjoying the feel of the soft wools, the cool silk.

After months of wearing nothing but buckskin, it seemed odd to have a choice of so many fabrics, so many colors and styles. Pink muslin. Blue silk. A pale yellow challis. Stripes and plaids and prints.

Blue had always been her favorite color. The silk felt cool and delicious against her skin. She put on a pair of stockings and half-boots, then brushed her hair until it gleamed.

She looked at herself in the full-length mirror and smiled at her reflection. It had been almost a year since she'd seen herself so clearly. She looked older, thinner. What would her parents think?

She tied her hair back with a white ribbon, then went downstairs, eager to see Jesse, but he was nowhere to be found.

Going into the kitchen, she asked Mrs. Moseley if she knew where he had gone.

"I believe he went to the stable, to check on his horse," Mrs. Moseley said.

"Of course," Kaylynn said. "Where else would he be?" Going into the pantry, she grabbed a couple of carrots, then went out the back door and ran down the path to the stable.

She found Jesse in the barn, brushing the roan.

"I should have known I'd find you here," she said, grinning.

Jesse shrugged. He felt a sight more comfortable out here, with his horse, than he did in the house.

Kaylynn glanced at the watch pinned to the bodice of her dress. "My parents will be home soon."

"I reckon they'll be glad to see you."

"I hope so."

"Why wouldn't they be? You're their daughter."

"I know, but they didn't want me to marry Alan. My mother wanted me to marry the son of an old school chum of hers." Rodney Farnsworth had been a nice man, with dark brown hair and blue eyes. He had been sweet and polite, and she had liked him a lot, but he hadn't fit her image of Prince Charming. She wondered now if she might not have been happier with the toad than the prince. "I guess my marrying Alan upset them more than I thought."

"What do you mean?"

"Well, I thought we'd keep in touch, through letters, you know, that Alan and I would come back to visit, but . . ." She sighed. "I wrote home every month. In six years, I think I got two letters from my mother and one from my father."

Jesse rested his arms on the roan's back. "I'm sorry, Kay."

She shrugged, as if it didn't matter, but he knew it did. He could see the hurt, the uncertainty, in her eyes. Putting the curry comb aside, he drew Kaylynn into his arms. Damn, but it felt good to hold her. He wished he had the right to lay her down on a pile of sweet-smelling straw and kiss her until she saw nothing, wanted nothing, but him. But this was not the time or the place. He didn't belong here, and all the wishing in the world wouldn't make him a part of this world.

He held her for a long time, one hand moving up and down her back, until, with a sigh, she moved out of his arms.

"We should probably go back to the house," she said. "My parents will be home any minute." She reached for his hand and squeezed it tightly. "I'm glad you're here. I know it's silly, but I'm really nervous about seeing them again."

Jesse nodded. He would stay, for her. He would meet her parents, endure their scrutiny and their questions, do anything Kaylynn asked of him because he couldn't do anything else. He wondered if she knew the power she had over him.

Hand in hand, they left the barn and walked up to the house. They entered through the kitchen because it was closer.

"There you are!" Mrs. Moseley exclaimed. "My, my, I'm so glad you're here. I didn't know if you wanted me to tell your mother and father you were home, or not."

"They're here?" Kaylynn asked.

"Just came in. They're upstairs, dressing for dinner."

Kaylynn's nails dug into Jesse's palm. She glanced down at her dress. "How do I look?" she asked.

"Beautiful," Jesse said.

"You look fine, child," Mrs. Moseley said, beaming at Kaylynn. "I've prepared all your favorites for supper. Go along now. Lord, this is a happy day."

Kaylynn nodded. Clinging to Jesse's hand as if

it were a lifeline, she left the kitchen and went into the back parlor. Her parents always spent a few minutes there before dinner, discussing the day's events over a glass of wine.

Moving to the liquor cabinet, she withdrew four crystal goblets and filled them with wine. Her hands were shaking so badly, she was surprised she managed to get the wine into the glasses.

She heard footsteps in the hall, the sound of her mother's voice, and then her parents were there, her mother slightly ahead of her father, and they were both staring at her as if she'd come back from the dead.

They had both aged in the last six years. Her father's hair, once a dark brown, was graying at the temples. There were worry lines in her mother's brow that hadn't been there before.

"Kaylynn." Her mother took a step forward, one hand outstretched, and then she rushed forward, tears streaming down her face as she enveloped her daughter in her arms.

Jesse stood back, watching the play of emotions move over Kaylynn's father's face as he watched his wife and daughter embrace. Tears glistened in the man's eyes.

Kaylynn looked over her mother's shoulder and smiled at her father, and he crossed the room, wrapping his arms around both women.

"Katydid," her father whispered hoarsely. "Thank God you're home."

Chapter Thirty-two

Later that night, Jesse sat at the dinner table across from Kaylynn, feeling like a fish out of water. Never in all his life had he seen such an array of silver and crystal and china. A fine white cloth covered the table. Tall white tapers burned in a pair of crystal candlesticks. An elderly man clad in a black suit hovered in the background, making sure platters were passed, wine glasses filled.

Jesse slid a glance at Kaylynn's parents. Her father sat at the head of the table. William Duvall was a tall, spare man, with shrewd green eyes and graying brown hair. He appeared to be in his late fifties.

Elizabeth Duvall was a few inches shorter than her husband. Her dark red hair was coiled in a neat bun at her nape. Her eyes were a lighter shade of brown than her daughter's. She looked slight, almost frail.

"Jesse, would you like anything else?" Kaylynn asked.

He shook his head. He had to agree that Mrs. Moseley was a fine cook. There was succulent roast beef, chicken and dumplings, potatoes and gravy, sweet corn, freshly baked biscuits that melted in his mouth. Just when he thought he couldn't eat another bite, the woman brought out a seven-layer chocolate cake and an apple pie, still warm from the oven.

Kaylynn clapped her hands with delight.

"Which will it be, miss?" the butler asked, hovering at Kaylynn's elbow.

"Both!" she exclaimed.

William and Elizabeth Duvall beamed at her. Earlier, when the first rush of excitement at Kaylynn's homecoming had passed, they had spent an hour in the parlor while Kaylynn and her parents brought each other up to date. Kaylynn had never told her parents that her husband abused her, and she didn't mention it now, nor did she tell them about the time she'd spent with the Indians. Jesse listened, saying nothing, as she apologized for not writing more often, for not being able to make it home until now. She told them that the stage had been attacked by robbers and that Jesse had kindly agreed to see her safely home. In answer to their question, she explained that Alan had not been with her when the stage was held up because he had stayed in San Francisco to see to several urgent business matters.

She went on to say that she and Jesse had become good friends during the journey, and that she had invited him to stay with them while he was in the city.

Besides leaving out the fact that she had been captured by Indians, she neglected to mention Jesse's line of work. He guessed he couldn't blame her for that. It troubled him that she hadn't told her parents they were in love, but he couldn't fault her for that, either. He was not the kind of man her parents would ever accept as a son-in-law. Her father and mother had both been starchily polite, but Jesse was acutely aware of her mother's revulsion, her father's misgivings. Well, he couldn't blame them. He wasn't the kind of man he'd want his daughter to marry, either, if he had one.

His gaze moved over her now. Here, in her own home, surrounded by those she loved, Kaylynn fairly sparkled. Between alternating bites of chocolate cake and apple pie, she caught his gaze, and smiled.

When dinner was over, they went into the formal parlor. Jesse had the feeling Kaylynn's mother had chosen this room to more clearly demonstrate to her daughter just how unsuitable and out of place he was, just in case Kaylynn might be harboring any ideas about him she shouldn't be having.

Feeling like a mustang in a room full of thoroughbreds, Jesse sat down on a dainty damask-covered sofa beside Kaylynn.

Her mother sat on a spindly chair. Her back, which was ramrod straight, did not touch the back of the chair.

"So, Mr. Thunder," Elizabeth said, smoothing her cream-colored skirts, "how long will you be staying with us?"

Jesse swallowed a grin. She didn't really want to know how long he was staying, but how soon he was leaving.

"I'm not sure."

Kaylynn looked at her mother. "I told Jesse he was welcome to stay as long as he wished." She glanced at her father, who was standing beside the fireplace, looking handsome and distinguished in a forest-green smoking jacket. "That's all right, isn't it?"

Elizabeth's hands fluttered in the air. "Of course, dear."

"Naturally, Katydid."

Kaylynn smiled at her parents. "That's what I thought." She turned to Jesse and patted his hand. "We have a lot of sightseeing to do. Jesse's never been to New York before."

William and Elizabeth exchanged worried looks, neither of which was lost on Jesse.

Elizabeth cleared her throat. "Tell me, Mr. Thunder . . ."

"Jesse. Just call me Jesse."

Elizabeth smiled, but there was no warmth in it. "Of course. Jesse. Tell me, what is it you do for a living?"

Jesse looked over at Kaylynn. "I'm a bounty hunter."

"A bounty hunter?" Elizabeth repeated.

"He hunts outlaws," William explained. "For money. Isn't that right?"

Jesse nodded.

"I see." Elizabeth looked at Kaylynn, obviously wondering if her daughter knew what sort of man she had brought into their home. "It sounds . . . dangerous."

"Yes, ma'am," Jesse replied. "It can be."

There was an awkward moment of silence.

Elizabeth came to the rescue with a complete change of subject. "I'm sure your friends will all want to see you while you're here, Kaylynn. What would you think about having a party—say, two weeks from Saturday?"

"That isn't much time to plan," Kaylynn exclaimed.

"A party is just what we need," Elizabeth said. "Things have been dreadfully dull this summer."

A fancy party, Jesse mused. One more way for her parents to show Kaylynn that he wouldn't fit in, that he wasn't good enough for her. As if he didn't already know that.

"I'd love it!" Kaylynn said. Two-and-half weeks would give her plenty of time to find a dress and take Jesse sightseeing. "How's Grams?"

"She's fine now," William answered. "She was quite sick a few months back."

"She was? Was it serious?"

William shook his head. "No."

"Good." Kaylynn looked at Jesse. "We'll have to visit her soon. I want you to meet her."

Jesse nodded.

"We'll need to get invitations out as soon as possible," Elizabeth remarked. "Tomorrow, I'll speak to Mrs. Moseley about the menu."

"I can't wait!" Kaylynn exclaimed, excited at the prospect of seeing all her old friends again, of wearing a new gown. Of dancing with Jesse. She smiled at the thought of seeing him in evening clothes. He'd look divine. "I can't wait!" she said again. "Oh, Jesse, won't it be fun?"

"Fun," he said.

Chapter Thirty-three

Kaylynn took him shopping the next day. It was an ordeal Jesse hoped never to endure again. He didn't know which was worse, waiting while she picked out fabrics and patterns at her favorite dressmaker's, or being measured for clothes of his own.

She picked out several shirts and cravats, wool trousers in gray and brown and black, a suit of evening clothes.

"Just charge it to my father's account," she said as they prepared to leave the shop.

"No," Jesse said. "I'll pay for it now."

"But . . ."

Jesse silenced her with a look. "I can afford it."

Apparently realizing she had hit a sore spot,

331

Kaylynn went outside to wait while Jesse settled the bill.

"I'm sorry," she said when he joined her on the sidewalk.

"I pay my own way," he said, taking her arm.

"I'll remember that," Kaylynn replied with a toss of her head.

"See that you do, woman," he replied with mock ferocity.

Walking down the street, he was aware of being stared at.

Some people were openly repulsed by his scarred face, some merely curious. He felt naked walking around without his gun, but Kaylynn had asked, with a winning smile, if he would please leave it home. He'd have done anything she asked just to have her smile at him like that.

The city itself was a busy place, filled with people in a rush. Hacks and cabs and carriages crowded the street. Men and women hurried along the sidewalk. Factory smoke filled the air, along with the shouts of the draymen, the sound of horses' hooves and carriage wheels. In the distance, a clock relentlessly chimed the hour, scolding those who were late.

Jesse shook his head. He much preferred the Indian way of life. The Cheyenne did not live their lives by the clock. They slept when they were tired, ate when they were hungry. There was always time to play, to visit, to gamble. The women went out in groups to gather food, thereby turning what could have been a chore into a time of laughter and conversation.

"I'm hungry," Kaylynn said.

"What?"

She looked up at him and smiled. "You look like you're a million miles away."

"Not quite. What did you say?"

"I said I'm hungry. Let's go in here and get something to eat."

Jesse looked at the shop she indicated. The front was painted white, with black grillwork. Flowers bloomed in yellow window boxes. A small French flag fluttered in the breeze. A sign painted in flowery script read *La Parisienne*.

He followed her inside reluctantly. The air was thick with the scent of fresh bread and coffee. Small round tables covered with green-and-white checked cloths were scattered around the room. Most were occupied by well-coifed women in expensive dresses.

Jesse felt like the proverbial bull in the china shop as several pairs of eyes turned in his direction.

Drawing Kaylynn closer, he whispered, "I don't think this is such a good idea."

She looked up at him. "Why not?"

"I don't belong in here."

"Don't be silly." Taking his hand again, she led him to a vacant table on the far side of the room. "*La Parisienne* has the best French pastry in the city."

French pastry. Jesse swore silently as he held her chair for her, then sat down. He didn't have to look to know that all eyes in the shop were watching him. He could feel the stares on his back.

"Kaylynn? Is that you?" The words gushed from the mouth of a tall young woman clad in a dark-green wool gown and matching floppy-brimmed bonnet.

"Regina!" Kaylynn stood up, smiling. "How are you?"

"Je vais très bien, merci, et toi?"

"Je vais bien."

The two women embraced, then looked at each other and laughed.

"I'm afraid that's about all the French I remember," Kaylynn said.

"It's so good to see you," Regina exclaimed. "It's been ages."

Kaylynn nodded. "You look wonderful, Reggie." But then, Regina always looked lovely. Kaylynn's mother thought it was scandalous that Reggie rouged her cheeks and painted her lips. Kaylynn had always thought it was gilding the lily, for Reggie was naturally beautiful with her silky blond hair, vivid green eyes, and peaches-and-cream complexion. All that, combined with her perfect hourglass figure, turned heads everywhere she went.

"So do you." Regina glanced at Jesse and frowned. "Who's your . . . friend?"

"Oh, I'm sorry. Regina Daniels, this is Jesse Yellow Thunder. Jesse, this is my best friend, Regina."

Rising, Jesse made a slight bow in the woman's direction. "Pleased to meet you, ma'am."

"The pleasure is mine, I'm sure," Regina replied. "Yellow Thunder, what an odd name."

"He's a Cheyenne Indian," Kaylynn said.

"Really?" Interest mingled with the curiosity in Regina's eyes.

"Join us, why don't you?" Kaylynn suggested.

"I'd love to, but I can't. I'm meeting Mother at Simone's." Regina laughed and glanced upward, as if asking for divine help. "And I'm already late."

"It was wonderful seeing you again," Kaylynn said.

"I'll call on you soon," Regina said. She leaned forward and kissed Kaylynn on the cheek, then turned and smiled at Jesse. "Very soon," she said in a throaty purr. "It was nice meeting you, Mr. Thunder."

Jesse nodded.

"*À la prochaine*," Regina said gaily.

"Yes, until next time." Kaylynn said. "She's lovely, isn't she?" Kaylynn remarked as she sat down.

Jesse shrugged. He supposed Regina was pretty enough, if you liked women who wore too much paint. Any barn could use a coat of paint now and then, he mused, but you didn't slap it all in one spot.

Kaylynn looked at him across the table, a speculative look in her eyes. "She certainly liked you."

Jesse shrugged. He hadn't missed the seductive look in Regina's eyes. Some women liked forbidden fruit.

"What did you think of her?"

Jesse grinned. "You're not jealous, are you?"

"Of course not."

"Good, 'cause I don't have time to think of anyone but you."

Her expression softened. "Oh, Jesse."

"*Bonjour, Monsieur, Mademoiselle*. Your order, please?"

"I'll have a croissant and a *demi-tasse, s'il vous plaît*," Kaylynn said. "Jesse?"

"Just a cup of coffee."

The waiter bowed slightly. *"Très bien,"* he said, and left the table.

"I used to come here all the time," Kaylynn remarked, glancing around. "It hasn't changed at all."

Jesse nodded. "It's . . . nice."

"You don't like it, do you?"

"Well . . ." He shifted in his chair. It was a delicate thing. He was surprised it held his weight without breaking.

Kaylynn looked around, only then seeming to notice that not only was Jesse the only man in the place, he also seemed to be the focus of every eye in the room. "Do you want to leave?"

He would have said yes if she hadn't mentioned that this was her favorite place. "It's all right. Can I ask you something?"

"Of course."

"Why didn't you tell your parents about being captured by the Cheyenne?"

"I should have, I know, but . . ." She made a vague dismissive gesture with her hand. "I just didn't want to have to talk about it. They would have been horrified, especially my mother. I just didn't want them to worry about something that was over and done. You understand, don't you?"

"Yeah, I understand." He had known white women who had been captured by Indians and then returned to their families. No matter how sympathetic people were, how understanding, they always wondered what had really happened, always assumed the worst. He couldn't blame Kaylynn for wanting to avoid that.

Moments later, the waiter reappeared with their

order. He placed a small plate with a crescent-shaped pastry in front of Kaylynn, along with a tiny cup of coffee. He set a large cup in front of Jesse, smiled at Kaylynn, and left the table.

Kaylynn took a bite of her croissant. Closing her eyes, she chewed it slowly, a soft sound of pleasure rising in her throat.

Jesse couldn't help smiling as he watched her. Kaylynn blushed when she opened her eyes to find Jesse grinning at her.

"What?" she asked.

Jesse shook his head. "Nothing."

"Tell me."

He laughed softly. "I've just never seen anyone who looked so happy when they were eating."

"Well, here," she said, offering him a bite. "Try it for yourself."

Obediently, he took a bite. It was good. Melt-in-your-mouth good.

"Well?" Kaylynn looked at him, a knowing grin on her face.

"It's good."

"Good! Just good?"

"All right. It's better than good."

With a smirk that said *I told you so*, she took another bite, chewed it slowly, then licked her lips.

Jesse swore silently, wishing he could lean forward and lick the crumb she had missed from the corner of her mouth. He quashed the other images that rose in his mind, thinking Kaylynn would be appalled by his lustful thoughts.

He was relieved when she finished the last bite.

* * *

Kaylynn decided to visit her grandmother the next morning. She had missed Grandmother Dearmond, and she was anxious to see her again.

Jesse was reluctant to meet any more of Kay's relatives, but he couldn't refuse, not when Kaylynn smiled at him, her eyes softly pleading.

Kaylynn's grandmother lived in a large two-story house made of white brick. It was set amid an expanse of well-cared-for lawn. Trees and flowers added shade and color.

An elderly woman dressed in a black gabardine dress answered the door.

"Miss Kaylynn!" she exclaimed, her blue eyes twinkling.

"Hello, Effie," Kaylynn replied. "Is Grandmother home?"

"She's in the library."

"Thank you, Effie."

"It's good to see you again, Miss Kaylynn. May I take your hat, sir?"

Jesse handed the woman his hat. Kaylynn took his hand. He managed a quick glance at his surroundings as he followed her. Though her grandmother's house was not so large as that of Kaylynn's parents, it felt warmer somehow. There were knickknacks everywhere, along with dozens of photographs in silver frames. The furniture was made of dark mahogany. There were lace doilies on the tabletops.

Kaylynn paused in front of a door at the end of a long hallway. Peering over her shoulder, Jesse saw a white-haired woman bent over a small cherrywood desk, apparently writing a letter. Bookshelves lined two walls. A large window let in the morning sun. A large gray cat lay curled in a padded rocking chair in the corner.

"What is it, Effie?" the woman asked, not looking up.

"It's teatime," Kaylynn said.

The woman's head jerked up, her expression one of disbelief, and then joy. "Kaylynn!"

"Hi, Grams," Kaylynn said, and hurrying across the floor, she knelt by her grandmother's chair and gave her a hug. "I'm so glad to see you."

"And I you. It's been much too long since you've been home."

"Yes. How are you? Father said you'd been ill."

"Pshaw, I'm fine, Kaylynn. Tell me, who's this you've brought with you?"

"Oh, this is Jesse." Kaylynn stood up, motioning for Jesse to enter the room.

"Grams, this is Jesse Yellow Thunder. He's a friend of mine."

Lynn Dearmond's eyes narrowed as her gaze ran over Jesse. "A friend, you say."

Kaylynn nodded. "I met him a few months ago. He was kind enough to accompany me home."

"I see. Why didn't Alan come with you?"

"He couldn't get away. Business, you know."

"Yes, business. Come closer, young man. Let me have a look at you."

Feeling like a horse on the auction block, Jesse did as the woman asked.

"That's a nasty scar you've got there."

Kaylynn gasped, wondering if Jesse would be offended.

"Yes, ma'am," Jesse said, pleased by the elderly woman's directness. It was refreshing to finally meet someone who spoke her mind, who didn't look at him furtively, all the while wondering what had happened to him.

"Bet there's a good story behind it."

Jesse nodded.

Lynn Dearmond grinned. "Involves a pretty girl, I'll wager. Maybe you'll tell me about it someday."

"Maybe," Jesse said, grinning back at her.

"Well, sit down, both of you," Lynn Dearmond said. She waved a hand toward the sofa, then picked up a tiny silver bell and rang it.

A short time later, Effie appeared in the doorway, a tea tray in her hands.

Lynn Dearmond laughed softly. "I see you've anticipated me, as usual."

"Yes, ma'am," Effie said. "I brought tea and cakes."

"Thank you, Effie."

"Will there be anything else?"

Lynn Dearmond regarded Jesse a moment. "If I'm not mistaken, I think Mr. Thunder would rather have coffee, isn't that right?"

"If it's no trouble." He looked at Effie. "No cream, no sugar."

With a nod, Effie left the room.

"Kaylynn, pour the tea, won't you, dear? Mr. Thunder, tell me about yourself. Judging from your name, I'd say you've got some Indian blood in you."

"Yes, ma'am," Jesse said, and spent the next hour describing life in the West.

They spent a few minutes talking about the upcoming party, and then Kaylynn stood up. "We should be going."

"You must bring Mr. Thunder to visit me again,"

Lynn Dearmond said. "I should love to hear more about the West."

Jesse nodded. "My pleasure."

Kaylynn hugged her grandmother. "Bye, Grams."

"Good-bye, dear. I'm so glad you came," Lynn Dearmond said. "It was nice to meet you, Mr. Thunder."

"Just Jesse."

Lynn Dearmond smiled and extended her hand. "It was nice to meet you, just Jesse."

"Thank you, ma'am," he replied, taking her hand in his. He smiled at her, surprised to find that he liked Kaylynn's grandmother very much. Of all the people he had met in the city, she was the only one who had made him feel welcome. Impulsively, he kissed her hand.

Lynn Dearmond grinned. "Handsome and gallant," she murmured. "You must come back and visit me again."

"I'd like that."

Effie was waiting for them at the front door, Jesse's hat in hand. "I'm so glad you stopped by, Miss Kaylynn," she said.

"Is she really all right?"

Effie nodded. "Yes, thank the Lord. And seeing you has done wonders."

"We'll be back soon. Take good care of her for me."

Jesse smiled at Effie as he took his hat from her, then turned and followed Kaylynn outside.

"So," Kaylynn asked as they walked down the path to the carriage, "what did you think of her?"

"I like her," he replied, and it was true. The woman was open and honest, and he valued that.

Shortly after they returned home, Regina came to call with Rodney Farnsworth in tow.

"I know I should have sent word we were coming," Regina said as she breezed into the parlor, "but we happened to be in the neighborhood, and . . ." Her words trailed off as her gaze came to rest on Jesse.

She looked, Kaylynn thought, like a hungry cat that had just discovered a bowl of fresh cream.

"Good afternoon, Kaylynn," Rodney said.

Kaylynn smiled. "Rodney, I don't believe you've met Jesse. Jesse, this is Rodney Farnsworth. Rodney, Jesse Yellow Thunder."

The two men shook hands.

"Well," Kaylynn said, "why don't we sit down."

"Good idea," Regina said. "I'd love to get to know Mr. Thunder better." She smiled at Jesse as she glided across the floor and slipped her arm through his. "I've never known a real Indian before," she said as she drew him toward the love seat. "Do tell me all about yourself. Are you married?"

Kaylynn had a sudden urge to scratch her friend's eyes out as she watched Regina flirt shamelessly with Jesse. She tried to hear what her friend was saying, but Rodney was telling her all about his latest victory on Trotter's Row, and how his new horse had beaten all the others. As if she cared.

And then Rodney changed the subject. "Why didn't Alan come with you?"

"Business," Kaylynn said.

"Too bad. I was hoping maybe you were tired of him."

"Oh?" Kaylynn leaned a little to the left so she

could keep an eye on Regina and Jesse. Regina was smiling up at him, apparently mesmerized by whatever Jesse was telling her.

"Maybe we could go out while you're here," Rodney suggested. "Dinner, a play."

"Maybe," Kaylynn said. Her eyes narrowed as she watched Regina run her fingertips along Jesse's forearm.

She was glad when Cora entered the room with the tea cart.

"Thank you, Cora," Kaylynn said. "That will be all."

With a nod and a curtsey, Cora left the room.

Pouring a cup of tea, Kaylynn carried it to Regina and thrust it into her friend's hand. "I don't remember, Reggie," she asked sweetly, "do you take cream?"

Chapter Thirty-four

Ravenhawk stood up, stretching. Pouring himself a cup of lukewarm coffee, he looked west and then east. When Yellow Thunder had turned him loose, he'd been determined to head back to the Dakotas, find a woman, and settle down. Now . . .

He looked up at the bridge overhead. He had spent the night camped in the ravine below the bridge. Once, about midnight, a train had passed over, the shriek of the whistle echoing like a siren call in the night. A call that said, *follow me.*

He'd never been farther east than Apache Junction. Never seen a big city.

He took a sip of the coffee. Grimacing at its bitterness, he dumped it on the ground.

A man ought to experience the big city just once before he settled down.

Grinning, he doused his campfire and saddled the Appaloosa. There was a town not far from here. He'd buy a ticket for St. Louis . . .

The sound of a train whistle shattered the stillness of the morning. It was an omen, he thought.

He was swinging into the saddle when he heard the explosion.

Alan Summers jolted awake. "What the hell was that?" Sitting up, he opened the window and stuck his head outside. Up ahead, he could see a plume of gray smoke.

"Somebody blew up the bridge!"

"What?" Alan glanced over his shoulder. On both sides of the aisle, people were leaning out of windows, trying to find out what was going on. There was a loud grinding of metal against metal as the train slowly screeched to a halt.

"The bridge! It's gone!"

"Look! Riders!"

"Damn. We're being held up."

Alan swore. A holdup! He looked out the window again in time to see a masked man climb aboard the engine.

Moments later, two masked men entered the passenger car.

"Get your hands up," one of them ordered, his voice gruff. "Now!"

Ravenhawk urged his horse up the side of the ravine. It didn't take a genius to figure out what was happening. The train was being robbed. Keeping out of sight, he watched as a masked man hurried the engineer toward one of the cars in the back. Having robbed a train or two himself, Ravenhawk figured the bandits were after a payroll.

The engineer stopped in front of one of the cars farther down the track.

The outlaw pounded on the door. "Open up," he hollered.

Ravenhawk couldn't hear the reply of the man inside, but apparently he refused, because the outlaw pounded on the door again, harder this time.

"Open the door, Sam," the engineer called out. "He'll kill me if you don't."

"Throw your gun out, nice and easy, Sam," the outlaw said. "Then lie down on the floor with your hands out where I can see 'em."

A pair of minutes went by, and then, with a loud creak, the car door slid open.

Ravenhawk grunted softly as a revolver skittered out the door to land in the dirt near the outlaw's feet. Apparently they weren't paying the guard enough that he was willing to risk his life to protect someone else's money.

The outlaw ordered the engineer into the car, then climbed in after him.

When both men were out of sight, Ravenhawk crept closer. Peering around the edge of the door, he saw the engineer and the guard sitting against the far wall of the car.

The bandit was cussing as he pushed a small black safe across the floor.

Moving quietly, Ravenhawk climbed inside the car. "Need some help?" he asked.

Startled, the bandit looked up. The last thing he saw was Ravenhawk's fist.

Moving quickly, Ravenhawk untied the engineer and the guard.

"You two stay put," Ravenhawk said. "Here." He

slipped the gun out of the bandit's holster and thrust it into the guard's hand. "Keep an eye on him."

"Who are you?" the guard asked.

"No time for questions now. Just do as I said."

Vaulting lightly to the ground, Ravenhawk made his way to the passenger car. Climbing up on the platform, he peered in the window. The outlaws had their backs toward him. One was watching the passengers; the other was moving down the aisle, relieving the passengers of their valuables.

Drawing his gun, Ravenhawk slowly opened the door and stepped inside.

Alan Summers glared at the outlaw, unable to believe he was being robbed. "Do you know who I am?" he demanded.

"I don't give a damn. Just give me your money. I'll take that ring, too. And that fancy watch."

Alan shook his head. "Go to hell."

Muttering an oath, the bandit grabbed Alan and hauled him to his feet. Alan's eyes widened as the second outlaw stepped forward and drove his fist into his belly. With a grunt, Alan doubled over, retching, unable to believe that anyone would dare strike him.

"Kill him."

Alan looked up, his blood turning to ice, as he found himself staring into the barrel of a gun.

He put up one hand, started to say he had changed his mind, when there was a shout from the back of the car.

Both outlaws turned, guns swinging to bear on the tall, dark-haired man standing near the door.

There was a blast of noise, the acrid smell of smoke. A woman screamed. The lady sitting across from Alan fainted.

When the smoke cleared, the outlaws lay dead in the aisle.

Taking hold of the edge of his seat, Alan pulled himself to his feet.

"You all right?" Ravenhawk asked.

Alan nodded. "Yes. Thanks to you."

Ravenhawk shrugged. Now that the excitement was over, he found himself wondering what had possessed him to get involved.

"We're all in your debt," Alan said. Closing the distance between them, he offered the stranger his hand.

There was a murmur of assent from the other passengers. Two of the men began returning the stolen property to its rightful owners. Mothers quieted their children.

Ravenhawk shook the man's hand, then turned to go.

"Wait!" Alan called. "Who are you?"

"Name's Ravenhawk."

"I could use a man like you."

"Is that right?"

Alan nodded. "I'm on my way to New York City. How'd you like to work for me?"

Ravenhawk took a good look at the man, noting the expensive cut of his clothes, the thick gold ring on his finger, the diamond stickpin in his cravat. "Doing what?"

"I'd like to hire you to be my bodyguard."

"Bodyguard?"

"I'll pay you ten dollars a day."

Ravenhawk swore. Ten dollars. A day. Damn,

that was good money, and even though he still had most of his share of the bounty money in his pockets, it wouldn't last forever.

"You just hired yourself a bodyguard, mister."

Ravenhawk sat back in his seat, the brim of his hat pulled down over his eyes. The bodies of the two dead outlaws had been put in the baggage car. The third bandit was in there, too. Ravenhawk's horse and the horses belonging to the outlaws had been loaded into an empty cattle car. The engineer had thanked Ravenhawk effusively for coming to the rescue. It was a strange feeling, being on the right side of the law.

Closing his eyes, he blew out a breath. The train was going back to the last stop. Word would have to be sent ahead, warning trains coming from the east that the bridge was out.

Alan Summers was as mad as hell at the delay. He was in an itching hurry to get to New York City, but this was one time when his money wouldn't help.

There wouldn't be any trains coming or going until the track was repaired. The engineer's best guess was that it would take at least two weeks, maybe three. But if Mr. Summers didn't want to wait, he could always buy or rent a carriage.

Mr. Summers decided to wait.

Ravenhawk grinned. It might take longer than planned, but sooner or later, he'd make it to the big city.

Chapter Thirty-five

The next two weeks passed in a flurry of activity as Kaylynn and her mother made plans for the party. Jesse rarely saw Kaylynn for more than a few minutes at a time. Servants scurried around the house, cleaning, waxing, dusting.

To avoid being in the way, Jesse spent most of his time outside. He whiled away several hours talking to the man in charge of the Duvalls' carriage horses. He went sightseeing, impressed, in spite of himself, by the mansions built by William Astor and A. T. Stewart. Stewart was the largest landowner in the city, the world's most successful merchant, and the proprietor of a huge department store. Jesse had heard Kaylynn's mother talking about the man one evening. Apparently a man of solitary habits, childless and almost friendless, he was excluded from aristocratic society because he was a tradesman.

Jesse had visited the East River, where a bridge was being built that would connect New York with Brooklyn.

But his favorite pastime was riding in Central Park.

He had thought to find seclusion if he rode early in the morning, before breakfast, only to find that that was considered the "fashionable" hour for equestriennes. Perched on sidesaddles, elegantly togged out in silk hats with flying veils, tightly buttoned bodices, and flowing skirts, crops in gloved hand, they were like nothing Jesse had ever seen before. No lady ever rode alone. They either rode in groups, attended by a gentleman, or with a liveried groom or riding master.

The "carriage parade," considered one of the sights of the city, took place between four and five in the afternoon. Jesse had seen crowds gathered along the walk that bordered the carriage drive that ran from Fifty-ninth Street and Fifth Avenue to the Mall. He had watched one afternoon, listening as a rather obnoxious man kept up a running conversation, pointing out the Jays, Livingstons, and Stuyvesants, who were members of the aristocracy. Also evident were the celebrities, notorious and otherwise, the *demimondaines*. Jesse had nodded, pretending to be interested.

His new clothes had arrived. They fit fine. They looked good. But he was uncomfortable wearing them. The phrase, a "wolf in sheep's clothing," came to mind when he looked at himself in the mirror. Kaylynn could dress him up in striped trousers and a silk cravat, but it didn't hide what he was. His callused hands, his scarred face, his rough speech set him apart from her set, as did his dark skin and unfashionably long hair.

He knew she hoped her parents would come to accept him, but he knew it wasn't going to happen. Oh, they were polite, painfully so. The servants tiptoed around him. He knew they gossiped about him behind his back, speculating on how he had gotten the scar on his face, why he refused to have help when he dressed.

After a week in the Duvall house, he knew he couldn't stay there any longer, knew that, as much as he loved Kaylynn, he couldn't stay in New York. He didn't belong here, and never would.

He watched her greet the friends who came to call. She tried to make him feel at ease, but he was always on the outside looking in. He was ignorant of the books they discussed, the people they knew, the memories they shared. She had told him several times that once she got back to New York she was never leaving again.

It would be hard to leave her, but it was for her own good. She would be better off without him. She was home, where she belonged.

It was time for him to go back where he belonged.

"Leaving? What do you mean?" Kaylynn stared up at him, her dark eyes like bruises in her pale face.

"It's for the best."

"Best for whom?"

"For both of us."

"No!"

"I got a room at the hotel today, while you were

visiting your grandmother. I'll be staying there until the train leaves on Saturday."

"But the party is Saturday."

"I'm sorry, Kay."

"I thought you loved me, that . . ."

"I thought so, too," he said. "I'm sorry."

He watched her eyes fill with pain. Almost, he told her he was lying, that he loved her, would always love her. But a clean break was the best. For both of them.

He watched her blink back her tears. Watched her lift her chin, straighten her shoulders like a soldier about to go to battle. She was a strong woman, with a strong spirit. She would miss him for a little while, perhaps shed a few tears, and then get on with her life.

Kaylynn looked up at Jesse, her heart breaking. She wanted to ask him what was wrong, beg him to stay, tell him . . . She clenched her hands. She wouldn't beg. If he didn't want her, then she didn't want him!

"I guess this is good-bye then," she said.

"I guess so," he said quietly. "Be happy, darlin'."

"Thank you," she said hoarsely. "You, too."

Knowing it was a mistake, he pulled her into his arms and kissed her, once, and then, slinging his gunbelt over his shoulder, he turned and left the house.

Kaylynn stood in the doorway, watching him go. Then, with a muffled cry, she ran up the stairs to her room. Bending over the commode, she began to retch.

Chapter Thirty-six

Elizabeth stared at her daughter, unable to believe her ears. "What did you say?"

"I think I'm pregnant."

A slow smile spread over Elizabeth's face. "Why, that's wonderful, dear. How far along are you?"

"I'm not sure." It couldn't be more than a month or so. Maybe it was too early to tell. Maybe it was just a stomach upset. But it wasn't, and she knew it. She was pregnant with Jesse's child.

"Does Alan know?"

"Alan?"

"Yes, Alan. Your husband."

"No. No, he doesn't know."

"Did you two have a quarrel?"

Kaylynn stared at her mother. A quarrel? With Alan? The thought was so ludicrous, she laughed.

You didn't quarrel with Alan. He said jump, and you said, how high? He said go, and you said, where?

"Kaylynn? Kaylynn, are you all right?"

She stared at her mother, unable to stop laughing, while tears rolled down her cheeks.

"Kaylynn!" Elizabeth shook her daughter's shoulder, her expression worried. "Kaylynn, stop that!"

Kaylynn shook her head. She couldn't stop laughing. Couldn't stop crying.

Elizabeth went to the door and opened it. "William! William, come here!"

Kaylynn took a deep, calming breath as her father rushed into the room.

"What's wrong?" he asked.

"I'm . . . I'm in the family way," Kaylynn said.

William Duvall smiled, and then, seeing the worried look on his wife's face, he frowned. "Is something wrong?"

"Alan doesn't know," Elizabeth said.

"So, we'll send him a wire and tell him."

Kaylynn took a deep breath. The time for truth had come.

"It's not Alan's. We could never conceive a child."

"What?"

Kaylynn looked up and met her father's gaze. "It's not Alan's baby."

Elizabeth and William exchanged glances.

"Whose is it?" William asked.

"Jesse's."

Elizabeth's eyes widened in horror. "The bounty hunter's?"

Kaylynn nodded.

"Kaylynn Elizabeth, how could you?"

"I love him."

"I'll kill him!" William roared. "Where is he?"

"He moved out," Kaylynn said. "He's leaving town."

"Like hell!"

"Father, don't. He doesn't know about the baby, and you're not to tell him."

William began to pace the floor. "There's only one thing to do," he said.

"What's that, dear?" Elizabeth asked.

"Let people think the child is Alan's, of course."

"Is that fair to Alan?" Elizabeth asked.

"I'm not worried about Alan," William replied. "I'm worried about Kaylynn's reputation."

"I left Alan, Father. That's why I came home."

"Left him!" William exclaimed.

"Yes."

"But why, dear?" Elizabeth asked.

Kaylynn took a deep breath. "I lied to you before. I didn't come home for a vacation. I ran away."

"Ran away?" William said. "I think you'd better explain."

She told them everything, how Alan had beat her, how she had run away, how the stage had been attacked by Indians. She told them about Ravenhawk and Jesse. Told them everything.

"And so," she said, "I'm getting a divorce."

"Divorce!" Elizabeth exclaimed. She looked at her husband. "Divorce, William. There's never been a divorce in our family."

"Perhaps we can avoid a divorce," William said. "We'll just tell people you came home to be with your mother, that you wanted her near you when

356

the child was born. There's nothing unusual about that."

"Of course," Elizabeth said. "No one has to know the child isn't Alan's. You can live here, with us. Lots of couples don't live together. Look at Flo and Roger Littlefield. She lives in France and he lives here."

"Say whatever you like," Kaylynn said. What did it matter, now that Jesse was gone?

William thought they should cancel the party, but Elizabeth protested, saying a party was just what they needed. Besides, the invitations had gone out, and replies were pouring in. It would be rude to cancel now.

The day before the party, Kaylynn went to visit her grandmother.

"Good afternoon, Miss Kaylynn," Effie said, smiling warmly. "How nice to see you again."

"Hello, Effie. Is Grams awake?"

"Yes," Effie said. "Come in. She's been hoping you'd stop by. She's out back, taking the sun."

With a nod, Kaylynn walked through the house toward the back entrance. She had always loved her grandmother's house. She remembered playing here when she was a little girl, holding a big ball of yarn while she watched Grams knit, standing on a chair in the kitchen while Grams baked gingerbread men.

She found her grandmother sitting on a padded bench in the grape arbor, reading a copy of *Harper's Weekly*. In spite of the warmth of the day, Grams wore a lacy black shawl over her shoulders; a light woolen blanket covered her legs. Her big gray cat, Theadosia, lay curled in her lap.

Grams looked up as Kaylynn approached, a smile of welcome lighting her face.

"Kaylynn, I had a feeling you'd come see me today."

"Did you?" Bending, Kaylynn hugged her grandmother.

Theadosia, never one to share her mistress's attention, made a soft, angry sound in her throat.

"Hush, Thea," Lynn Dearmond admonished. "Have you ever seen such a possessive creature?" she said, fondly stroking the cat.

"Never," Kaylynn agreed.

"Go along with you now, Thea," Lynn said. She nudged the cat gently off her lap, then smiled at Kaylynn. "How's the party coming along?"

Kaylynn shrugged. "Fine. Everything's fine."

Lynn Dearmond studied her granddaughter's face. Kaylynn had always been a lovely child, with a winning smile and laughing eyes. She was still lovely, but . . .

"What is it, child? What's troubling you?"

"I never could keep a secret from you, could I?"

"Never," Lynn replied. Closing the magazine, she put it on the table beside the bench and patted the seat beside her. "Sit down and tell me what's wrong."

Kaylynn sat down beside her grandmother, and the whole story poured forth in a torrent of words and tears.

"And now he's leaving," Kaylynn said, sniffing. "I love him, Grams."

Lynn Dearmond smiled faintly as she patted Kaylynn's shoulder. "Yes, I can see that you do." She shook her head. "I just can't believe what you told me about Summers. Oh, I never cared for the man myself, but he seemed a decent sort."

"Father doesn't think I should divorce him. Mother is worried about the scandal. They don't seem to care about how I feel."

"Of course you should divorce him. And I shall tell your father so the next time I see him."

Kaylynn smiled through her tears. Grams had always taken her side.

"I wish I had told Jesse about the baby," Kaylynn said, sniffling. "Maybe he would have stayed."

"You did the right thing."

"How can you be so sure?"

"Listen to me, child. I'm an old woman, but if there's one thing I've learned in life, it's that a man stays with a woman because he can't live without her. You might trap him into marriage by telling him about the baby, but he'd never be happy, and neither would you."

"I thought he loved me."

"How do you know he doesn't?"

"He's leaving! If he loved me, he'd stay."

"Look around, child. From what you've told me, he wouldn't fit in here, in your world. Some men aren't made for ballrooms and the like," Lynn said, her voice suddenly wistful. "Some men have to live wild and free. It doesn't mean that he doesn't love you. . . ."

"Did you ever know a man like that?" Kaylynn asked, her own troubles momentarily forgotten.

"Yes, indeed. Before I met your grandfather, I fell in love with just such a man. He asked me to go West with him, but I was afraid. I didn't want to leave my comfortable house and my friends. I was afraid of the kind of life he led."

"Are you sorry now that you didn't go with him?"

"I've been sorry every day of my life."

"Maybe I should go with Jesse . . ."

"Did he ask you to go with him?"

Kaylynn shook her head. "No."

"Then let him go, child." Lynn Dearmond took Kaylynn's hand and gave it a reassuring squeeze. "I know it's hard, but let him go. If he loves you, if it's meant to be, he'll be back."

Chapter Thirty-seven

The train pulled into New York City late Friday afternoon. The city was unlike anything Ravenhawk had ever seen. It was quite a change for a half-breed Lakota who was used to miles of endless prairie and dusty little cow towns. Tall buildings lined both sides of the street. There were horses and carriages and people everywhere, all of them in an itching hurry. He saw women in fancy dresses and big hats adorned with flowers and feathers and colorful ribbons. Men in city suits and black bowlers. A Chinaman with a long black queue decked out in something that looked like baggy silk pajamas.

Ravenhawk followed Alan down the street toward the hotel, aware of the curious stares of the men he passed, the lingering glances and smiles of the women. He tipped his hat to a pretty dark-haired young woman and laughed out loud when an older woman, obviously her mother, took the girl by the arm and ushered her across the street.

When they reached the hotel, Ravenhawk opened the door for Alan, then held it for a rather buxom blond woman wearing a dress in an eye-popping shade of pink. She paused in the doorway, her deep blue eyes gazing at him as if he were a banquet and she hadn't eaten in weeks.

"Have we met?" she asked.

"No, ma'am," Ravenhawk replied.

She smiled up at him. "Perhaps I can arrange it."

"I'd like that," Ravenhawk drawled.

She tapped his shoulder with her fan. "I shall see what I can do."

She granted him another smile, then swished out the door in a rustle of silk and satin.

Ravenhawk watched her sashay down the street, then walked across the floor to join Summers, who was standing at the desk.

"I'll be needing another room, as well," Summers was saying. "Preferably one adjoining my own."

"Yes, sir, Mr. Summers."

Alan signed the register with a flourish and handed the pen to the desk clerk. "Any messages for me?"

"Yes, sir." The man pulled a folded sheet of paper from under the desk. "This arrived last night."

Alan took the paper and read it quickly, a slow smile spreading over his face. With a nod, he folded the paper and slipped it in his coat pocket.

He glanced at Ravenhawk. "I signed for you,

too. Let's go. I want to clean up before dinner."

Ravenhawk nodded. Being a bodyguard was the best job he'd ever had. It was certainly the easiest. Except for dispatching the train robbers, he hadn't done anything except follow Summers around. He glanced around the hotel again as he followed Summers up the stairs. Yes, sir, he was living high on the hog now.

John Porter took a puff on his cigar. "Yes, sir, Mrs. Summers is here. I've seen her several times. She looks well. The Duvalls are giving her a welcome-home party tomorrow night."

"Is that so?" Alan smiled, thinking of the welcome he had in mind.

"Yes, sir. I overheard her talking about it with her mother just yesterday afternoon."

Ravenhawk stood near the window, his back to the room. He had little interest in Summers's wife. He was more concerned with John Porter. Unless he was very much mistaken, Porter had been a passenger on the stage out of Twin Bluffs. Porter hadn't recognized him when Alan introduced them, although he'd asked if they had met before. Since then, Ravenhawk had been aware of John Porter's gaze on him more than once. Sooner or later, the man was going to remember who he was. Ravenhawk grinned at his reflection in the glass. Not that it mattered. He wasn't wanted for anything in this part of the country.

He ran a hand around the inside of his shirt collar. Summers had insisted that he get rid of his buckskins while they were in the city. A quick trip to a tailor shop, and Ravenhawk found himself wearing a fashionable black suit and a white linen shirt. He regarded himself in the glass. Even though he was aware of his good looks, he'd never been particularly vain. Still, he had to admit he'd never looked better. There was a new suit of evening clothes hanging in his room, together with a pair of shiny black shoes. He had argued that he didn't need any new duds, but after seeing himself in the mirror, he had changed his mind. Maybe clothes did make the man. He had to admit he looked damn good in his new suit. Little wonder Porter hadn't been able to place him. He doubted if his own mother would recognize him now.

"Well," Porter said, rising, "if you won't be needing me for anything else, I'll be heading back to Frisco."

Alan nodded, and the two men shook hands.

It was with a sense of relief that Ravenhawk watched Porter take his leave. It could have proved embarrassing if Porter had recognized him and mentioned it to Summers.

"Here."

Ravenhawk turned around at the sound of Summers's voice. "What's this for?" he asked as Summers handed him a glass of bourbon.

"We're celebrating," Alan said.

"Oh?" Ravenhawk took a sip, savoring the smooth taste of the whiskey. Never, in all his life, had he tasted anything so fine.

Summers nodded, a satisfied grin playing over his face. "Tomorrow night I shall take back what is mine."

Ravenhawk nodded. Summers had been rather close-mouthed on the train, saying only that he was going East to meet his wife. "Taking back what is mine" sounded ominous somehow, leaving Ravenhawk to wonder if the reunion was going to be a happy one. But that wasn't his problem. He smiled as he emptied the glass in a single swallow. The pay was good and the whiskey was smooth. What more could he ask for?

Jesse sat in a far corner of the saloon, a glass of whiskey in one hand. Tomorrow was Saturday. The day of Kaylynn's homecoming party. The day he was leaving town.

Three days had passed since he last saw Kaylynn. They had been the longest three days of his life. Time and again, he had left his hotel room, determined to go to her, to tell her he loved her, and every time he had turned back. She deserved better than a worn-out bounty hunter. She already had more than he could ever give her, more than he could ever hope to give her.

He lifted the glass and drained it in a single swallow. "Be happy, darlin'," he murmured.

Picking up the bottle, he refilled his glass. Maybe, if he got good and drunk, he'd be able to forget her.

And maybe pigs would fly.

A clock chimed in the distance. This time tomorrow, he'd be on his way back where he belonged.

Chapter Thirty-eight

Kaylynn smoothed her skirt over her hips. The gown, of dark russet silk, complemented the color of her hair and eyes and made her skin glow. It was a lovely dress, simple yet elegant, with a square neckline that was almost daring, long sleeves, a fitted bodice, and a full skirt. It felt heavenly against her skin.

Almost as wonderful as . . . She shook the thought aside as tears stung her eyes. She would not think of him! And yet, how could she help it when his child was growing within her womb?

She studied her reflection in the mirror. She looked the same as always. Her stomach was still flat. No one, looking at her, would guess her secret.

Downstairs, the grandfather clock chimed the

hour. Pasting a smile on her face, she left her room.

It was time to go down and greet her guests.

Kaylynn stood between her parents, smiling and nodding and pretending she was having a good time. And she was. Really. It was nice to see all her old friends again. They were all there, the girls she had grown up with, gone to school with, laughed with, dreamed dreams with. They all looked happy and prosperous.

Dinner was a huge success. Mrs. Moseley had outdone herself. The table was beautiful, set with china and crystal, candles and fresh flowers. The food excellent, the wine the best that money could buy.

Kaylynn looked at the bounty spread on the table, at the platters of meat, bowls of fancy potatoes and vegetables dripping butter and sauce, and thought of the winter she had spent with the Cheyenne, how they had almost run out of food before the snow melted and the warriors had brought in fresh meat.

She tried to pay attention to the conversation around her, but she seemed trapped in the past, remembering the time she had spent with the Cheyenne, with Jesse and Ravenhawk. Mindful of her queasy stomach, she ate little.

When the meal was over, she couldn't help noticing that there was enough food left on the table to feed Mo'e'ha and her family for a week.

From the dining room, they moved into the ballroom. A five-piece orchestra struck up a waltz, and Kaylynn watched her mother and father take the floor. They made a handsome couple.

Kaylynn moved around the room, speaking to her guests, getting caught up on the lives of her friends, congratulating Heather on the birth of her twin sons, wishing Cynthia happiness in her forthcoming marriage, laughing as Lucinda related her daughter's latest prank. She waved at Regina, who was surrounded by men, as always. They all seemed to be happy with their lives, husbands, children. None of them seemed to have a care in the world.

Feeling a little queasy, she slipped out of the ballroom and made her way into the library and shut the door. It was quiet in the book-lined room. A single lamp turned away the darkness.

She wandered around the room, fingers trailing over the top of the desk, the back of her father's chair, the spines of the books on the shelves, resting on a volume bound in dark blue cloth. *Love Poems and Sonnets to Win a Lady's Heart.*

Jesse had left town today. She had hoped he would come to see her before he left, had thought he would at least send her a note of farewell.

She pulled the book from the shelf, remembering the day by the lake when she had recited poetry to Jesse.

She opened the book to the section titled "My Spirit's Songs," thumbing through the pages until her gaze came to rest on one titled "Night Dreams."

"I just can't seem to get it right
I'm wrong by day and wrong by night,
I really think this feeling never ends.
Why can't I have a normal life,

SPIRIT'S SONG

Not filled with all this pain and strife,
Why is it that we have to be just friends?

If I was there with you right now,
I know we'd never wonder how
We could please each other when we meet.
I'd kiss your lips and brush your hair
And show you just how much I care,
I can't imagine anything as sweet.

But you are there and I am here,
This is the thing that I most fear,
That we will never meet in warm embrace.
Darling, tell me I am wrong,
Sing for me, my Spirit's Song,
Tell me that you long to see my face.

Tell me that you long for me
Tell me how you long to be
With me every minute of the day.
Tell me, when I long for you,
That you are there and feel it, too,
Listen to the words I long to say.

I long to tell you how I care,
I long to show you I'll be there,
When all the world around you comes apart.
And when I think of your sweet kiss,
My darling, just remember this,
No one else will ever have my heart.

So, here's to us, here in the night,
Our burning love our only light,
To lead and guide us through these lonely
    times.

Here's to love and joy and peace,
And memories that will never cease
As long as I can love you in my rhymes."

She took a deep breath and blew it out in a long sigh. She had been so certain that Jesse loved her, that somehow they would be able to have a life together, that he would be there when she needed him.

She glanced at the page again. "I long to show you I'll be there, When all the world around you comes apart . . ." That was how she felt, as if her world were coming apart.

She put the book back on the shelf, refusing to give in to the melancholy sweeping over her. She had wanted to come home, to New York, and she was home. She had wanted a party. Why wasn't she enjoying it? The orchestra was playing a reel; she heard the faint sound of laughter. Grams always said there was no use crying over spilt milk, and she was right. Jesse was gone, and all the crying in the world wouldn't bring him back.

She ran a hand over her hair, blinked back her tears, and left the library. Tears hadn't accomplished anything when she was captured by the Cheyenne; they wouldn't help her now.

Forcing a smile, she entered the ballroom. It *was* good to be home, to see familiar faces.

Walking around the edge of the dance floor, she made her way to the punch bowl, determined to have a good time. Her parents had spared no expense this evening, she mused as Cora handed her a glass of champagne. The least she could do was enjoy it.

"Hey, Kaylynn."

She turned at the sound of a familiar voice. "Oh, hello, Rodney. Are you having a good time?"

He lifted his glass in a toast. "As always, darlin'."

She made a dismissive gesture with her hand. She had never really liked Rodney Farnsworth. He was a terrible flirt. He had called on her several times before she announced her engagement to Alan, declaring that he loved her, but she had never taken him seriously.

"You're lookin' real pretty tonight," he remarked with a wry grin.

Kaylynn frowned at him. "You're drunk."

"Nah." He shook his head, his grin widening. "A little tipsy, maybe. So, darlin' how long are you gonna be in town?"

"I don't know. And I'm not your darling."

He moved toward her, leering. "You should have married me, Kaylynn. I've got just as much money as old Summers."

"Yes," she said, trying to keep the mood light, "but he holds his liquor better."

Rodney grunted. "So, where is Alan?"

"He couldn't get away."

Rodney cupped her cheek with his free hand, and then, before she realized what he meant to do, he kissed her. "Any man who'd let you out of his sight is a fool."

"Who are you calling a fool?"

Kaylynn's eyes widened at the sound of Alan's voice.

Rodney straightened and whirled around, and Alan punched him in the face. Rodney staggered backward, the glass falling from his hand. There was the sound of breaking crystal. Blood spurted from Rodney's nose.

371

"Get the hell away from my wife," Alan said.

Rodney pulled a handkerchief from his pocket and held it to his nose. "Sure, sure," he said. "I didn't mean anything."

Alan glared at him. "Get out."

Suddenly sober, Rodney Farnsworth did as he was told. Alan Summers was not a man to trifle with.

"Alan." Kaylynn breathed his name.

"I knew you would run home, sooner or later."

Kaylynn took a deep breath in an effort to calm the panic rising within her. She wanted to tell him to go away, to leave her alone, but she couldn't seem to speak. She could only stare at him, at Rodney's blood splattered across the front of his white linen shirt.

"Quite impolite of you to have a party and not invite your husband, don't you think?"

She nodded, suddenly aware that the orchestra had stopped playing, that everyone was watching them.

Alan held out his hand. "Shall we dance?"

She stared at his hand, the same hand that had broken Farnsworth's nose. The same hand that had hit her more times than she could count.

"Kaylynn, I said let's dance."

She knew that tone of voice. It said don't argue with me, or you'll regret it.

Her hand was shaking as she placed it in his. He saw it, and smiled.

His fingers curled around her hand, squeezing, squeezing. Tears welled in her eyes, and she blinked them back.

Slowly, he loosened his hold. "Later, I shall expect a day-by-day account of where you have been this past year, and what you have been doing."

Kaylynn nodded. She knew that look. Knew he meant to punish her later, when they were alone.

A man moved up behind Alan. It was a day of surprises, she thought. First Alan, and now Ravenhawk, though she hardly recognized him.

He stared at her, and she had a sudden urge to laugh. They were like two kids playing grownup, she thought, she in her fancy ball gown and Ravenhawk in evening clothes.

For a moment, their gazes met. When he would have spoken, she shook her head, silently asking him not to interfere.

Alan smiled at her, a cold, heartless smile. "I don't think we'll dance, after all," he said. "I think it's time you and I got reacquainted."

His words sent a chill down Kaylynn's spine.

Summoning every bit of courage she possessed, Kaylynn jerked her hand from Alan's grasp. "No."

Alan's eyes narrowed ominously. "No? Have you forgotten how much I detest that word?"

Kaylynn shook her head. "I haven't forgotten anything."

Alan stared at her, his eyes dark with rage. "I see I shall have to remind you of your place," he said, and she had no doubt he was looking forward to doing just that.

Kaylynn ran her hands over her arms. She was suddenly cold, inside and out. "I'm not going anywhere with you."

Alan laughed, and the sound sent shivers down her spine.

"You are my wife." He bit off each word, his voice rising. "You will do as I say. You will go where I go."

Lowering her arms to her sides, she clenched her fists. She had survived an Indian attack. She had won the respect of old Mo'e'ha and her son. She had escaped from Vance Sandler, been kidnapped by outlaws. She would not be cowed by Alan Summers. Not anymore.

"No," she said, boldly meeting his gaze. "I won't."

He stared at her in stunned disbelief, unable to believe she would defy him. "Damn you!" Shaking with rage, he drew back his hand and slapped her.

Kaylynn reeled backward, her cheek stinging from the blow.

"What's going on?"

Relief washed through Kaylynn as her father came striding across the dance floor toward them.

"Mind your own business, Duvall," Alan said. "This doesn't concern you."

"Now, see here," William Duvall exclaimed. "Kaylynn is my daughter—"

"Kaylynn is my wife, old man. Don't interfere."

"Now, see here—"

"Alan, don't!" Kaylynn screamed the words as Alan drove his fist into her father's stomach. Her father doubled over, and Alan drew back his fist, ready to strike him again.

"I wouldn't."

Alan stopped in mid-swing, his gaze darting toward the man who had spoken.

"Jesse!" Kaylynn breathed his name, her heart pounding with joy at the sight of him.

William Duvall straightened up, one arm wrapped around his middle.

Alan took a step forward, as if to strike Kaylynn's father again, and Jesse hit him. Once. Hard.

Alan dropped to his hands and knees, blood flowing from his nose.

Kaylynn flew into Jesse's arms. "Jesse. Oh, Jesse. Thank God you're here."

His arm tightened around her waist as his gaze moved over her face. "Are you all right?"

"I'm fine, now."

Kaylynn glanced around, wishing she could just disappear. She saw her mother standing on the edge of the crowd, one hand at her throat. Rodney Farnsworth was leaning against the far wall, a half-smile on his face as he stared at Alan. It was obvious from his expression that he was enjoying himself at Alan's expense. Regina stood nearby, her eyes glowing. She had always enjoyed watching men fight over her. Kaylynn had never understood why.

Alan stood up. The lower half of his face was spattered with blood, his eyes were cold and hard, like chips of ice-blue glass.

Ready and eager for a fight, Jesse put Kaylynn behind him and took a step forward.

"Afraid I can't let you touch her."

Alan laughed softly as Ravenhawk stepped up beside him, his pistol drawn.

Jesse stared at Ravenhawk.

"What the hell are you doing here?" Jesse asked.

"I work for Mr. Summers," Ravenhawk replied.

"Doing what?"

"Protecting him from men like you."

Jesse glanced at the gun aimed at him, then looked up and met Ravenhawk's eyes. "He had it coming."

"That may be true, but she's his wife."

"She wants a divorce."

"I'll never give her a divorce," Alan said. "Never."

"Whether you give me a divorce or not doesn't matter," Kaylynn said. She stepped in front of Jesse, his presence giving her the courage to face Alan. "I'm not going back to San Francisco with you. Not now. Not ever."

"You're my wife," Alan retorted. "You'll do as I say."

Kaylynn shook her head. "Not anymore."

Overcome with fury, Alan sprang forward, his fists lashing out. Kaylynn tried to avoid the blow, but he was too fast for her. She grunted with pain as he struck her across the face, twice, bloodying her nose and cutting her lower lip.

Heedless of the gun aimed at him, Jesse lunged forward. Catching Alan by the scruff of the neck, he jerked him around and drove his fist into Summers's face with all the force at his command.

Alan reeled backward. He came up hard against the table behind him. Punch splashed over the sides of the bowl, staining the white damask cloth that covered the table.

Lifting his hand to his jaw, Alan glared at Jesse. "Ravenhawk!" he shouted. "What the hell am I paying you for? Do something."

"Yes, boss," Ravenhawk said. And holstering his Colt, he punched Alan Summers in the jaw. The sound of his fist striking Alan's jaw seemed to echo off the walls.

It was a very satisfying sound.

Alan Summers crumpled to the floor like a wet dishrag.

William Duvall smiled.

Rodney Farnsworth applauded.

Jesse turned and drew Kaylynn into his arms.

Ravenhawk blew out a deep breath. "Looks like I'm out of a job. Too bad, too, cause he serves great whiskey."

Chapter Thirty-nine

They were all gathered in the library. William Duvall sat behind his desk, his arms folded across his chest. Elizabeth stood behind her husband, looking slightly dazed.

Alan stood near the hearth, a damp cloth pressed to his nose. Every few moments, he touched his jaw, as though unable to believe that anyone had dared strike him.

Ravenhawk stood near the door, one hand resting on the butt of his gun.

Kaylynn sat on the sofa. Jesse stood behind her.

"All right," William said. "Will someone please tell me what the hell is going on?"

"I don't owe you any explanations," Alan said, his tone surly. "But if you must know, I came to take my wife home."

"You're not taking my daughter anywhere. She told me why she ran away." William glanced at his daughter's face. Her bottom lip was swollen where Alan had struck her.

"She belongs to me," Alan said. "I keep what's mine."

"She's not going anywhere with you," Jesse said quietly. "And if you ever try to see her again, I'll kill you."

"You can't threaten me! You're nothing but a dirty half-breed—a bounty hunter." Alan snorted. "You're nothing but scum."

Jesse didn't argue; he just fixed Summers with an icy stare.

"You heard him," Alan said, glancing around the room. "He threatened me."

"I'd do what he says, if I were you," Ravenhawk remarked. "He's ruthless. I ought to know."

Jesse snorted softly, then turned to glare at Summers again. "Kaylynn wants a divorce. You're gonna let her have it. Is that understood?"

"She's my wife," Alan retorted. "She'll do whatever I say."

"Not anymore." Jesse smiled. It was not a pleasant expression. "You can give her a divorce," he drawled, "or I can make her a widow. The choice is yours."

Alan's face paled visibly as he glanced from the bounty hunter to Ravenhawk. The look on Ravenhawk's face told him that Yellow Thunder was not given to making idle threats. "I'll give her a divorce," he said.

Ravenhawk looked at Yellow Thunder. "So, are you gonna marry the lady?"

"I don't see as how that's any of your business."

Ravenhawk shrugged. "Oh, I think maybe it is."

Jesse scowled at him. "What the hell are you talking about?"

"Well, she's a mighty handsome woman. Pretty soon she'll be a free woman, one way or the other. Divorced or widowed, it don't matter to me. If you don't want her, I reckon that leaves the field open." Ravenhawk smiled at Kaylynn. "If Yellow Thunder isn't interested, sweetheart, I am."

Jesse moved around to the front of the sofa, so that he stood between Kaylynn and Ravenhawk. "I warned you once," he said, his voice deceptively calm. "Leave her alone."

"You're in love with her, then?"

"Damn right."

Ravenhawk grinned broadly. "Maybe you ought to tell her."

"Maybe you ought to mind your own damn business!" Jesse took a deep breath, then turned to face Kaylynn's parents. "Would it be all right if I spoke to Kaylynn alone for a few minutes?"

William and Elizabeth exchanged resigned glances.

"I think that's up to Alan," William said. "He's still her husband."

Jesse looked at Alan. "Well?"

Ravenhawk stepped forward and tapped Alan on the shoulder. "You heard him. He wants to be alone with the lady."

"Hell, he can have her," Alan exclaimed, and storming past Ravenhawk, he stalked out of the room, slamming the door behind him.

William Duvall smiled at Ravenhawk. "Well done," he remarked. "Come along, Elizabeth," he said, and taking his wife by the hand, they left the room.

Ravenhawk grinned at Jesse. "Good luck, bounty hunter," he drawled. He turned to leave, only to come face-to-face with the most beautiful woman he had ever seen. She had hair the color of cornsilk and eyes as green as new grass.

"Kaylynn," Regina said, her voice low and sultry. "Why don't you introduce me to this handsome gentleman."

"Regina, this is Ravenhawk. Ravenhawk, this is my best friend, Regina Daniels."

"Ravenhawk?" Regina purred. "What an interesting name."

Ravenhawk grinned at Regina, amused and pleased by her admiration. "I'd be glad to tell you how I got it," he said.

"I can't wait." Regina placed her hand on Ravenhawk's arm. "I know a place where we can be alone."

"Suits me," Ravenhawk replied. He grinned at Kaylynn, then escorted Regina out of the room.

Jesse muttered an oath as Ravenhawk closed the door.

Feeling suddenly shy and uncertain, Kaylynn clasped her hands in her lap. "Why did you come here tonight?" she asked. "I thought you were leaving."

"I thought so, too."

"What changed your mind?"

"You did." Jesse raked a hand through his hair. "Kay . . . Dammit, I'm no good at this."

"At what?"

He made a sweeping gesture with his hand. "I don't belong here, Kay. I don't like the city. It doesn't fit me." He rubbed his scarred cheek. "I don't fit it."

"No one's making you stay."

"You are."

She looked up at him, her heart pounding in her breast. "What are you trying to say, Jesse?"

"I love you, Kay. I want you to be my wife. I'll do my best to make you happy, to be the kind of husband you deserve."

"Is that a proposal?" she asked.

"Yeah, I reckon it is." He took a deep breath. "So, what do you say?"

"Oh, Jesse."

"Is that a yes?"

She nodded, her eyes filling with happy tears. "Did you really think I'd say no?"

"I wouldn't blame you if you did. Your friends are gonna think you're crazy."

"I am. Crazy about you."

"Kay." Dropping to one knee in front of her, he wrapped his arms around her waist and held her tight. "I love you."

"I love you."

"I'll try to make you happy."

"You already make me happy." She smiled at him. "I have something to tell you."

"I'm listening."

"We're going to have a baby."

He stared at her a moment. "We are?"

Kaylynn nodded. "I'm pregnant, Jesse. I hope you don't mind."

A slow smile spread over his face as he sat back on his heels and then, very gently, he placed his hand over her stomach. "I don't mind, darlin'," he murmured. "Why didn't you tell me before?"

"I couldn't."

"Why not?"

"I wanted you to stay because you loved me, not because you felt it was your duty."

"I guess I can understand that. I'm sorry I've behaved like such a bas—such an idiot. Can you forgive me?"

"There's nothing to forgive. Grandmother Dearmond told me you would come back if you really loved me. I guess she was right."

Jesse nodded as he drew Kaylynn into his arms. "I'll always come back to you, Kay," he drawled softly. "I love you, my Spirit's Song."

"And I love you," she replied tremulously, and lifted her face for his kiss.

Chapter Forty

Music filled the air. Kaylynn smiled as she placed her hand on her father's arm and they began to walk down the long white runner that led to the gazebo. Her mother had wanted a big church wedding, but Kaylynn had wanted to be married outside.

Alan hadn't given them any more trouble about the divorce and had, in fact, arranged it in a remarkably short time.

Kaylynn had insisted on inviting only family and close friends. She was, after all, a divorced woman. It had caused quite a scandal, but her mother and father had handled it surprisingly well.

She looked around, wanting to imprint the memory of this day forever in her mind.

The yard looked lovely. Baskets of flowers were everywhere. There were white wicker cages filled with doves. Large round tables spread with white cloths were scattered around the yard.

She looked up at her father and smiled.

"Be happy this time," William said, squeezing her hand.

"Thank you, Papa."

Kaylynn met Jesse's gaze as she walked toward him, felt his love reach out to surround her. How handsome he was! His hair fell past his shoulders, long and black. He wore an elkskin shirt and leggings that were the color of cream, and a pair of new moccasins. Long fringe dangled from the sleeves of the shirt, and from the outer seam of the leggings. The yoke of his shirt was beaded in blue and yellow.

Ravenhawk stood beside him, resplendent in a black cutaway coat and striped trousers. Surprisingly, he had taken to city life like a duck to water.

Elizabeth had been appalled when Kaylynn insisted that Jesse wear buckskins instead of a cutaway coat and cravat. Jesse had been pleased.

Heads turned as she walked down the aisle. Regina sat near the aisle, her gaze fixed on Ravenhawk. The two had been practically inseparable since the night they met.

Grandmother Dearmond smiled at Kaylynn as she passed, and Kaylynn smiled back. Once again, Grams had been right.

They climbed the three steps to the gazebo, and the musicians fell silent.

Kaylynn's gaze met Jesse's again and everyone else was forgotten.

"Who giveth this woman to be married to this man?" the minister asked.

"Her mother and I do," William said, and giving Kaylynn a kiss on the cheek, he placed her hand in Jesse's.

"Dearly beloved, we are gathered here today to join this man and this woman in holy matrimony . . ."

Jesse squeezed Kaylynn's hand, and she smiled up at him. She looked radiant, he thought, more beautiful than he had ever seen her. She wore a gown of pale pink satin that managed to be modest and provocative at the same time. She had left her hair unbound at his request; it fell over her shoulders in glorious waves.

"I love you."

He mouthed the words, but Kaylynn heard them, clear and beautiful within her heart. "And I love you."

". . . now pronounce you man and wife. You may kiss the bride."

Jesse turned her toward him with gentle hands. "Hello, wife," he said.

"Hello, husband," she replied.

Drawing her into his embrace, he kissed her gently. And then he kissed her again, kissed her until she was breathless.

As from far away, she heard her mother gasp, heard Regina's laughter. Someone—Ravenhawk?—applauded.

The minister leaned forward. "You may want to save a little something for later," he whispered, and she heard the laughter in his voice.

Jesse was grinning when he let her go. "Don't

worry," he told her with a wink. "I've got plenty left for later."

Jesse's gaze moved over her, slowly, lovingly, as if he wanted to imprint her image on his mind, and then he kissed her again, ever so tenderly, and in that kiss was his love and devotion and the promise of forever.

Her family came forward to congratulate them, and then they went into the house for cake and champagne.

A short time later, Kaylynn took Ravenhawk aside for a moment, and then she went upstairs to change her clothes. Her father has given them a trip to Europe for a wedding present. Tonight, they would stay in the best hotel in the city.

Ravenhawk herded everyone outside so they could bid Kaylynn and Jesse farewell; then he slipped around the side of the house.

Moments later, Kaylynn emerged.

A hush fell over those gathered outside.

"Kaylynn, you're not wearing that!" her mother exclaimed, horrified.

"Hush, Elizabeth," Grams said. "She looks lovely."

"William, what will people say?"

"Who cares what people say? She always loved to play dress-up," he said, smiling.

"I think she looks fabulous," Regina remarked. "Where can I get one?"

Kaylynn ignored them all, her gaze fixed on Jesse's face. He looked surprised, and then pleased.

"You look beautiful," he murmured as he took her hand. More beautiful than he had ever seen her, he thought. She wore a tunic of soft white doeskin. Long fringe dangled from the sleeves. Tiny bells had been sewn to the fringe, and they tinkled merrily each time she moved. The yoke of her tunic was beaded in the same pattern as his shirt. Her hair fell down her back and over her shoulders, gleaming in the sunlight.

"So beautiful," he said. "Thank you."

She smiled up at him, then turned as Ravenhawk came around the corner of the house, leading Jesse's horse.

Jesse lifted Kaylynn into the saddle, then vaulted up behind her. Feeling as though her heart would burst with happiness, Kaylynn wrapped her arms around Jesse's waist.

Ravenhawk grinned as he handed Jesse the reins. With a whoop, Jesse touched the roan's flanks. The mare reared, forelegs pawing the air, then spun on her hocks and galloped across the lawn.

Kaylynn laughed out loud as Jesse loosed another war cry. At last, she thought, she had found her prince, and although he had come to her in the guise of a Cheyenne warrior, she knew that this time she would live happily ever after.

Epilogue

Two years later

Kaylynn smiled at Regina. "They're at it again."

Regina nodded. "Shall we go see what they're arguing about this time, or just let them kill each other?"

Kaylynn laughed. "Do you think they'll ever see eye to eye on anything?"

"I doubt it."

"Come on," Kaylynn said, hauling herself to her feet, "we'd better go referee."

"I suppose." With an effort, Regina stood up. Her baby was due in a few weeks, and she was finding it harder and harder to get up and down.

She looked over at Kaylynn and grinned. They were both pregnant and both due within a few weeks of each other.

They found the men in the kitchen. Jesse was standing beside the table, his son in his arms. Ravenhawk was sitting down. They were glaring at each other.

"What are you two fighting about now?" Kaylynn asked. Crossing the floor, she took her son from his father's arms. "I don't know how this child sleeps through all your bellowing."

Jesse jerked a thumb in Ravenhawk's direction. "This fool thinks we ought to start raising buffalo."

Ravenhawk surged to his feet. "Who are you calling a fool?"

"You see any other fools in the room?" Jesse retorted.

"Boys, boys," Regina said. "If you can't play nice, we'll have to send you to your rooms."

Jesse and Ravenhawk both glared at her, glared at each other, and then burst out laughing.

Kaylynn laughed, too, happier than she had ever been in her life.

"Let's go watch the sun set," Jesse said. "I can argue with that idiot any time. Besides, I've got something to give you."

"A present?" Kaylynn asked.

Jesse shrugged. "Sort of."

"Here," Regina said, "I'll put your son to bed."

"Thanks, Reggie," Kaylynn said.

She placed her son in Regina's arms, then followed Jesse out onto the porch.

"Well, what is it?" Kaylynn asked.

"I . . ."

"You what?" she asked, intrigued.

"You like poetry so much, I . . ." He took a deep breath, then pulled a sheet of paper out of his back pocket and thrust it into her hand. "I wrote you one."

"You wrote me a poem?" She unfolded the paper, more touched than she could say as she began to read.

What do you give someone who has given her
    all to you?
What do you give to a heart so true?
Do you give love?
Yes, unfeigned.
Do you give joy?
Yes, unrestrained.

And what do you say to a love that's true?
What do you say when she gives it to you?
Do you speak of love?
Yes, many times.
Do you speak of joy?
Yes, with reasons and rhymes.

What do you think of one so dear?
What do you feel when her love is near?
Do you think of love?
Yes, in my dreams.
Do you feel joy?
Yes, deeper now, it seems.

Where will this lead when our journey's o'er?
Where will it be and will there be more?
Will there be love?
Yes, deep and strong.
Will there be joy?
Forever, my Spirit's Song.

"Oh, Jesse," she murmured. "I love it."

"Ever since that day, when you recited that poem by the lake, I've thought of you as my Spirit's Song." He smiled at her. "It fits you, you know."

"Thank you, Jesse."

"I love you, Spirit's Song."

"And I love you, Jesse Yellow Thunder."

Jesse drew her into his arms, content to hold her. He was the luckiest man in the world, he mused, and he knew he could ask nothing more of *Maheo* than to spend the rest of his life with the woman in his arms.

"Pretty sunset," he said, thinking it shone over the ranch like a benediction from the Great Spirit.

"Yes," Kaylynn replied.

"We've got company coming," Jesse remarked.

"Really? Who?" She followed his gaze, frowning as she saw a man walking toward the house. "I don't recognize him."

"I do," Jesse muttered.

"What are you doing?" Kaylynn asked, her eyes widening as Jesse drew his gun and held it behind his back.

"Excuse me," the man said as he approached the porch. "I lost my horse a few miles back and I was wondering . . ." The words died in his throat as he recognized Jesse. "Damn," he muttered. "Of all the rotten luck."

With a grin, Jesse leveled his pistol at Phil Barnett.

Barnett shook his head, his expression glum. "Damn!" he exclaimed ruefully. "This is where I came in."

Dear Reader,

I must confess, if it wasn't for the man to whom this book is dedicated, *Spirit's Song* would probably never have taken shape. I was muddling along, not sure if I would ever finish what I had started, when I met SpiritWalker in an online chat room. He encouraged me, made me feel like I could do it, like I *had* to do it.

His help was invaluable. Not only did he give me some wonderful advice on Indian lore and some great insight on male POV, he suggested part of the plot line as well. I really feel that this book is his as much as mine. So, my thanks again, SpiritWalker. I couldn't have done it without you.

Most of the poetry in the book is also his.

Madeline

"Lovers of Indian romance have a special place on their bookshelves for Madeline Baker!"
— *Romantic Times*

Ruthless and cunning, Ryder Fallon can deal cards and death in the same breath. Yet when the Indians take him prisoner, he is in danger of being sent to the devil—until a green-eyed angel saves his life.

For two long years, Jenny Braedon has prayed for someone to rescue her from the heathen savages who enslaved her. And even if Ryder is a half-breed, she'll help him in exchange for her freedom. But unknown perils and desires await the determined beauty in his strong arms, sweeping them both from a world of tortured agony to love's sweet paradise.

_3742-4 $5.99 US/$6.99 CAN

Dorchester Publishing Co., Inc.
P.O. Box 6640
Wayne, PA 19087-8640

Please add $1.75 for shipping and handling for the first book and $.50 for each book thereafter. NY, NYC, and PA residents, please add appropriate sales tax. No cash, stamps, or C.O.D.s. All orders shipped within 6 weeks via postal service book rate. Canadian orders require $2.00 extra postage and must be paid in U.S. dollars through a U.S. banking facility.

Name_____
Address _____
City_____ State_____ Zip_____
I have enclosed $_____ in payment for the checked book(s).
Payment <u>must</u> accompany all orders. ☐ Please send a free catalog.

DON'T MISS THESE OTHER HISTORICAL ROMANCES BY MADELINE BAKER

Feather in the Wind. Black Wind gazes out over a land as vast and empty as the sky, praying for the strength to guide his people, and he sees her face. Susannah comes to him in a vision, a woman as mysterious as the new moon over the prairie, as tender as springtime in the Paha Sapa. And he knows his life is changed forever. To the writer in her he is an inspiration, but to the lonely woman within he is a dream come true who will lure her across the years to fulfill a love beyond time.

_4197-9 $5.99 US/$6.99 CAN

Lacey's Way. Lacey Montana is making a long trek across the plains, following her father's prison wagon, when Indians suddenly attack the wagon, kidnapping her father and leaving her helpless and alone. By helping the wounded Matt Drago, part Apache and part gambler, she finds someone to help her locate her father. Stranded in the burning desert, desperation turns to fierce passion as they struggle to stay alive on their dangerous journey.

_3956-7 $5.99 US/$6.99 CAN

Dorchester Publishing Co., Inc.
P.O. Box 6640
Wayne, PA 19087-8640

Please add $1.75 for shipping and handling for the first book and $.50 for each book thereafter. NY, NYC, and PA residents, please add appropriate sales tax. No cash, stamps, or C.O.D.s. All orders shipped within 6 weeks via postal service book rate. Canadian orders require $2.00 extra postage and must be paid in U.S. dollars through a U.S. banking facility.

Name_____
Address_____
City_____ State_____ Zip_____
I have enclosed $_____ in payment for the checked book(s).
Payment <u>must</u> accompany all orders. ❏ Please send a free catalog

DELANEY'S CROSSING

JEAN BARRETT

Virile, womanizing Cooper J. Delaney is Agatha Pennington's only hope to help lead a group of destitute women to Oregon, where the promise of a new life awaits them. He is a man as harsh and hostile as the vast wilderness—but Agatha senses a gentleness behind his hard-muscled exterior, a tenderness lurking beneath his gruff facade. Though the group battles rainstorms, renegade Indians, and raging rivers, the tall beauty's tenacity never wavers. And with each passing mile, Cooper realizes he is struggling against a maddening attraction for her and that he would journey to the ends of the earth if only to claim her untouched heart.

_4200-2 $5.50 US/$6.50 CAN

GOLDEN DREAMS

ANNA DeFOREST

After her father's sudden death leaves her penniless, Boston-bred Kate Holden arrives in Cripple Creek anxious to start a new life, her elegant upbringing a distant memory and her dream of going to college and becoming a history professor long-forgotten. But the golden-haired Kate soon finds that the Colorado mining town is no place for a young, single woman to make a living. Then desperate circumstances force her to strike a deal with the only man who was ever able to turn her nose from a book—the dark and brooding Justin Talbott.

As skilled at passion as he is at staking a valuable claim, Justin vows he'll taste the feisty scholar's sweet lips—and teach her unschooled body the meaning of desire. But bitter from past betrayals, the wealthy claimholder wants no part of her heart. He has sworn never to let another woman close enough to hurt him—until the lonely beauty awakens a romantic side he thinks has died along with his ideals. For though bedding her has its pleasures, Justin is soon to realize that only claiming Kate's heart will fulfill their golden dreams.

_4179-0 $4.99 US/$5.99 CAN